T

THE WAR ANGELS

THE WAR ANGELS

AN ASTONISHING SOUL SEARCHING JOURNEY OF ONE MAN . . . AND THE HEROIC FAITH OF AN ENTIRE VILLAGE AGAINST SATANIC FORCES

A NOVEL

WRITTEN BY

RONALD L. GAISER

Based on a story by
Gerald Gaiser

authorHOUSE®

AuthorHouse™ LLC
1663 Liberty Drive
Bloomington, IN 47403
www.authorhouse.com
Phone: 1-800-839-8640

© 2014 Ronald L. Gaiser. All rights reserved.

Book cover Illustration: Fred Levinson / Los Angeles, CA
Cover Design / Author House / Bloomington, IN.

No part of this book may be reproduced, stored in a retrieval system, or transmitted by any means without the written permission of the author.

Published by AuthorHouse   02/11/2014

ISBN: 978-1-4918-3491-6 (sc)
ISBN: 978-1-4918-3490-9 (hc)
ISBN: 978-1-4918-3489-3 (e)

Library of Congress Control Number: 2013920731

Any people depicted in stock imagery provided by Thinkstock are models, and such images are being used for illustrative purposes only. Certain stock imagery © Thinkstock.

This book is printed on acid-free paper.

Because of the dynamic nature of the Internet, any web addresses or links contained in this book may have changed since publication and may no longer be valid. The views expressed in this work are solely those of the author and do not necessarily reflect the views of the publisher, and the publisher hereby disclaims any responsibility for them.

DEDICATIONS

THIS BOOK IS DEDICATED TO MY FATHER, WHO WAS A FLYER IN THE U.S. AIR FORCE, A CREATIVE WRITER, AND A SPIRITUAL MAN OF GREAT INTEGRITY. ALSO, MY MOTHER, WHO STAYED BY HIS SIDE ASSISTING HIM IN HIS NOBLE PURSUITS.

CONTENTS

PROLOGUE xi

PART I: THE MOUNTAIN VILLAGE 1
  CHAPTERS 1-22

PART II: THE WAR ANGELS 79
  CHAPTERS 23-40

PART III: THE STEEL RING 143
  CHAPTERS 41-58

PART IV: THE LONELY LOVERS 217
  CHAPTERS 59-67

PART V: THE SKY QUEEN 259
  CHAPTERS 68-82

ACKNOWLEDGEMENTS

First, my father for telling me the story, and my mother for her encouragement; Barnaby and Mary Conrad for taking me under their wings at the Santa Barbara Writers Conference for so many years; Elizabeth Lyon, at the Questa College Editing workshops, for making me see what I really needed to do as a novel writer; Laura Taylor for her 'spot on' editing advice, and passion for my story; Mathew Pallamary for his friendship and editing help; Joe Kolkowitz for his friendship, sense of humor, and good ideas; Monte and Nicole Shultz for all their support; Ilona Klar for her friendship, belief in me, and agent-like support without whom this book would not have been published; Cho Ying Hon for her help and support; all the great people at Author House, a 'new author' division of Random House / Penguin; Fred Levinson for a great cover illustration; all the other people whom I may have inadvertently left out, I express my great appreciation, and thanks. And . . . to God, for making everything possible.

NOTE

Szabla is a Polish word. It is pronounced Sha' bla, and means saber, or a blade of sorts. In the context of this story, it is a nickname used in the same way Wolf, Bear, Swifty, or Shorty might be used.

PROLOGUE

POLAND 1936

Szabla's heart ached as he lifted Basha over a steep jagged edge on the mountain path and carefully lowered her onto a bed of crumbling rock. Her hand felt soft to his touch as it gripped his big arm, dwarfed against his bulging muscle. Brushing his straw colored hair out of his deep blue eyes, he glanced at her. He hadn't believed her the night before when she told him they were done. Like an oozing stab wound, he hadn't much time to stop her from leaving, or his life's blood would be gone. Delaying every step, he guided her down the trail toward the great gorge where the tributary river roared out of the Tatra Mountains toward the Vistula. Below he saw the mouth of the canyon separate into two smaller rivers, each winding their different ways into the flatlands.

Closer to the bottom end of the trail, he eyed her with longing. One of nature's true beauties, she looked shapely with soft skin and long dark hair, and unusually strong and intelligent for her twenty-six years. *Where would she go? Who would protect her? Who might steal her from him? Would he ever see her again?*

"Winter is coming, it will be hard! There's trouble in the cities."

"I'll manage," she said.

When they reached the bank of the river, she peered across its rapids. Cold spray wafted over them and water-pounding rocks rang in his ears. He raised his voice above the din, "After all we have been through these past years, you can still leave?"

"I can't go on with the killing, stealing, and living like animals in this wilderness. I'm not a bandit! I don't know who I am anymore!"

He grabbed her arm.

"You are part of me . . ."

"I need time to think. I need peace and quiet. Let me go."

The tears in her eyes told the truth, she still loved him. Turning his back on her, he stared out where the rivers parted, searching for something to say. The last few years had been hard since they sought refuge in the mountains from the law, but they had done the only thing they could. He turned around, hoping to reach out and pull her close, but she had already left.

He stood still, holding his breath, watching as she ran down the right side of the river where the waters disappeared behind foothills and reappeared further on, stretching out in rolling rows toward the low horizon.

He felt like the mountain, and she the river, carving a deeper gorge in him then the scar from his past, which seemed a lifetime of conflict. If he had still been Pawel Pajak, the boy of his youth, he would have gotten down on his knees and prayed for her not to go, but he was Szabla now, the bandit with no faith in God anymore. *After what we have been through, how could there be a God?* Szabla felt justified in his killing. How could anyone blame him? Most did not, especially his band of men who faithfully followed him into the mountains.

His eyes blurred as he watched his dreams and desire for a family of his own vanish. Basha seemed to evaporate in the rising vapors around the bend where the river grew calm.

"That's it, she's gone," he muttered.

His nose twitched from the smell of sweat on his sheepskin vest. His clothes felt heavy from perspiration and the dampness of the gorge as he climbed back up the path, but heavier still was the scar on his heart. He gasped for breath when he finally reached the top to find Durcansky waiting for him. Szabla could not hide his grimace from his tall, lean friend, who had stuck by him since the beginning of his troubles with Basha.

"She will come back." Durcansky said, as Szabla sat down on a rock, unable to speak. He gazed out across the vista of southern Poland at the foothills and its winding rivers, squinting at the dark clouds entering from the western border of Germany, wondering what made Durcansky think that she would come back.

His attention wandered across the landscape below and decided that after winter, he would go back down into the cities to find her if he could. "One winter should be enough time to find herself," he said aloud, then motioned Durcansky to follow him up into the mist to their hidden camp in the mountains above.

PART I

THE MOUNTAIN VILLAGE

1

THREE YEARS LATER

Basha Mickiewicz looked out upon the bright morning sun filling the village square from her small room above an artisans shop. At the intersection, a dirt road crossed the main street. Large smooth stones covered the middle of the square extending a few feet past each of the four corners. She cracked a window open and enjoyed the aroma of fresh baked bread from the corner Bakery shop. The rays of sun warmed her skin in the high altitude, the way it had when she first came to the village of Praznik two years ago. It seemed like the perfect place to hide.

Basha had been told by a friend in Krakow, who once had lived in the village, that Praznik's few people, mostly peasant-farmers, Catholics, had lived there for centuries. Cradled high in the snow-capped southern mountains of Poland, Praznik had always depended on its remoteness for security and protection. For centuries, wars, pestilence, famine, and the changing political fortunes of Poland, with its historically shifting boundaries, had passed them by.

Basha had also heard of times when the village had known some famine, but the forests, mountains, and streams with their natural abundance of wildlife offset any real hunger. Eventually their remoteness had cost the villagers of Praznik oblivion on the maps of Poland. It seemed to Basha that even God had forgotten about them.

Basha shook the dust from the curtains and sneezed. *Poor old Jarod.* She loved the white haired old man with the crippled leg and felt grateful that he had let her rent the small room above his shop. It was all she needed and she was happy taking care of him.

She reached up and dusted his hand made violins, guitars, and religious artifacts that hung on the walls for sale. As she dusted, Szabla crossed her mind. It had been two years of peace and quiet for her in the village. When Szabla found her below in the city, she ran again. Smiling, she thought how smart it had been to hide up in the mountains. He wouldn't think to look for her right under his nose. She had found time to forget about him, time that she needed to discover who she was again, and what she wanted.

Basha heard the bell above the front door ring and watched Jarod hobble into his shop. She hurried to him, smiled, and patted him on his bony shoulder with affection.

"Today I will clean the windows so you may see and feel the sunlight in the entire shop." She took his finely carved lacquered pinewood cane and hung it next to the door reluctantly releasing it from her hand. She liked its smooth touch and the smell of pinewood in his shop while he worked. With an arm around his shoulder, she helped him to the table, where he placed a paper on the counter and tapped it with his finger. In a slow heavy Polish dialect he said, "The Germans have established Poland as the new temporary residence of Satan and his hordes. Those living in the flatlands call it the beginning of the second Great War."

Basha shrugged, "We are far from the flatlands. Tell me what beautiful things you are going to make out of wood today." Jarod's wrinkled face turned from grim concern to a smile, lifting her spirits.

"I'll make tea for you, and then get to the windows."

"You have gone through so much for your age, yet you still keep such a positive attitude. I'm telling you, you are a wonder Basha Mickiewicz. Some man will snatch you away from me soon."

"I'm not interested in men right now, don't worry!"

Reaching for the old teapot on the black iron wood burning stove, she poured steaming hot tea into a big ceramic mug Jarod had made in his kiln in back of his shop. *It was true*, she thought as she stirred tealeaves. She was at that age, yet she felt comfortable with her regained inner strength and the new worldly wisdom she was learning from Jarod. *What did it matter if she was still unmarried going into her prime? Many of the villagers sought her advice as if she were as wise as Jarod.* She suspected it was one of the reasons they had so readily accepted her.

"Thank you Jarod, thank you for everything."

"For what?"

"You have been so kind these years, taking me in, teaching me, and helping me understand myself and these people in the village

"Bah,—I got the best deal. I thought you city girls were quick learns. Look who's helping who."

When she settled into working behind his bench, Basha kissed him on his forehead and stepped outside. She reached for the cloth in a bucket to clean the windows when she noticed three villagers walking toward her followed by a group of refugees. Wiping her hands on her apron she flicked a lock of her long black hair back from her forehead and raised her eyebrows.

She didn't know any of the rag tag group of refugees that followed behind them. Johan, the butcher, a big stalk of a man spoke, "These people are fleeing from what they call a holocaust in the cities below. They want us to help them." Basha scanned the group, "Where is Tearses, and the other elders?"

"We can't find him, and we need to do something."

She listened to several refugees babbling at the same time. She eyed their ripped and torn formal city clothes that seemed out of place in the Mountains, and felt sorry for their obvious hardships they had been through.

"Wait, slow down, one at a time." she said.

A worn-out man beyond his real age and in great anguish stepped forward. Basha hoped she hid her pity from the refugee standing in front of her. A torn beat up black rimmed hat hid most of his long gray braided hair. Her heart went out to him when she looked compassionately into his eyes. Calmly she asked in Polish, "Where do you come from?"

"Krakow—you can't imagine the cruelty. Everywhere there is war! They are massacring whole cities and villages, killing women and children, and anybody who opposes them. They have returned Poland to the Middle Ages."

Basha thought of Szabla, the one person who still chased her. Because of him, she had come to Praznik to get away from killings.

"Who—Who are they?" *Maybe*, she thought, *this refugee would know something about where Szabla was.*

"Germans, the Germans!"

"Did you see any Germans, or bandits on the road coming up to the village?"

"I'd rather face bandits than Germans. They're everywhere; there is no place to hide. No one is safe!"

Basha saw many villagers shading their eyes, watching something from the mountain rim with great interest. She strode past the refugees stopping when she heard one of the women start to pray.

A German column with four motorcycles, an armored half-track, and four trucks were grinding up the narrow mountain road. Two trucks filled with guttural shouting soldiers bounced along in front of two empty trucks. Even from far away, she flinched at their guttural shouts.

They pulled into the center of the village with brakes screeching loudly. Nazi swastikas covered the side of their trucks and armbands.

Basha slowly backed up, picked up her bucket, and watched the villagers scatter. Some of the refugees ran around the corner and down an alley, while others seemed rooted and remained unmoving.

She stepped behind a shadowed alcove watching from the shadows. Nazi soldiers swarmed out of their vehicles into the town square like foraging ants out of a nest rounding up all the men in the village, and bringing them to the square where they separated them from the women and children. A tall Nazi pushed Jarod out of the door.

"Stop, please, I don't know anything."

Basha covered her mouth and shrank further into the shadows. Basha was about to step out and say something about Jarod's leg when she heard the Nazi officer with a scar down his neck spit out the word, "Juden? Juden?"

The men of the village shifted their feet and relaxed. Basha let out her breath. *If the men of the village were not too concerned, why worry? After all, they were only looking for Jews.*

2

"Juden?" The voice sounded louder and more demanding now. *Why were Jews so important?* Several Nazis dragged some of the newcomers to the village, ignoring their cries and forcing them to lie in the dirt a few feet in front of the alcove where Basha stood. Her stomach muscles tightened and hot blood rushed up her back. She instinctively moved further back, and then the officer looked straight at her and sauntered over to the front of the alcove, lit a cigarette, and smirked at the people on the ground. A deeper foreboding surged through her veins and she shivered from the cold wall against her shoulder. She fought off a nauseating desire to run, yell at the officer, or do something to stop all this.

The Nazis continued through the village taking all the able-bodied men from twelve years old and forced them into the two empty trucks. The villagers at gunpoint remained standing, staring at the Jews in the dirt before them as the Germans went from house to house in a frantic search. She knew it was beyond anyone's comprehension what else they could be searching for; they had all the men and Jews. *There was nothing of value in the village. There had been nothing of value in the village for years.*

She cringed as the Germans smashed furniture and huts. She raised her hands to cover her ears. *Why didn't they just tell them what they were seeking?*

When the soldiers dragged out the wives and children of the men lying in the dirt, it was too much. Feeling like a cat raising its back, Basha clenched her fists, and gasped for breath as a swelling in her throat held back her words. Propelled by an inner force she stepped out of the shadows to confront the Nazi officer, but before she could, Jarod stepped in front of her.

"If you take these men who will harvest and work the farms?"

A slow smile creased the Nazi officer's lips. He raised his pistol and fired directly into the old man's face. The smoking empty shell flew into the alcove landing at Bashas foot. She screamed, "NO".

Three German soldiers stepped over to the huddling group of men, women, and children, scrutinizing the Jews and refugees of the village, then at the smiling officer. He barked orders to separate the children and stand them in a line front to back. Basha felt like she had turned into stone, unable to speak or move. Jarods head lay in a puddle of blood before her.

"This is how we deal with runaway Jews," the officer said, and fired into the body of the first child with his Luger sending the nine millimeter bullet through each child's chest and blasting a bigger hole out their back, and into the next one in line. Eight children dropped like lifeless ragdolls, heads jerking back, and arms flailing out from the bullet's impact. Men and women screamed and wailed in protest. The officer nodded and the soldiers fired at the rest of the refugees. Where once there were living human beings lay a bloodied mass of torn flesh in the dirt.

Basha vomited. She heard the Germans climb into their mechanized beasts and start their long grind back down the mountain road. She looked up with blurry eyes and saw the Nazis taking the young lifeblood of the village, leaving behind the remaining villagers, shattered and shocked. In tears, Basha picked up Jarods cane and held it close to her body spitting out her words.

"The Devil has come to the village. Praznik will never again be the same."

For a long time no one moved, even though several of the village huts were on fire. Basha felt frozen in a nightmare. After moments that seemed like hours her ears pricked awake at the new sound of the crackling flames. She smelled the musty smoke in the crisp mountain air and tasted the leftover bitterness of her own regurgitation.

Tearing her eyes from the dead bodies, she saw the remaining villager's senses finally return. Beata, Marta and other women moved about clumsily, unable to decide on where to go or what to do. Some went to their homes; others wandered aimlessly. She watched some of them stumble over to the mountain rim and stare down the deserted mountain road looking for their men. With shaky legs, Basha bent over to Jarod. He had no face left. She flopped down again, weeping as she put her apron over his head.

After a while, she started walking toward the old village chapel. She felt the weight of torrential satanic winds pushing her back to the square and the slaughtered people. She had to pray. She needed to find meaning and answers about what happened and what to do about it. *Why had this happened to Praznik?*

The chapel was dark and musty as she creaked open the one good door. She moved toward the altar and reached out blindly fumbling on top of the altar brushing aside years of cobwebs around a group of candelabras. She blew dust off the box of matches she found, and lit a single candle. As the light glowed dim, she saw the broken pews and chapel in disrepair. She got down on her knees, folding her hands.

"Why God, why do you do this thing to us?" Was it what I did? What has the village done wrong? Why Jarod? What about the men of the village? What about the souls of the Jews? What about the harvest? What do I do now? How have we wronged you? God, show me what it is we should do!"

Basha waited all night for an answer. None came.

The candle burned down and went out, and in the darkest hour of the morning, she saw a vision of the chapel, bright and new, everything repaired and shining. The altar glowed from a column of light entering from above. It was then that Basha made a promise to God.

"I will rebuild the church. I only ask to please forgive me, all of us, for being away from you for so long" She prayed for forgiveness, then remembered what the refugee had said; maybe bandits would be better than Germans. Exhausted and emotionally depleted, she knew she had to find Szabla after all, even though he was the last person she wanted to see. He had protected her in the past. She would bring God back to the village, and bring Szabla here for protection. She thought of the villager's spiritual neglect and all the past wrongs she had committed with Szabla and prayed aloud, "Please God, stop me if this is the wrong decision and not your will." She collapsed on the stone floor, and as the earliest light of dawn seeped through the holes of the chapel walls, she fell into a deep sleep.

3

BUDAPEST, HUNGARY

At 6:30 pm on a humid August summer evening, Dr. Aaron Estreicher walked out of Elizabeth hospital and down the long concrete steps toward the rock part along the Danube River. His healthy well-shaped body topped with curly dark hair and thick eyebrows moved with certain direction. Putting his glasses in their case in his white shirt pocket, his face now looked younger than his 38 years. He was clean-shaven with smooth white skin from being indoors.

He never advertently pushed his privileges as the chief resident surgeon of the largest and most modern hospital in Budapest, but today he decided to leave early, preferring to walk the Buda side of the city where he worked and lived between the Margit Bridge and the Lenchid chain bridge.

"How could I be so stupid?" He mumbled. *Father had always been a smart surgeon during the aristocratic era; I had a thriving practice, with patients from every station in life, from charity cases to the very rich. Even the old order nobility would consider no other doctor but me. I never hurt anyone, and I never refused a case. It didn't matter whether they could pay or not.* His footsteps creaked on the cobblestones along the rock part. He could have taken the streetcar south to the chain bridge, but he needed to sort out his thoughts.

Walking along the side of the rocks at the water's edge helped. He smelled an occasional angler's catch as they tossed their lines into the still looking surface of the river. He enjoyed looking at the Geraniums, even though there was no detectable fragrance. *I have position, wealth; happily married to a beautiful wife, two children and I have accomplished most of my goals in life.*

At Clark Circle, he caught the streetcar leaving the river heading west along Allagut Road, up into the rich green foothills of Buda. A German patrol car with several Nazi officers rolled along next to him. He stared blankly at it before it turned away from his sight. The ancient stone houses he passed always reminded him of the aristocratic hideouts of decadent nobility from a thousand years past giving him a twinge of guilt that he lived in the quiet luxury of this beautiful part of town.

In spite of my achievements there is still that one thorn in my life that makes everything I have achieved, seem to count for nothing in the country I love. I am still a Jew, which means I am still a victim of illogical hatred, discrimination, and humiliation, I, the great doctor still have to suffer in silence to survive this wretched anti-Semitism. The streetcar rolled up to Varos Ter on Istenhegye Ut and stopped. He jumped off and took a deep breath. The air seemed cleaner and purer than any other part of the city. He loved the big Oak trees that lined each side of his street interspersed with small ponds latticed together with stonewalls and walkways. He was especially fond of his house. To him, it looked like a little white Gothic style stone castle, with a view overlooking the city.

I never got involved in petty intrigues at the hospital and refused to engage in covert Hungarian politics. I only wish to advance my career with the recognition of my ability and interest in medicine, not because of political associations, because I am a Jew, it seems I must go through this despair of changing status.

Climbing the steps to the front of his home, he heard beautiful music from next-door. It drifted out the upstairs turret where his neighbor, the famous composer Kolday was rehearsing. *Ever since the Nazi madness has spread over Europe my status has changed. I should have seen it coming when Germany ceded Slovakia and the Carpatho-Ukraine to Hungry after its takeover of Czechoslovakia. I was complacent about the Hungarian—'Jewish Problem'. Now this German poison has permeated all of Hungary. How could Hungary ally itself with this disease? Why did it take me so long to wake up?*

Opening his front door, he soaked in the ruby red lips and delicate white skin of his lovely wife standing there to greet him. He kissed her, pulling her perfect breasts into him, and stroked her soft blonde hair. He entered the foyer placing his things on the antique hall table below the large chandelier. He couldn't stop thinking even though his wife said, "Doctor, dinner is almost ready."

"Thank you darling, I will be with you and the children shortly."

Up to now, my only fear has been for my Jewish friends and close associates, but when those gentiles whom I professionally associated with for so many years began to draw away, I should have known the waves of hate were lapping at my heels. My few friends who remained loyal tried to warn me and told me to flee the country, but I couldn't believe the incredible stories of what was happening to Jews throughout all of Europe, and now Hungary.

He plopped down at his desk in the anteroom and shoved his mail aside unable to get out of his brain. *Hungarian Jews being rounded up and refugees pouring in from other countries overrun by the Nazis, the Einsatzgruppen that followed the victorious German armies, and the eyewitness accounts of their mass shootings, now here in Hungary. My God! What have I done?*

He went into the dining room, sat down with his family, and looked at his meager plate of vegetables. His wife wept silently.

"What is it Ilona?"

"There is nothing Kosher anymore, anywhere!"

"Not even on the Pest side of town?"

"The butcher over there wouldn't sell me any meat."

He watched his children bow their heads and pray, but they didn't touch their food.

"Sosha, show your little brother how much you like vegetables."

"Father, I ate my friend's sandwich today at school. It had meat in it. She said it was all right. They had plenty of meat at their house."

"Why can't we have meat Father?" Tobias chimed in. He saw their eyes looking expectantly at him. A pang of guilt chilled through him.

"We will, wait and see." He said half believing it.

"I haven't heard or seen Sonia or any of her family all summer. Where have they taken her? What have they done with them? I want to know, but nobody says anything."

He answered once again the same way he always did for the children's sake.

"Don't worry. I will look into it."

4

In the quiet of their bed, Esteicher rolled over to kiss his wife and gently caress her soft back. "I can't," she sobbed. He rolled her over and looked into her wet beautiful blue eyes. Finally, it was impossible for Estreicher to continue deluding himself.

The increasing restrictions made the future painfully obvious. It was time to escape from the insanity that surrounded him, that even now reached into the operating room and prevented him, Hungary's greatest surgeon, from operating on any so-called Aryan gentile. He didn't dare tell Ilona that. His practice had been steadily dwindling, his former patients, rather than risk the permanence of a concentration camp, chose the expediency of a temporary illness that at least allowed a chance of recovery.

"Don't tell the children yet, but we are leaving Hungary." He saw Ilona rub her eyes and look up at him.

"We won't take anything."

"What about your mothers Jewels?"

"Of course we will take them and all the money we have saved along with a few valuables we can carry."

"Where are we going Aaron?"

"To Sweden! They have indicated they would appreciate my services there."

"But I . . ."

"Get ready my love, we leave soon."

Estriecher wrapped her in his arms and held her close kissing her on the head, then on her neck, shoulders, and everywhere. She responded with shivers.

* * *

Several days before their scheduled secret departure, Estreicher was called by a patient and informed by his neighbor, the great composer Kolday, that his family had been arrested along with other Jews in the area and taken to a place of detention.

"Even the children?"

"I'm sorry Aaron, yes, all of them." The voice on the other end of the phone was sympathetic. Although badly shaken by the news, Estreicher kept his emotions in check.

He systematically called every politically important person he knew or had ever been acquainted with. The majority of them refused to speak to him. Those that did spoke guardedly. One of these, a politically active party member high in government circles, whose life Estreicher once saved, agreed to make inquiries, but he also suggested Estreicher turn himself in to the local police in the off chance that he too might be arrested and taken to the same detention camp as his family.

Estreicher reported to the station nearest his residence, and watched as an officer found his name on a list within the covers of an ominous looking black book. Instead of arresting him, the officer handed him a special identity card.

"You will continue reporting to the hospital, Heir Esteicher."

"And my family, where are they?"

"They are in safe custody. When the time is right you will be informed of their whereabouts."

* * *

Dr. Aaron Estreicher remained at the hospital, no longer commuting from the house and empty bedrooms, the playthings left un-gathered, his wife's purse still on the hall table. The reminders of his loved ones proved too much for him. He lived at the hospital, returning once a week to check the house until informed that the house was no longer his, and new occupants resided there. There were no belongings given him. The police had confiscated everything.

At the hospital, each day became like the day before. He performed his functions almost by rote, never smiling, yet trying to appear normal in a world of growing insanity.

Each day at five o'clock, he made the same call to the same government official whose friendship he now hung on to tenaciously, careful of his questions, careful of his tone of voice, careful not to offend and cut off the only remaining possibility of ever finding his wife and children again. The only real information he received was the official statement that his family was arrested as non-citizens and considered stateless.

Each day rolled on and became weeks of an endless chain of anguish. His bitterness grew against himself for the self-delusion and ignorance of the danger that had enveloped his family; against the Germans for perpetrating their crime against humanity; against the Hungarians who joined the murderers; and against God for allowing the horror of murder, rape, and pillage that became a daily occurrence wherever the Nazi flag flew. He chafed at the irony of his position when the hospital began receiving wounded Hungarian soldiers from the incursion into Yugoslavia.

Several months later, the hospital filled with soldiers from the Russian front. Hungary allied itself with the Nazi regime in both invasions. There were days so crowded with operations and death, that even those associates who were the most vituperative toward him forgot for a time the man wielding the scalpel so effectively was a non—Aryan. He stole glances at them during especially delicate and dangerous surgery as they marveled at his skill, not realizing that except for his bitterness, all his emotions were tightly boxed and put away with his lost family.

Occasionally during a lull in the hectic wartime activities of the hospital, when his subordinates found the time to recall his seemingly steady cold nerve, they would remember what he was, and accuse him of being subhuman and emotionless, conveniently lumping him with the other Jews.

Once he had been a source of pride and encouragement to the medical staff. Now he was an irritant. His skill was no longer a prod to their own abilities, which helped raise their level of competence, but an embarrassment. He was a Jew and his medical prowess made them look bad. He felt certain his days were numbered and that they looked forward to when it would happen.

Estreicher found it more and more difficult to reach his friend in the government, and he realized what this man's initial act of kindness might seem to others. Esteicher's dependency on the man for any sign of hope had grown into a collaborative danger that could threaten the man's own world and family. It came as no surprise when his former friend told Estreicher that it looked hopeless. When there was any news, he would see that the 'good doctor' was contacted. In the meantime, Estreicher understood his reasons for not wanting him to call any longer.

The moment came when he had exhausted every possible source that could assist him in finding his wife and children. He knew it was over before this final door was closed, because he had already reached the end of his own resources, spent the remainder of his savings on the last bribe, begged the final unsympathetic clerk, and was once and for all rebuffed by dangerous men in authority. There was no one left to see or any place to go. He was restricted to the city limits.

With this final cut off, it seemed that he had lost the last contact with his family. Relegated to the vault of his memory, only the hope of a miracle could release them.

5

BERLIN, GERMANY

Earnst Von Rhinestock felt like a thousand needles were pricking his leg. He blinked open his eyes several times as he struggled to regain consciousness. Everything looked like he was viewing it through a thin layer of gauze stretched in front of him. It all seemed white, then a blurry white figure slowly moved around him. *Am I dead?* He asked himself the question and tried to focus on where he was. He didn't believe in heaven and even if he had, he was sure he would be bound for hell. Then it seemed as if another layer of gauze came off his eyes and his vision started to clear. There in front of him was a blonde woman, a nurse.

He convulsed with a shake from a pungent medical smell in his nose. "Daffa Gomme!" He managed to spurt out in a half-cracked voice. "I'm in a hospital, a stupid hospital."

"Gooden Taaq, Heir Rienstock," the nurse exclaimed cheerfully. He didn't feel cheerful.

"Where am I?"

"You are in a hospital in Berlin, try to rest now."

He lifted himself up to get a better look at his surroundings and himself. He took in a window on the left, a dresser on the right, a medical cart with a tray of various drugs and appliques. There was only one bed in the room. At least he had a private room he thought.

"What happened to my plane?"

Waiting for the nurse to answer, he watched her adjust his leg and give him another shot of morphine.

"You will please relax Heir Reinstock; you are going to have visitors this afternoon. Heir Goering himself is coming with a film crew to decorate you on behalf of the Fatherland; you must be in good shape." He was restless and wanted answers.

"How long must I stay in the hospital?" he demanded, as if he hadn't heard a word she had said.

"The doctor will see you after Heir Goering's visit today. He will explain everything to you." Von Reinstock laid his head back on the pillow and started to feel the effects of the morphine running through his veins, tingling and anesthetizing each section of his body from the entry point of the needle. He struggled to keep conscious as long as he could. He tried to recall the events that had brought him to the hospital. His mind fuzzed then he was clearly looking through the gun sights of his Folk Wolf 190 high above the English Channel.

Peering through the cross hairs, he fired a burst at an English spitfire attacking a group of Henkel Bombers over Dover. He was the leader of the German fighters flying escort for the bombers. As another spitfire swooped in on the lead bomber, Earnst singled him out and chased him.

"They will be missing you at the dinner table tonight," he yelled as he let loose a quick burst at the spitfire. He tensed his grip as he looped around following the smoking plane down to sea level. Skipping over the waves heading toward the shore Earnst again lined him up in his sights. "There's nowhere for you to go except down." He fired all his guns longer than usual and the spitfire splashed into the water in a ball of flames. Earnst jerked up on his stick and his Folk Wolfe climbed up into the sky.

Looking out over the water, he could see the white Cliffs of Dover as the bombers passed over them. He thought about when he had convinced Goering that he could still fly after his first crash and injury in Poland. In a fantastic demonstration, he arranged with his own Folk Wolf back home, he had shown Goering he was still an Ace to deal with. It was a happy day being reassigned to combat duty. He felt an uneasy feeling that the present battle was passing him by, and without haste quickly pointed his plane back into the fray.

"Wing man, Straus, where are you?"

"Just above you sir."

Von Rhinestock circled up into the mass of bombers again searching for his wingman. Just as he reached the Henkel's protection zone, out of the corner of his eye he saw two spitfires, guns flaming, coming down strong on Straus. He helplessly watched his friend plummeting toward the ocean, a smoke trail streaming behind him. "Jump Straus, Jump." Earnst saw Straus arching into oblivion then his wingman became a circle of white foam on the water as his plane went under the waves.

Von Rhinestock immediately heard the sound of 'taka, taka, taka, taka' as bullets riddled his plane. "Shiesa" he yelled and tried to pull up on his stick. It was too late. A bold spitfire had singled him out and was pouncing on him. Oil began spraying into his cockpit from a ruptured oil line.

Earnst felt like his adrenaline line ruptured inside himself, and gushed through every vein as he pulled the canopy lever. His canopy flew off and he was ejecting when his plane simultaneously exploded flinging him into the sky. Fortunately for him he was not unconscious as he spun around in the air and saw the sky above with planes dotted everywhere, then the white caps on the sea below, then the shore, then the sky, then the sea, then the planes, then the sea.

As he tumbled through the smoke, bullets, and planes, he somehow ripped his parachute cord and heard a large popping sound as his chute opened and jerked his arms almost out of their sockets. While drifting down he searched the sky for his plane but couldn't see it. The explosion disintegrated it entirely in mid-air with no trace. Once again, he had eluded death. Wondering how long he could play this chess game with the hooded scythe carrier; he looked down at the ocean coming up fast and then inflated his life jacket. A glob of blood filled his right eye and he couldn't see out of it. He struggled to bring his right hand up to his eye and touch the blood. He felt his forehead, following the blood streaming down his face, and touched a piece of metal sticking out of his cap. However, the biggest piece was in his leg. Can I swim? With all the adrenaline pumping through him, he didn't feel his wounds from the metal fragments that had riddled his body when his plane exploded. Now the nausea and pain was beginning to fill his stomach. As the adrenaline subsided through various locations, his whole body began aching. The pain from his leg was the sharpest.

Again, he looked down at the ocean through his left eye and in the distance; coming from France, he could see a boat. "One lone boat, let it be German." Then he hit the cold water hard and before he blacked out, he thought of skiing in the Swiss Alps, and falling in the cold snow.

He couldn't remember or visualize the German U-boat commander pulling him out of the water as the report on the side of his bed read. Von Reinstock didn't feel pain anymore in his leg, in fact his whole body was numb and his mind began to blur, his last thoughts were; *I am an Ace, and one of Germanys Wonderkind. I have survived another crash that should have killed me,* and the cost, he looked down at his body and just as he passed out he mumbled, "— Only one leg."

6

Basha awoke from the chill air feeling as old as the crumbling stones of the chapel around her. A warm column of sun filtered through a hole in the wall and illuminated the head of the statue of Mary Mother of Christ, the only representation of faith left in the village. Basha blinked at the statue and thoughtfully recalled the plan she had promised God the night before. She got up with great resolution and hurried back to her small apartment above the shop in the village square. She packed a meager bundle of food for three days and set off for the high mountains.

She had passed the bodies and smell of the dead un-moved in the village square. The villagers remained tightly gripped by shock and fear in their homes. She only stopped to tell one of the elders, Tearses, of her leaving.

"You know more about the village than anyone else, and you were Jarod's oldest friend. We need someone who is strong enough to rebuild and do the harvest. Szabla can do it, and protect us at the same time!"

"You know what the villagers think of him! You don't really know what you're bringing back." Tearses white beard wagged as he spoke, while warning her of possible consequences. She agreed with his wisdom, but she had made up her mind what the village needed now was Szabla's type of leadership. They had to trust her. However long it took to find him she was convinced it was the right decision.

"A villager who talks too much has given you away, and Szabla knows you are in Praznik," Tearses told her. "He is actually camped nearby. Be careful."

"So, he is here. In these mountains near the village?" She thought of Tearses words and realized what it meant; Szabla had found her again! *I will search for his camp in a few well-hidden places.* Then she left the village.

Basha climbed deep into the mountains. With each step, she reflected on the past. She used Jarod's cane as a walking stick as her thoughts turned to the villagers. The rumor in the village was that Szabla had killed her fiancé. She knew the truth, but had left the rumor alone not wanting to disclose the whole story to everyone. However, Jarod had known, she was glad she told Jarod that Szabla was not to blame. She poked the earth with the cane to see how damp it was. She stopped at a clearing near a stream and glanced back at the beginning fringe of the forest that covered her trail into the high mountains. She was sure of it. No one followed her. Bending down, she soothed her lips with water from the cool mountain stream, then spit and kept climbing.

Late in the afternoon dense shadows filled the high forest. She reached a rise on a little knoll, stopped to rest, and surveyed a tiny-cratered valley a few hundred feet below. A little further on the top of the rise was a group of large jagged rocks. Thinking she heard voices, she crept up to the top of the outcropping and looked down upon a well-hidden strategically located camp. She felt it best not to walk into the camp at that moment because of what seemed like an intense meeting going on. She decided to stay perched in the rocks, listen, and watch for an opportune time to enter. She noticed several men gathered in a circle. She squinted at the one man in the center and then she saw him.

"Szabla! Yes, he is still every bit Szabla." Basha flicked her hair back remembering that like the primitive ancient weapon he brandished, now his namesake, he also was a tool for killing. She felt a chill go down her back. Basha would recognize him anywhere, a large burly man with a full head of hair, and a mustache the color of summer hay. Then the chill turned warm. She had rejected his longings for her, but now something kept pulling her toward him. His nose at one time had been broken and the break set in such a way as to give his still handsome face a fierce-like appearance. Part of her admired how he seemed immune to the harshness of the elements around him. She imagined his hard body beneath those ragged peasant clothes. She wanted to get closer and with the stealth of a mountain cat crept to the bottom of the knoll near the outer edge of the circle.

Basha's heart beat rapidly. Several even tougher-looking men than Szabla shoved two ragged and emaciated refugees to the ground at his feet. Blind rage almost made her surge to her feet. She wondered why she had come. The men on the ground trembled as if they faced their last judgment day. Basha's mind went red at this sight, remembering the refugees slaughtered by Nazi's.

7

Szabla felt keenly alert, every muscle ready to respond, but kept his expression a composed blank of deceptive innocence. Out of the corner of his eye, he saw something move on the edge of his camp and motioned two of his men with only his eyes to check on it. Then he examined the two men at his feet. Szabla made his voice gush out slow and heavy, and said, "Tell me why I should not kill you."

A man in an old worn-out Polish army uniform jumped up and hurled his words at Szabla, "It's unpatriotic."

Szabla placed his hand on the big knife hanging on his belt and stared the man down. The soldier quickly retreated, sat down, and averted Szabla's eyes.

Nevertheless, the words still rang in Szabla's ear. There was a time when he would never have tolerated that kind of insubordination. He would have immediately killed the two men, and then sliced the throat of the man in uniform. He gripped his knife handle then released it.

He turned back to the two men on the ground and then strode around the circle studying all his men. Everyone knew his normal policy toward refugees found in the mountains: if they looked strong and capable enough, they were assimilated into his band. If they looked weak and unable to survive the rigorous hardships that awaited them as his followers, they were killed and buried on the spot. His band had begun to include former Polish soldiers, and his practice of killing the weaker recruits had grown subtler.

As he continued to circle the men, he locked eyes with each man's gaze. The occupation of being a bandit had become difficult and more complex. Not only was it dangerous to travel out of the mountains, or travel in a large group because of those accursed German airplanes, but new attitudes were popping up like poison mushrooms among his followers. Lately his men expressed the startling desire of killing and looting Germans for no other reason than the bandits were Poles and the Germans were Germans.

Szabla found this confusing and unsettling. There was no doubt that the Germans had brought changes with their invasion of the lowlands.

He stopped where the Polish soldier had sat back down and said directly to him, "It is my decision to make!" Several of his men sat down in solidarity with the uniformed man and other Polish refugees. This gave the man who had spoken the courage to stand up again. Szabla glanced over his shoulder and saw his friend Durcansky and his most trusted men adjusting their weapons.

Suddenly, with great clarity, Szabla saw the truth staring him in the face; He was no longer the leader of just a band of common outlaws and bandits. He was in reality a leader of patriots. He squinted one eye, and lowered his brow. They had become a strange band of Polish partisan heroes. He was a Pole and every man in the camp was a Pole, with the exception of Sediva who was a Czech, and a very good man with a rifle. As Poles, they all had a common enemy now —the Germans.

"It is true; we are all Poles, except for Sediva. All of us." He gestured to the circle. He looked at the two men kneeling before him and said, "And as a partisan, I spare you in the name of Poland."

Then he saw all the men cheer. Szabla let his shoulders relax in great relief. The two refugees rose and everyone hugged and patted each other on their backs. With one clever stroke, from his cunning predatory mind, he realized he had averted a civil war in his camp. Szabla congratulated himself for he now bound the group together in a spirit they had never displayed before. He didn't try to repress his wide smile showing his gapped two front teeth. His men chanted, "Partisans, Partisans, Partisans." Szabla nodded his head vigorously, enjoying his brilliant victory.

During all the commotion, the two men he had sent to the edge of his camp came back and dropped a bundle wrapped in a cape at his feet. *Another refugee*, Szabla thought and ripped off the cape. The entire camp gasped and quieted when a woman, Basha Mickiewicz, struggled to her feet before him.

8

Szabla blinked. Was he seeing things? No, it was the women of his deepest desires, the one with soft hair, dark eyes, smooth skin, and his beloved. Yet, in these three lonely years, she had come into the full flower of her maturity in the most hazardous of times. The one, who years ago, forced him to turn outlaw.

Basha was about to speak, but Szabla held his hand up to stop her. He looked around at his men.

"This conversation should be private."

He took her by the arm and moved under a tree away from everyone. He nodded his head for her to speak. She spoke, sounding as if she did not know him. "I have come from Praznik." Her words tumbled out as she told him what had occurred with the Nazis. He listened, his brain filling with rage and his heart felt pinched from the slaughter. Once again, he could not believe there was a God. How could God allow humans to do such things to children, even if they were Jews? A metallic chill coursed through his body like when his mother had read him scary stories about monsters. He catalogued it in his mind knowing that somewhere later in time he would make the Germans pay for this.

Basha paused to catch her breath in remembrance, then Explained, "The harvest with no men left to help the village, how can we bring in the harvest and feed the people?"

As she continued, Szabla could not keep his eyes from slowly caressing and undressing her even under all the clothing she wore. The coat that hid her supple breasts bulged just slightly, her scarf hiding her silky hair falling across her shoulders. Those full pouting lips and her fragrance like mountain flowers. He still admired her, could still feel that dormant smoldering desire that only waited seeing her again to fan itself into flames. He knew that she was aware of his intense scrutiny, yet she chose to ignore it, even though one time she had invited it. He knew how hard she could be, how easily she could dismiss the emotion so plainly written on his face as when in the past she chose even to ignore her own feelings toward him.

His trouble with her had occurred long before the invasion of the Germans. It made him recall the old days when he could have had her as his own. If he only would have settled down and become a farmer, maybe gone with her to Praznik, to that village of ignorant peasants, things would be different. As their eyes held in their embrace of the past, she shook her head and broke the spell. He had not heard all she had said and she repeated the question.

"Well. What do you say? Will you come down to the village?" His thoughts were still elsewhere.

"I have not seen you in a long time," he said, sounding surprisingly formal. "Yet, I can easily believe we have not been apart but only a few short days." He saw her pause to reflect on his attitude. She glanced at the setting sun.

"For me, it has been long, very long."

"Of course it has. But seeing me again, like this, doesn't it seem to you we haven't been apart?"

"No." She tightened her scarf from the evening breeze.

He let his disappointment show with a frown. Then, recovering, he smiled. "Have I changed much?"

"As always, you remain the same."

"You too. Only now, each time we meet again, I can discover some new thing of you that reminds me of our past. Those things we felt. What we still feel, if you would admit it." He felt renewed determination to win her back so she would never leave him again.

"I have told you before. That is gone between us."

"Is it? Or are you running away as you did before, hiding from the truth." He rolled down and buttoned his shirtsleeves.

"There is nothing to hide. What we had was of another time. It's no longer even a memory for me." She crossed her arms on her breasts and looked away.

Szabla lowered one eye and squinted at her intently. "You lie poorly. Your voice betrays you, as even your action in coming here. No matter what you do or say, I know you, Basha Mickiewicz. The past is still alive for you as it is for me. And it is because of that alone I have allowed you to find my camp and to see me."

"If this is so, then give me your answer," Basha said, hands on her hips, changing to the reason for her appearance at his camp.

"What?" Behind him, he could hear the crackling of the evening campfires. The smell of wood burning trickled through the trees and into his nostrils and made him think of those stupid villagers.

"Will you come down to the village? We need your men for the harvest. Some of the houses have been destroyed. They need rebuilding. They've taken away all the young men. I told you."

"Who?" Now Basha came closer to him, almost in his face. "The Germans. You haven't been listening."

"Yes. I have been listening. I have been listening to nothing. Why should I come to that village? Why should I want to do anything for them? Praznik!" He spat, barely missing her. Turning his back, he walked away from her then turned towards her again and said, "They tried to hang me. Hang me! And now you want me to come and be a farmer for them. You want me to care for them. You want me to bring them food."

"Yes."

Finally, he had but one more word. He walked back over to her and shouted, "No!" Then, he returned to the partisans while Basha followed him, crunching pine needles, and speaking as she went.

"You call yourself a patriot," she said.

"I never said I was a patriot."

"But you never said you were a bandit either, but you are. You are a jackal, living off your fellow countrymen."

"What do you mean? We are partisans."

"Bah! You are worse than the Germans! You are a traitor!"

Szabla rolled his eyes and shook his head at her futile effort. Bronislaw, Szabla's newly acquired son, barely sixteen, of slender build, jumped up, and came over to them.

"He is no traitor! He is a patriot," Bronislaw said, his young voice cracking. Basha laughed long and hard. "He is a fat jackal who is afraid of his own shadow and terrified of Germans." Bronislaw rushed towards Basha but Szabla restrained him.

"A traitor who needs a boy to protect him," Basha said while shaking Jarods cane. Out of the corner of his eye, Szabla saw his men watching, some with amusement, others with disdain.

"You go too far, Basha," Szabla warned. He felt his whole plan to win her back slipping from his grasp. He wished the conversation had taken another direction.

Basha pointed the cane at the boy and waved it in his face tauntingly.

"Who is this boy who needs a good whipping?"

"This is my son, Bronislaw."

"Your son?" Basha guffawed with a choke. "Your son?"

"My adopted son." Basha pointed the cane at Szabla.

"Well, my boy. Study your adopted father. Study the ways of this wolf and this life he leads. Maybe someday we can curse you as well!"

Szabla and everyone in the camp watched as she batted the ground with the cane and headed down the trail.

Szabla ran up to the top of the knoll, caught his breath and a last glimpse of her in the twilight threading her way from the high mountains back down to the village. He thought, *Gone again!*

9

Dr. Estricher's mind translated to his whole body and soul that his only salvation now was to work and wait at the hospital. He felt a new resurgence of the will to live blossom within as he lost himself in the unending number of patients he treated. Once again he watched as his dedication, not to humanity, but to medicine and skill, won him admirers and to a degree, a modicum of protection. Yet his bitterness grew inside and eventually sought an outlet.

After several months, he still had not heard a word of his wife and children. He resigned himself that apparently his family had joined the countless other families who had vanished in the maelstrom of an old Europe in the process of disintegration.

He could see his situation steadily growing more hopeless and so he began to plan an escape. As a non-Aryan, he had no passport and therefore could not travel, that is in the normal manner of civilized people. It was obvious to him that unless he acquired a passport or permit, he could never leave Budapest. Because he was a Jew, he could not qualify for either. It was then he realized the only other choice was to acquire a new identity.

He became obsessed with the problem of obtaining a new identity and he thought of it daily. It occupied his mind, creating a new purpose and activity for his skill that gave him a strange sort of sustenance.

I must escape permanently—without any possibility of capture, he muttered under his breath while devising a brilliant plan. He knew exactly what would happen to him if he left Budapest.

Using his position at the hospital, and his relationship with some of the military personnel who were patients, many of whom were not aware that he was a Jew, he began to make discrete inquiries.

"How is your wound this morning Heir Gustav? How in the world did you get into our bustling city? Our records show you had no permit or passport only your military ID, —Lieutenant Hedrick Gustav of the SS."

"Ah doctor, first, my wound seems to be healing fine thanks to you. That bottleneck traffic at the bridge checkpoint was the worst. Imagine, I had to wait over two hours before they could see who I was and wave me past. But of course most travel is easy with military ID."

"Of course. So, have our fine nurses here contacted any of your relatives for you?"

"Oh, yes. They did reach my wife."

"Will she be coming to visit you?"

"No no, she cannot she is in Germany. It's hard enough for the military to get over the border now with all the checkpoints, and for a civilian, next to impossible without a special permit, it's all so much trouble."

"But for a wife, it would be worth the trouble wouldn't it? And a man of your position should have no trouble getting his wife a permit."

"Maybe if I was a colonel, and had influence back home. However, I am just a man who takes orders. I always do what my commanding officer tells me. He likes me you know."

* * *

Estricher made it a point to be there when Heir Gustav was well enough to be discharged several weeks later.

"I hope I don't see you again Heir Gustav."

"You are a funny man Doctor."

"I understand your commanding officer got your wife a permit to come see you."

"Doctor, you know very well you talked to him."

"Yes, well I thought he should know you were a man of courage and strength, and in these times that should be rewarded."

"Yes, quite amazing really. My wife will be here tomorrow, but only for two days, then it's back to the front for me."

"May I recommend a romantic place on Margit Island for you and your wife during your stay?"

"You Hungarians, always thinking about romance. That would be very nice Doctor; I'm in your debt. You will have to come out and share a bottle with us."

"Ah, I appreciate your generosity but as you see here I am in great demand. In any case, may I have the honor of assisting you in your wife's travel arrangements and your accommodations?"

"I can see why so many of our wounded soldiers hope to come to this hospital, the service and convalescing is impeccable, but I won't be recommending it."

"Now who's the funny man?"

Estricher smiled, took Gustav's papers with the special permit the commanding officer had given the lieutenant for his wife, and made all the travel arrangements. He soon knew as much about the required documentation for wartime travel as the most arrogant clerks he dealt with while making travel accommodations for relatives of his patients. In this way, he also became familiar with military customs and manner as well as the privileges of rank.

His awareness to the details of the military establishment and his observance of the ease in which doors opened to certain men in uniform decided him finally on his plan of impersonating one of them.

It would be simple he thought. From the growing number of terminal cases that filled the basement and morgue of the hospital, he would select an officer most closely fitting his own description. Certainly, with just minor alterations to his own personal appearance he could make himself resemble the military identity photo the officer carried. A disguise would only be necessary as far as Vienna; he pictured it, because there he had friends he knew would help him. From Vienna, he could continue on to either Switzerland or Spain, where he heard there were already a growing number of expatriates. He could even choose to head directly north to Sweden, a country where some of his relatives had fled in earlier years. There were all sorts of possibilities once he had definitely decided to put his plan in action. It was now only a question of days, or even hours. He now felt prepared to make his move immediately the moment any opportunity presented itself.

10

One morning, an opportunity presented itself. It was the doctor's duty to check in several new patients for special surgery, and then he saw the man. It caused an immediate increase in Estreicher's heartbeat. It was an army captain and although Estreicher would have preferred an officer of higher rank, the man had a close enough resemblance to him to make him realize the moment had arrived.

On the report, Estreicher read the captain had already undergone a serious operation to save his life, but was sent back for a second to remove a bullet still lodged near his spine. The officer was a staunch Nazi party man and therefore Estreicher, silently thankful, was not allowed to operate on him. If he had, his own conscience would have prevented him from doing anything but utilizing his utmost skill to save the man. Instead, another doctor, one whom Estreicher considered the worst surgeon at the hospital was given the task of operating.

The next afternoon the officer was dead, and Estreicher carefully stole his credentials. Estreicher originally had not intended to impersonate a German, although he spoke the language, he had prepared a Hungarian officers uniform, hidden in the basement of the hospital. On seeing the German captain in the morning and identifying him as a distinct possibility, he had removed a German uniform nearest his size from the morgue storage closet and smuggled it to his room.

That evening, after making the necessary changes to his own appearance, shaving his mustache, lightening his hair, narrowing and changing the shape of his eyebrows, he left the hospital. Inside a closed booth in a public restroom next to a church, he changed into the uniform and headed for the Deli train station on Alkotas Ut.

He waited nervously several hours before the next train, and once again thought of his wife and children. Then he saw the public phone and decided, regardless of the risk, to make one final call to the government official that had once professed to be his friend. When told the man was out for the evening, Estreicher lied as to whom he was and demanded to know his whereabouts. The call was government business, and he was given the information. He placed another call, this time to one of the larger hotels in Budapest. The man at the other end seemed stunned at hearing Estreicher's voice.

"Yes, I do have new news, I don't feel comfortable talking over the phone, can you come to the hotel?"

"No. It's impossible. Please tell me. Are they alive or dead?" There was a hesitant pause. Then, "Dead."

"The children too?"

"Yes."

"When?"

"Several months ago."

"Where?"

"In the Polish Ukraine."

"How were they . . . ?"

"I don' t know."

"Were they alone? Were there others?"

"Some."

"Some—what do you mean some? Hundreds? Thousands?"

"I don't know . . . Estreicher. I am sorry. But listen, listen Estreicher, we are even now. Do not call me again. Ever! Do you understand?" A long silence passed.

"Estreicher? Estreicher, are you there? Hello?"

11

Eastriecher stared out the window of the train the next morning as the monotony of the clacking track spurs lulled him into another depressing stupor. Forcing himself to pull out of the negative dive, he reached for the morning paper left by someone on the seat next to him. Thumbing through to the second page his eyes refocused on a small article with the by line 'Elizabeth Hospital Administration Embarrassed Last Night'. The hospital had reported Estriecher to the city police as missing. When the police came to investigate they revealed Estriecher was a Jew. The special secret police were immediately called in to assume responsibility. It was obvious the man had fled.

The official version carried by the state news bureau was simple, and to the point. 'After a highly delicate and successful operation on a brave German war hero, this Jew had secretly administered a fatal dose of the wrong drug into the arm of the helpless victim. The Germans have offered their own police assistance, and Hungary was being actively combed for this heinous criminal.'

The shock sent his adrenaline flowing. *They already know who I am!* He looked up and out the window and realized another jolting shock. In his anguish over the loss of his family, he had taken the wrong train and was now crossing over the boarder to Czechoslovakia not Vienna. Recovering from his initial surprise, there was nothing he could do now but ride on to the next stop and change trains. During the short ride to the next station, he began to think that maybe his mistake had not been so misfortunate after all. *Now that his family . . . maybe Sweden would be the better destination.*

By the time the train reached the next station he had decided on Sweden and prepared to travel the entire distance in his present disguise. As the smoke cleared, he saw a group of German soldiers, Gestapo, divide themselves into pairs, and begin making their way to the coach doorways.

Furtively, Estreicher assessed his situation. He seemed trapped. He stood up and tried to appear casual. Then moving as quickly as possible without attracting attention to himself, he moved through the crowded cars in an agony of slow motion. He was in a continuous struggle to stifle his impulse to keep from shoving the unconcerned passengers aside and dash through the train. To do so would be like strapping a target to his body. Finally, almost to the end of his nerve, and growing more frantic by the second as he approached the last cars of the train, he suddenly found himself in the baggage and storage car. He entered the baggage car cautiously, and then quickly searched for a place to hide. Though the car was crowded with luggage, packages, and several crates, it was obvious that with any systematic search, he would be quickly discovered anywhere he might hide.

He rapidly reached a point of desperation. His eyes caught an ornate coffin resting against the far wall. He stood over it and stared. It was a heavy coffin, constructed in the style reserved for Hungarian royalty of years past. The entire coffin was covered with brass ornamentation, and on the lid of one side was an elaborately designed cross. Pausing only for a moment, Estreicher quickly forced open the coffin and stared at the corpse inside. It was a man, slight of build, who in death, even with closed eyes, seemed to look up at him with a serene expression. The body was dressed in a cassock. The man was a priest, the sight of him so completely unexpected that Estreicher froze in surprise for several moments. The sound of shouting men outside the train brought him abruptly back to his present desperation. Glancing around with a feeling of some guilt, Estreicher moved the corpse onto its side and climbed into the coffin, gently closing the lid.

Once inside the coffin, his breath sounded like a racing steam engine and he thought he could detect the faint odor of embalming fluid. He felt cramped and uncomfortable in the confining space of the coffin, but was too frightened to move. He tried not to think, waiting patiently for the train to move again. He thought he heard the outside door of the baggage car open, and the sound of voices nearby. He tried to calm his breathing so that he could listen, but it was impossible to distinguish any of the sounds so that they were intelligible.

In a short while, his breathing had calmed considerably and his eyes became accustomed to the interior of the coffin. Inquisitively he discovered tiny shafts of light coming through cracks in the side and along the line of the lid. He looked as far as his eyes could see without moving his head. He deduced that warping and age apparently caused it. Estreicher wondered about the coffin. Had it been used before?

In the quiet of the coffin, he could suddenly hear the ticking of his watch. He tried to bring his hand up to see but the body next to him made it impossible. Then he decided to stop his fidgeting and relax to the degree the cramped interior of the coffin would permit. He would remain perfectly still and wait. At least he would try to. Given enough time, they would give up their search and he could emerge again, reborn from the dead.

He waited for what seemed like a sweating trip through eternity. In only a short while, the sudden jerking of the coffin and a sense of motion reached him. He continued to wait until the clicking noise of the rolling wheels on the track and the gentle rocking of the baggage car had remained steady for a time. Then with an easy shove, he exerted pressure against the lid. It remained closed. He exerted more pressure against the lid. Then he strained. The lid was solid, refusing to budge. He wanted to scream as his breath began racing again. He tried several more times then, lapsed into an exhausted stillness.

He became calm again as he began to reason out the situation. He did not recall seeing any locking devices on the outside of the coffin. He did originally have to pry it open. He figured the age of the coffin had also warped the lid and it must have jammed shut again, but it remained shut.

For hours, in unsuccessful repetition, he exerted pressure on the lid wherever he could. No matter how hard he tried, it refused to budge. Then, because of the shortage of oxygen in the restrictive space of the coffin, he became too weak to continue the struggle. Finally, in exhaustion from his whole experience from the last two days, he fell into a deep sleep.

12

For two days and nights, the coffin remained on the train with Estreicher inside. By the beginning of the third day, Estreicher had already accepted his fate as the train rumbled on to a destination that could result in his being buried alive.

He awoke and slept in fits. His weakness calmed him, but his mind, when he was awake and not dreaming of hell, was active. His thirst became excruciating. He lost all sense of time and there were moments when he felt he had died and was in some sort of transitory state before hell. When he thought of hell, he thought of God, and the paradox that he should think of him when he was on his way to hell. For the sin of not thinking of God seemed to be the reason he was now on his way to eternal darkness.

During those first thoughts of God, he was bitter, contemptuous, and unbelieving. He thought of his father and what an orthodox man he had been and what a staunch believer he had remained until his death. Estreicher thought of his own youth and his coming of age and how the injustice and brutality of the world had disillusioned him and made him angry with a God who could allow all this to happen. It was ridiculous to think of God as a grand old man who had picked the Jews as his chosen people and then proceeded to allow their massacre and destruction wherever the Jew settled and stayed for long. It was nothing but rubbish, and a fairy tale, and Estreicher had refused to believe in it any longer.

What was worse, he became indifferent to God. Yet, the irony of it all, was that those with whom he agreed about the proud stubbornness of the Jew refusing to assimilate and give up this nonsense, forced him to remain a Jew, ethnically if not religiously. Persecution kept him a Jew along with millions of others. The law of survival was too strong for him to attempt to stand-alone.

At the end of the day, when the light in the baggage car faded, and the little shafts of light in the coffin darkened into nothing, he felt it was over for him.

The next morning when the shafts of light returned, he thought once again of his wife and children and how God had failed even them, they who still believed and had managed to practice the faith no matter what seemed to be happening in the world around them. Then he realized his rationalization, and knew he failed his family. That it was not God who was at fault. It was his prideful self-delusion of importance. He wept as he recalled his life. How happy he had been with it. When he thought of all the wonderful things he had done for his fellow beings with his medical knowledge and skill, he cursed the injustice of it all, and the imponderability of the fate that had killed his family, and had sent him to a living death. He gnashed his teeth bitterly and once more sank back into the stupor of recalling his past, hovering in a netherworld of strange haunting images.

When he came to again, he seemed to have recovered his senses. He felt more alert, almost refreshed. He knew that eventually the train would stop and the coffin would be removed from the baggage car. All that was required was for him to wait. At the proper moment, he would pound on the lid and someone would release him.

To occupy himself he now systematically began to review his past as a surgeon and recalled many of his successful operations, performing them over again in his mind. A startling revelation came to him as he did so, a sudden clarity of truth that washed the last dregs of self-pity from him. He had enjoyed being a surgeon and looked up to as some great wizard who held the secret of life and death in his scalpel. He realized it had nothing whatsoever to do with a desire to serve humanity, and it was all for Estreicher. It was about how it made him feel. It had fed his self-righteousness and his charitable works performed under the public glare of those around him that had made him proud. Whatever he had done, he had done for himself, regardless who were the recipients of his beneficence. He had been amply repaid in fame and wealth for all his work, so where was the injustice?

His mind became inactive for a time and then he became conscious of the corpse beside him, conscious that is, of the man, or life force that had given the body life. *What had I done to deserve this fate?*

Estreicher recalled the serene expression of the corpse and wondered what sort of man this priest had been. He could almost smile when he thought of how shocked this priest would be if he knew that he was sharing his final resting-place with a Jew, maybe even for an eternity. He wondered what the priest had accomplished with his life, and tried to recall what little knowledge he had of Christianity and priests.

Estreicher had a great deal of Old Testament knowledge from his youth, having diligently studied Torah, but only a smattering of New Testament and Christianity. Christianity and especially those that believe in it made no sense to him. It was incongruous, based on his own painful experience with alleged Christians, that those who worshipped a Jew as the Son of God should be among the greatest Jew haters in the world. How many times had he heard Christians call Jews Christ killers then to go on illogically and preach that his death was necessary to pay for all our sins, that He chose of his own volition to sacrifice Himself as the lamb of God.

When shafts of light streaming into the coffin faded that night, fear and exhaustion had made Estreicher delirious. He moaned loudly and his body twitched nervously. He dreamt wild dreams. Someone had stolen his body, and the priest had taken his place. He could see the priest standing in his place at the hospital in Budapest, operating. He saw the priest kissing his wife and playing with his children. He saw the priest taking his Toraha, and he screamed in protest but no one could hear him.

Then he became the priest and everyone who saw him made the sign of the cross and smiled at him knowingly, aware of his impersonation. Now as the priest, he was in the operating room about to perform an operation on a German officer in uniform lying on the table. With the scalpel between his fingers, he reached to make the first incision through the uniform and he looked at the man's face, stunned to find it was himself. And as he watched, the man in the German uniform who was himself, opened his eyes and smiled up at him, and as he did so the scalpel turned into a cross and he fainted.

13

Once again, Estreicher came to his senses and this time he was aware of stillness, and unnatural quiet that made its presence felt so that he weakly moved his head to determine what had happened. It was the fourth day, although he hadn't realized it at the time, and there was no rocking motion, there was nothing but silence.

He knew immediately he was no longer on the train. He felt a coldness coming from the sides of the coffin and he cried out in terror. While he was unconscious, they had buried the coffin. He was buried alive! He desperately began to groan aloud at his doom. There was nothing left for him to do now but die, or pray. *To whom? To what? There is no God. Then die,* He refused to listen, but his thoughts raced on in a forlorn search for survival. Pray? For what? For a miracle, he asked himself contemptuously. For a miracle like the one that had saved his family? Or a miracle like the one now letting thousands die? What rot, what hopelessness. He wanted to live, and to the priest in the coffin beside him he said, in a croaking voice, "Help me to pray. I have forgotten how." The priest refused to answer him.

"If you're with God now, help me. You can't be angry with me for sharing your coffin. I need help. I'm sorry for my ignorance. I don't remember how to pray. If Jesus is your God, ask Him to teach me. I'll listen. Let me live and I'll listen. Help me to escape and I'll believe. Don't allow me to be buried alive." He paused, waiting desperately for an answer. When there was none, he said,

"Jesus, if you are the Son of God, save me and I'll do whatever you ask. Like Jacob served Laban, I'll serve you for as long a period as you want me to. Only save me!"

Suddenly he seemed to hear the sound of voices. He listened and he was certain of the voices. They were outside the coffin, the sound of many people speaking. Then, there was only the sound of a single clear voice and with a palpitating heart, Estreicher heard the unmistakable intonation of a liturgy, and he knew it was for the man beside him. As he listened quietly, unable to distinguish the words, he also knew it was for him. He felt an unfamiliar assurance; an unfamiliar peace come over him as he listened with the realization his prayer had been heard. With damp eyes, he spoke out softly.

"Thank you."

Estreicher waited for a long while after the sound outside the coffin had ceased before he shoved quietly on the coffin lid. It opened easily and he sat up stiffly. As he had assumed, he found himself inside a large church, and he clumsily climbed out of the coffin. It was as if he had arisen from the dead and he looked up at the unfamiliar face of the crucified man on the cross above him. "Thank you." He croaked hoarsely. "Thank you."

It was night and he was alone. Except for several candles, the church was dark. During the last of his dark sojourn, he had fouled his clothes. He staggered about until he found a washroom where he cleaned up and relieved himself.

Afterwards, still stumbling, he searched through the private rooms behind the altar, looking for a change of clothing. The only clothing he could find was in the vestry closet. There were several cassocks of different sizes and a heavy overcoat. There was no choice. He had to do what was necessary. He found a cassock that would fit him, and taking it, and the heavy overcoat, he returned to the washroom where he stripped off the German uniform and spent considerable time washing himself. Then cautiously he put on the cassock, and as he fit the cloth over him, he seemed to derive a certain sense of comfort from it. He removed only the money from the uniform before rolling it up and putting on the heavy overcoat.

Returning through the vestry, he noticed several small prayer books and a set of beads on a desk. He stuffed them quickly into his overcoat pocket. Then remembering the priest again, he walked back out to the coffin resting near the altar. He now moved one of the candles to cast sufficient light inside the coffin. As he did so, he discovered a small book and a set of papers that had become wedged behind the priest. Holding the documents to the light, he was amazed at what he held. It was the priest's personal prayer book, several letters, and his passport.

Wetting his lips with his tongue, Estreicher opened the passport and saw smiling at him the same serene face of the man whose coffin he had shared. Father Jan Kabos, the passport read, he was Hungarian! *Hungarian? Then why was his body shipped out of Hungary? Of course, this must be his church. He must have died on a visit and they sent him back to his church, to the people who knew him, for burial.*

Estreicher dismissed the puzzle, only glad that it had happened at the proper moment to allow him to escape. He pocketed the documents and passport that had belonged to father Kabos and paused long enough to look down at the face in the coffin and ask forgiveness for stealing his belongings and to thank the priest again. He closed the lid then changed his mind and reopened it, moving the coffin slightly so that the face of the dead priest was in the visual direction of the crucifixion.

Estreicher blinked his eyes at the sight of the small city in Czechoslovakia he was in now. There was a river that seemed only a block away, and he immediately disposed of the rolled up German uniform by securely tying and weighting it with some heavy stones then dropping it in the river. It sank with only a few quiet bubbles as it descended. Then carefully ripping up the German identity papers, he scattered them over the flowing water, watching them disappear. He faced north, in the direction of Sweden and began walking.

Soon he was in flight again, and he thought how strange, being pursued for his Christian activities. Wherever he went in the guise of Father Kabos, he gave succor to whoever called upon him, clumsily at first, but growing better with time. Wherever those of the faith took him in, he gave comfort, and in return received comfort.

With a bumbling mixture of old testament knowledge and a smattering of the New Testament sacraments he was gleaning from the prayer books, he went from town to town, village to village, avoiding the larger cities, preaching comfort and the messages he found in the prayer books.

Moreover, along the way through observation of religious layman and the assimilation of much literature, he found the ability to conduct a formal mass whenever called upon to do so. He felt no guilt, but almost a divine calling similar to those disciples he was now reading about in the bible, brought forth from their own strange backgrounds to preach the word.

In spite of the fact that he became known to the Gestapo for his illegal preaching, and was considered an outlaw priest, he found the door always opened to him. The law for sheltering such an individual was death, but he was welcomed and sheltered by all he met. He found himself continuously astonished at the people who called themselves Christians, welcoming, and sheltering him. For no matter what had happened to them, regardless of the depth of their despair, none had lost faith in God. They were long-suffering and penitent, certain of having sinned, but willing to wait for God to show them his mercy.

Finally, there came a time, a moment he could not exactly put his finger on, when he began to believe in what he was saying. He believed the message of salvation, and he made a vow to God that if he were ever to escape this madness, he would keep the promise he had made in death, and he would make full restitution for any sin that he might be committing in his ignorance.

He kept moving, on many occasions staying just one jump ahead of his pursuers, who he felt were very much aware of his weird zigzag pattern through the countryside, thereby eluding them. Many times, he was questioned by sympathetic local police, but not held. Twice he was arrested and thought it was over. By some providential intervention, he escaped harm; the first time being ransomed by a prelate of the area who claimed to know him. The Second time, after inadvertently having revealed his knowledge of German, he was picked up on general suspicion, later released through the sheer incompetence of his captors who could not find his name on any list. He escaped only a short time before the routine arrival of the Gestapo at his place of destination.

At last, he found himself in Poland, having been detoured from his original journey, and at the same time, he finally came to the end of his stamina. He asked God for help as he staggered into a small village where he knew no one. He graciously accepted an invitation to a meager dinner by a conscripted laborer who told him where he might hide from the Germans until he was sufficiently well again to travel. As he ate, he listened and discovered it was a village not even important enough to be on the map of Poland. It was a place where they needed a priest, and men, a place where an outlaw priest could easily hide and be useful.

After memorizing the route, blessing the man and his family, knapsack on his back, Estreicher rallied his last bit of strength and left town. He proceeded out of the lowlands and started the long climb into the mountains, heading for the village the laborer had called, Praznik.

14

Several days after Basha had left his camp, Szabla reluctantly brought some of his men down to the village. As they sauntered into the square, he noticed the villagers peeping out their windows and doors surprised at his sudden appearance. It amused him to see them so frightened. Szabla felt that some of the eyes were the same eyes that unjustly tried to hang him many years ago. He had helped this village before. He had brought them food from the forests and supplies they could not afford. What did he get? They turned around and had him arrested for possession of stolen goods.

Szabla wondered if this time Basha's commanding personality could keep the villagers listening to reason. He watched her come out of her apartment into the street and confront him face-to-face.

"I am here to help you with my men," he said, looking around at the gathering villagers at the meeting place in the square. He thought if he helped Basha with the village she would come back to him. He and his men stood to the side and waited silently while Basha called all the villagers to assemble, they were mostly women and elders.

Szabla squinted at his men perusing the women with wanton eyes, and then looked at Basha to see if she noticed.

"This man is a partisan now fighting the Germans."

"He is a bandit, how can we trust him?" One of the women yelled out.

"Times change, people change." Basha retorted.

There was mumbling amongst the villagers. Szabla saw in that moment that Basha was becoming the intermediary between himself and the villagers. He didn't think she could keep the peace if they were stupid again, and he had to show who was stronger. Szabla was surprised to see Basha, by the strength of her will and the common sense of her wisdom, become the real leader of the village. Another of the villagers shouted, "Why should we give him a chance?"

Basha replied. "He is a Pole, and we all must band together to protect ourselves from the Germans. He can rebuild our huts, help with the harvest, and show us how to protect the village. We have no strong men, we need him, and I have his word he will only help us." Basha looked at Szabla. He nodded approvingly so all could see him agree with every assurance that she gave the villagers about his being there to help and keep them safe. "He is a thief and will only bring trouble. If he steals from the Germans they will come here again." Some of the women nodded in agreement.

"You see Basha; they would rather freeze and starve than be saved by me. I am leaving, let them starve."

"Wait, give them your promise you will only protect us and not steal or kill Germans anywhere near the Village." Szabla thought a moment, he would have given his word to Basha, and strategically he would do that anyway. Even though he hated to promise this village anything, he had to do it for her. He looked at the villagers and his men staring at him in anticipation, waiting to see what he did next. He looked at Basha and said, "All right, I promise!" Then Szabla saw one of the elder men step forward,

"That's too easy, make him swear on the bible. Then it's not just us he has to account to." He held up a bible. All were silent.

That was too much. Why should he swear on the Bible? What was worse, Basha had gone over to the elder, taken the Bible, and was standing in front of him holding it up.

"You push me to far woman." He mumbled under his breath.

"Swear, or be gone," She barked loudly.

Szabla was ready to leave. He turned around and saw his men and thought, he didn't believe anyway, so what's the difference. Then his cunning mind made him say,

"If I swear, then this village must listen and do what I say to protect it from the Germans". Szabla saw all eyes were not on him now but on

Basha. She looked at everyone then at Szabla. "Done, now swear!" Szabla reluctantly put his hand quickly on the bible. "All right, I swear."

"Good. Don't think this changes anything between you and me. You still sleep in your camp."

Basha's words stung again and Szabla realized it was going to take time. He would wait; he had waited three years he could wait a little longer. Then, in front of everyone, he instructed his men, "Each one of you will pick a house to rebuild. Double up if you have to. You will also work the fields and bring in your households share of the harvest. After the day's work is done you will return to the camp." Then he explained how they would set up lookouts and an alarm to secure the perimeter around the village. A plan would be devised that everyone must follow in case the Germans came back. That was all for now.

* * *

It was not easy at first, but slowly in the months that followed, Szabla saw and heard the villager's feelings toward him and his partisans grow friendlier with trust and appreciation. Eventually he and his men felt truly welcomed. He was now considered a true partisan, and as such found the new admiration and respect of him by most villagers something he desired. He began to feel and even behave like a patriot, allowing some of his men to move into the village of Praznik and become an integral part of its life and wellbeing. As he promised, he skirmished far afield from Praznik to protect the village and his partisan camp.

After the harvest, Szabla and some of his men left the village. He trekked with them to the Vistula and San rivers and once had gone as far south as the supported territory of Slovakia. He was disappointed they had found little to nothing in the way of food supplies. They had managed only to replenish their ammunitions and arms taken from a few German patrols. After their long trek, he and his men actually looked forward to coming back to Praznik.

During his time away, he observed that below the village of Praznik the world grew darker. Poland had become the graveyard of hope and decency in the human spirit, a playground for the forces of evil in the world. It seemed to him that no cry of anguish could penetrate the cloud that covered Poland. Men, women, and children of all ages were being gobbled up in the furnaces of the German destruction.

As he led his men back into the mountains toward Praznik, with their booty from the flatland raids, something was cogitating in Szabla's mind again. A strange pattern began to form that Szabla did not understand, or even notice at first. He had watched and pondered a single thread in a seemingly insignificant occurrence, in the great panorama of Poland's anguish, attached itself to another thread, and that thread attached itself to another. He had witnessed people who were unused to emotion finding them overcome with feeling. He wondered at the professional soldier discovering the human beneath his uniform. The clever became stupid, and the peasant grew wise. Hardened murderers demonstrated compassion. People who did not know of God became his active agents. To the few intelligent minds and the faithful he had spoken to, the ones who could see this pattern slowly forming everywhere, it meant only one thing to them. God was preparing to return to Poland. Szabla wondered at a ridiculous notion he had heard on many occasions and shook his head in disbelief. Now he concentrated his efforts on getting his men safely back home. Yes, he thought *where ever Basha is was home.*

15

Basha was uneasy and somewhat restless during the time Szabla was away. She had gone down to the flatlands in an attempt to discover what had happened to the young men of Praznik, and had barely been able to get back through the German lines from a seemingly fruitless trip to Krakow. She did return to the village with two nuns, two very pale and sickly women of the cloth. She made a promise and now she was keeping it. It was irritating to Szabla, but she hoped God would be pleased she was rebuilding his house in Praznik.

Basha kicked down part of the dilapidated doorway to the old chapel. Dust flew around and up everyone's nostrils causing the weaker-looking nun standing next to her to sneeze. The shorter nun, the paler of the two, was called Sister Theresa Mieczislaw. The taller and apparently healthier woman was Sister Anna Pulaski. Basha glanced at them and grimaced at the thought that if anyone were to look at them, they would see the two nuns had undergone severe hardship. She still needed to ensconce them in the chapel as part of its renovation and the rejuvenation for the soul of the village, keeping her promise to God.

Basha was surprised how readily the nuns had accepted her offer to come to Praznik immediately. They had told her the Germans had killed their priest and burned the church they lived in. She watched the nuns look appallingly at the chapel. Then she saw two of the elder men look disapprovingly at the nuns. The villagers did not accept them, and looked upon them almost the same as they looked upon the rundown Chapel. It was a large structure built of stones and mud. Basha rationalized it was like most of the huts and homes in Praznik, and she spoke her thoughts aloud, "the roof has been neglected for a long period but we can fix that." In the daytime with the sun shining through, she saw many openings between the stones and knew it would be dreadfully cold in winter. The chapel had never been designed for anyone to live in. Fortunately, before she left, Basha had asked some of the villagers and the partisans who had stayed behind, to help rebuild the structure. She looked again at the nuns as they watched a few of the women trying at the last minute to make it livable for the sisters. She could see that the women of the village were very superstitious and doubtful; they wondered why she had brought the nuns back to Praznik.

"Do we need more women in the village?" one of the elder men asked her. Basha again was taken aback by the attitudes.

"I don't think they want us here!", Sister Anna Pulaski said, while brushing dust off the alter. "Maybe we could stay with you." Basha could promptly install the stronger of the two women at the chapel, and keep the other with her until she was well enough to live there. Basha stopped Beata, who was bringing water to the workers and asked her, "Please go and get some of the linens I had instructed the women of the village to make, and tell them to bring the household items back as well."

Sister Theresa started brushing off the pews, and Sister Anna went in front of the statue of Mary, knelt down, and began to pray. Basha and the workers briefly stopped to watch them.

Glancing about the chapel again, Basha caught a glimpse of Szabla peeping in through the window as the nuns went about tidying up their new living space. She was glad he was back, walked over, and rested her arms on the dusty windowsill surprising Szabla. "Well, what do you think?" He shrugged and said, "Did you miss me?"

"I'm talking about the nuns and the chapel."

"Why do you waste your time on this old chapel and bring back more mouths to feed?"

"I made a promise to God." Basha said, as she saw Szabla give up, shake his head and in parting say, "Good, then let God feed them."

* * *

As time went on, Basha thought Szabla and the villager's relatively quiet acceptance of the nuns was because no one believed they would last through the winter.

One sunny spring morning, after winter had come and gone, Basha brought fruit to the chapel for the nuns. She stopped at the front door to say good morning to Beata, who was milling about the entrance.

"So, they are still alive?"

"Go in and you will see for yourself" Basha replied.

"I just wondered if they were alright."

"What is it you really want to know?"

"Well, where are they from, and who are they?"

Basha shrugged and entered the chapel. The villagers had finally accepted the nuns and Basha did not think it was important for anyone to know of their past, or where they came from. By now, it was too late.

Basha could see that the beginning of spring was bringing a healthier glow in the two nun's appearance. The sisters had definitely survived the winter. Basha still felt their voices were weak, and they appeared frail looking and quite apparently city-bred to the villagers. They were unused to the ways of peasant folk. Besides, the villagers realized that although these nuns were women of God, they were nonetheless, still women. Basha hoped what they would ultimately accomplish would be God's continued protection and wellbeing of an almost soulless group of people. She said to herself, *"After all, any contact with God is better than none."* She knew the nuns would make the village aware of God but probably were not strong enough to lead them to Him.

Even Basha was surprised when the entire village showed up for the Easter Sunday mass, including Szabla and some of his men.

16

Several days after the village's Easter mass, Basha walked to the bakery while contemplating the disappointment the villagers had with the quality of Sunday's service.

Then, she saw something happen that brought the most definite change to Praznik. It was the mysterious arrival of Father Kabos. She gasped at the sight of him in the middle of the street like an apparition of St. Peter arriving at the gates of heaven, staggering into the village, his clothes disheveled, a bruise on his forehead, his shoes worn through, his lips cracked. She noticed immediately he had the appearance of another refugee who had not eaten for some time. She wondered how he could have gotten past Szabla and his men. He arrived from nowhere in the midst of the harvest. No one saw him come up the mountain road, if that indeed was where he came from. No one saw him come down from the high mountains.

Basha knew the secret trail to Szabla's camp was well guarded so he must not have come from that direction. She felt something different, a strange aura about him, and instead of questioning him, she brought him to the tavern and took care to see that he was washed, clothed, and fed by the innkeeper and his wife. They were concerned about who he was and where he came from.

When Father Kabos recovered sufficiently to tell Basha who he was, they were all stunned. "A priest!" She knew it must be Gods will that sent him to the village. She had to figure a way for Szabla and the villagers to accept him without more feelings of trepidation, which she was sure they would all have.

In the tavern, that evening Basha stood behind the long polished wooden bar. She liked feeling her hands on the smooth surface as she leaned forward onto it and told the elder wise ones in the village about the stranger that had arrived. She glanced at the priest quietly sitting at a table by himself in the back of the tavern. She wanted them to accept him, and let him stay in the village even though they all had misgivings.

The elders were mumbling back and forth to each other, then Basha spoke, "He is a man of God, and we need the priest. After all, if believing in something good that you have not yet seen isn't faith, what is? And the nuns need a priest for mass."

Tearses, sitting in a semi-circle of chairs in front of the bar with the other elders said, "Where there is someone pursued, there are pursuers." Basha knew Tearses spoke with true wisdom, but she continued to plead the priest's case.

"But a priest! Where would you send him?"

Basha knew that they all were aware Praznik was the last of civilization before the high mountains. They couldn't send him there! "What would God say? No. He should remain in the village."

Basha waited patiently while the elders discussed the priest. First it was yes, then it was no. She heard one of them say, "Look what happened in the past when strangers were taken in." Then she heard another say, "Yes, but in Praznik, a village that years ago could barely sustain a traveling priest, a village that God sometimes forgot even existed, now had in it three of His representatives!"

Basha thought, *Yes, it was incredible.* Yet, although they had no idea what it might portend, the elders finally accepted it as a great sign, then Tearses stood up, "It is said, there are no coincidences, and God has a reason for everything he does."

"So you have decided he stays?" Basha asked. Tearses looked back at everyone and then said, "Let us speak with this priest."

Now she felt the time was right to introduce Father Jan Kabos to the elders. At least he was a man of the cloth, he would be stronger than the nuns would and she felt Tearses in all his wisdom would feel comfortable with him. Basha had been watching Father Kabos listening and taking it all in at the back of the tavern. Then he stood up, walked forward to the bar, and in a calm but firm voice assured them, without going into explanation, "I have no specific pursuers to my knowledge. In any case, I have no intention of staying. I am attempting to reach Sweden and will leave soon."

Basha Mickiewecz listened to him and narrowed her eyes with a sudden growing uneasiness. She found herself drawn to him, but also felt he was lying about something, and whatever it might be was only meant to obscure some truth about him. She wanted him to stay now more than ever. She wanted to know what he was hiding. As an extra precaution Basha said, "Let's bring him to the chapel and introduce him to the sisters." With that, they headed for the door. The other villagers who had been waiting outside the tavern for a verdict about Father Kabos now followed them to the Chapel.

When they arrived at the Chapel Basha was quick to note Father Kabos's sudden shyness with the nuns and found this curious, his behavior feeding the uneasiness she had felt earlier. The congregation stood in the Chapel as she introduced Father Kabos to the nuns. Then she heard Durcansky ask if Father Kabos would hold mass for the village this weekend, he said, "I will go to the upper camp and bring some of the men down for the service." Father Kabos hesitated for a moment before consenting, but Basha was quick to catch this, and her heart skipped a beat.

"It can wait. It has waited this long. The good Father can tell us when he is ready. Another week of rest is what he needs. Is that right, Father?" she asked.

"Let us see." Father Kabos said in a reticent manner. Durcansky shrugged and left. Basha caught up with him by the time he had almost reached the secret trail. He looked at her, startled, and when she caught her breath she said, "Tell Szabla not to send anyone else down until I tell him." Durcansky closed one eye the way Szabla always did. "Basha, is there something wrong? What is it? The priest?"

"Why did you mention the camp?" She said sharply.

"You don't . . . You think . . . do you think I would not kill him if I thought he was a traitor. Do you think I would be afraid to kill a priest?"

"No, Durcansky. You can kill anybody. You are good at doing that. If the priest is to be killed, I'll ask him if he would let you do it. All right? Go, stupid. Tell Szabla what I have said."

Durcansky turned from her and she watched him disappear into the brush of the trail. Basha suddenly felt used by the devil and guilt ridden.

She sensed a knot in her stomach beginning to grow. Had she been away from things spiritual and sacred for so long that when a man of God did arrive, she became uneasy? She felt confused by her own actions and thought of father Kabos's manner in the chapel that had seemed so unlike a priest. It had made her suspicious. *Had she become uneasy because of herself or the man? Why shouldn't his manner seem strange? How long had it been that she had stood so close to a priest? She had done an evil thing casting suspicion on a man of God.* She made up her mind; she would have to confess this sin, *but to whom? Surely not the priest she had become suspicious of.*

17

Szabla silently crept up stairs to Bashas apartment. When he reached the top, he opened the door and that familiar smell of wood-berry pedals from her permeated the cool damp air. He had sensed these feelings many times in the past. He wanted her and could feel the swelling in his blood making him salivate at the thought. When he gently woke her from sleep with caresses on her back, she peered up at him, said nothing, but pulled away. He watched her with disappointment and admiration as she slipped her clothes over her still firm naked body, the sight of which had never failed to excite him.

"Turn your eyes, you horny goat."

"Horny goat, huh? Well this goat still has the kind of milk that would do you good!"

"I want nothing from you until you prove you love something or somebody more than just yourself and stop the kill, kill, kill! He turned his head even though it was dark to make sure she could not see his reaction to her words. He waited until she dressed and then he lit the oil lamp.

"What about the priest?"

"There is nothing."

"Durcansky says you think he's a spy."

"Durcansky is a fool." He watched Basha get up, turn her back on him, and move to the table. He followed her.

"Basha, don't play games with me. I will go see this priest myself. If he is a spy, I'll kill him." In a burst of anger, Szabla whipped out his knife and drove it into the table an inch from Basha's hand. "I'm protecting this village. No games!"

"I thought he was a German."

"Why?"

"I don't know. He didn't act like a priest."

"What's his name?"

"Jan Kabos."

"Hungarian, huh? Maybe that's why you didn't recognize him. He's not one of us. But you don't think he's a German anymore?" Basha slowly shook her head. She reached for the flimsy comforter on the small bed and wrapped it around herself.

"Aah! First he's a priest; then he isn't. Then he's a German. Then he isn't. I'm going to kill him, get it over with.

"What if he is a priest? Would you kill a man of God? What do you believe in anymore? Anything?" She sat down on the corner of the small wooden bed, her feet firmly on the floor.

"I don't know God anymore. I just know he's a man and if he isn't a priest, he can bring the Germans here again."

"The sisters would know." Basha said.

"These Germans are clever. Two days, that's all I give you." Szabla bent over the bed and stuck his face close to hers. He knew she could smell the earthy wilderness on him.

"And if the Germans come sooner, you tell them the sisters know who or what he is. If the sisters don't know, then you tell the Germans. Two days. You understand?" Then he reached out to touch her hand and sooth her, but she jerked away. He stood slowly, and then left as silently as he had come.

Szabla's frustration was excruciating. He whacked the bushes with his knife and cursed as he made his way back to the upper camp. He was fuming. *How could she reject me? Most women succumbed to me for just my looks and presence. She was different, she had always been different,* and she was the only one he truly desired.

He tore off his goatskin vest and shirt, then the rest of his clothes, and threw them next to a creek. The moon glistened on a waterhole made by some large boulders rolled into the creek that ran along the side of the path. It damned the flowing water making it deep enough to dive into. He dove in and welcomed the cold pain pin pricking his entire body. It calmed him, and bursting the surface for breath, he felt better. *What did she mean; love somebody or something more than himself. I love her; she must know that.* He let the flow of the creek move him in its slow current as he thought about what she had said. *Proof? What kind of proof did she want? Didn't I bring my men down to the village to help? Didn't she see how I protected the village, reaped the harvest, mended the huts, cared for her? Why did she ask if I believed in anything anymore?* Maybe he didn't believe in God anymore. Nevertheless, he believed that Basha was meant for him! He was sure he believed in that. He climbed up on one of the boulders and watched the water drip off his hairy chest. He heard a call from a wolf in the forest, and then looked up at the moon. It was as if that call had come from somewhere deep inside of him.

He vowed aloud, "She is my family! I'll do whatever it takes to win her back." Then, he screamed up to the moon,

"I can change!"

18

"Oh, yes, most assuredly he is a priest."

Sister Theresa not only verified to Szabla that Jan Kabos was a priest, she said that both she and Sister Anna had noticed his unusual behavior, but they felt it was only because of the extreme hardship he had suffered fleeing from the Germans. Szabla accepted her explanation, but only grudgingly. *I'll keep my eyes open for some evidence that the priest is a spy* he thought as he walked up the stairs and entered the chapel. It was Sunday, and Szabla sat in the pews suspicious again of Father Kabos' stumbling manner through the mass. He sat scrunched next to Basha, his big body warming her. He decided after the mass to approach the priest.

"I want to see his papers," he leaned over and told Basha. "Not at church." Basha pleaded and grabbed his arm. He shrugged her off and followed the priest outside onto the steps in front of the chapel where Father Kabos shook hands and bid the villagers a good day. When it was Szabla's turn, he confronted the priest, "Father Kabos, if that's who you really are, I would like to see some proof of that on paper." Surprisingly enough, Father Kabos produced some papers from under his robe, and they were in perfect order. The picture and everything else that Szabla's limited reading and education could discern appeared to be correct. Szabla looked at Basha and she displayed a disapproving smile.

"Do you know how easy it would be for anyone to produce a set of false papers similar to the ones you hold in your hand?" Father Kabos said, yanking them back from Szabla's grasp. Szabla squinted and lowered one eye.

"How would you know that Father?"

"If you knew God, my son, you would know that I am not your enemy."

"Priest, I know man, and man is my enemy, and you're a man. Be careful, priest."

* * *

Szabla saw that for some time after their confrontation, Father Kabos was careful. He had regained his strength and appeared healthy again. However, Szabla noticed the priest began to postpone his departure from Praznik, much to the relief of the villagers and Basha. When he inquired why the priest was staying, they told Szabla, "Maybe he realized the enormous hardships that awaited him in his attempt to reach Sweden. Maybe with the pressure of that unknown pursuit removed, he's grown comfortable and feels safe here." Szabla thought, but held his tongue, *possibly the two nuns had convinced him there was a flock that needed his care more in Praznik than in Sweden.* Basha said, "After all, there were many religious duties that the nuns could not perform for which a priest is needed." Whatever the real reason Szabla could see that the villagers were all glad Father Kabos had not gone. This made him even more suspicious and frustrated. It was as if the priest was using his charms to influence the people of Praznik into letting him stay.

What was even worse, he had watched Father Kabos continue to delay his departure until eventually the need for the priest to speak of it seemed to leave him, and the possibility of his leaving was no longer a topic in Praznik. It seemed his stay would become permanent.

Then there had been Szabla's discovery that the good father was trained in the medical arts even more than in the spiritual. First in religious matters, until he grew to know the villagers, he would stumble and at times seem unsure of himself; Then Szabla saw he was immediately knowledgeable and sure of himself when treating anyone in distress because of worldly ailments. In addition, as time passed, Szabla realized it was apparent to all in Praznik that this priest was accepted as a different man now, not just 'the priest', he was 'Father Kabos or 'Father' to everyone. Beyond all the positive evidence and contradictions, Szabla still doubted Father Kabos was truly a priest.

* * *

Shortly after the discovery of Father Jan Kabos' skill in the medical arts, Szabla walked toward the Chapel to pay him a visit. He had concluded he was being foolish by not deriving the benefits of the priest's ability. He thought of the many men in his camp in the high mountains that were in need of medical attention and the fact that it could be his for the asking disturbed him. He knocked on the Chapel door anyway. "Yes, my son what can I do for you?"

"It's not for me, it's for my men."

"What is it?"

"I need you to come to my camp and help them; they have wounds and need medical attention." Szabla had convinced himself that it was more important to see that his men were fit than to worry about a stupid obligation to a priest. Father Kabos agreed immediately to help the men.

"That's not all they probably need."

"Will you come?"

"It is not because of you but because of God I do this."

"I'm sorry father but I must blindfold you." Szabla held up a long scarf.

"Szabla, you're a greater fool than I thought. Do you think a blindfold would prevent me from finding the camp if I wanted to? I'll go on my own, when God gives me the time and the leading, and not when you think I should. Otherwise Szabla, you will have to take care of the men yourself." There was nothing for Szabla to do. What else could he do? Now even he needed the priest, and the priest's refusal goaded him with no alternative than agreement.

From that day on, without any further words between Father Kabos and Szabla, he observed the priest making regular trips to the camp in the high mountains. He tended not only the medical needs of the partisans, but their spiritual needs as well. To Szabla's surprise, just by Father Kabos's presence, several of the men were even converted to belief in God again.

To Szabla, with the exception of the priest, life in Praznik continued as close to normal as possible before the Germans had come. The fields were planted, and some of the partisans, mostly the wounded and the tired, came down and settled in the village. Some came to live openly with the women who had lost husbands or sons. Szabla saw the dismay of the priest, while others took some of the women in marriage. A child was born, a death occurred from natural causes. Szabla realized that to any casual observer and the world below. It seemed that life had been going on this way in Praznik for years. Szabla knew the villagers were not the same and they had not forgotten that first visit of the Germans. Their husbands and sons, the heart and soul of the village, were still gone. They lived in dread of a second arrival, whether because there might be something the Germans could want in Praznik, or because of the partisans. He wasn't sure which it was, but knew it was his job to protect them. Weather he was gone or not, the one thing that always remained the same was his two men stationed permanently along the mountain road whose only duty was to warn the village and the camp of anyone or anything coming up the mountain toward the village. He felt that when the Germans did return, the village would be warned. They would gather up all the children and hide them in his camp until the Germans left. It was a simple precautionary plan and a procedure that relieved some anxieties. That is, until there occurred another life changing event even unforeseen in the beginning by Szabla. Nevertheless, considered even by him, and the entire village, another act of God, which supplied a new thread to be sewn into the steadily growing mosaic pattern he continued to see affecting the lives of those inhabiting this unimportant village called Praznik.

19

Szabla had been gone for more than a month that summer. He had taken with him Durcansky, Yanov, Sediva the Czech and two other men from the camp above Praznik. He tried to stay in Poland close to the Czechoslovakian and German borders where the countries meet near the Neisse River. He kept his men very active, penetrating a short ways into Czechoslovakia, blowing up a small military storehouse, destroying several German trucks, killing more than a dozen Germans, then jumping back over the border. Much to Szabla's relief, Sediva's long-range ability with his rifle had made it exceedingly safe, and they had scouted interesting areas for a future foraging raid with a larger force.

Szabla glanced at his men and knew they were hot, tired, and hungry when they stumbled onto the small depot switching station. Cautiously approaching, his eagle eyes saw just three soldiers guarding the depot. With one quick glance, he had taken in a rickety wooden shack and a short raised platform that ran along the main track. A second track ran parallel to the main one for some distance. It was a spur line that held several boxcars on it. Szabla thought this was probably the reason for the guards. Two of them were walking slowly along the track bed, their rifles slung carelessly at their shoulders. The other guard was standing on one end of the platform, sheltered beneath an overhang. He was seriously eating away at what looked like a chunk of rabbit meat. Szabla stared at the man's mouth for some moments, watching him eat, and then at his boots and knew they couldn't pass up food and some additional clothing, and no telling what else in those boxcars. It was dangerous, but there were trees and mountains nearby that could hide them. He glanced at the shack and the single telegraph line that ran out the side to one of the poles along the tracks.

Szabla crouched behind the low embankment, nodding to Durcansky, who had already unsheathed his knife, his cold blue eyes telling Szabla that his comrade was ready to kill. Szabla extended his hand in the signal for the other men to lay low and wait. In what had become routine, he again surveyed the terrain, knowing that their survival depended upon his judgment. He shaded his eyes against the bright rising sun, and for a moment felt a trickle of sweat run down his side. He shifted his feet, keeping muscles taut, ready to spring, but he also felt the deep fatigue in his muscles that spoke of too many missions, too much killing, and urged him to leave. He ignored the saboteur within and made himself focus on the woods, thick with scrub oaks and walnut trees about ten meters away. Barely half a kilometer beyond the station, raised craggy mountains with endless hiding places, and Szabla knew they would need to hide from the planes that would come searching in this war that seemed without end.

Szabla saw Durcansky catch his gaze. His friend could practically read his mind. His raised eyebrows told Szabla the danger and knew what Szabla had concluded: they would safely make their escape into the hills this time. Szabla wondered if there would be a time when this would not be true.

Now he studied the shack only ten meters in front of them. They could not approach the guards from the blind side behind the boxcars. The only choice was to spring on them from behind the embankment. *Too dangerous, but what other choice do we have?*

Szabla, hands sweaty from the summer heat, drew his knife. He surveyed his men strung out along the embankment. He nodded at Yanov and pointed at the two men next to him, sending hand signals. He sent Durcansky in the lead. As they crept along the track embankment, he felt his nostrils fill with the odor of hot oil, dust, and the metallic smell of the rails. He sensed the familiar rush well up, consuming him, taking residence as a pulsing ball in his solar plexus. *We will kill them*, even though he knew it would be very tight.

Szabla saw the three soldiers on the platform, their backs to them. If they do not turn, if Yanov and the others did not get there in time, Szabla was certain Sediva would make short work of them with the rifle, maybe even before he and Durcansky made their attack. Szabla felt his chest swell with pride. Sediva the Czech loved to shoot his rifle, so deadly with that scope on it.

Szabla tapped Durcansky on his shoulder. The men now moved as close as they could, just a few meters from the shack, it's faded red paint peeling from the half-baked rotten wood. Suddenly one guard shouted, "Da druben!" A chill raced down Szabla's spine. The other two guards whipped around, and the three strode across the platform to stare at the embankment.

Szabla's mind raced. He and his men had mere seconds before discovery. Now those seconds elongated into the eternity of the attack. He stood up, feeling like a giant, a titan bull and rushed forward. The nearest guard, taken aback as if Szabla was an apparition, stumbled backwards into the second guard. Szabla saw the flash of fear in the man's eyes. In several thrusts of his knife, in a deadly arc that he honed into perfection so many times before, Szabla slashed the throat of the first man, his lifeblood spraying out, and then he stabbed the guts of the second guard, watching both crumple into a bloody heap at his feet. Szabla withdrew his knife. When he looked up, he faced the third guard, his rifle raised at him, point blank, and as the moment froze, he watched the Germans finger touch the trigger.

Szabla heard a single shot, and he shook himself out of the killing dream. The third guard fell to Sediva's rifle at the same time Yanov and the others rushed the shack. Szabla followed. It was empty. There was no one else. It was over, this time.

Szabla leaned against the windowsill as his men ransacked the shack taking what little food they found and anything else of value. They stripped the dead men, taking their coats and boots. Then they went over to break into the boxcars and discovered them empty! Szabla was disgusted. He turned and saw the padlocked lever protruding from the track bed, the vertical bar used to switch the main track to the spur line. He blasted the lock open and threw the switch in anger at the empty boxcars. *What would Basha say, all this killing, for what . . . nothing?*

20

Szabla decided to take his men back to Praznik without further delay, and had begun the climb into the foothills above the station. As the shack gradually diminished in his view, he was startled to hear in the faint distance the whistle of a train. Worry was something he rarely saw on Durcansky's face, but there it was. His friend was asking with only a contortion of his brow, how long do we have? In that instant they read each other's mind, if the train carried German troops they could be in for very serious trouble.

Szabla glanced back at the train. Its closeness urged him to close up their ranks hurrying his men along at a faster pace. His glance had revealed a very long train emerging from behind a group of trees, but he couldn't tell whether it was the kind used for carrying troops. His experience dictated that; not all troop trains were pulled by heavily armored engines followed by flatcars bristling with guns. He tried to conceal his own nervous strain of the impending danger. This time he saw his men's overwhelming curiosity gave their fear momentary pause. Breathing heavily, they stopped to rest and all gazed down the hill. The engine came first, the rest were cattle cars filled with something non-discernible because of the distance. Szabla noticed the train looked as if it missed the switch, but then suddenly it turned, abruptly changing tracks, screeching into the spur line and slamming into the empty boxcars. The engine veered over the edge of the embankment. In a great mortal anguish of gushing steam and crunching metal, it tilted and rolled onto its side plowing and twisting over several of the cars behind it before the train tore in half.

Many of the first cattle cars broke open while the second half of the train remained on the embankment. Fire began spreading out from the engine. An explosion rocked and destroyed the first part of the train. Szabla watched his men riveted in fascination, but they were all shaken from their visceral grip when the wind carried up the sound of many screaming voices. From out of several of the overturned cars, there erupted a stream of little figures that began to scatter. Szabla and his Partisans continued watching with increased amazement as a good many of the figures headed directly for the hills. He grabbed Durcansky's binoculars and peered down at those coming in their direction. He stared in disbelief at what he was now observing. Those little figures that looked like children were in reality just what they seemed. Rubbing his eyes, he focused the binoculars on the train. There too he could see children still pouring out of the cattle cars, ragged, emaciated, stumbling, and panicky children running everywhere.

The sudden cracking sound of rifles brought his attention to the last half of the train, which appeared undamaged. Many German soldiers had jumped from the train and were now firing at the fleeing children. A machine gun began to bark from the top of the train and over the landscape, many of the children seemed to stumble, fall, and not move again. Szabla and the partisans stared in morbid wonder at the scene unfolding before them. A second machine gun was set up on another of the boxcars and began firing at the desperate figures moving toward the partisans. German soldiers continued pouring out of the train firing and running after the fugitives. Szabla and his men grew uneasy as the first of the children reached the foothills just below them. The children had discovered the trail and were forced to bunch up. The path leading into the hills was narrow and a few German soldiers were making for it and gaining on them. At the same time over the hills, the children were still scattered and climbing frantically for their lives.

Suddenly, the brush parted before Szabla and a child appeared. He was bruised and bleeding, wearing a trembling mask of fear as he stared in terror at the partisans. The men froze, startled and speechless by this unexpected confrontation, but immediately Szabla grabbed the child, patted him on his backside reassuringly, and pointing to the mountains behind them, whispered kindly, "go!"

Szabla now sprang into action. He ordered the men to fan out and stay low out of sight. He told them not to fire at any of the Germans if it meant revealing their position. He knew they were all experienced enough on how to use their weapons concealed by the constant rifle fire without fear of discovery by the pursuing Germans. Just as long as they could shoot the Germans without those near the train seeing them, they were safe.

He and Durcansky stayed close together crouching while the other men spread out. Szabla watched, as children would appear, popping suddenly through the high grass or brush freezing at the sight of the partisans. His men would signal them on, sometimes having to grasp one who would attempt to turn back not knowing the partisans were friendly. Then he saw the German pursuers stomping through the brush and Szabla immensely enjoyed their startled expressions upon seeing him or Durcansky. The Germans surprise was fleeting and immediately changed to pain as Szabla's knife, or a bullet from Durcansky rocked them back off their feet. It had been a long time since Szabla had gotten so much pleasure from killing.

Szabla saw Sediva the Czech also greatly enjoying himself as he began sniping with deadly accuracy at the climbing soldiers. When the soldiers reached the tree line, they were lost from sight by those below. He continued to see his men revel in this turkey shoot. Sediva eyed the machine gunners atop the train. He knew it could be fatal to all of them if the Germans became aware of their presence. Even so, Szabla realized Sediva was rapidly running out of targets and already picking off Germans in the high grass as well as waiting for them to break into the trees. He gave his great whistle to pull back just as Sediva was about to take a shot at one of the machine gunners. Then Szabla saw the Germans head on top of the train explode like a watermelon from Sediva's bullet, and the Germans metal helmet landed with a resounding bounce on the top of the train and rolled off. *Too late,* and cursed out-loud. Szabla ordered his men to retreat still staying low. He decided to deal with Sediva later.

Feeling very anxious, Szabla prodded his partisans forward into the hills that now became steeper. He heard the noises from the train fading in the distance. *Just get deep enough into the mountains and the Germans will lose our trail.* He kept everyone moving at a steady pace, keeping under cover of the trees as much as possible. He constantly scanned the sky and listened for the sound of any aircraft. They traveled for almost an hour before he gave the signal to halt and saw his men looking at him expectantly. He knew the men were thinking maybe he was going to kill Sediva now, but he stopped for another reason. They were being followed; he listened for several moments but could hear nothing.

21

Szabla and his men waited, their weapons held at ready. Szabla watched the trailhead, listening intently until finally some distance away he heard the sound of pursuit coming through the forest. The sound grew closer and he exchanged grim glances with the partisans. Then the first of the pursuers parted the heavy growth and came through the entrance of the trail.

Szabla took aim then saw a boy; an emaciated boy of about twelve year's old holding tightly to an even skinnier and younger girl who he was all but dragging after him. He saw the boy pause as he came into the small clearing and glanced about trying to determine the correct direction to follow while gasping for breath. The trail seemed to have vanished and he was having a difficult time trying to locate it again.

Szabla and the partisans stepped out of hiding and the boy froze when the fierce looking men appeared from behind the brush. The little girl began to whimper. Szabla saw another child appear running up behind them and stopped cold at the sight of the men. Then two more ran up behind at such a panting pace they all collided and fell.

The rest of the partisans emerged and both groups stood staring at one another: Szabla could see his men were just as amazed as he was, and the children showed fear and uncertainty. Even while the partisans stood there quietly appraising the small figures Szabla saw yet another child appear. His first instinct was to send them off in another direction, but in fact, it had been himself that previously pointed the first child in the direction of their retreat. Szabla surmised they were all in great jeopardy if there were many more of these children on the trail behind them. For like geese being picked off by a hunter at the tail end of a flight, the Germans could easily bring them down one at a time until they finally caught up with the partisans.

As dangerous as it was, Szabla decided he must now wait for a while and pick up any of the children who still might be straggling behind them. If he waited an hour, the thought of wasting so much time sent a surge of anger through him, he would certainly be able to pick up any other of these frightened scarecrows who were following. *But then what? Could I leave them behind once whatever number was still coming, or could I send them all off in another direction? If the Germans were following these children, how far behind were they?* He would have to wait and see. He deployed the men and had the children wait further up among the trees, Yanov guarding them.

Only a half hour had elapsed before Szabla's calm expression changed to concern for their inactivity, and his anxiousness of the possibility of pursuers closing in on them. There hadn't been any more children stumbling into the clearing for at least ten minutes now. Szabla glanced around once more then signaled the others and they moved to where Yanov was waiting beyond the clearing with all the children.

Szabla counted twenty-four children of various ages and of both sexes. They ranged from what looked like a five-year-old girl to an almost man-sized boy. He noticed none of them spoke, including the little ones. They remained mute; their eyes glazed with fear.

Looking at their sorrowful condition, Szabla was greatly irritated at his dilemma. He couldn't possibly send them off in another direction. In their present state, they'd wander over the countryside and attract even more attention, eventually leading the Germans back to him. There was no other choice. He had to bring them along, and he angrily gave the order to move out, with himself leading the column. Then a comforting thought occurred to him, *this would show Basha he was thinking of someone else beside himself.* He ordered Durcansky to remain behind for a short time in case they had missed any children, or the Germans were closer than they knew. Then another thought came to his mind, *or Basha might think he was a fool.*

* * *

A day later into their climb, Szabla watched Durcansky come up the trail. Szabla listened with concern as Durcansky told him the Germans were practically breathing down their necks. The Nazis had mounted a concerted effort to both catch those who had attacked the switching station causing the train wreck, and to find the escaped children who were scattered over the hills and forest.

Szabla's strategy was stop and go, hide and detour, all the way for many days until they hit the Sudeten mountain range. It had taken him almost a week to reach there and they were still far away from Praznik. He made a decision and gave the order to send Sediva ahead of them, alone to the village, to see if it was safe to come home to Praznik.

Szabla stared out over the mountains with his binoculars and saw Sediva on a ridge ahead of him waving the signal that it was safe to come home.

By the time they reached the village, Szabla couldn't believe that each of the partisans was carrying one of the children on their backs. They were done in and ragged, even for partisans. All of them had a pale gaunt expression so that in some strange way to Szabla they seemed to resemble each other, as if they were part of one large harrowed peasant family. He trooped them into the village, twenty-three children, and the partisans. He had lost one of the smaller Children who died of pneumonia along the way, and was buried in a small grave somewhere on the side of a mountain.

After the incredulous sight of all those children, and hearing their story with embellishment, Szabla saw most of the villager's hearts went out to these helpless ones. He thought it seemed strange they immediately were so prepared to assimilate them into their lives without disagreement.

22

Joseph, a boy of twelve, looked at all the children then quickly studied the villagers. He was a boy with ideas and suspicions about everything. He had already gotten to know many of the children even before the Germans had rounded them up and crowded them into cattle cars on their way to the death camps. He watched a woman who seemed to be in charge of the villagers talk to a priest and then back to the villagers.

He heard one of the villagers say, "But they look like Jews, they should be shunned. Remember what happened to the last Jews that were here." That was all Josheph needed to hear. He felt the pressure of all the children relying on him to keep them safe. He knew they all looked to him and his inseparable friend Nicholas, and the girl Marisha for guidance. They considered him the smartest, Nicholas the tallest and strongest, and the blond haired blue eyed Marisha the kindest. He scanned the street in the square for any exits out of the village. *How could we all get out, run? No. The partisans were blocking the entrances to each street. Besides, even though some of us would escape they could just shoot us.*

Joseph knew it had been an act of desperation on his part to follow that big man, the leader, in their escape from the train. He wouldn't have if he had not witnessed the partisans killing those cruel German soldiers with such obvious satisfaction. He saw all the children's eyes had now turned to him again for his leadership. He could see they were upset and frightened, their wide searching eyes seemed to stick-out from what his mother would have called, soul-starved depths that made them appear old in their suffering. They were all undernourished and remained mute unless someone spoke to them. Then he heard the priest, the one they called Father Kabos say, "How could you even consider turning away these innocents." Joseph listened as the few village complainers were strongly over-ruled by the priest and the woman they kept calling Basha. However, for him and the children, who had experienced all the horror of an adult world gone mad, it was frightening to find themselves among villagers who were gentiles, which meant they must be like all the others . . . Jew haters! Joseph knew their recent past had made it difficult for them to trust any gentile adult, let alone these strange villagers. He did not forget there had always been anti-Semitism in Poland and with some very bloody violent strains, but like the common cold, it came and went, and there never seemed to be a cure.

Joseph cringed at the memory of one particular bad period of looting and murder when his parents informed him of God's promise which had always prevailed: that the Almighty would never allow the Jews to be destroyed, but keep them alive as a sign to the world of the wonder of His holy word. Joseph still believed it, but barely, considering what atrocities he had experienced in his short life.

Joseph looked into the faces of the children showing their concern and tried to reassure them as the villagers discussed their fate. He had seen the longing, sympathetic looks, and the touching of the children by some of the villagers, and recognized it for what it was, yet he remained suspicious.

"What are they going to do to us?" one of the younger children asked. "They are peasants, their men are against the Germans. You saw how they fought them." Joseph answered. "But those others in the cities made war and killed the Germans, but they also beat and killed Jews."

"They were different," Marisha said.

Then Joseph saw his friend Nicholas step forward and smile at the smaller children, and then he said, "But if they are like the others, then we will run away from them too. We can live by ourselves here in the forests and the mountains. We can hunt game, and fish, and plant food."

"And if some of these villagers are friendly, they might even give us food and what we need to hide in the forests," Marisha said, cheering the younger ones by her smile and reassuringly touching many of them. Joseph glanced at one of the older boys who still stood mute, staring at Marisha in despair. He was tall for his age, and he watched her keenly.

"Don't worry, Paul, whatever happens, all of us will still be together. One day, you will get better. You'll see. I know." Marisha's soothing words were not enough. The boy, Paul Geller, just continued to watch her, his eyes beginning to water. She squeezed his shoulder warmly. She remained silent for he was mute, and had been so for the last six months of their horrible journey.

Joseph was now slowly moving all the children towards an alley he had picked out where there was no one at the entrance. He had a plan and was about to send Nicholas to scout it out. Then, Joseph saw the villagers all turn and smile. They approached the tightly grouped circle of children and began to mingle with the smaller ones, speaking somewhat soothingly, and attempting to draw them into conversation. Joseph put his hand on Nicholas's shoulder holding him back while several of the village women began to study the boys and girls individually, discovering in a friendly manner their names and background. Joseph didn't like what he heard. They informed the children they were going to take care of, and watch over them, already asking some if they would care to come and live in their homes. Before any of the children answered, many began to look at Joseph to see his reaction to what was happening. Joseph shook his head and glanced at Marisha. She nodded. "It's all right. They mean no harm."

"That is true, children," Joseph watched the priest say, standing in among them and patting several on the head. "I'm Father Kabos, and these people mean only to help you. You have nothing to fear from them."

"We are Jews," Joseph suspiciously said.

"I know."

"And they still want to help us?" Father Kabos nodded and smiled. "Why?" Joseph asked, glancing at the milling villagers who were succeeding in overcoming the initial fear of many of the younger children.

"Why would they want to do anything for us?"

"I think you and the others will do more for them than the other way around. You may even be an answer to prayer for many of them. You see almost all of their own sons and husbands were taken by the Germans, or are in hiding, or fighting somewhere in Poland.

Joseph looked perplexed at this. He saw Marisha and Nicholas exchange glances and then Joseph was surprised to find several of the villagers smiling at him. Marisha turned back to face Father Kabos.

"I don't understand, but I believe you."

"Do you, my child."

"I am Marisha and this is Joseph and Nicholas." She turned to Joseph who was now very anxious. "Maybe we should trust them, Joseph. If they were going to hurt us, wouldn't they be doing it now?"

Joseph looked at the other children eagerly waiting for his decision. He saw Father Kabos studying him with a compassionate stare. Joseph tried to think quickly what to do. It could be a trap. Now is the time to run before it's too late.

Joseph in an instant of thoughts agonized over the hard lessons he had learned in dark alleys, back streets, cellars, and the hostile environment of a Europe preoccupied with its own destruction. Like most of the other children born into European minorities, he was the first to suffer as their ordered world collapsed around them with the death of parents, brothers, sister, and relatives.

Only action, not words count on a planet that has never known a single moment without the death of some animal, or human life. Only fools rely on the good will of people to protect them. He remembered how he had escaped the clutches of the Germans time after time, constantly eluding the authorities that were cataloging all Jews into ghettos to help ease the logistics of the final solution. Joseph thought of Nicholas, and Marisha, who had tried to calm the younger children as they had done so often at the orphanage before the Nazis took them to the death trains.

Marisha told them stories and tried to make them laugh. Most of the children cared for each other. Nevertheless, the cold and hunger began to take its toll and only the miracle of the train accident, and the breaking open of the cattle cars had saved them. *The partisans brought them to this village but why?*

He finally, but reluctantly, nodded his acceptance of the villagers, giving his temporary approval. He thought of the partisans again who had freed and brought them back to the village and possibly a new life. *Because of those fierce men, once again they would have a chance to live, only this time with a new set of adults, so strangely willing and eager to be their parents.*

Though Joseph remained suspicious and reticent about his new foster parents, he could see that the children were no match in the end for the overwhelming power of love. To the great pleasure of the villagers, after a period, all the children began to respond to their affections. Soon they were headed off to their new parent's homes.

As Marisha parted Joseph looked in her eyes, she stopped and went over to him, as if to give him something. The woman taking her home waited patiently for a moment.

"Do you think the Germans will find us here?"

"I don't know, at least not for a while." Joseph prayed that they could all take a brief rest until they were strong enough to continue their flight.

"I think its ok for now, I will see you tomorrow." Joseph watched Marisha walk away and he turned to his surrogate parents and wondered how far away the Germans were.

PART II

THE WAR ANGELS

23

Major Greg Marvin looked out the window of his B-17; the sky filled with brilliant maniacs performing in what seemed to him a suicidal circus. He blinked his blood-shot eyes at the four Luftwaffe Me 109's coming directly at his plane. He re-gripped the wheel as the great Fort shook violently, spitting out its own stream of bullets from the top turret and nose guns at the closing Messerschmitt's.

Major Marvin turned his head as the fighters went by on the right, and he heard Novak, the right waist gunner shout excitedly over the interphone, "Hey. I think I got one!"

Major Marvin turned his head to the man on his right, his copilot, Lieutenant Dave Harper, young and inexperienced, and only on his third mission. Marvin spoke quickly through the interphone, "Knock off the shouting." Then he re-glued his attention to the airspace before them.

He was handsome, and being a former football athlete with good hands and a calm manner, was perfect for the aircraft commander of a B-17 bomber. At twenty-eight, he was the oldest man aboard and would be the first to agree that flying was definitely a young man's game.

He was proud of his plane, The Sky Queen, and his crew. They were the lead ship in the second squadron in the highest formation. He glanced outside again and knew they were about to get all hell thrown at them.

Now he saw the sky over Germany dirty with airplanes and falling debris. A long line of Flying Fortresses filled a corridor of the sky that was surrounded above, below, and in between with black ugly exploding mushrooms of flak. He watched as bursting shells of sharp jagged metal pieces reached out to rip into planes and men, sent skyward by determined anti-aircraft gunners on the ground. From outside that great air corridor, he saw hundreds of smaller planes darting in and out and between, their passage marked by a multitude of tracer lines.

A sudden explosion off to his left grabbed his attention, turning his head he held his breath as one of the Forts disappeared in a blinding flash, scattering a mass of debris into the path of the planes still pushing on. The other bombers closed in, filling the gap created by the dying plane. Parachutes blossomed white in the black sky of exploding flak. The rain of falling brown and white jumpers was everywhere. Falling B-17's, German fighter planes and the crisscrossing path of tracers confused his sight.

Although the fierce running air battle was raging over many miles following the great stretched-out force of bombers, Marvin was conscious only of the staggered squadron formation of his own group. He maneuvered The Sky Queen through the raging fury and the many faces of death coming against them. He kept an eye on the large stream of bombers moving across the sky, forging steadily and deeper into Germany.

Marvin's hat was loose on his head from the sweat beads creeping out from under the brim. He saw more German fighter groups arrive probing for weakness. Then the worst came, the American fighter planes that were escorting the Bomber squadrons reached the limit of their fuel range, and his stomach dropped as he saw them turn back. That left the B-17s with their only hope being the protective staggered box formations they flew.

"We can do it boys, were gonna get through this and reach our target, drop our bombs and go home." He reassured himself as well as his crew.

Marvin then started counting each type of aircraft and equipment the German war machine was using, mumbling their names as he saw each go by. He saw them use single-engine planes, twin-engine planes, and even four-engine bombers for observation and tracking. They used machine guns and 20-mm cannons. They used air rockets fired from planes and intense and effective concentrations of flak from the ground. They dropped air-to-air mines and bombs from above, filling the sky with more-debris and-deadly shards. In addition, the Germans used their own bombers as launching platforms for their more powerful rockets and cannons.

Then, they came with devastating frontal attacks; from high and low positions and from the tails of the formations; they struck at the bombers in single groups of three or four; they hid in the sun, coming into view at point blank range, or they hid in the vapor trails, surprising hapless bombers from the protective box-screen.

The calm voice of Stiles, the navigator, came over the interphone. "Nine minutes to IP." *Nine minutes,* Marvin thought. *Nine minutes.* It didn't seem possible that anything could survive this much carnage for nine more minutes. The Germans were everywhere.

Several holes appeared in the left wing and a piece of the right wing slowly bent itself up and broke off. Marvin moved the control column slightly and could feel the sluggish response. He could see Harper felt it also as they once again exchanged a brief glance. Marvin couldn't help notice and feel the fear of his copilot as he saw the strained eyes staring out above his oxygen mask as if he was hanging onto a cliff by his fingernails. There was nothing he could do but fly the plane. His contribution to their survival was limited.

Marvin knew it was the enlisted men who had to keep them alive. The gunners who were blasting away, fighting off the ambition of those German bastards wanting to destroy his ship, The Sky Queen. Soon he knew it would be Ryan, the bombardier, who would have his turn. The whole purpose of the mission was to get Ryan over the target and give him his turn. During the last important moments while making the run over the target, he would put the control of the ship in his hands.

"Check. We're at the Initial Point," Marvin heard Stiles, the navigator, say, "Roger, I've got it." Suddenly Marvin jumped up in his seat as a large piece of black metal, part of some falling debris, spun by the top turret, nicking the Plexiglas cover, and plowed into the vertical fin shearing off part of it. There was a momentary loss of control as Marvin quickly compensated and brought the plane back in line.

"What was that?" Marvin barked into the throat mike. Ballard the flight engineer, who also doubled as the top turret gunner, responded. "We've lost part of the vertical fin, sir."

"How much?"

"About half"

Marvin moved the control column slightly and again could feel an even worse sluggish response. With part of the vertical fin gone and the damage The Sky Queen had already sustained, he worried as controlling the ship was becoming more difficult. Marvin knew they were too close to the target to abort now and even if they weren't, as long as they were airborne, he'd push on.

24

"Fighters at nine o'clock high!" Ballard shouted as the top turret guns began hammering away.

Marvin realized that The Sky Queen was now the new primary target as a string of Me-210's at ten o'clock rolled over in uniform precision and came at them in a perfect sequential attack. Every gun in the plane facing the Germans was brought to bear and began hammering away. The first two fighters flew past undamaged. Then the third blew apart sending a chunk of its fuselage into the right wing of The Sky Queen. Time after time, Marvin's stomach contorted and knotted up as the B-17 paused in flight for less than a second, as if some invisible giant hand were swatting the air away from the ship, leaving nothing to ride on.

Marvin glanced quickly in all directions, the plane was on AFCE, Automatic Flight Control Equipment, and Ryan was in complete control of The Sky Queen as they approached the target. Then he saw the Me-210's coming head on in waves of three. He gave a quick glance at his co-pilot, at the low squadron, and ahead at the mushrooming clouds of smoke caused by the first bombing groups, and now beginning to obscure the target. He sat with a feeling of continued helplessness as Ryan, through the controls of the bombsight, brought the ship to bear on a straight line to its final target.

The ship lurched convulsively and Marvin grabbed the wheel. He knew immediately, they had taken a hit and a bad one. There was a gaping hole somewhere in the ship. Then, feeling the sudden rush of cold air flooding into the Fort on his cheeks, it almost dried the sweat near his eyes.

"Check in. Everyone okay? Harper said quickly, breaking the radio silence.

"Up front," Ryan's voice came weakly through the earphones. "We caught one."

"Shall I take it?" Marvin asked into the throat mike.

"Stay off the wheel Major. It's still mine," the bombardier's voice responded instantly.

"Roger."

Marvin listened as Ryan now went into his usual monologue he performed almost ritualistically on every raid. "I'm opening the doors, baby." The plane trembled slightly as the bomb bay doors opened. "Steady, baby. Don't move. I've got you covered. I told you not to move Stupid Krauthead. Take that. Bombs away!"

Marvin felt the plane tremble as the load of bombs emptied from the Fort and the ship lifted itself in relief.

Immediately Marvin retook control of the Fort, closing the bomb-bay doors and dipping the left wing, preparing to swing around for the reassemble point and regrouping in formation for the trip home.

At first, the response of the rudder was slight, then the rudder went completely mushy, and Marvin instantly realized in a pang of despair that somewhere in the Fort, the flight control cables had been severed or severely damaged. With part of the rudder already gone, his lateral control had been mostly all by ailerons. Now he felt nothing, or hardly anything.

His nightmare escalated and white flashes were going off in his brain when the propeller on the number two engine began to 'run away', out of control, the vibration shaking the Fort so violently it seemed that the engine was about to tear itself off the wing. Marvin feathered the number two props by mechanical instinct and killed the engine. When the propeller finally turned into the full feather position so that the blades were streamlined to offer the least wind resistance, he observed that one of the blades was completely gone and his body slowly went into a state of numbness. Desperately raising the left wing Marvin could see the plane had already gone too far and had not even begun the turn. The third group, what remained of them, was already formed and beginning to pull away. He tilted the right wing and attempted to bring The Sky Queen around to the right. Again, the controls were mushy and unresponsive. He turned and shook his head at the frightened copilot. He glanced out his window and he could no longer see the other formations. He looked quickly at his compass and was overwhelmed and sickened with the knowledge that The Sky Queen had bought it.

How could he see the formations? My God—they were flying in the opposite direction. The bomber groups were heading for home, The Sky Queen deeper into Germany.

25

As the war raged all over Europe, Basha saw life become almost normal in Praznik. She heard the sounds of laughter from children again and watched the villager's and even Father Kabos play with the children.

Basha helped Father Kabos set up the chapel as a temporary school and there was talk of constructing a permanent one. They were both happy when many of the villagers talked of legally adopting the children to reside in their individual homes. Yet for all the love and new beauty that had come to Praznik, there was still, deep inside Basha, the fear of the Germans, and she listened, as it became a topic of concern for many of the villagers and elders of Praznik.

"What if the Germans did return? What would become of the children? What of the partisans who had settled among them?" Basha could see that everyone knew the population of the village had grown to a number even greater than before the Germans had come. What of the priest . . . and the sisters? She heard the villagers naively talk; surely, a man and woman of God would be safe. She thought, but weren't they all men, women, and children of God.

Finally, Basha called a great meeting with most of the population of Praznik present, for which Szabla and many of the other partisans came down from their camp. She expressed her feelings and a plan was developed. A mile into the mountain behind Praznik was the outer edge of the forest. In that forest was a gully whose location only Szabla and a very few others knew. At the first sound of alarm from the partisans on the mountain road, all the children and those partisans who were not in the fields at the time would gather at the chapel. From there, Father Kabos would lead them all to the secret gully and await the word telling them the Germans had gone. There was no need to provide for water, as a small stream nearby would be able to amply supply them.

Basha and Father Kabos participated whole-heartedly as the plan went into effect and a rehearsal was started which came off with stupendous efficiency. However, she noticed the first rehearsal uncovered a glaring weakness that was immediately apparent and required a strong warning to those involved. When the group arrived at the secret gully Father Kabos said, "I discovered that four of the younger children were not present. They were still in the village, off playing in a stand of trees just a short distance from one of the houses. If the Germans had come into the village and interrogated these children, all would have been lost."

Basha then made a decision and said to everyone, "Even though it may prove a strain in some cases, especially during harvest time, all the parents and adopted guardians of the children must know at any given moment, where their children are!"

After the second rehearsal, the elders approached Basha, and Tearses said, "The presence of even one child could give the plan away and therefore all the children must be sent into the forest with the priest along with any personal belongings that might betray the lives of all of them."

Suddenly, Basha realized, there was no time for another rehearsal as the daylight alarm of the flashing mirror warned her of the approaching Germans. This time, as she looked down the road she saw a short motorized column straining its way up the mountain road. It was only a single car and a small truck, preceded by many motorcycles with sidecars. Behind the truck, pulled along on wheels, was a deadly looking gun that appeared to have seen much use. When the column finally motored into the square of the village, Basha and several of the older men and women stepped forward. A large heavyset German officer in an overcoat, gloves and cap, demanded to see the men of the village. Basha, with just the right amount of hatred, explained what had occurred when the other Germans had come to Praznik.

"What about the fields and the harvest. We can see there has been a recent harvest here."

"That is true."

"Well then?"

Basha indicated the elders who stood morosely in the square before the German.

"You are lying," the German said in a raised voice. "They're too old."

"Not if one wants to eat. Not if one wants to live. You can see for yourself. There are no men here, no young men. They've taken them all away. This is an old village with old people."

"What about the children? I see no children here. Where are your children?"

"Except for the young ones, they too were taken with the men. As I've told you, we are old people. We have no children."

The German officer suddenly barked an order to search the village. He stood silently smoking a cigarette while the soldiers obeyed his command. One of the soldiers returned and spoke in a low voice to the officer. He turned to Basha.

"What about your church?"

"Yes?"

"It's been used recently."

"We use it to pray." The German laughed harshly. "For what? For our deaths?"

"No. For your salvation."

The German slapped Basha across the face, causing her lip to bleed. She said nothing but continued to stare at him.

"Pay attention. We are looking for criminals, and the children of Polish traitors, and Jews. In spite of our decency to these pigs, they have bitten the hand of kindness we have extended to them as children. They've shown their inferior breeding. They must be made to pay for their crimes." Basha bravely interrupted, "We don't understand."

For a moment, it looked as if the German would strike her again. Then he said, "We are looking for escaped Jew brats, and we have good reason to believe some of them may be in this area." Basha shook her head in bewilderment and the German officer stared at her grimly then addressed all of the villagers. "In these mountains there is a group of traitors who plotted the destruction of one of our trains to free these brats. We intend to find these traitors and the escaped brats and punish them. Punish them severely. Anyone . . . anyone at all who has any information concerning these traitors and does not immediately report it will be responsible for the death of everyone in this village. You will all be shot, and the village burned to the ground. Is that understood?" Basha nodded slowly and kept on nodding as the Germans left the village and started down the mountain road. She walked over to the rim and stood watching them for a long time, deep in reflective thought.

That evening, she told the priest all that had happened and what was said. Then she voiced the fear that had so suddenly grown within her as she had watched the Germans depart. She had no fear for herself, but only for the children . . . all of them. The children would never be safe and protected here, never. The Germans would come repeatedly until one day they would be caught. Father Kabos tried to reason with her anxiety but she was beyond being calmed by his words.

"I know Father, God rules the spiritual world, but the Germans seem to be the real masters of this one, and eventually they will destroy us all if they are allowed to continue.

"Are they so strong?" Father Kabos asked her.

"Can they ever be stopped," she said angrily at the frustration of their helplessness.

"Their strength comes from the world's weakness. The best time to have stopped them was at the moment they stood revealed for what they are."

"Then is Szabla truly the smart one? Is the only hope for us to become killers? To behave as animals without mercy, to live by cunning and stealth?"

"I don't believe it is sinful to live intelligently in order to escape conflict of one's enemies. But killing can only lead to more of the same."

"But if we do nothing, will it not still result in the same destruction for us by these sons of evil? It seems the only true choice is the way of Szabla. Either we fight them or die!"

"We all die eventually. It is how we have lived which gives meaning to that inescapable moment when it comes."

She shook her head painfully, having expected him to be passive, but still torn by this unhappy situation they faced. "Father. I see the future for us here, and it does not look well. These evil ones will return. We cannot hide from an enemy who continues to seek us out because we dare breathe the same air, and stand upright, who treat us as things not human."

"If one has no choice, then one must do battle, I expect."

She was surprised at this; his agreement of what she knew could very easily happen if they were backed into a position of no retreat. She said,

"One can do battle only if one is strong enough, Father. Otherwise one is quickly overcome and all chance to succeed is lost."

"Then the moment you are strong enough is the moment to resist."

"Even if we lose?"

"Even then."

"I fear desperately for the children," she said. Then she touched his arm, her hand feeling the strength of him beneath the cloth. "And I fear for you also. Very much." She dropped her head as Father Kabos looked long and hard at her, and then in a soft voice said, "We must pray, daughter. We must pray." They did.

Nevertheless, as righteous as they felt their case was before God, the answer to their prayers still did not come; neither Basha Mickiewicz, nor Father Kabos, knew specifically what to pray. So they just prayed for the safety and protection of the children and the village, and of course, the destruction of the Germans. Basha witnessed many of the other villagers who felt the same fear as Basha now also began to pray.

26

That afternoon the chapel filled with the children of the village, Father Kabos was instructing them in his favorite pastime. He told them a story from the Old Testament in his familiar way, displaying his abundant knowledge of all the people and events.

He spoke as if he knew them personally, and it came to him what to pray. That is, it actually came to the children first, but he recognized it immediately for what it was. He saw the sisters caught by the power of his voice as he told the biblical story of Elisha, and the children listened with unusual interest.

"Elisha had saved the children of Israel many times from the evil plans of the King of Syria, and his attempted invasions. The King of Syria in his anger and frustration had decided to send a large detachment of soldiers and many chariots to capture Elisha and destroy him." He paused, the atmosphere in the chapel suddenly appeared to change and a tension filled the air, a sense of anticipation seemed to hang over all of them as Father Kabos studied the faces of his listeners.

"And so while Elisha and his servant slept that night, the Syrians slowly and stealthily surrounded not only the house that Elisha was sleeping in, but the entire city. When they awoke they were surrounded by that fierce army of Syrians and it looked hopeless.

"Now because Elisha was a prophet and a man of God, he was not afraid. You see, children, he had the ability to see angels. Elsiha's servant, who was still terribly frightened, couldn't see anything. Elisha told him not to be frightened. There wasn't any need to worry because there were more for them out there than were against them. Well, this poor servant couldn't understand a thing Elisha was talking about and just continued to shake in fear. He probably thought Elisha must be crazy, acting so cheerful. Then Elisha asked God to show what it was he saw that no one else did. What do you suppose happened? The spiritual veil lifted from the eyes of Elisha's servant. Suddenly the man could see that an army of angels surrounded those Syrians, and all of them dressed for battle! And when Elisha prayed again, both he and his servant escaped right out from under the very noses of that Syrian army."

Father Kabos continued until he finished the story and for several minutes, there was absolute silence in the chapel. Then Marjan, a red-haired boy that was never far away from his younger sister, spoke up.

"Were those really angels?"

"The bible says they were, my son"

"Did they have guns? The boy asked, not skeptical, but very much interested.

"Angels don't have guns," someone else said. Then Nicholas, his expression already betraying his own doubts concerning the story, said scornfully, "How could they be soldiers if they don't have guns?"

"They must have tanks too, another boy said.

"You can't have an army without tanks." One of the girls spoke.

"Don't be silly. They didn't have tanks in those days."

"Well, if they didn't have tanks, what did they have?'

"Spears."

"Spears?"

"Spears and chariots. Isn't that right, Father?"

"Yes, that's right, daughter."

Nicholas now stood up and leaned toward the children who had voiced their opinions. "Well, if they didn't have guns, I don't see how they could be soldiers." Father Kabos smiled. "You see, they weren't exactly soldiers. They were angels."

"You mean angels with wings?"

"How can angels with wings fight. They'd get in the way."

Another boy entered the discussion now, recalling one of his own experiences with these alleged heavenly beings.

"I once saw some angels in a big building in Prague where I used to live, and they didn't look like they could do anything at all."

"Silly. Those were statues," the girl Marisha said. Marjan, the first boy to speak, rose to his feet and faced the others. "I never heard of angels fighting, or being in an army. How could that be? I never saw a picture of an angel that was fighting."

"Well, Marjan, the bible does tell us that an army of angels did surround those Syrians and were ready for battle." There was a moment of silence and suddenly Marisha spoke up loudly, because in an inspired revelation, she knew the only kind of beings they could have been. "Then they must have been War Angels!" she said smiling.

"There are all kinds of angels in heaven, aren't there?"

"Well these must have been war angels." Now Father Kabos heard everyone speaking and adding their own opinion, but the question was settled. They all agreed that these truly must have been a special group of angels that were like soldiers, but not really. After several more minutes of discussion, the chapel quieted down and Father Kabos was preparing their mood for the prayer before dismissing them, when Tomas, a boy who had listened to everything in solemn and long contemplation, raised his hand.

"Yes, my son?"

"Father. Are there war angels today?"

"I suppose so. Yes, there are."

"Like those that did that to the Syrians?"

"Yes."

"Would they do it to the Germans? Would they do it to the Germans if we prayed for them to do it?"

"I . . . I . . ." Father Kabos glanced helplessly at Sister Anna. "If that was what we really wanted. Yes, I think so." Nicholas excitedly rose to his feet again. "Let's pray to kill all the Germans." Father Kabos looked at the boy and reflected sadly. Then he shook his head.

"We can't pray for that."

"Why not?" Nicholas asked stubbornly.

"They're bad like the Syrians were."

"They're worse. They kill everyone," Marjan said, bitterly agreeing with Nicholas.

"Children, We can't ask God to kill anyone,"

Father Kabos protested mildly, yet disturbed by the direction the discussion had taken.

"Why not?" Nicholas asked.

"It's only fair. Isn't it?"

"They killed my Mommy and did naughty to my sister," Hester, Marjan's little sister said, speaking up now in her small voice.

"And they killed Grandma too."

Suddenly, Father Kabos saw the children were out of control. Their faces changed from innocence to anguish and anger. They all began shouting and speaking at once, all voicing the same angry cry, "Kill the Germans, Kill the Germans!" finally, and with great difficulty, Father Kabos calmed them down.

"Children, Children. God has said thou shall not kill. We cannot disobey the commandment of God."

"The Germans do!" Nicholas, who had remained standing, said, "They don't believe in God, do they?"

"Some of them do."

"Not the soldiers though." Father Kabos had to admit, "It doesn't appear that they do, my son."

"Then why do we?"

"What?"

"Believe in God."

"Because he is greater than anything. Greater than any man, or ourselves. He is definitely greater than the Germans."

"Then why doesn't He help us?" Father Kabos thought for a while before answering. "I don't know. It certainly isn't because we don't need help."

"Maybe it's because we never prayed for help," Marisha stood up and said astutely. "I prayed all the time, but they still killed my father," a boy said. Sister Anna now stood up and the children grew quiet as they watched her. Father Kabos glanced at her expectantly.

"Maybe it was because none of us prayed for that which was right in the eyes of Our Lord. Maybe it was because we prayed for what it was that we wanted and not what was in His divine will." Marjan spoke.

"Sister Anna**,** if we prayed for those War Angels, would that be in His divine will?"

"It might, if it were not for killing."

"For deliverance?" father Kabos said, looking at her uncertainly. "We could pray for deliverance that God might send some of his War Angels to deliver us, mightn't we?"

"I don't know," Sister Anna said.

"I can't see the harm in it. I don't see how if we all prayed now, together, for God to send us some of His War Angels that it would be against his divine will. Would you

Sister Anna? Would you, Sister Theresa?" Sister Theresa who had been in silent prayer throughout the discussion, exchanged a glance with Sister Anna then looked compassionately at Father Kabos, and the children, and shook her head.

"Well then," Father Kabos said, with reverent happiness, "Let us all be upon our knees and pray for deliverance." He paused several moments as he collected his thoughts. "Our merciful Lord," he began slowly. "We . . . all of your faithful children, come before Thee and ask that Thou cleanse us from all sin and purify our minds and hearts. Our gracious heavenly Father, we ask Thee for mercy and deliverance. We ask Thee to send us Thy 'War Angels' to intercede for us in this time of woe and strife, where we have seen our countries invaded and brutalized, where we have been separated from our loved ones, where we have seen them murdered before our eyes, where our homes and possessions have been taken from us, where . . ." he paused once again, realizing that he was about to be carried away by his own feelings, as if he himself were interceding for them all. He waited and then continued, more calmly. "Father, Thou knowest my heart and I now ask not for myself, but for all these innocents. I ask this in belief, and lord, Thou knowest what I mean." Suddenly Father Kabos could detect the hushed atmosphere in the chapel. All of the children were watching him with a sort of faraway gleam in their eyes. He felt uncomfortable. Then looking at the two nuns, he added hurriedly, "In the name of the Father, and of the Son, and of the Holy Ghost. Amen. You may leave now, children."

As the children filed out of the crowded chapel, Father Kabos watched Sister Theresa keep her hands clasped tightly together and said silently, "Grant this, Lord Jesus." One of the girls asked him on the way out, "Why do you pray to a Son, and a Ghost, Father?"

"Another time my child, another time." He replied in a distracted way.

27

Major Gregg Marvin was in mild shock, and in his worst nightmare. As he swiveled his head taking in the cockpit, it seemed everything shimmered in a white heavenly glow, and was weightlessly floating in space moving in slow motion. He heard no sounds and only his thoughts were in real time. After what seemed an endless moment he started to hear an echo. He struggled to listen carefully as the echoing words of "What's happening, sir?" slowly brought him back.

"What's happening, sir?" Ballard said again, leaning down from the top turret. A confused bedlam of voices suddenly flooded through Marvin's earphones as he felt the reality of their condition hit the crew. They all became aware of death reaching out for them as the Fort continued on its lone course away from the rest of the squadrons. He slapped the back of his neck hard a couple of times.

"Knock it off!" Marvin shouted. "Watch the sky!"

"Bogies at nine o'clock high!" Dunham, the left waist gunner shouted. The guns began clattering again.

Marvin and the crew knew they were stragglers now, a single Fortress in a hostile sky, easy prey for any fighter that wanted to come after them.

Marvin watched the number one engine start to smoke badly yet the manifold pressure stayed up. Then the flames began appearing in long bright tongues that licked greedily at the wing. Marvin punched the number one extinguisher button and the flames disappeared; yet the engine continued to trail smoke. He moved the number one mixture control to the off position and feathered the propeller. He opened the cowl flaps in an attempt to cool the engine and blow out the fire. Then he turned the ignition off, but the smoke poured out black and dirty.

Marvin quickly increased the rpm of the other two engines while struggling angrily with the controls. He was flying on two engines now with no power on the left side. They were already beginning to lose airspeed and altitude. He stared out the window, *one stall on the remaining two engines, and were through. It looks like we already bought it, we are just hanging on by a prayer!*

For some time, Marvin watched fatefully as the sky around the damaged B-17 grew peaceful, and their flight took them further off course deeper into enemy territory. Then he started evaluating in disbelief the holes in the controls and didn't notice the attackers right off. When they began to get closer, he could see them clearly. A small group of fighters had suddenly appeared from the east in a clumsy strung out formation, coming straight at The Sky Queen without going for altitude and making easy targets for the American gunners. In moments of hectic short firing, one was down and three were obvious hits and damaged. Marvin thought it curious that the formation then broke off and headed back the way they had come.

He watched two more German fighters appear, they were different, fresher, and smarter, Me-l09's, and they climbed ahead of the Fortress, gaining distance and height. The first fighter made a slow turn at 11 o'clock high and came down head on, blasting away at the cockpit. Marvin yelled out a profanity as part of the Fort's windshield shattered on the copilot's side, sending a spray of fragments through the pilot's compartment into Marvin's side. He had turned away at the last instant to protect his face, none of the pieces penetrating his thick flak jacket. He saw something slam into Harper's arm with a snapping sound. Harper groaned but hung on, the pain keeping him fully conscious. He could hear Ballard's guns in the top turret and Novak on the right waist gun as the fighter closed, passed, and then veered off. Then he heard a quick burst from Haply in the ball turret. Marvin was acutely aware there hadn't been any fire from the nose guns of The Sky Queen at the first approach of the fighter.

"What's going on down there," Marvin yelled. "Stiles! Ryan! You jokers asleep?" When there was no response, he poked the bleeding Harper, who was in mild shock, but still functioning. "Harper, get down to the nose and see what's going on." For a moment, Marvin hoped they might have jumped, parachuted out after the carnage of the last attack, but he knew better. A queasy feeling settled over him as Harper disappeared into the forward compartment of what was left of the nose.

Marvin saw the horizon slipping and knew they were losing altitude steadily now and the number one engine was still smoking badly. He could hear they were still under attack, but by fewer fighters. Ballard, the top turret gunner and Novak, the right waist gunner were still blazing away. Occasionally, a sporadic burst would come from the tail section, signifying that Shaw; the tail gunner, was still alive and hanging in there.

Marvin put on his flight goggles and looked through the shattered windshield, and ahead there seemed to be a range of mountains rapidly approaching them. Out there, the same Me-109 was doing a slow climb to 11 o'clock high again.

As Marvin held tightly to the control column, he knew The Sky Queen was dying, and she had sustained mortal damage. The rudder, the fuselage, the wings, and now the control cables were all mangled, frayed, the plane bleeding to death. He was certain the nose had taken a direct hit of some sort, and he could swear he was seeing a beginning wisp of smoke trailing from the number four engine. There were pieces of the fuselage flapping in the wind. The plane was losing altitude, and was too low for any of them to bail out.

"Poland. That must be the border and Poland up ahead." Marvin spoke aloud.

He looked out at the cold sky around them and he could see only the two fighters lazily gaining altitude before coming in for the kill and putting the bleeding Fortress out of its misery. Marvin felt the quickening despair of the worst kind of helplessness, the kind you know disaster is coming, but seems to wait forever for the end.

28

The first fighter swooped down and raked the entire right side of the Fort, stitching a neat set of holes through a long section of the fuselage. Then the fighter broke off the attack and wagged his wings at the second fighter with what seemed like a signal. One of the Germans remained high, but both fighters circled the bomber and discontinued their attack. It seemed miraculous to Marvin that such a thing was occurring. *What were they doing, or thinking? Why don't they finish us off?* Then he watched them come closer as if they were going to escort the fortress to safety.

Marvin heard Novak start blasting away at the closest fighter. Seconds later, Ballard's guns joined in. Marvin saw the German fighter roll over to get out of the sudden surprising line of fire. It pulled away, but not fast enough, and was hit. Trying to gain altitude, the German veered left, crossing over the Fort. Dunham blazed away fiercely as the fighter crossed over into his area of fire. Marvin heard Dunham cheer loudly as the German fighter burst into smoke, and disappeared behind the mountain they had just buzzed.

In a trance-like stupor, Marvin held onto the wheel as The Sky Queen continued to lose altitude and more mountains loomed menacingly ahead. He heard Haply say something about the ball turret. Marvin was well aware Haply occupied the most dangerous position to be trapped in during a fire, or when a Fortress was losing altitude heading for a possible crash landing. He left his post before getting the word. "Watch it, Swifty, the Kraut's coming up the tail." It was Ballard in the top turret. "Six o'clock, Swifty. Six o' clock!"

"I see him," Swifty, the tail gunner yelled. Swifty began blasting the second fighter in rapid short bursts. Marvin tried to gain more altitude as the mountains grew higher again. He strained at the control column, almost oblivious to Swifty's machine guns and the hammering of the top turret. Outside, along the tree line the ground appeared splotchy and white with snow.

"It looks like they've had snow here already," Marvin said. Then he said sharply into the mike, "Harper. What's happening?" Harper, his voice weak with pain, came over the interphone, "The whole nose took one. It's all twisted in."

"What about Stiles and Ryan?"

"Tony's dead," Harper's voice crackled through Marvin's earphones. He could barely hear him.

"Say again."

"Stiles bought it, sir. Ryan's still alive but he's out cold. Concussion I think. I can't budge him. Everything's a mess. His leg's jammed into the nose. Part of its hanging outside, sir."

"Can you move him? I'm going to belly in."

"You can't do it, sir. You'll kill him."

Suddenly the guns started chattering again. "Watch the Bogie. He's at 11 o'clock," Ballard cut in, already pouring long bursts at the German.

Marvin looked through what was left of the dirty speckled windshield as the German came at them, the brilliant flashes along its wings showing all guns blazing. Then along with the top turret guns, Marvin could hear the additional noise of one of the nose guns as Harper joined in. He wondered how Harper was holding the gun. The Me-109 crossed in front of the cockpit and disappeared to the right of the Fort. Suddenly it was in view again, this time going straight up, hanging on its nose in a stall as one of its wings came off. Then it turned over on its back and spiraled crazily from view as a single parachute suddenly blossomed open and drifted after the plane.

29

Somehow, Marvin knew instinctively the battle was over. There were no more planes in the sky. It was clear all around him. Only the crippled roar of the engines rattled out as he felt the fortress taking its last gasp. Marvin pulled back on the control column. They had reached one of the higher mountain ranges and The Fort gained some altitude as they cleared another ridge. Marvin heard Novak's voice come in loud and clear over the interphone. "Where are we and what's going on?" Marvin ignored Novak, speaking quickly into the mike.

"Harper. Are you certain you can't move him?"

"Couldn't be surer."

"You know what a wheels down landing will do to us on a plowed or rutted field."

"You're the pilot, sir. You're sure to kill him if you belly in, Major."

"Ballard. What's topside?"

"Clear sky, sir. No fighters anywhere."

"Swifty?"

"Clear here, sir. Not a Kraut in sight. Major, there's an awful lot of cables flopping around loose all over the place. Sir, I got a big whole back here and I can see the stabilizer, and its shot up. Are we gonna bail out?"

"We're too low to jump, kid. Everyone to crash stations on the double. Harper, get up here and give me a hand."

A few moments later, Marvin saw Harper stagger into the cockpit covered with blood. Marvin could see Harper's arm hanging limply at his side. Harper had taken off his oxygen mask and Marvin dropped his own off and frowned at Harper's arm.

"Sorry, sir." Harper said as he struggled into the copilot's seat and painfully strapped himself in.

"Caught a bad one. Can't move the arm. I think I've bought the farm. I'm beginning to fuzz out."

The number four engine began to cough and Marvin reached for the landing gear switch on the control pedestal and couldn't find it. Glancing down, he could see the indentation where the switch was hit and broken off. It was a pattern of strafing holes that had climbed and shattered some of the gauges along the instrument panel. He suddenly realized with amazement the landing gear was already down and probably had been since the switch was first sheared off, the bullet undoubtedly throwing it. He had no idea when it might have happened. It could have been at any time during those ferocious fighter attacks on the Fort.

Then with another sickening sensation, he realized now what had caused the strange behavior of those last two German fighters, the two that had broken off their attack and had approached The Sky Queen with their wheels down. They were acknowledging The Sky Queen's universal sign of surrender that all flyers adhered to when seen, and the crew not knowing the bomber's gear was down had blasted the two Germans from the air!

30

Luftwaffe Colonel Ernst Von Reinstock was in the upsetting throes of conflicting emotions. In one sense, he was extremely happy, taking pleasure in his new activities, pitting his intelligence once again against the enemies of the Fatherland.

He stood in the center of a newly constructed one-story building located near Frankfurt, and looked out over his little kingdom. It was a small building, crowded with a good number of Germans wearing the uniform of the Luftwaffe.

Stacked tightly against all the walls but one, various pieces of electronic and communications equipment blinked with multicolored lights, and jangled strange bells. Large bulky cables ran from the great variety of gear to one wall, which was cut to allow passage to the outside where cables, were separated and spread apart heading in all directions. Reinstock observed with careful interest, a gigantic map of occupied Europe. It was fixed on the far wall with Germany in the center and a small bulb emanating a steady red glow showing the location of the building he was in from which all distances on the map were calculated.

A long narrow platform separated the map from the rest of the room. Near the platform were numerous desks occupied by German aviators busily engaged in answering the constant ringing of the field phones. He observed the German airmen continuously rising from their desks, going to a large box at either side of the platform, extracting a small flat piece of metal in the shape of a four-engine aircraft, and hanging them at various locations on the map. Each of the metal aircraft had a hole in the nose in which a red flagged short pin could be pushed through to hold it.

Reinstock's lips parted with a grin of satisfaction at the smoothness of his system he had created. He had made sure that each plane was numbered and beneath the map were several pads of preprinted narrow thin cardboard sheets. After the enlisted men working the map pinned each metal plane up, one of the small cardboard sheets was marked with the corresponding number and tacked up beside the plane. On the cardboard slip, there were ten lines with space for the ten names, or classifications of the downed flyers belonging to each aircraft. Rienstock knew that anyone, including Hitler himself, studying the intense activity going on in this large noisy room, hearing the incessant blare of the radio reports of the air war now in progress, and raging over Germany that the purpose of the operation would be immediately apparent. His single most obvious design of these men in motion was to account for every allied aircraft shot down over German territory, and to keep track of the number of enemy flyers who might be loose or attempting to escape from any particular area. He was proud of his effective and deadly method to finish off what German fliers and anti-aircraft batteries had wrought.

All of this was his brainchild, so of course he was the most interested in the operations' success. Reich Marshal Goering had personally given him the authority to proceed, and so far, the operation had been extremely effective. He had breathed it into life, and his very presence gave it the driving sustenance that guided its accomplishments. He was aware that everyone in the room knew many an allied flyer was dead or captured because of his fanatical determination of a once great German flier who continued to pursue the enemy even when he was no longer able to fly.

The efficiency of his operation continued to please Reinstock. At the same time, he found himself chafing with frustration. *Here I am, one of the greatest air aces Germany has ever produced, grounded, forced to defend the Fatherland against these accursed Americans inside a shack!*

He knew he was still able to fly in spite of what the doctors had said. He still had the courage and the will power. The iron cross and a breast full of ribbons could attest to his bravery and the skill to match. *Yet here I am, on the deck, while Germany is undergoing some of its gravest hours.* The only thing that prevented him from disobeying orders, and stealing a plane if need be, was that the Fuehrer himself, on receiving his last decoration, had ordered him to remain at this post on the ground.

He continued to chafe at the fate that kept him chained to a desk rather than with his comrades in the sky. While his eyes still roamed over the ever-changing board, his thoughts were with the Luftwaffe pilots high over Germany, and he recalled the thrill of the pursuit and battle of high-powered machines, where ability and the will to win could survive anything the enemy might throw at him.

Then a flicker of pain crossed his face and betrayed the weakness that had finally grounded him. He mused at what he had become, shaking his head at the wonder of it.

Beneath the sharply pressed material of his Luftwaffe uniform was a body that was no longer completely his. There were wires in his left elbow and in his right knee. There was a metal plate in his skull, and another one in his shoulder. His lower left leg that fitted so well into its polished officers' boot was artificial. Part of his skin no longer even had any resemblance to the original layer changed by countless skin grafts. Scar tissue covered the entire left side of his body from his last flaming crash.

Another flicker of sharp pain cleared his mind and he walked over to the map and surveyed the growing line of downed aircraft. The line was now heading in the other direction as the Americans began their long trip home from the target.

Reinstock smiled as he saw the metal planes steadily tacked up, and his thoughts went back to the high air over Germany and his comrades. Somewhere in that vast arena of airspace, his brother Hans was still flying for the both of them. His brother was young, hardly a man yet, but he was skilled. Reinstock knew his brother honored him. He had spent many hours teaching him the vast difference between just being a good pilot, and one with the ability to survive. He had shared the battle-wise skill of his experience as one of Germany's great fliers, and he was confident his younger brother would be as great. In the air war, if one was skilled, it took only a short time to achieve greatness.

Then a plane presently tacked up on the border of Poland, obviously miles from the returning line of American aircraft caught his glance.

"What is that?" Reinstock asked an aviator flagging it.

"An unconfirmed report sir, it's from civilians sighting a low flying smoking aircraft."

31

The number two engine started to cough again, bringing Marvin's attention to the immediate problem, landing about thirty tons of crippled Fortress. If they ditched or bellied in, they'd kill Ryan for sure, but the chances for the rest of them surviving would be much better. A wheels down landing could wipe them all out. He chose to try to keep Ryan alive.

Marvin looked at the control panel again. The landing gear warning light on the panel was shattered and the landing gear warning horn hadn't been working, even on their last two missions. Marvin made a quick visual check from the left-hand window and could see the left wheel was down.

"Down left," he said loudly to Harper.

Harper glanced at him for a moment before he understood. Then struggling with his good arm, he looked out the right window. He could see the wheel down on the right side. "Down right," he said. Marvin nodded, inching the flaps down. He glanced quickly at the airspeed indicator, which was still operative, noticing the decrease in airspeed. He began to cut back the throttles carefully while staring intently at the ground coming up from below.

The white snow blotches covered larger areas now and he could even make out what appeared to be large snowdrifts. Visibility steadily became much worse as small patches of fog blurred his vision. Then suddenly there was a great green forest area with high trees just a few hundred feet before them and he frantically jammed the throttles forward, goosing the engines barely in time to trim the tops of some of the higher trees.

He went through another patch of fog that turned to mist and stayed with them. Marvin exchanged a glance with Harper, then once more peered intently through the windshield desperately searching for an opening, and level ground with a minimum of obstructions where he could bring her down. *Right now, I'd settle for just about anything that even looked flat.* Once again he began easing back on the throttles and the airspeed decreased. The strain was getting to him and he was certain he was about to crack and bring them all too sudden flaming death.

Finally, there was a break in the mist, and through the tree line he saw a clearing up ahead, a snow-covered valley that beckoned in promise of safe haven. He cranked the flaps down to full flaps and cut the engines. The Sky Queen was now fully committed to the earth and destiny. Immediately he cut all the fuel and ignition switches bracing himself. He grasped the wheel firmly as the big Fort began to settle rapidly.

An eerie sensation came over him with the sudden silence of the dead engines and the wind whistling through countless holes of the crippled ship. It almost forced him to close his eyes.

The splotchy white earth quickly rose up beneath him and ahead he could see the pure white of what looked like the gentle mounds of snow drifts, or jagged rock waiting deceptively covered to lure him to disaster. At the last moment, he pulled the wheel all the way back into his stomach and the plane settled with the nose high and the tail wheel hitting first. Marvin applied pressure on the brake pedals gingerly, then heavily, and the brakes squealed in protest as the plane bucked.

To Marvin's complete surprise, the plane continued to roll forward in a long slow skid until the gradual slope of the earth began to turn the Fort toward a great stand of trees that rapidly grew larger and it appeared as if they were going to smash into them. Then the plane skidded completely around and came to a rocking convulsive halt, burying itself into a great white mound of snow.

For a very long time, nobody moved, and everything was silent except for the whistling wind.

32

Szabla motioned Yanov, Durcansky, Sediva the Czech, and several of the other men to get down. They were all high up in the snow line apprehensively watching a strong German patrol as they moved through the foothills away from the position of the partisans. Szabla had observed the smoke in the sky while it was still some distance away. Then he heard the increasing sound of the roaring engines and was startled to see the great ship come over the far mountain ridge and pass right in front of them, almost level with their altitude and close enough for Szabla to catch a glimpse of the occupants before the plane disappeared over the next mountain.

Szabla came back to earth when Durcansky punched him in the arm and pointed where the plane had disappeared. Szabla shrugged, he had already seen it. So did Yanov. The partisans understood what they had to do. Then Sediva the Czech threw snow at Szabla to attract his attention, and pointed down into the foothills. Szabla saw the Germans had stopped and were discussing the plane that had just gone over.

While the partisans watched, Szabla involuntarily shivered as it started to snow again and the cold wind of the mountain whipped frigidly against his face. He felt it was unusual weather for this time of the year and was certain the early snow boded great trouble ahead.

Szabla contemplated if this was just the normal German patrol, which the Germans seemed to make about once every six weeks, or whether they were looking for him and the partisans. Either way, as long as the Germans were down there, they could not move. He kicked snow with his foot in frustration knowing a jagged bluff hid them, but a move in either direction would expose them to any German that might happen to look up. Szabla was almost certain they weren't looking for them because he still confined the activities of his partisans to a great distance from Praznik. Any of his men who even accidentally did something that would jeopardize the location of their camp, no matter how slight, was a dead man. He had already killed two of his own men for violating this rule when they had visited a village below Praznik to spend some of the money they had liberated from the bodies of Germans killed in a previous ambush. His justice was swift and he dispatched them both using his knife. This was too close to the village.

Szabla stole another peek around the jagged rocks below. He watched the German patrol split in two. The larger number of soldiers were continuing in the same direction as before, away from the position of the partisans, while eight of them headed off in the direction of the plane and the dissipating smoke trail. Szabla waited until the larger group was no longer in sight then signaled to the others to follow as they too set off in the same direction as the eight Germans.

A short time later, Szabla still had the small German patrol in sight, but he began to wear a worried frown as their struggling trek through the continuously falling snow was bringing them nearer and nearer to the mountain range that housed the village of Praznik, and higher up, his own camp.

Sediva poked him again and motioned with his rifle that they should kill the Germans now. Szabla could see Sediva could do it easily. It would be like killing ducks and Sediva hadn't used his rifle on any Germans since the train wreck. Szabla knew Sediva's hatred of the Germans momentarily blinded him to the absolute authority of Szabla. Then, astonishingly to Szabla, Sediva the Czech raised his rifle as if to fire, Szabla punched him, sending the suddenly startled partisan reeling into the snow.

Szabla watched Sediva's face flare red as he reacted angrily, and then Szabla reached for his knife, which seemed to appear as if from nowhere. "I let the machine gunner on the train go, but this time you will not give away our position."

He now saw Sediva's face fill with terror at the sight of the blade. He watched Sediva change his whole demeanor immediately realizing the only way to save his life was to cool down and profusely apologize.

Szabla accepted Sediva's apology for his momentary lapse. Szabla nodded once, and already dismissing the incident from his mind, ordered all the partisans to move on.

Szabla continued to trudge his men after the Germans, remaining on the high ground and being careful to keep out of sight. He wondered if he would have really killed Sediva, also a friend since the beginning of his bandit days. The going was painfully slow and tedious but his type of tracking they were familiar with, and he hoped their caution would be rewarded and they would not have to kill the Germans. Killing the Germans might bring even more of them into the area in search of this patrol and the plane.

It was just getting dark when he saw the Germans suddenly stop and surprisingly start back over their same trail, apparently giving up the search, but heading straight for the partisans.

33

Rienstock went into a mode everyone in the room knew so well. His inquisitive predatory mind was ticking towards the moment when he would figure out all the answers needed to find, capture, or kill the men from the metal plane on the big board.

"Could it have been one of ours?"

"I'm checking that now, Colonel."

"It's too far from the main line. It must be one of ours." Reinstock watched the aviator move back to his desk and began making a series of calls. His attention returned to the battle pattern on the map. He observed a new shorter line into France, a raid that was occurring simultaneously with the American deep penetration into Germany. Looking at another area on the map of France, he noticed several of the slips covering a raid of almost twenty-four hours ago, still incomplete. He counted quickly and was surprised that there were almost thirty Americans still unaccounted for in that earlier raid.

"Kramer," he shouted, and across the room, a junior officer snapped to attention and hurried over. "Yes sir," he said, with fear and respect.

"Kramer, what is happening with these planes? I know it does not look like we are involved in a shooting war because you are not in the sky or behind a gun. You are, Kramer. We all are. Your gun is your brain. Your bullets are your pencil, your voice, your ears, and your intelligence. Now if I am not disturbing your dreams too much, why are those planes still there? What are you doing to remove them from the board?"

"I've contacted both the SS and Army groups in that area, sir. The foxhunt plan has been put into effect in each of the districts involved. In the Rouen district, we could not use the civilian population for obvious reasons."

"So?"

"There is an armored group in the area that is now assisting in the search and I expect a report momentarily Colonel."

"Alright. See to it." Kramer saluted sharply, returned to his desk, and began cranking the phone with renewed vigor. Reinstock turned and saw the aviator who had been checking on the downed plane in Poland approach him.

"Sir."

"Hoffman"

"The defense group in that area has not returned to the field. They have again interrogated the civilian observer who now claims he did not actually see the American go down, but observed him to be on fire, smoking badly and under attack by three of our fighters."

"What squadron is presently stationed at the closest field in that area?"

"The 22nd, sir." Reinstock raised an eyebrow and smiled. *Hans's squadron, Excellent.* It would give him an opportunity to speak to his brother and get a firsthand account of some of the air action.

"As soon as possible, contact Luftwaffe Lieutenant Hans Reinstock and tell him I wish to speak with him. Interrupt me when you reach him."

"Yes, sir."

"What about the squadron and confirmation of the American?"

"The 22nd is landing now, sir."

"Good. Inform their operations officer what we wish to know, and have him call us immediately upon finding out."

"Yes, sir." The aviator returned to his desk. When Reinstock glanced back at the map, he could see Kramer removing two of the planes tacked up in the area of Rouen, France. Another aviator was beginning to fill in some of the names on the remaining slips. Of the almost thirty unaccounted for Americans of just moments ago, there were now only four missing. Reinstock smiled and rubbed at the pain in his left thigh. Limping, he walked back to his glass enclosed office and sat down.

Sitting at his desk, he poured himself a large measure of Cognac and gulped it down. While he waited, he lit a cigarette and smoked it slowly.

He looked up, surprised to see Hoffmann approaching already. Hoffman entered and informed him that Luftwaffe Captain Beck, the 22nd squadron commander himself was on the phone. Reinstock dismissed Hoffmann waiting until the door closed before lifting the phone and saying,

"Reinstock."

He listened patiently for the confirmation of the American going down as Beck spoke to him in the respectful tone of a subordinate officer and one who regarded him as a national hero. It seemed incredible, but suddenly Reinstock comprehended the call, and it was not really about the American bomber at all. It was about the tremendous air battle over Germany and the great loss suffered on both sides. It was about Hans. When Beck spoke about Hans, he spoke quickly, without embellishment. He told about the returning squadron and the call concerning a lone American B-17 on its way to Poland.

"Most of the squadron was already short on fuel, but Hans and several others checked out the coordinates and gave pursuit. From the account, the bomber was already under attack and damaged when the first units sighted the plane. The Americans fought them off viciously with skill and determination, downing several of the fighters in a matter of minutes. Then Hans and another plane arrived to find the bomber smoking badly but still flying and alone. When Hans and his wingman dove in for the attack, the Americans perpetrated a murderous deception and lowered their wheels in apparent surrender. Then, in utter dis-regard of the ethics of air warfare, shot down both fighter planes when they closed to guide the bomber in. Hans, taken by surprise, died, and went down with his plane. The pilot of the second fighter had parachuted out. It was an infamous breech of international law!" Captain Beck barked angrily.

"Something these American gangsters should be made to regret." Reinstock remained silent for several moments, until Beck was almost certain the man had hung up.

"And the other pilot survived?"

"I'm afraid not. He managed to parachute out, but was badly shot up. I am sorry about your brother Colonel, Hans was a good pilot."

"They were both good pilots," Reinstock said softly. What about the Americans?" Captain Beck told him that the fortress was heavily damaged, yet he could not confirm that the plane had gone down.

"When last seen, it was still maintaining altitude, although one engine continued to stream smoke."

Beck had notified Air Defense, alerting them to the bomber, and they had scrambled the nearest fighter squadron to the area. Beck once again gave his condolences to Reinstock on the loss of his courageous younger brother and informed him he would call the moment anything additional concerning the Americans came in. Reinstock slowly hung up and for a long time sat staring into space, lost in the mental image of his younger brothers young and happy smiling face, his eagerness to get into the fray before all the glory was gone. His younger brother, who until this moment, and his father, were the only members of his immediate family not killed by the war. His mother, both his sisters, and an older brother were already dead.

Now only he and his father remained as the last two surviving members of the Reinstock's, a once proud family, which had given everything, and then some, to the new order that was to make Germany great for a thousand years, but had managed to bungle it all away. *What a waste for Germany that the war was being run poorly.*

He started another cigarette then abruptly crushed it. His jaw clenched in a tight grim determination, he slowly stood up, and then forgetting the pain in his leg strode from his office back into the large room. "Kramer!" he snapped loudly. Immediately, Kramer was standing before him. "Yes, Colonel." Reinstock did not answer him but walked quickly to the map where the lone unconfirmed metal plane was flagged. Kramer hurried along behind, careful to stay just far enough back to keep from bumping into him. Reinstock's finger first traced a vertical line that followed a path on the map dissecting the plane, and then his finger followed a horizontal line across the map that ran close to it.

"Kramer."

"Yes, sir."

"I want all the detail maps we have in the areas surrounding these coordinates. I want them at once."

Kramer was about to salute in acknowledgement.

"Wait, Kramer. Listen carefully. At any time, day or night, wherever I am, whomever I might be talking to, immediately inform me of any change in the status of this plane. Do you understand? I have taken a personal interest in what has become of it, and especially the crew. I want them." He turned and faced the others and pointed.

"I am talking about this particular plane. Let there be no mistake."

He saw the room grow ominously quiet; no one bothering to answer the ringing telephones as they curiously watched him. He could see it was obvious to everyone how emotionally upset he had suddenly become, causing most to listen with quiet concern, hoping to hear the possible explanation for this surprising behavior in their normally undisturbed Colonel.

"I want them," Reinstock repeated loudly, addressing the entire room. "And if anyone shirks their responsibility in assisting me in bringing these murderers to justice, they will find themselves joining these Americans and what I have in store for them."

He scanned the room, which remained silent for several moments longer, everyone disappointed, but still curious, then the room picked up its normal level of activity.

Reinstock walked over to a table that Kramer had cleared and was already spreading his maps. He impatiently helped open them and began studying the markings with meticulous attention. From the corner of his eye, he watched an officer come cautiously up to Kramer and whisper in his ear. "What is it Kramer?" He demanded. "Sir, one of our patrols spotted a low flying smoking plane somewhere in these mountains."

Reinstock's attention turned to the single metal plane that hung at the border of Poland, and he noticed the number assigned to it. His face was grim as he spoke through tightened lips. "Well, number 145. We shall see. Yes, we shall see."

34

Marvin, motionless and silent, but slowly coming to his senses, looked out the cockpit at the gently falling snow. He had no idea how long he'd been out. He rubbed his face and then became aware of the silence around him from the ringing in his ears. He glanced to his right and was surprised to discover that Harper was gone from his seat in the cockpit.

"Ballard, Shaw, Novak. You guys all right?" he said, speaking into the dead throat mike breaking the silence.

"Harper, can you hear me?" He waited only seconds then unbuckled, and climbed down into the forward compartment. He found Stiles' body, riddled with holes and one arm gone. His nausea started to come back to him. He moved Stiles aside and saw Harper and Ryan. They were both unconscious. Harper's arm hung oddly at his side and his face was pale and beaded with perspiration. Ryan looked almost normal, yet there were burn marks over his flying suit and it was apparent the man was in shock, possibly from the explosion, or maybe the loss of blood, or even the pain of whatever had happened to his leg. It appeared as if Harper had applied a tourniquet to Ryan's dangling leg to stop the bleeding and then had probably passed out.

Then Marvin heard something behind him. It was Ballard, and after seeing the blood spattered compartment, he said softly, "Have they bought it?"

"No. Harper and Ryan are still alive. Help me get Harper out of here so we can work on Ryan." He and Ballard dragged Harper as far back as they could and attempted to move Ryan.

"It's, no good. We've got to cut him free from the outside." From behind, he now heard the voices of some of the other members of the crew. He saw Novak climb through from the catwalk, coming around the radio compartment and the top turret platform.

"Are you guys all right up there?"

"Yeah," Ballard answered.

"What about the rest of the guys?"

"Miller got it. I just saw him . . . part of his head's blown clean off." There was a pause,

"Who else?"

"Dunham's nicked, but the rest of us are okay.

"How about the old man? Is he okay?"

"I'm all right," Marvin said from behind Ballard where Novak still couldn't see him.

"Some of you men get on the outside and help me free Ryan's leg. Break out the small saw from the toolbox and get out there."

Marvin glanced out from the opening in the ship at the fading light. Dark clouds were moving in fast and an ugly storm was about to engulf them. Inside the forward compartment, it was already too dark to see.

"Break out some light," he said to Ballard. Then shouting, "You men out there, climb in through the forward hatch and give us a hand. We've got to move Lieutenant Harper out of here before the storm hits us." Ballard called down through the hatch. "Novak, over here."

"It's too damn cold out here," Novak said.

"All right, let's get him back to the waist compartment. At least he can stretch out there." Upon giving orders he watched Ballard quickly take off his flack suit and help Novak back into the ship. He knew that with their flying clothes on, both Ballard and Novak were too bulky to move Harper. Then Novak stopped and removed his flying clothes, but he watched Novak at once begin to shiver. Slowly and painstakingly, with Novak standing on the closed bomb bay door to do it, Marvin watched them manage to get Harper into the waist section and lay him gently on some insulation they had ripped from one of the bulkheads. Dunham, in pain, had closed the gun hatches. Now, except for the light coming from the main entrance hatch to the ship, the waist section was dark.

Marvin had put some insulation around the broken open nose of the plane and had gotten a flashlight. He felt the fatigue hit him and he wanted to sit down for a moment and light up a cigarette but he didn't. He looked up to see Ballard stick his head in.

"How is he, sir?" Ballard asked quietly.

"Alive, but barely."

"Should we move him?"

"I don't think it's a good idea, but we're going to have to. It's too cold in here with the nose open the way it is. I've bandaged him and the bleeding's stopped.

We've got to get him someplace more conformable and warm."

"I'm sorry, sir. Ryan was a good egg."

Marvin glanced at Ballard and mused at the words, 'good egg.' If Ryan were conscious and able to, he undoubtedly would have slugged Ballard.

"What about the others?" he asked.

"All in the waist section, major."

"Come on, then. Let's try and get Ryan back there."

The snow was no longer falling gently but swirling in biting bursts and gusts. Several of the crewmembers on the inside reached out for Ryan and easily lifted him though, Ballard following. Before climbing in, Marvin took a last look at the gathering storm and the foreboding mountains. The clouds engulfed them, swallowing them in a silent fury as snow whipped in mini-twisters.

"What's it look like, sir. I mean, where are we?"

"Somewhere in Poland. There's absolutely nothing we can do until daylight. We don't know the terrain or the disposition of any Germans in the area. We don't know what's out there. Hopefully it will clear, and in the morning we'll try to get a bearing on our location. Now let's get some sleep."

Marvin listened and watched the men crawl into separate sleeping positions, with some groans, snorting, and a few wisecracks then they settled down. By mutual consent, they all closed in for warmth, like a squadron of penguins in there bulky flight suits creating a large heap of arms and legs, the proximity of their bodies warming them.

Marvin lay next to the mass of men and finally dozed off and dreamed he was at the controls of The Sky Queen still high in the air over Germany, and under heavy attack.

Outside the black fury of the massive snowstorm raged into the night.

35

Szabla awoke to the sound of planes. He opened his eyes, looked out from his snow-covered shelter, and saw them. There were three, single-engine Junker dive-bombers, ugly aircraft, with the pilot seated in front and a second man, a machine gunner, facing to the rear. It was the hated Stuka; the plane that resembled a vulture, and in the first days of the German invasion had so easily destroyed the Polish armed forces wreaking death and havoc throughout the land.

Szabla recalled how they had bombed and strafed civilian refugees on crowded roads, destroyed the Polish air force on the ground, and decimating what remained of the famed Polish cavalry after the German armor had run over and crushed it.

He watched the planes flying in their familiar wide V reconnaissance formation. He felt they were obviously searching for something or someone, not just seeking their usual random targets of opportunity. As they passed over his position, Szabla was certain the planes were not searching for the partisans. *They couldn't have missed the German patrol already it had been too soon.* Then he remembered, *it was the big plane, the one that had been smoking so badly. It must have gone down in the mountains. Good.* He hoped all the Germans on board had been killed. *That many less would save that many more of their bullets, w*hich were growing scarcer these days.

He signaled the others to get up and look at the sky. It was an overcast morning but the storm had passed, and the snow had stopped. From where he stood, he could see all the way down into the rolling hills and one of the nearby valleys. A fresh powdered blanket of snow covered everything. It had been a long time since he had seen this much snow. He cursed, loud enough to startle the other men. *Travelling in snow was always dangerous. It left tracks. It was like an arrow pointing to a target.* He knew for partisans who must be like the wind in their coming and goings, snow could mean disaster.

He glanced again at the sky and there was no sign of the sun, or the possibility of warmth that would even begin to melt the snowfall. He felt their best hope was snow again, but it didn't look like it would.

All the men were up and near him as he studied the mountain range ahead of them searching for hard ground high enough and hidden enough to cover tracks. He cursed again. He cursed the Germans; he cursed the Stukas; and he cursed the big German bomber for its stupidity in crashing in his mountains. Because of the snow, the trip back to their camp was going to be long and dangerous even though they were less than a day away from it.

Forced to take a roundabout route, he knew making a track near the village would draw attention. They might even make the tortuously long climb up that hard, open mountain road and pass through the village, something that Szabla had only done once before. He cursed and ordered the men to move out and they started moving along the steep slope of the mountain keeping toward the ridges and rock.

* * *

Marvin woke to the sound of three planes. He opened his eyes and listened, as the sound of the approaching aircraft grew louder. He jumped up, quickly opened the main entrance hatch, and crashed through a wall of snow that had piled up during the night. He lay there, unmoving and watched as the flight of three planes passed and continued on over the next range. He made them out to be Stukas and remained prone for several minutes before standing. When he turned back to the plane, he saw The Sky Queen completely covered with snow. He glanced around the surrounding terrain and noticed that everything was covered with great white drifts of it; the trees, the ground, the hills, the mountains up ahead and the path the plane had taken coming in. He was sure they hadn't been seen.

He noticed they had landed on the flat bed of a small valley surrounded by high trees on three sides. Seeing the trees, Marvin found it incredible that he had landed without hitting any of them. He thought it was truly a miraculous landing and remembered his parents driving to church one Sunday after a big snow. The car skidded on the ice, swerved into a big snow bank, and saved them. He thought that was miraculous.

Marvin studied the overcast sky and the immediate surroundings. Then he saw Ballard and some of the others climb out of the plane. They studied the mountains that seemed to rise on all sides.

He focused on his crew. Shaw, in almost boyish delight, trudged out a short ways to the nearest drift then cupping some snow in his hands, turned back to the others and said, "Look at all this snow."

"Don't track it up," Marvin commanded. "Those planes were looking for us."

"What planes?" Shaw asked.

"Germans, stupid," Haply said.

Marvin walked completely around the Fortress and felt a sense of reassurance. He was confident now that the German planes had not seen them and if the weather remained cold and the snow covering the ship didn't melt, they would be safe for a while. He came around to find Haply and Shaw pelting each other with snowballs, laughing it up, while Novak shook his head in disgust at their frivolity.

"Novak," Marvin said loudly, bringing Haply and Shaw back to their present predicament. "You and Haply head for those trees over there and start rigging up a litter for Lieutenant Ryan. Shaw, see what you can scrounge up in the way of food and supplies. Pickup any weapons from the ship that we might be able to carry, and Shaw, pick up the escape kits from Miller and Stiles. Ballard, see what you can do for Lieutenant Harper and Dunham."

"I'm okay, sir." It was Dunham. He had come out to join them, and although he moved stiffly, he seemed all right. "Really, I'm feeling great."

"Good. Right now, you stay with Lieutenant Harper and take it easy until we need you. Okay, men, let's move it. Come on . . . go!"

"Sir, there's really nothing more I can do for Lieutenant Ryan. He needs medical attention bad. Lieutenant Harper seems to be doing better.

His arm is still numb but painful to move. I think he'll be able to get around though."

Marvin glanced at his wristwatch and realized how long he'd been asleep. He felt a twinge of guilt.

"I'm going to try and get a fix and find out where we are, if Stiles' gear isn't too badly shot up. Frank, do you feel like taking a walk?"

"A walk?" Marvin pointed. "Right up to that mountain." High enough so you can see what's on the other side of that ridge? Follow the tree line then cut up to that bluff. The tracks won't be so obvious."

"Major. You think there might be people around here somewhere? You know. Maybe farmers, or friendly types who could help us?"

"I doubt it. Sergeant, this whole mountain range looks isolated. We run into anything up here, you can bet it's going to be a German patrol searching for us. But, you never can tell, we could get lucky."

Ballard trekked off, and Marvin climbed back in the ship through the forward escape hatch.

36

It was startling to Marvin, in the subdued morning light that was filtering into the compartment, to see the body of Stiles again, this time looking very unreal, his face glazed over with a frosted appearance. Stiles was completely covered with snow. The insulation Marvin had previously stuffed into the opening of the ship's broken nose was caved in by the wind, and snow gusted into the compartment.

Marvin pulled in the rest of the insulation and kicked out the snow to light the forward navigator's compartment. He found some of the maps on Stiles' table. All the electronic navigation gear was shot to pieces. He was stunned at the realization of the beating the forward compartment had taken. They had all taken a beating in the air battle over Germany, but down here, seeing it in a quiet light, Marvin almost wept at the carnage these two men must have encountered. It was over for one of them, maybe both if Ryan died, but God, they didn't go quietly! They fought on against the overwhelming fanatical German fighters, wounded, and bleeding, they stayed at their guns to the very end.

There were bullet holes and twisted metal everywhere. The bombsight had taken a direct hit by a cannon shell, yet strangely, it was not destroyed. The drift meter, near Stiles' table had been shot off the wall. Every compass face and dial either was shattered or had a bullet hole through it. The control panel was unrecognizable and Stiles' interphone jack-box with the small oxygen regulator completely shot away.

Looking at all the twisted wreckage of the forward compartment, Marvin took off his gloves, rubbed his face hard, and muttered softly to himself. "You poor guys really took it."

Finally, he broke from his morbid anguish and brought himself to the task of determining their location. He searched for the maps. When he found them, he discovered that even the maps had bullet holes in them! Finding a pencil, he did some rough calculating. He searched for the slide-rule but couldn't find it. Going from one map to another and then back again, he figured the time over the target, the airspeed at the time of his loss of complete rudder control, and the approximate length of time they remained airborne from leaving the target until their forced landing. He was exceptionally careful in his time estimate because of his experience in knowing that where time seemed like hours during an air battle it was always in reality only accurately counted in minutes. He finally arrived at a rough approximation of their location and felt certain he couldn't be too far off.

Then he tried to match the topography of the map with the physical aspects of what he recalled of their immediate surroundings. He was astounded at where he thought he was. It didn't seem possible they had done what they did without some divine intervention. In a brief quiet moment, he thanked God.

He circled the area on the map where he thought they had landed. He was about to recalculate the entire painful effort when he heard Novak and Haply outside returning to the ship and being greeted by Shaw. He frowned as he realized Shaw hadn't come in to remove the escape kits from the bodies of Stiles and Miller. He wondered if Shaw already accomplished it and he'd been too busy with his calculations to notice. He wondered whether to check if the kits were gone and then decided it could wait. Marvin returned to his calculations and rechecked some of his figures again until he was satisfied it was correct.

Marvin finally exited through the hatch again and saw that Novak and Haply had completed the makeshift litter. They had very cleverly used some of the ammunition belts covered with ripped pieces of insulation across two sturdy-looking tree limbs. Although the litter seemed heavier than necessary, it looked serviceable, and was what he wanted.

Shaw had put the survival kits and several other things into a makeshift pack and stood near them outside the plane. He also had two

.45 pistols, one which he had taken from the body of Stiles along with his escape kit the other from Lieutenant Harper, who because of his broken arm, had gladly parted with it. Shaw had also removed the flare gun and he was holding it and the two .45s in his hand along with the small box of flare cartridges.

The sun was breaking through the clouds and the snow became damper as it melted off part of the ship in tiny glistening rivulets. Even through the covering of snow, Marvin could still make out its outline. The props and forward nacelles were plainly visible. Seeing it from the outside where he stood, the snow covered over the many ugly holes in the fuselage.

No matter how you cut it, it was incredible to Marvin how he managed to bring the battered Fortress safely to earth in such a perfect wheels down landing in the middle of nowhere on hard-packed snow.

Marvin looked at The Sky Queen; she just stood silently parked in its normal sloping angle. The poor girl didn't know where she was and probably thought she was parked at the hardstand back home in England. The snow was fooling her. The fact that The Sky Queen did look undamaged and flyable under its white blanket was what really sealed its doom to Marvin. They'd have to burn it.

Their instructions had always been explicit. No flyable, repairable, or usable piece of equipment must ever fall into German hands. Already too many American planes were being flown by Germans. A group of German-flown P-47s once attacked the Sky Queen.

"We're going to burn the plane," Marvin said aloud, confirming the decision by voicing it. Haply, you and Shaw bring out the bodies and we'll bury them." Haply and Shaw stood there stupidly without moving, as if they hadn't heard him.

"Well, hop to it," Marvin said.

"Sir, Shaw started uncomfortably.

"Sir, why do we have to drag them out and bury them? Why can't we just burn them in the plane? They won't know the difference."

"We will," Novak said angrily. "I'll do it, sir," he said, starting forward. Haply grabbed him. "Are you bucking for something?"

Novak deliberately and with an ease born of familiar strength, removed Haply's hand from his arm and said, "Ralph, you know something, you stink!"

"Anytime you want to make something of it, try it." Haply reported quickly.

"Knock it off!" Marvin bellowed angrily. "If I hear anymore guff, I'll kick the crap out of both of you. All right, Sergeant, bring out the bodies. Haply, you and Shaw find a spot by those trees and start digging." Novak laid both bodies beneath one of the wings, covering their faces with cloth.

Marvin knew how distasteful Novak's chore must be to him and he marveled at the waist gunner, a husky man of twenty-three and of Polish extraction, he was a tower of quiet efficiency and strength. A bo-hunk was what he called himself, but he was a far cry from that label.

Marvin was pleased that he had recently put him in again for another Technical Sergeant. He deserved it. Novak was a good man, possibly officer material.

37

Marvin stared up at the bluff, searching for another good man, Ballard his engineer, and top turret gunner. He could make him out high up, a small moving dark spot on the landscape off to the side of the bluff. Marvin had great confidence in this man, Ballard. Married, almost twenty-six and mature for his age, only twenty units away from an engineering degree. Ballard displayed an impressive amount of intelligence, both in human wisdom and technical expertise. Marvin had always felt fortunate in having Ballard as a crew member and had, along with Ryan, Stiles, Novak, Shaw and Haply, been with The Sky Queen on all nineteen missions of this last tour. Dunham had been with the Queen for fifteen missions. This had been Miller's first and last mission, no one really knew him at all. He arrived a stranger, and died the same way. Marvin didn't even know yet whether the man was married or had a family, and here he was burying him.

Marvin thought about another newcomer to The Sky Queen, but not quite a stranger, Lieutenant Dave Harper, the copilot who had replaced Henry, the original copilot killed three missions ago. *Was it only three missions ago that Henry had the top of his head blown away?*

He remembered Henry now as dependable, someone whom he had grown to like and shared perilous times with during camaraderie of numerous sky passages until a burst of flak had ended the relationship in a spray of blood and brains. Harper had replaced him and this was only his third mission, and quite possibly his last. Marvin glanced over at Novak and waited as he approached.

It was obvious the Sergeant was upset. His face had lost its color and he appeared reluctant to speak. "Sir," he began then paused and indicated the place where he had brought out the bodies. "Sir." We've got a problem. I don't have all of Miller. Part of him is still inside."

Novak paused again before continuing. "I don't think I can go back in there again to look."

"Okay. Let it go," Marvin said sympathetically.

"Just get their personal effects together."

"You want me to bring them over there?" Novak asked, indicating the trees where Shaw and Haply were busily digging away.

"No. Leave 'em be.

Novak joined Marvin as he watched Ballard in the distance on the snow-covered mountain. Ballard appeared a slow moving dark patch on the white snow as he neared the crest high above them.

Dunham dropped out of the main entrance hatch and came over to where they were standing. Frowning, he stopped directly beside Marvin, who now continued to stare up at the slow progress of his climber. "Sir." Lieutenant Ryan is conscious and groaning up a storm. He's acting kind of wild. I can't get him calmed down."

"Can you give him another shot of morphine?"

"I don't think there's any left."

"There should be some in those packs Shaw put together." Suddenly Marvin grew tense as he observed something on the mountain above Ballard. He said to Dunham, almost impatiently, "See what you can do for him. I'll be there in a minute."

Dunham nodded to Marvin and quickly located the packs near the fuselage. He rummaged through them and found two first-aid kits with morphine. He took one and climbed back into the plane.

Marvin walked forward several steps squinting his eyes. There in the slight mist above Ballard and to the right of him was a group of moving figures! "Sergeant," Marvin spoke out softly without turning his gaze from the mountain. "Yes, major." Novak responded, glancing at Marvin Curiously. "Up there, to the right of the bluff above Ballard. Do you see anything?" Novak frowned then walked even further toward the slope of the mountain than Marvin, staring up and shading his eyes with his hand. "It looks like soldiers. Maybe eight or ten men."

"Do you think they can see us?"

"I don't know, but they sure see him."

They watched anxiously as the figures suddenly changed their course and headed for Ballard. He was standing motionless against the crest and didn't seem to notice them. Before Marvin could move, Novak ran for the slope and started climbing, yelling as he struggled up a short ways.

"Frank! Frank! Get out of there. Behind you!"

Then it appeared that Ballard had either heard Novak or seen them, because now he came to life and began running and tumbling down the hill in a direct line toward the plane, the other figures chasing behind.

38

Marvin heard a sound like the crack of a rifle, and watched as Ballard seemed to trip and roll. Then he was up again and running a zigzag course madly down the slope as he heard the crack of other rifles and tufts of snow began spurting around Ballard.

Marvin saw Haply and Shaw come running at the first shot and were next to him near the plane. Marvin spun around and began shouting, "Dunham! Dunham! Break out the waist gun! Hurry it up! Where are the .45s?"

He saw that Shaw had already picked them up and tossed one to Haply and the two of them pushed past Marvin and Novak, blasting away at the figures coming down the slope. They fired until the weapons were empty and then they just stood there foolishly, not knowing what else to do next.

"Haply, Shaw, you dumb-heads. Get out of there!" Marvin shouted to them. "Get the thirty caliber and ammunition from the nose. Snap to it. Novak, get back here!" Marvin and Dunham struggled to set up the machine gun and bring it to bear on the slope. Ballard was almost home and Novak was shouting, "Come on, baby. Keep running!"

Marvin dashed for the main entrance hatch and in a few moments was moving Dunham aside and taking his place behind the .50-caliber machine gun. He was sighting it as Ballard in a surprising leap finally tumbled to the bottom of the slope rolling past Novak, who suddenly found himself in the forward position, the crew behind him, and the advancing figures above. Marvin knew Novak could not make it safely back, and saw him drop behind a protruding boulder and take cover.

Marvin opened up with the machine gun then Ballard crashed through the snow underneath the plane to the protection of the main landing gear and dropped behind the closest wheel.

The clattering of the machine gun sounded flat to Marvin as it echoed off the snow-covered mountain and the figures descending suddenly froze in their tracks. He was firing a long burst and used the gun hose-like as he traced a pattern in the snow toward the still figures. They scattered and disappeared. Marvin kept hammering away at the area, in short bursts now. Then he heard the other machine gun somewhere outside near the ship as Haply and Shaw blasted away at the mountain.

The figures had vanished behind the big snowdrifts. Marvin stopped firing. Haply and Shaw kept at it for some moments longer, then they too stopped.

"Ballard. You okay?"

"Yes, sir."

"Haply, you see anything?" Marvin shouted more loudly, staring intently at the slope where the figures had disappeared from sight. Ballard, down below, relayed the question, and then called back the answer to Marvin, "Nothing."

"Can you see anything from where you are?"

"Not a thing."

Suddenly a bullet pinged through the metal skin of The Sky Queen, barely an inch from Marvin's shoulder. A second ping banged loudly by his ear and another bullet hole appeared near him. Yet he could see absolutely nothing out there but the plowed up tracks the running figures had made and where they abruptly ended. He opened up with the machine gun again, plowing up geysers of snow where each of the figures tracks had ended. He emptied another belt of ammunition and stopped. He waited, straining his eyes for some movement, for any sign of them. Then a ping and another bullet hole appeared in the metal skin near him.

"We haven't got a chance in here. Let's get outside behind some cover!" Dunham said wildly, starting for the hatchway. "Hold it, Sergeant," Marvin said, grabbing his arm and restraining him. "We'll go, but we'll take the other gun with us." They unhooked the other machine gun from its mount, and with Marvin carrying the gun and Dunham the ammunition, they dropped through the main entrance hatch into the snow beneath the plane. They rapidly set the gun across an old fallen tree trunk back from the slope, using it as a make shift mount. Then Marvin studied the two men out forward of the ship who had brought out the other machine gun.

"Haply, Shaw," he called out. "Work yourselves over to the trees and then around to the trail." He indicated the area where Ballard had originally started crawling toward the small stand of trees, carefully moving the machine gun with them.

"Novak," Marvin called out to his waist gunner still tucked behind the boulder at the base of the sharp slope.

"Stay put and watch yourself."

"Yes, sir." Novak responded crisply.

Then Marvin heard what sounded like a shout. Everyone heard it this time. Marvin listened and it was definitely someone shouting, causing them to freeze in position, waiting intently as the voice came again. Someone was yelling at them in a guttural, German-sounding series of commands. Their silence, mostly surprise, encouraged whoever was yelling at them to continue. Dunham whispered, "Can you understand what those Krauts are shouting about, sir?" Marvin shook his head. At first, he thought he could understand some of it, but the more he listened, the more it sounded like a sort of badly pronounced German, yet not really. More like Slavic. Finally he called, "Can any of you make out what he's saying?"

"Sounds Czechoslovakian or Polish to me," Ballard said, his voice carrying clearly in the crisp air. "Maybe they think we're partisans and found the plane," Dunham said. Novak listened to another burst of shouting that were definitely commands of some sort then turned to the others. "That's what it is all right," he said. "Those Germans think we're Polish."

"Cut it, Sergeant," Marvin said, watching intently.

The same voice out there was still talking, only now the tone had changed somewhat as Marvin listened, silently cursing his lack of linguistic knowledge.

"Sir. They're Polacks!" Novak shouted, suddenly smiling.

"Are you sure?"

"Am I sure? That guy sounds like my father talking."

"What is he saying?" Novak shouted something in Polish that sounded like gibberish to Marvin. There was a pause from the man who had originally called out, and then a strong voice shouted a question. Novak answered and then stood up. Before Marvin could order him back down, a hulking figure rose from the snow. Keeping his rifle aimed in their direction, Novak turned to shout back at the surprised crew in English, "Don't shoot. These guys are not Germans. They're Polish." Novak spoke out again in Polish and then another figure rose, almost directly in front of Marvin, pointing his gun startling him. "It's okay." Novak said reassuringly. "They're partisans."

39

Marvin slowly stood up and called out in what he hoped would still sound friendly.

"Haply, stay with the gun."

Then Ballard stood up and some more of the partisans appeared until eight of the toughest-looking men major Marvin had ever seen were standing in a semicircle facing them, their rifles still pointed warily in their direction. Shaw and Dunham cautiously came out with their hands in plain view and the husky blonde man with the full mustache the color of summer hay wearing a fierce expression stood in the center of the waiting partisans. Then he stepped forward and spoke rapidly in Polish.

The partisan leader directed his voice toward Marvin. He could identify him as the shouter. Then the partisan and Novak quickly engaged in a hot argument, their voices loud, both men punctuating their differences in a variety of impressive hand gestures. Dunham whispered to Marvin, "That tough bastard must be the leader."

"Mean looking isn't he. Must scare the hell out of the Germans," Marvin said. Marvin listened and the conversation seemed to take a sudden turn for the worse and grow even more unpleasant. For a minute, it looked as if it was going to turn ugly, and Marvin said loudly, "Haply, hold the gun and stand up!" Haply stood up, holding the gun pointed at Novak and the partisan. He was only yards away and would be deadly at that range. At the sight of Haply and the machine gun, the partisans fell silent. Then after a moment, he resumed talking but this time with a definitely milder tone. Novak motioned for the partisan leader to remain where he was.

"Major Marvin," Novak called, heavily accenting the word 'major'. "Major Marvin, would you step over here please?" Attempting to look casual, Marvin sauntered over.

"Yes, Sergeant, what seems to be the problem?" Up close, the partisan leader was craggier and meaner looking and he reeked of something that smelled like garlic.

"Sir, they want us to surrender."

"Surrender?" Marvin burst out, glancing sharply at the large burly partisan who had warily watched him approach.

"Aren't these men Polish partisans?"

"That's right, sir."

"Do you have any doubt that these men are Polish partisans?"

"No, sir."

"Then why aren't they behaving like Polish partisans?"

"I don't know. All I know sir is that this man here, their leader, Szabla by name, wants us to surrender. He says they won't kill us."

"Now isn't that nice! Why that son of a . . ." Marvin faced the leader fully. "Novak, translate. My name is Major Greg Marvin of the American Army Air Force. American Air Force. Do you understand?"

"He does, sir," Novak said, after translating and getting a response, a curt short nod.

"You are . . . Polish partisans. Right? You hate the Germans. We hate the Germans. You fight the Germans. We fight the Germans. Poland and America are friends. Allies.

How can one friend surrender to another? Not when they are friends and allies. Does he understand?"

"He does, sir." The leader began speaking rapidly now, with more emotion as Novak listened carefully, waiting at the end to make certain the man had finished.

"Sir, he understands. He still says we have to surrender. If we do, he won't hurt us. If we don't he'll kill us . . . and he has no more time to waste. He's afraid the German planes may come back."

Marvin frowned and let his eyes take in every man of the crew standing out there. Then he said, "What do you think, Novak?"

"I don't think we have a choice, sir."

"Okay," Marvin said. "Tell him we have two wounded with us. One of them badly hurt." Novak did. "He says they have a doctor in their camp."

"He wins. Put down the gun Haply. Novak, tell him we surrender."

40

As soon as Novak had finished translating, Marvin saw the eight partisan's spring to life. One of them instantly moved the two machine guns away from the Americans while another told them to stand together. Two of the partisans climbed into the plane through the main entrance hatch, and moments later one of them stuck his head back out the side window to shout something.

"They want us to get Lieutenant Ryan and Harper out of there," Novak said.

"Shaw. Haply. Bring out Lieutenant Ryan." Marvin commanded.

They cautiously brought the litter over to the ship and carefully lowered Ryan into it. Then Harper appeared and the men helped him through the hatch. Except for his blood shot eyes and the loss of feeling in his arm, Marvin observed that Harper had recovered somewhat and was able to function on his own. Someone had rigged up a sling for his arm and he walked slowly away from the plane to where the rest of the crew stood watching.

Marvin could hear the two men inside the ship kicking and ripping things in their search for guns and other items of value. Turning, Marvin saw one of the partisans going through the pockets of the dead men under the wing while another was beginning to remove their boots.

Marvin stomped over in a fury and knocked the boots from the hand of the nearest man, knocking him down.

"What are you doing?" he shouted, unable to contain his anger. "Get away from those men!"

The fallen partisan struggled up from the snow onto his feet and angrily pointed his rifle at Marvin intending to shoot, when the leader, the one called Szabla, barked something at him and the man reluctantly lowered the weapon, but not before glaring a promise at the American of some future deadly encounter. Marvin inaudibly let his breath out knowing it had been close. Szabla came over to Marvin and poked him with his knife, saying something in Polish.

"He says don't touch any of his men again or he'll kill us all," Novak translated.

Marvin and the rest of the crew watched helplessly as the partisans stripped the bodies. The partisans took everything leaving only the underwear, which was unusable because of the rips and frozen blood.

"And these guys are supposed to be our allies," Dunham whispered bitterly.

When it was apparent the partisans had finished their ransacking of the plane and the bodies, Marvin approached Szabla and told him with motions of his hand he was going to bury his men. Szabla looked at Marvin for only a second then nodded.

The ground was frozen beneath the snow, making the earth too hard for the crew to achieve any depth as Marvin watched them dig. They lowered the bodies into a shallow grave and covered them with the cold frozen dirt. Major Marvin said the eulogy, the Lord's Prayer, and was quite surprised to see the partisans stand respectfully near the grave. When the prayer was complete, they reverently made the sign of the cross.

Szabla gave the signal for them to pick up the wounded Ryan, and indicated they were all to move out. Marvin informed him they had to first burn the plane. Szabla stared at him blankly. Marvin in his anxiousness forgot about Novak and tried to make Szabla understand. He just looked at him. Picking up the flare gun Marvin pointed it at the plane. Finally, he lit a match and held it under the wing to show him. Szabla got the picture and in a quick movement, knocked the flare gun and match from Marvin's hands. In an angry burst of language, Szabla waited for each sentence to make sure Marvin understood.

"You are not to burn the plane, now or later. Burning the plane would reveal their presence in these mountains. This would endanger others as well as themselves. Burning the plane would mean smoke.

Smoke means fire. Fire will bring the Germans. He says if anyone tries to burn the plane, he'll kill us all."

"I don't know sergeant, Marvin said grimly. "I'm beginning to worry. Why does he keep threatening to kill us? You sure he's Polish." Novak nodded. "Absolutely, sir."

Marvin listened while Szabla shouted something unintelligible again and all of them began moving away from the area. The partisans indicated where they wanted the Americans and the crew slowly fell in. Six of the partisans led out front and were soon fifty yards ahead. Marvin worried about Haply and Shaw carrying the sedated Ryan, glancing over his shoulder he saw the remaining two partisans bringing up the rear.

No one spoke, the only sounds being the heavy breathing of the crew as they forced themselves to keep pace, but carrying Ryan was making the going slow. One of the partisans up ahead stopped to shout back at them. When Novak started to translate, Marvin interrupted. "I know. I know. He wants us to keep up. Ballard, Dunham, you two grab onto the litter and see if we can't make it easier." With four of them carrying the litter now, they picked up their pace a bit. The partisans continued slowly to pull ahead, having to stop periodically to allow the crew to catch up.

Marvin wondered at first about their direction as the partisans continued their march through the low areas hugging the slopes bordering the valleys. They were not heading for the high mountains where he assumed they would have their camp. The more he thought about the direction they were taking, the more he realized what good sense it made. Down in the lower hills the sun was warming the snow and already it was beginning to melt, wiping out any tracks the group might leave. If a German patrol discovered the plane, which Marvin felt was only a question of time, *they might easily assume from all the tracks on the slope around the plane that the crew had escaped back up the mountain with the partisans. Were the Germans that stupid?* Marvin knew they weren't. *Why hadn't this partisan, Szabla, who seemed clever enough, decided on wiping out the tracks, or at least letting them burn the plane? Maybe he was the stupid one and not the damn Krauts.* The one thing Marvin did feel certain about was their only safety right now was in putting distance between them and the plane.

Marvin began to encourage the crew, passing an occasional upbeat remark among them, attempting to display a confidence he didn't have as they all trudged on trying to keep pace with the partisans leading them far ahead.

After a while, he grew too winded to talk and just concentrated on the simple act of keeping up, helping Harper along now as they continued on what seemed to be an unending march.

PART III

THE STEEL RING

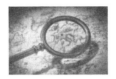

41

Colonel Ernst Von Reinstock was pressed for time. He knew in order to find this particular crew of Americans; he must begin at once to put into action the machinery for their capture. Before he could devote his full attention to the task, there remained one disturbing chore he was required to perform.

As distasteful as he knew it was there was no way for him to escape this chore, and it was one that he must attend to by himself. He had to see his father and tell him of Hans. He would go see the old man and tell him of his youngest son's death, getting it over with as quickly as possible, and before the official notification. He called for an appointment and got one immediately. It was only a short flight to the factory, he was quickly ushered into the offices of the old man. He always felt they were somber offices made of oak-lined paneling with aged carvings of a Teutonic era, giving the room the cultured appearance of a museum. Placed irreverently over the walls, and many of the carvings, were blueprints, charts, graphs and various displays used by his father in managing the vast plant his office rose above and looked on like some great watchtower. In a strange sort of way, seeing the charts and displays on the walls reminded Reinstock of his own operations group. The difference here however, was that the old man was dealing with industry and production quotas while Ernst dealt with human lives, the capture of downed enemy airmen, who in flight had been intent on destroying factories very much like this one owned by his father.

Earnst watched as the old man rose from behind his antique desk to greet his son. The old man, Karl Reinstock, seemed to have aged even more than the last time Ernst had seen him. Ernst observed the war was obviously continuing to take its toll on his father. To speed him on his decline, there would be another sapping of his vitality with this latest news concerning Hans.

Ernst had not seen him since the death of Ernst's mother, which had occurred during an allied bombing raid. He had never been close to his father and each new tragedy in the family had seemed to estrange them even further. Hans, who Ernst had always looked after and protected, had been his father's favorite, and his hope for the future.

Ernst wondered how his father viewed his appearance now as he leaned on his cane and stood before the old man in his smartly tailored uniform, pinned with its many decorations. He was an older son who had bitterly disappointed his father. Yet, up until the death of his mother, his father had never failed to visit him whenever Ernst had been wounded or confined for illness. He continued to do so regardless of where he was, or the practical flying distances between them at the time.

During Ernst's furiously successful career as a front line pilot there had been many visits. While flying in defense of the Fatherland, Ernst had been wounded many times. After the death of Ernst's mother, the old man seemed to have lost heart concerning his son's many air victories, and his visits abruptly ended. It was, Ernst suspected, as if suddenly he counted his elder son already dead.

The old man now offered him a chair. "I've ordered some tea," he said. "As you know, a habit of mine I picked up in my Oxford days. If you prefer cognac or schnapps . . . ?"

"No, Tea will do nicely." Ernst seated himself and waited for his father to do the same. Instead, the old man remained standing while his secretary, a slim blonde woman, entered and served tea from a silver teapot and left the tray on a table between them. Ernst was familiar with the daily ritual his father had first encountered as a visiting student in London in his younger years, and had happily accepted the custom he brought back with him. He had claimed it as a wonderfully inspired idea of the English, something that added a needed touch of civilization, a refreshing pause in the affairs of a cruel world.

Ernst watched the old man wait until his secretary closed the heavy door behind her, then he seated himself opposite his son and carefully sipped his tea. "Are you well?" He asked finally.

"Yes. And you?",

"I am well. That woman, Gerta, wasn't it, the one in Berlin. Are you still seeing her?"

"No. That's over with."

"A pity. I think she gave you a touch of humanity. Something you sorely needed."

Ernst smiled slightly. He had already determined not be drawn into conflict with his father no matter what the insult or rage heaped on him. He had no idea how the old man was going to react to the grim news he was about to reveal, but he was prepared for anything, and to forgive what came. Staring across at his father, suddenly he was struck by a strange premonition. Watching the old man sip at his tea so English-like, he became aware of the future.

In spite of his realistic attitude toward the world and its primitive beliefs, and his own pragmatism against anything metaphysical or religious, he suddenly knew somehow that this would be the last time he would ever be seeing his father.

"And how do things go for us?" the old man asked politely.

"I should be asking you that, Father. You would know better than I, considering your access to the inner circles of industry."

The old man nodded. "Then putting it more directly. How goes it for you?"

"It's not flying. At least I'm still involved in some aspect of it. Occasionally I can still take a plane up, in the line of duty of course. As you know, the Fuhrer has personally forbidden me to fly in combat."

"So now you engage in other forms of combat."

"There is a war."

"Is that what you call it? Let me ask you. Have you seen the camps? I don't mean those used to hold allied prisoners. I mean the others."

Ernst knew exactly what his father referred to, just as he knew what the old man's position would be. "Yes. I've seen them."

"Do you know what's going on in those camps? Have you actually observed what we are doing to people, to other human beings?"

"Those people are not human beings. They are inferior races, enemies of our country. What happens in those places are really not your concern. Why do you go, if it upsets you?"

"I have no choice. It is where we get our labor these days to keep the factories going. That slave labor builds our war machines. The blood of those unfortunates keeps everything oiled and running. It's perfect, economically speaking. You see we don't have to feed or care for any of them. They cost us nothing. We work them until they die of starvation or overwork, or simply succumb to the brutality of the guards. Of course, their deaths are nothing like the clean kills at 10,000 feet you were so pleased to brag about to your Mother and Hans. Out of the sun, a swift dive, a short burst, and another medal, isn't that how it was? The glory of a rich and stronger Germany, with no room for weaklings or decency, is that a Germany to be proud of? We must do away with the Christian Messiah and follow a new one, a madman who will lead us to a new and better Promised Land. The day you preached that poison to me was the moment I should have stopped you by whatever means possible. I and the other thousands of fathers who were so preoccupied with our profits and anything that might interfere with them."

With restraint, Ernst let him go on. The old man smiled grimly as he paused a moment in reflection. Then he continued. "We just stood by and did nothing. We actually believed this insanity would heal itself in time. We remained mute, like sheep. What fools we were. Any action, at whatever the cost, would have been a small price to pay compared to what we are now paying over and over."

"Father, you are speaking treason."

"I am speaking truth," the old man flared angrily. "The same truth that drove you from my house and keeps you away because of the one time I did have the courage to tell you my opinion of our glorious leader and his thousand year Reich."

The two suddenly became silent. The memory of that moment between them renewed the animosity of the past. Ernst was determined to press on and finish the purpose of his visit.

"I must tell you, Father. This is not just a visit. I have a painful duty to perform."

"No need. I already know." Ernst was genuinely surprised.

"There's no reason to be surprised. What other purpose could possibly bring you here. It could only be about Hans. He's dead, isn't he?" Ernst nodded.

He saw the old man take a deep breath, as if receiving a blow. He remained in silent reflection for some moments then once more became aware of Ernst.

"Thank you for coming, he said. At least you still have a semblance of family loyalty, something that monster hasn't completely taken from you and perverted."

"Those are dangerous words. Even I couldn't protect you if they were heard by some others."

"What will they do? Kill me? Your Mother is dead. Now Hansy is gone. What is left for me? You? . . . Tell me, are you satisfied what you've done to your brother with all your talk of a new order, and the glory of raining death on your fellow man from the sky."

Suddenly Earnst perceived the old man was overcome with an intense sadness and tears began to well up in his eyes. "Hans, my poor lovely boy. He wanted nothing more in life than to play the piano, to bring the joy of his music to others. Dead now. Such a waste."

Ernst watched quietly as his father quickly recovered then picked up his cup again, finishing the tea. Ernst, his voice hard and menacing said, "I want you to know that I intend to find those men who killed Hans, the crew of a particular American bomber."

"And naturally you will kill them."

"Slowly, if they are taken alive. We will have our revenge."

"Not ours. Yours. I want no more deaths on my hands. Whatever you do will be for your own inner reasons. It will have nothing to do with poor Hansy or me. I know you, my son, and that perverted honor of yours. It's not that Hansy was killed, but for you, his death has to be a personal affront. What really matters is that somehow, whoever these men are, it's you they've done it to, not Hansy."

The old man put down his cup, pushing aside the service tray. Ernst rose and stood stiffly erect, facing his father.

"I will find them. They won't escape, believe me."

"I believe you, unfortunately." The old man turned to the desk and pressed the interphone switch, signaling his secretary it was time to re-enter. The old man faced his son once more.

"Was there anything else you wanted to say, Ernst?"

Ernst observed his father for a long moment, and then shrugged in resignation. "No. Nothing more. Goodbye, Father." The old man nodded. Neither felt the need to shake hands.

Ernst Von Reinstock turned and left the offices of his father. As he did so, his hatred of those particular Americans increased another notch. It was one more thing that they're killing of Hans had put him through, the grief at his younger brother's death, and now this humiliating uncomfortable interview with his father. He vowed to inflict as much physical pain on the Americans as this experience had emotionally caused him to suffer. He renewed his determination to see every one of them in his grave. His hatred actually dimmed some of the constant pain caused by his old body wounds as he focused on his plan to locate the downed bomber and capture its crew.

42

Marvin's feet crunched the snow. He could see the gradual change in the area around them from barren cragginess to steep places of semi-cultivated farmland. They passed several small farms that appeared to be nothing more than mud-like huts surrounded by roughly furrowed ground. Marvin found it difficult to imagine these farmers plowing their fields on these steep slopes.

Marvin reached a flattened crest of ground and a road ending at the base of another series of mountain ranges. However, the column of partisans, much to Marvin's surprise, turned sharply up hill and they were now on what looked like a tortuously winding mountain road of rutted dirt and rocks.

Marvin watched his men gasping for breath and beginning to stagger at the climb while the partisans marched on, maintaining a steady pace. He studied Ryan's face, the wild expression, and the rolling eyes attempting to focus, and it was painfully clear that unless he received medical attention soon he would be the next man whose dog tags would be carried in Marvin's pocket. He used the last ampule of morphine on Ryan that morning, and as the painkilling effect wore off, Lieutenant Ryan began to groan with increasing pain.

"Novak," Marvin called, turning his head, but still walking, "Ask him how much further to the camp." Novak did, and then replied to Marvin, "He says, not long."

"Tell him Lieutenant Ryan must have medical attention and that we're exhausted and can't go much further," Marvin said, slowing his pace this time so the men behind him began to catch up.

Marvin cocked his head to hear Novak speak to Szabla, but this time instead of replying immediately to Marvin, Novak seemed to be engaged in an earnest conversation with him. When Marvin saw Novak break off the conversation, he hurried to catch up. Novak waited for him and the two men resumed walking together.

"Well, what did the brute have to say this time?"

"Sir, he's not very impressed with us."

"Oh?"

"He's been watching us stagger along and thinks we're like a bunch of women." Marvin thought about it for a moment before replying, "What about Ryan? How much longer?"

"He says we're going to pull off the road around the next bend and stop at a farm there. He is going to send one of his men ahead to bring the doctor back."

Marvin was too tired to continue the conversation and resumed his concentration to keep from stumbling. They finally passed the bend in the road and one of the two partisans up ahead stopped and turned while the other kept moving without changing pace. Marvin noticed them signal him by silent pointing across a rocky furrowed field toward a farm in the distance.

It was small, but much larger than some of the others they had seen along the way. It seemed to Marvin this one was comprised of two buildings: a small hut and something that looked like a barn, appearing much larger than the house.

When they were close enough to make out several men and women near the structures, the partisans seemed to grow tense as they flanked out from their column. They approached slowly in a more attentive attitude, their weapons held a little higher.

Marvin understood their sudden change from a seemingly tired ragtag group back to a disciplined band of partisans practicing an obviously familiar strategy. He wondered just what nationality the farmers were. It seemed they were of the same nationality as the partisans; Poles, but from the tone of the conversation there was no love lost between them. A middle-aged man dressed in very ragged peasant clothes, apparently the owner of the farm, was already protesting vigorously by the time Marvin was close enough to hear. While the farmer used his hands extensively to express his emotion, Szabla barely moved, his lips growing into a thin hard line, waiting until the farmer finished venting his anger.

Szabla pointed to the Americans, Marvin in particular and said something to the farmer that sounded final. When the farmer began to protest again, Szabla struck him, hard, knocking the man down. The farmer, a brute of a man, and not easily intimidated, angrily reached for his pitchfork and threatened the partisan. With a speed and agility that impressed Marvin, and the rest of the crew, Szabla's knife flashed out and the blade stuck through the startled man's hand into the shaft of the pitchfork. Just as quickly, Szabla withdrew the knife and the farmer meekly allowed himself to be disarmed, holding his bleeding hand, and staring at it with amazement.

Marvin saw Szabla bark something guttural at him, and pointed to the barn. With the last of their remaining energy, the crew staggered the few yards into the barn.

43

Inside the barn, away from the wind, Marvin felt quiet and warm. At the sight of the hay piled in a great heap along one side of the barn, the crew trudged over and sank into it with expressive moaning and groans, sprawling with outstretched arms and feet, their expressions turning to relief.

Marvin watched the men of his battered crew almost enviously as he remained standing, waiting for Szabla to enter. When he did, he saw Szabla's surprised look to see the American leader still standing up waiting for him.

Marvin remained silent until several more of the partisans came into the barn and cautiously took positions seating themselves on the opposite side away from the Americans.

"Novak, ask him how long before the doctor gets here." Marvin could already see the partisan's answer and said, "Ask him about food. How long it will be before we can have some."

When Marvin heard the question asked he saw Szabla and his men laugh contemptuously. The others grunted strange words among themselves and a few of the partisans smirked at the Americans. Novak started to explain, but Marvin interrupted him. "Never mind, sergeant. I got the message.

Szabla spoke in a low tone with apparent finality then turned his back to the Americans. He sat down and lit something that looked like a leaf rolled tightly to resemble a cigarette. One of the partisans, the one who was now wearing Stiles' flight jacket, held up the pack of American cigarettes he had found in it. He offered it to Szabla who took one, and after lighting it, took several more for his pocket before passing the pack around.

"Did he say where we were?" Marvin asked Novak. "No, sir." He said . . . you talk too much. You asked too many questions." Then Marvin's attention went to Dunham, angrily watching the partisan's obvious enjoyment of Lieutenant Stiles cigarettes, said quietly, "Would I like to get that crew in my sight. Man, just one long burst."

"What for? You'd miss 'em, even at this range," Novak said, making himself comfortable.

"What did you say?" Dunham asked.

"You couldn't hit those guys if they froze, grew targets all over'em, and turned into sitting ducks."

"What?" Dunham said, incredulous at Novak's remark.

"Hey listen, did you see me knock those Krauts down. man, I got four destroyed on this mission. Did you see me get that last Kraut? Wham, wham, wham. Did I chop him up or didn't I!"

"You only got three."

"What do you mean three? I got four!"

"You got three. That last one was a probable."

"Probable? You trying to start something? Ballard confirmed it. And Haply saw me chop that FW. Right, Haply?" Haply groaned. "Shut up, you guys, will you."

"Listen to him," Dunham said. "He sure got out of that ball turret fast."

"Dunham, if you're trying to get to me, forget it," Haply said, not moving, lying with his eyes closed. "Can it, Sergeant," Marvin said to Dunham.

Ryan began moaning again and Marvin watched him helplessly, unable to do anything for him. As he studied Ryan's painful expression, he thought of the odds against his recovering, of his ever getting home again, knowing the comfort of relationships based on love not just the companionship of survival. He wondered about the Lieutenant's family. *All they'd ever receive would be a telegram expressing regret over their loss. They would never really know what happened to Ryan, if he were to die. They would never know how or where. How could you explain to the bereaved, your son or husband is dead somewhere in Poland . . . we think. He's missing in action would be easier and the most likely. Your son or husband is missing in action somewhere over Germany. Don't give up hope. He has every chance of being a prisoner somewhere, and as soon as the Red Cross can possibly locate him, you will be notified immediately.*

He could envision the next of kin of Lieutenant Stiles, and Corporal Miller, receiving those telegrams. He wondered at the hope those telegrams of missing in action would raise. *The hope would last until the end of the war, while each day the families would continue to pray for some word, not realizing their loved ones, with broken and shattered bodies were buried, almost naked, in a common unmarked grave somewhere in Poland. They would never know. Even after the war when it was finally all over and those that would come home had already done so, those families would always believe that someday their loved ones would still return.*

Marvin shook his head as if trying to change the direction of his thoughts. Looking at the remainder of his crew, he wondered how many of them would join Stiles and Miller in some unmarked grave in Poland. He pictured himself in a cold wet grave and shuddered at the image.

There had to be a way to get back. He knew of the French underground that smuggled downed flyers back to England. He had also heard of other flyers downed in France, who on their own had made it across to Spain and returned to fly again. *There must be a Polish underground. They'd been involved in the war longer than anyone else had. They certainly would have established an underground by this time. The partisans were themselves evidence of Polish resistance, a fact there must be some sort of organized warfare still going on. If they could find others who might be more receptive than these partisans, possibly someone more educated might, or who spoke English, maybe they could explain the importance of their desire to return.*

Marvin's thoughts continued in his search to resolve their predicament for what seemed like several hours, but in actuality was only a short time. The sound of someone hurriedly approaching the barn from the outside interrupted his thoughts. Several of the partisans stood up and waited expectantly. The barn door opened, and to Marvin's complete surprise . . . a priest entered.

44

Father Jan Kabos had been in the midst of his daily devotion with Sister Theresa and Sister Anna when they were rudely, interrupted by the bearded partisan who had noisily clattered into the chapel. It was Sediva the Czech, who had no great love for priests or the church.

Father Kabos watched Sediva tell them of the foreign strangers they had captured who were in need of medical attention. Sediva smiled at the obvious annoyance of Father Kabobs when he informed him of Szabla's command to come at once. Father Kabos was even more annoyed when Sediva refused to leave until the priest was ready. Sister Theresa offered to accompany him, but before he could refuse, Sediva grunted a flat no.

As Father Kabos packed his German medical satchel, the one Szabla had brought back especially for him after an ambush of a German staff car, he attempted to glean additional information from Sediva. "Who were these strangers? How many were there? Where did they come from? Were the Germans looking for them?" The Czech's reluctance to discuss anything with him created nervousness in Father Kabos, who hadn't experienced it since his first meeting with the villagers of Praznik. At that time, he had no interest in Praznik and his feelings had been difficult to disguise. That was much earlier when he did not intend to remain, only continuing on to another destination far from Poland. Now he was vitally interested in the village, the people, and their welfare. Even more so, he was concerned for the children, those who were the flesh and blood of Praznik, and its future. The children, rescued from certain oblivion, were now the spiritually adopted sons and daughters of Praznik. His fear was not so much for himself, although he had great reason to fear for himself, but for the children. He could not love them more had they been from his own body.

Following Sediva down the mountain road, carrying the heavy satchel and wearing the bunglesome overcoat that the sisters had made for him during the last unusual cold season, he thought of the danger the presence of strangers could bring to all of them.

Sediva the Czech, preceding him down the mountain road, kept motioning for him to hurry, he was obviously enjoying the priest's discomfort. *Had Sediva intentionally slurred his words or had he said Englishmen? He could have meant partisan. Either way though, a wounded man, whether partisan or Englishman, could mean only one thing. The wounded person engaged in an act of war, or some illicit operation, and had engaged the enemy in some act of violence, thereby calling attention to themselves. Somewhere, by this act, a signal of violence informed the Germans there was a man, or men capable of creating a disturbance, or causing harm. That person, or persons, must be routed out and removed.*

Father Kabos groaned to himself at the stupidity of Szabla for coming this close to the village and putting them all in jeopardy. *Maybe arrogance had finally made him careless.*

They left the mountain road and cut across the hard slope until they sighted the farm. Then Sediva paused to let the priest catch up with him, directing him to the larger structure that was the barn. Father Kabos made his way alone to the farm. The closer he came to the farm the more frightened he became. When he finally entered the barn and saw those men staring at him in their strange uniforms, his knees trembled.

45

Marvin caught the priest glancing nervously at the partisans, then at the Americans. Szabla spoke rapidly and pointed to Ryan moving in pain on the litter. The priest was wearing a cassock covered by a heavy coat. The lower portion of the cassock had been slit up the center, then wrapped around each leg, giving the appearance of extra trousers. Marvin thought that was smart considering the snow outside. He quickly assessed him; the priest was a man with dark and unusually intense eyes that seemed to bore right through Marvin as he glanced at him. In his right hand, the man carried a German military medical satchel.

Pausing for only a moment to study the flyers, he knelt beside Ryan and felt his forehead, then reached for his wrist and took his pulse. He frowned as he saw Ryan's leg. He stood up again and removed his coat. He asked Szabla something in Polish and Szabla pointed to Marvin. The priest nodded at Marvin and then shocked him by saying in remarkably good English, "I'm father Jan Kabos, and a doctor. Szabla tells me you are the leader of these men."

Marvin's surprise at the priest's ability to speak English almost caused him to stammer. "Major . . . Major Marvin, Father. Major Gregg Marvin."

"English?"

"No, Americans."

"Americans? You're a long way from home, Major. What are you doing here?"

"Our plane was hit over Germany and we were forced to fly on. We crash-landed several miles from here, and these men found us."

"You were lucky they did. The Germans are searching for you, Major. We saw their planes fly over this morning and they know of your presence in the area."

"Father, we'd like to get some medical attention for Lieutenant Ryan here, and some rest, and something to eat. If possible, get in touch with the Polish underground so we can get back to England. The sooner we're on our way, the better it'll be for all of us. We'd certainly be in your debt if you could get that across to these local resistance people."

"Unfortunately, that may be difficult." The priest narrowed his eyes at Marvin a moment, then let himself glance at the exhausted crew who were watching him with intense anticipation. The priest reflected a moment then came to a decision. "In the meantime, let us see what we can do for your lieutenant. I should tell you he may not live, but I will do my best."

Marvin nodded. The priest knelt beside Ryan and opened his satchel. Searching only for a moment, he quickly brought out a large pair of scissors and began to cut away the ripped pant from the twisted leg. Marvin watched the priest's deft movements and grew more impressed as the man continued to work. He noticed the partisans draw closer.

They too watched the priest with great interest as his skilled hands moved with incredible sureness. Then Marvin was taken aback when the priest suddenly stopped and looked up at him. "You'll have to hold him now. I must pull the bone and set it. The pain will be intense."

While the priest waited for the Americans to get into their positions around Ryan, he said something in Polish to the partisans. One of them casually ripped off a board, and measuring it against Ryan's 'good leg broke the board again making it the same length as Ryan's leg. He gently laid it beside Ryan.

"All right. Hold him," the priest said. So quickly did he do it, the bone manipulated and reset with expert knowledge; it was over before the men holding Ryan realized he had finished. The priest nodded to them and they stood up, but continued to observe his rapid movements. He now cleansed the wounds in Ryan's upper thigh and hip. Using a scalpel, he next removed what looked like a piece of shrapnel from his side. Then he sutured the wounds closed, and taking what was obviously an old roll of cloth, wrapped Ryan's leg using the board as a splint. When he was through, he once again took Ryan's pulse and then stood up.

Marvin, still impressed by what he had witnessed, spoke quietly. "Father, I don't know too much about medicine, but I'd venture to say that if ever I saw a man that did, you're it."

The priest looked at Marvin gravely. "I'm afraid my knowledge is minimal. Your lieutenant may not live through the night. He's lost much blood. If he lasts the next six hours, he may survive."

"Well, Father, what can we do?"

"There isn't much more you can do for him, my son. I think before I leave he should be given extreme unction."

"I'm afraid that is one thing you can't do for him, Father. Lieutenant Ryan is Protestant. Father Kabos looked startled. "Oh. In that case, all we can do is pray for him."

Then, Father Kabos observed Harper propped against the barn wall, his arm in the sling. He came over and knelt beside him, gently examining Harper's arm. Harper met the priest's eyes and gave him a crooked smile.

"I'm Jewish, Father. But you can pray for me."

Father Kabos responded with a curt smile and nodded yet remained absorbed in the study of Harper's arm. After searching through his bag, he found his remaining supply of painkiller and injected it into Harper's arm. Harper flinched. Then Father Kabos, holding tightly to the arm, felt along its entire length until he was satisfied. He jerked quickly at the shoulder, jolting Harper painfully, his eyes watering. Now the arm looked more natural. Finally, the priest cleansed Harper's wounds and wrapped the arm, carefully replacing the sling when he had finished. "Nothing very serious, Lieutenant. It's not broken. Possibly a minor fracture and dislocation. Without x-rays, of course, I can't be certain. But under the circumstances, you will eventually be all right. Just keep the arm wrapped and don't use it."

Harper shook his head, definitely impressed by the authoritative manner of the man. "Thank you, Father."

Marvin, with some amazement, watched the priest slowly refill his medical satchel and then checked Ryan again before standing. "I'll have to leave you now. Is there anyone else here that might need my attention?"

"Dunham?" Marvin said. Dunham stood up and removed his flight jacket as well as his upper clothes. He stood shivering while the priest examined him. The wounds were superficial, but the priest treated them, and finished by putting bandages over both wounds.

When Dunham had redressed, the priest asked if there was anyone else. "Father, is there any way you might convey to these men . . . these partisans, that we're friends. That we need food and rest."

"Major, they are well aware of who you are. These people are very poor here, but someone is bringing something down for your comfort."

"From where? Is there a village near here?"

"I can't answer that, Major. The less you know, the safer it is for all of us."

"Look, Father, we're not trying to hurt anyone. We're all on the same side, aren't we? At least I thought we were. Are you in the same war as the rest of us?"

"I am not fighting at all, Major. But these men are. They are soldiers, of a sort. They are fighting the war against the Germans."

"Then will you tell them who we are, and that we are also fighting Germans."

"They know, that's why you are not dead."

"Then why are they keeping us prisoners?"

"You're not prisoners, my son, You're being protected. You don't know these mountains or the people. You may stumble into a German patrol, or you may leave a trail that would draw the Germans to you."

"Why should that worry them . . . or you for that matter?"

"Because if you did, the Germans would move into this area and that is something none of us who live in these mountain want."

"What are they hiding? What are you hiding?"

"Absolutely nothing, my son."

"Then why the double-talk?"

"That is a phrase I'm not familiar with."

"There's something you don't realize, Father. Somehow, I'm not getting the picture across to you. The United States of America is engaged in a war with the enemies of Poland and we're common allies. You can stand here and hand me a bunch of pap, but these characters are keeping us prisoner."

"Major, let me assure you that these partisans are your friends. They may be difficult to understand, but they are interested in your survival. However, their survival is meshed with yours, and they will not allow you to put them, or the people who live in this district in jeopardy. I suggest you do what they tell you. Szabla is a hard man, but he's no fool. He will save you if he can. Yet if you disobey him or get in his way, he's quite capable of killing all of you."

"He's pointed that out to us already."

"I'll return in the morning to see the Lieutenant. If he should die before then, please send one of the partisans to tell me."

"Why?"

"The trip is quite exhausting and I'd rather not make it unnecessarily." Marvin stared at the priest in silent disbelief. "Goodbye, major. Good luck," the priest said, walking out of the barn. "I shall pray for the Lieutenant."

Novak came up behind Marvin and whistled. "Now that is a priest who wears a cloth of a different color. Would you believe it? I don't know which one of these two Polacks is more cold-blooded. What was eating him anyway, sir?"

"He was frightened."

"Scared? Of what?"

"I don't know," Marvin glanced over to Szabla, who was watching them curiously, "Come on. Let's try talking to the big cheese again.

46

Marvin kept his eyes on Szabla as Novak translated. Marvin began by telling Szabla who they were and what had happened to them. He stressed the importance of the American daylight bombing raids, and how badly they were hurting the Germans. By this time, all the partisans were interested in the conversation. Marvin led up to the news of the vast armies of America now coming to England and how someday these armies would be landing on the continent of Europe to liberate the occupied countries. Szabla nodded his head approvingly and Marvin thought that at least he was making progress. He explained how the bombing raids were weakening the German defenses and destroying their war potential.

Then, very slowly, he told him what a premium flyers were to their mutual cause at this time because they had to be the front line until the invasion of Europe. He explained how long it took to train flyers and why it was essential therefore that they, the crew of this great bombing plane, get back to England to continue the offense against Germany. Szabla grunted his understanding.

Marvin said, "Once you put us in contact with the Polish underground, we'll be on our way and once again bombing the hated enemies of Poland."

Szabla asked Novak to explain what Marvin meant by Polish underground. When Novak told him about the French underground and their activities in helping downed fliers and that Marvin wished to contact with the Polish underground who took care of this type of operation in Poland, Szabla laughed with great amusement. Speaking something to his men, they too joined his laughter. Marvin was certain he and the crew were the butt of some derisive comment.

When Szabla stopped laughing, his face grew serious and he spoke very slowly and very carefully. He said, "There is no Polish underground. The only Polish underground are the dead. Poland is a dead country, without life. The only things that move in Poland are the Germans and the trains. And most of the trains that run in Poland go to the great smoking camps with the many chimneys from which no one ever returns."

Marvin stared at Szabla soberly, giving up for the moment, realizing there was nothing he could do for the present that might swing the partisan over to assist them in getting home again. It was now painfully obvious to him that they would have to escape from the partisans before they could do anything else. There was nothing for them to do but wait and see whether or not Ryan lived or died, they'd still have to remain cautious and hold themselves alert for an opportunity. The thought occurred to Marvin that the longer they waited; the more difficult it might be for them to escape.

Marvin thought of the priest, trying to determine whether he was their friend or enemy. *The priest, with luck, could be their key to getting away. The priest, Father Kabos as he called himself, seemed well educated and knowledgeable regarding the partisans and their attitude toward the Americans.* He had noticed the respectful and quiet warmth, if you could consider any attitude of these partisans as warm; the men seemed to regard him. *If they could somehow reach the priest and make him their ally,* Marvin felt they might eventually persuade Szabla to lead them to safety, or at the very least, let them try it on their own.

Just then, Marvin saw one of the partisans bring in a large cloth sack and several bottles of what looked like wine. The sack contained a large quantity of black bread and cheese, which the partisan had simply dumped on the barn floor over some spilled straw. After Szabla and his men had taken their pick, he motioned to Marvin and the crew to help themselves to food. The bread was very hard and the cheese was dry, but the crew ate their portions with relish, Shaw, and haply even taking seconds.

Afterwards, the men smoked, without conversation. The fatigue of the last several hours and the lack of sleep in the snow-covered plane the night before finally caught up. Marvin's eyelids began to droop with sleep. One at a time, Marvin watched his men dozing off until Ballard and Marvin were the only two awake. Ballard moved over, closer to Harper, then waving his hand at Marvin, dozed off. Marvin put his back against one of the barn posts and tried to stay awake. He lit a cigarette and kept his eyes on the partisans who were watching his struggle with curious interest. One of them laughed as Marvin's head fell forward, the jerk of his head startled him awake. Then finally, he too fell asleep.

    Twice during the night, it seemed to him he was awakened by Ryan's feverish cries. Once, he thought Ballard had gotten up and done something to make Ryan comfortable because the moaning stopped. Then, once again, Marvin crash-landed his plane in the black pit of exhausted sleep.

47

The next morning Marvin watched Ryan awake, his appearance had improved considerably. He was still pale, but there was a definite difference in him. He had passed the crisis point during the night while everyone around him had been asleep and he was now on the mend, which at first was not immediately apparent to the others. Marvin and the rest of the crew stared at him with sober faces. When he smiled, they responded with wide grins.

"How you feeling?" Marvin asked.

"Sore as hell and weak, but I think I'm going to make it, sir. Where are we?"

"Poland."

"Poland?" Marvin explained where in Poland he thought they were and how they'd gotten there, including the present difficulty they were having in getting the partisans to understand them. Marvin frowned when he saw Ryan observing the partisan's staring at him from the far end of the barn. Then he saw Ryan become aware of his leg, and the tight wrapping, as he glanced questioningly at Marvin. "It was a priest! Apparently he had some heavy medical training."

"A priest?"

"Probably saved your life." Ryan glanced around somberly at the other crewmembers before shaking his head in amazement. "You feel well enough now to eat something?" Marvin asked. Ryan nodded, and Marvin reached over to a wooden bowl taking some of the black bread and dry cheese. He tore off a chunk of bread and carefully broke off a piece of the cheese, holding them out to Ryan.

"It's not exactly the Ritz, but it isn't too bad." Ryan frowned at the unappetizing appearance of the black bread and cheese, but after Ballard propped him up on the litter and broke the bread and cheese into smaller pieces, he went at the food hungrily.

"Last thing I remember was getting hit and my leg going through the fuselage," Ryan said after a while. "Who got me out?"

"I did," Harper responded. Ryan glanced at Harper, observing his arm in the sling. Harper smiled.

"You were too heavy." Ryan nodded with a slight smile and continued eating, carefully chewing and swallowing each piece before starting another.

Marvin had seen all the partisans, except two, leave the barn some time before dawn. He had begun to wonder what had become of them, and how long he and the crew would have to remain in the barn. Then Dunham said, "Novak, tell those guys I have to urinate. Where do we do it?"

"Same here," Shaw said quickly. Novak informed the partisans, and all of them were marched out into the cold morning air behind the barn. They could now see how isolated and alone they were here on this farm, nothing but rolling hills and mountains in a vast countryside.

Afterwards, Marvin heard the crew keep the conversation going among themselves, discussing the raid, their narrow escape, and at last, their present circumstances. They had skirted the issue because of Ryan, only touching it tentatively and then moving away from the subject. They kept returning to their problem, and now Marvin watched Haply work himself to the point of bringing it into the open.

"Sir, how long do you think we'll be here? I don't mean here in the barn. I mean in Poland, in these mountains. The war is still going on and I don't think we're doing our side any good just sitting around waiting for someone to come and rescue us."

"What did you have in mind?" Marvin asked, already knowing what Haply was leading to.

"Making a break. It'd be nothing to jump those two jokers. I could almost do it myself. We jump them, take their guns, and get moving."

"All of us?"

"Sure."

"Sergeant, I don't think you fully appreciate where we are. We're in Poland. Poland isn't exactly a place where you catch a bus ride back to England. It's a long way. You're talking more than a thousand miles. Maybe one man, who knew the language and was very lucky, he might make it. Maybe, but there are eight of us, Haply. I don't think we could just all saunter up to some railway station, and buy ourselves a ticket to England."

"If that's the best way to do it, why not."

"And what about Lieutenant Ryan? I wouldn't say he was exactly fit for travelling right now, would you?"

"Sir, never mind me," Ryan said. "If my condition is holding any of you back, foget it. I'll manage. There isn't any sense in all of us getting captured."

"See, that makes it easier already."

"Haply, how does it feel to be a skunk?" Novak said.

"I'll bet you'd even leave your own mother if she were on that stretcher, wouldn't you."

"That's a crock and you know it. You just won't face the fact we're gonna have to do it sooner or later anyway," Haply said, viewing the somber expressions of the crew,

"Lieutenant Ryan knows it isn't personal. If we don't make a break while we got the chance, we're liable to be stuck her for the duration or worse, captured by the Krauts."

Novak had not moved, but remained stiffly watching him. "Listen, Novak. The rules say it's our duty to try to escape if we're captured. And that's what I'm for doing."

"Yeah, but I don't remember where it says we have to step on our own guys if that's the easiest way out."

Shaw came over and stood between Novak and Haply, but then looked at Marvin first. "Maybe if we split up, sir. Pair off in teams. A couple of guys together. Then some of us would have a chance of making it."

"That sounds good," Dunham said.

"What do you say, Swifty?" Haply asked Shaw, "You want to team up? We'll break out of here together. You and me."

"I don't know. What are we going to use for food? Besides, how do we get out of these mountains? I don't even know where we are. And I sure know you don't."

"The Major knows. All he has to do is point us in the right direction," Haply said assuringly, as if to convince Shaw of his own knowledge.

"And after we're pointed. What then? You got any idea how many countries we'd have to cross? About three whole countries, that's how many. One of them being Germany. And I sure don't feel like walking through Germany. Now that is something that really scares the pants off me."

"We could make a go for Switzerland. It's a whole lot closer." Shaw thought it over and then said, "That sounds better. Not much, but better. I'm for doing something besides just waiting around."

"Then how about closing your mouth," Novak suggested angrily, amazed at the discussion that seemed to have already consigned Ryan to abandonment.

"Listen, you ignorant Polack, you may like it here with all your relatives, but I don't. I'm for breaking out, you hear? If you even think about stopping me, I'm going to climb all over you."

"Haply, if you weren't such a little punk, I would've clobbered that mouth of yours long ago."

The major watched the two men with interest. When Harper realized that Marvin did not intend to stop the growing conflict, he quickly spoke up. "Don't we have enough problems without you two behaving like idiots," he said strongly. "Knock off the personal crap and let's just get back to the original discussion, okay?"

Now the major realized Shaw was eyeing Novak with hostile interest, perking up at the possibility of tangling with the husky Polish waist gunner. "Novak, I'm your size. Any time you feel like clobbering someone, I'm ready. So if you want to play tough, just keep leaning. I'd love to straighten you out."

"Shut your mouth, Swifty. I don't need anyone fighting my battles," Haply said with growing anger, then turned and faced Novak, moving closer. "Come on you damn Polack, let's see what you can do."

Novak glanced helplessly at the Major, but he was now determined to teach the feisty tail gunner a lesson. "Okay, squirt, come on," he said. "It's time you got your spanking."

48

With a savage surprising burst of fury, Haply rushed Novak and tackled him head on, crashing them both through the barn doors and outside the barn. The partisans and the crew followed them out, shouting, the partisans obviously enjoying the strange behavior of the Americans.

Then, Haply grappled with Novak hanging on to his back to prevent him from getting up. Novak finally shook Haply off and jumping to his feet got a clear swing at him, stunning haply so that he fell and remained motionless.

"You stupid Polack," Shaw said in sudden anger at the ease in which Haply got beaten, and came at Novak. This time Novak was ready and he side-stepped easily, and connected perfectly with his right hand, sending Shaw into a dazed heap on the ground.

Marvin waited to see if either Haply or Shaw wanted another dose. As they recovered and saw Marvin watching them, shaking his head in exaggerated long sufferance, they were embarrassed. "Okay, clowns," Marvin said. "Are you satisfied? Can we get back to the conversation now or do you two still want to continue playing cowboys and Indians?"

They all trudged back into the barn, Haply and Shaw wearing sullen expressions, Novak rubbing his cheek.

"Now all of you supposed NCO's listen to me," Marvin said firmly, his voice hard with barely concealed anger. He hadn't shirked his responsibility earlier by not interfering, but had used his silence to allow the crew to open up and reveal their true feelings, releasing the tension of the growing frustration of their present predicament. Marvin knew the release would make it much easier to control and lead them when he finally reached his own decision regarding any escape attempt. He had been around too long and survived to many disasters caused by the impulsive decisions of others to go off now on any half-cocked venture.

"You are all members of the United States Army Air Corp, and as such are subject to the rules and regulations thereof," he said, glancing at each of them individually as he spoke. "Striking another member, or any act of violence against another serviceman, or any insubordination to a superior rank, is a definite court martial offense. Haply, Shaw, you may have forgotten, but Sergeant Novak just happens to outrank you two. Which means both of you are guilty of striking a noncommissioned officer, a serious breach of conduct. Just because we are temporarily in the middle of nowhere doesn't mean that suddenly it's a free-for-all with everyone making their own decisions and just ignoring the rules of military conduct. Because if you think so, forget it. I'm here to tell you different. Starting right now, if there is one more drop of trouble from anyone, the man responsible is going to get busted, court marshaled right on the spot. If that isn't enough for some of you, I'll take whatever additional military discipline is necessary. Is that understood?"

When there was no response, Marvin repeated, "Is that understood?" The men all nodded in agreement. Marvin could see a drawing together of the men at this reminder of their responsibilities, and his authority of command.

"Now let's get down to the main problem facing us. Escape, yes I'm for it, and in almost any way possible. But not by taking out these two goons watching us, and then having the rest of those partisans breathing down our necks. It'll be tough enough having to dodge Germans, let alone having a band of partisans tracking after us at the same time. Our best bet for the moment is to attempt to convince the men it's in all our interest for them to help us get home. If we can't, then we'll have to consider more drastic action, and take our first opportunity. Whatever we do, we're going to stay calm and wait until we can determine the odds."

Marvin fell silent as he waited patiently for his words to sink in. The crew remained motionless, thoughtfully digesting everything the major had said. Shaw and Haply exchanged an awkward glance. Then Marvin continued.

"One more thing we've got to consider, and that is the Krauts are probably looking for us right now. If we go traipsing off, marching around out there without knowing where we are, or where we're headed, we're going to be spotted and scooped up before we've gone ten miles. What we have to do now is just sweat it out until we have a better chance of pulling anything off. Hopefully by that time we'll have some sort of plan." The men remained thoughtful, realizing the truth of Marvin's words. Then Haply said, in almost childish sincerity, "I'm sorry, sir. I guess I just got carried away." Then he glanced over at Novak. "No hard feelings? "Novak shook his head and clapped him on the shoulder, then dropping his hand lower, rubbed his back affectionately. Shaw said,

"Same here."

Marvin gave them a nodding smile of assurance then seated himself comfortably, settling back against a post and closing his eyes. The rest of the crew spread out around the barn and followed Marvin's lead in attitude, keeping their conversations to a minimum and quietly resting.

After almost two hours of waiting, Marvin saw Szabla and the partisans reappear, giving no indication of where they had gone during the night. There were more men now than last time, and all of them armed. Szabla, through Novak, informed Marvin and the others they were moving out and were going to be travelling along the outer edge of a mountain road. As he did not wish to take any chances of Germans discovering him, he warned them that if they revealed themselves in any way, or did not immediately drop to the ground when ordered, he instructed his men to shoot. The camp was still several hours away.

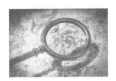

49

Marvin found that his muscles were sore from the previous day's march. He was surprised to discover that his walking ability had not diminished, but rather had improved. The road kept winding, first in one direction, then with a sharp curve veered back in the opposite direction.

Eventually, coming around one of the turns, Marvin caught his first glimpse of Praznik. He became aware they were approaching a village of some sort. He was certain it must be the one both Szabla and the priest had mentioned; *it must be the village they claimed our presence had put in jeopardy.* It was difficult to see the village from the mountain road. Only on an occasional curve did he even catch a glimpse of a rooftop. It was only at the very top of the road, as he came over the crest, that the entire village came into view. As he reached the top, the sudden appearance of the village caused him to stop for a moment, and a rifle quickly prodded him on.

Walking slowly, he stared at the villagers who had come out to see the straggling Americans in their strange uniforms. It was obvious to Marvin how bulky and bear-like they were in their flying clothes and he mused at the impression they must be making on these people. Under his own jacket, Marvin had begun to perspire from all the exertion.

Glancing around, he noticed the great number of children and older people. He also caught a glimpse of a pretty face here and there, and was intrigued at the lack of men in the crowd. He wondered if they were all partisans, or if the men were just up in the hills somewhere. A partisan angrily motioned for Marvin to keep his eyes forward and on the man ahead of him. Marvin picked up the pace and closed the gap that had grown between him and the others.

Then, the partisans abruptly halted and indicated the Americans were to fall out and wait. The crew staggered over to one of the structures and flopped down, resting their backs against a wood wall. Marvin was conscious of the villagers who had followed along with them, and were now standing off a short distance. He couldn't help but smile at the curious interest the kids were taking in the crew. The kids studied them with a sort of open wonder, their faces a mixture of peculiar expressions. The crew became naturally curious, and when Novak in an attempt to be friendly spoke to them in Polish, some of the children jumped back startled. They acted as if they had never heard anyone speak their language.

He watched them quickly bunch up in a circle and began talking in a curiously excited conversation among themselves, their faces flushed, their small bodies fidgeting nervously. Again, the bunched group suddenly moved apart like the opening petals of a blooming flower as the children turned, came a safe distance closer, and stood off watching the Americans.

Two of the younger girls smiled at Novak, and he responded pleasantly, asking their names. At the sound of Novak's voice, they were once again startled. When Novak persisted, asking them once more, the two girls exchanged a conspiratorial glance and giggled as only very small children can, causing Novak to chuckle at them. Then he politely told them his name.

One of the older children, a girl, came forward to stand beside the two little ones, and just stared incredulously at Novak. She was completely unnerved by his easy use of Polish. She quickly turned to the other children and spoke in rapid hushed tones. Novak could only understand some of it, but what he overheard still made no sense. Marvin thought we must look strange to these children.

Two older boys, obviously showing off for the rest, courageously walked up closer to the crew. When Shaw whistled a greeting and displayed a great smile full of teeth, they skedaddled away and the crew couldn't help but laugh.

Marvin shook his head in amusement at the weird antics of these kids and turned his glance toward the adults, the villagers who were still standing off at a distance continued their strange vigilance.

The curious behavior of these people was not lost on the rest of the crew. They too were aware of the intense interest their presence was causing among the villagers. Each attempt to communicate with them was met with peculiar silence, and a stony scrutiny.

Then, out of one of the larger huts, Marvin saw a woman emerge, followed by Szabla approaching without hesitation, stopping close enough so that any of the crew could have touched her if they had dared. She glanced over the Americans for a long moment. Marvin could see that she was different from the other villagers. She gave the appearance of solid maturity, yet was obviously young, in her early thirties possibly, with an air of almost regal authority on her. An inner strength shone forth from behind dark and penetrating eyes. Marvin thought she was the most interesting yet attractive woman he had ever seen, and he was surprised at his own reaction to her striking appearance.

He watched Szabla waiting silently beside her while she continued her perusal of the crew, her eyes finally resting on Marvin. He stared back and could have sworn he saw a flicker of interest in the woman's eyes. He smiled. She did not respond. She turned abruptly away, and with Szabla, walked back to the hut from which they had emerged.

Marvin saw there were several other young peasant girls watching them, some of them considered pretty enough in any environment. Caught up by the memory of the woman with Szabla, he thoroughly scrutinized them. Marvin was certain that she had to be someone important in the village. Aroused by his interest, he wondered if she was Szabla's woman, and was determined to find out.

One of the peasant girls giggled and Marvin turned to see Dunham going through a ridiculous routine of changing expressions on his face as if he were some clown. Several of the other villagers found him amusing, but it was apparent Dunham was performing for just an audience of one, the slim pale girl who stood closer than the other women did. She was young and pretty. Finally, Dunham grew serious and just casually looked her over. Then, he smiled that Kansas farm boy smile, and she blushed and turned away, glancing nervously at her companions to see if any of them had noticed.

Marvin turned again toward the hut where Szabla and the woman had entered, his thoughts of her already beginning to disturb him. He was convinced that whoever she was he felt their fate, for some reason, rested on her decision.

50

Americans? Americans! A strange breed of boyish-looking men, Basha thought. *To think that there were Americans here in Poland, from a land thousands of miles away, but seemed like millions, it was incredible.*

She had known, just as all the others in the village that America was involved in this war and had been since 1941. The fact that America was in the war had raised their feeling somewhat, but no one truly ever expected to see one, not in Poland. She felt that America was a make believe place with make believe armies. Yet, here they were, in Poland, in the very mountains where Praznik lay hidden from the normal gaze of the Germans.

Father Kabos entered the village chapel and sat down heavily on one of the crude wooden benches, deep in thought. From the corner of his eye he saw Sister Theresa and Sister Anna staring silently at his strange expression, unsure whether to disturb him or not. They glanced at each other and decided on continuing their devotional prayers, certain that he would be joining them shortly. He continued his thoughts with the arrival of the Americans in the area. *Regardless of how they came, it was certain to bring the Germans. The mere fact that just this morning the German Stukas had flown over Praznik was proof enough. At this very moment, a German column could be starting up the mountain road. What would they do if they discovered the children? What would they do if they discovered the partisan camp above the village? If the Germans came this time, they would arrive with enough troops to search not only the entire village, but also the forest behind it, and even the covering mountains above it. They would discover the children's hiding place or Szabla's camp, or both.* He shuddered when he thought of either consequence. *What about himself? What if they discovered who he was?*

Father Kabos smiled. Strangely, he no longer was concerned with his own safety. He was more concerned with the children and the villagers. In addition, what might happen to Sister Anna and Sister Theresa? He maintained his smile as he thought of what a changed man he had become. How most of the bitterness and hatred had left him and how different his life had become when compared to the fame and comfort of his former life. The ways of God were indeed strange.

Then he thought of God. *Of course, what a fool I am for not thinking of Him sooner. My own life had changed. What had changed it? The hand of god. Was this the hand of God, or that of Satan bringing these Americans here and threatening the safety of the village, and the innocents, the children? Yes, I will pray. God will give me the calmness and the answers I need. I will also pray for the deliverance of the Americans and that God would let them escape from these mountains, removing the danger of any German search party discovering them near the village.*

Father Kabos walked to the altar and knelt before it. He prayed long and earnestly, and then listened for God's answer. His mind raced furiously. *Was there some un-righteousness within him that prevented him from receiving?* He knew his agreement with god was still binding; the covenant he had made with Him because of his miraculous escape was always uppermost in his mind. He had been faithful on his part and had performed all the duties and functions that were required of him. *In fact, hadn't I even done more than I had agreed to, having gone as far as converting several people to Christ? Then so had God. Yes, that was true.* God had answered all his prayers. As many as there were, he had answered them. Then Satan spoke to his mind, and he recognized the devil's thought, but he listened. *Certainly, God had answered all his prayers . . . all the tiny ones. What about the big ones? What about the children and the village? What about Sister Anna? She was growing more ill every day. Didn't you tell God that one or two more years in this climate would kill her? Oh, no. God certainly doesn't answer all prayers!*

Father Kabos rebuked Satan and asked god to forgive him for listening. He stayed on his knees in penitence until the cold floor finally forced him to stand.

It was time for the afternoon instruction and many of the children were already arriving. He could hear their young boisterous voices coming from the chapel.

Father Kabos smiled at the sisters and said, "The Lord's work must go on." He was quite surprised to find the chapel filled with most of the children, young and old, and a surprising number of the villagers. He stood before the altar and made the sign of the cross, hurriedly the way he usually did. Then he turned to the children and smiled, ready to begin the class instruction, which the chapel was used for in the afternoon, and evening, except on important holidays. Perplexed by all the expectant faces staring at him, Father Kabos frowned. His glance went from face to face trying to discern the meaning of their barely suppressed excitement. Finally, with a trace of wonderment he looked out at the class and asked, "What is it my children?"

Marjan stood up, then Nicholas and then Marisha. Nicholas spoke. "Father, is it them?" Father Kabos rubbed his forehead, unsure of the question. "I don' t understand." Marisha said more loudly, with a touch of impatience.

"Father, is it them?"

"Is who them, my children?" Father Kabos asked, shaking his head with a little smile of bewilderment.

"Them, Father! Them! A child's voice spoke up. "The strange men in Lekach's barn," Marjan said quickly. "He said they were dressed strangely and they spoke in a way he couldn't understand." Nicholas completely ignored Father Kabos' bewildered look.

"Bronislaw said Yanov told him they came in a great bird from the sky!" He began to understand at last. Even at that, he was unprepared for the response when he asked nervously, "Do you mean the men who accompanied Szabla? The others?"

"Yes," Marisha said impatiently. "Yes, the angels. 'The War Angels.' Is it them? Have they come to protect us?"

"Tell us, Father," Marjan said. "What do they look like? Do they look like the ones in the pictures?"

"Did they bring chariots? What do they look like?"

Then all the children began talking at once and the priest stood before them in dismay, with complete comprehension now of what had occurred.

"Children, children," he said loudly, capturing their attention immediately. "Children, there has been a misunderstanding here. Those men . . . those men . . ." he was about to explain, but changed his mind. He realized that if he told them, and if by chance they might be questioned by anyone, their knowledge of the Americans presence would put them all in grave danger, the children and the village. He was trapped, and if he told them the truth who the strange men really were, it could be disastrous, yet it was impossible for him to lie, *but what is truth?* Trapped in a paradoxical dilemma, upon reflection, he realized what if it really was true? *What if these men were the answer to prayer? Didn't the Bible say that God's way was not man's way, nor were his thoughts the same as man's. Must God answer prayer in the way men expect Him to?*

Father Kabos decided to walk a thin line, keeping as close to the truth as possible without revealing too much. Even this decision was taken from him when Nicholas asked, "Is America part of heaven, Father?" *Bless his innocent heart, Lord,* Father Kabos said silently to himself before answering. "No, child, it is a land that is far away from here."

"Bronislaw said Yanov told him he thought the men came from America."

"That's just another country," Marjan said, frowning.

"Then they're just people like us. They couldn't be angels."

"Yes, they are! Didn't we pray?"

"If they came from America, they're just people. I know about them," Marjan said.

"My uncle lives there."

"They could be in disguise," Marisha said. "The Bible says angels come in disguise. Doesn't the Bible say that, Father?"

"Yes it does, child."

"Well, you saw them, Father. Were they angels?" Nicholas asked. "Is it them? Have they come?" Marisha asked again. "Tell us, please," Marjan asked. Leaning forward on his bench, Father Kabos' heart went out to all the children in compassion and love. *How could he withhold information they already had?* "Children, I don't know" he began.

"They say they come from America, and it's a far off country. So they are different in the way they speak and what they wear. Yet it is incredible . . . hard to believe that people from another country so far away would be in our mountains. If they were angels, then they're disguised in a way so we cannot tell them from any other human. They are definitely men of war. We did pray for 'War Angels'. Because they do claim to come from America, a country also in mortal combat against Germany, we must protect them. They are strange to our land and the Germans will be looking for them. They may come right to this very village in their search to find and destroy these men and therefore we must be alert and careful in whatever we say or do. Because the Germans may come here again, you must always be careful to let your parents and elders know where you are at all times."

He paused and waited expectantly for their reaction. Then, after a long while, Nicholas said, "How can we protect angels? They must be only men."

"God may have sent them here for a reason, Nicholas," the priest told him.

"What for?"

"I think we'll know that in God's time."

"I think He disguised them for protection. That's why they probably don't have wings either." Gilda said, and then another young girl stood up. "I think they **are** angels and God sent them as Americans to test us."

"For what?" Marjan said grumpily. "Why would he do 'that?"

"To see if we deserve them. God might have many places He could send his angels because of the war. He could send them to Russia if He wanted to. He's testing us that's what."

"I don't believe it. They're just men." Suddenly Father Kabos smiled with inspiration.

"Children, I have a wonderful idea. Let us all pray and thank the Lord for sending these men, whoever they are, and ask for His blessing and protection of them. I'm sure we can all agree on that, and I'm certain it would please our Lord."

After the prayer, Father Kabos attempted to begin the normal classroom instruction but Joseph immediately interrupted, standing again, frowning, he expressed his concern at the priest.

"But how can we really find out if they're angels?" Before Father Kabos could answer, Marjan piped up, "We could ask them."

"They wouldn't tell us if they were," Joseph responded quickly. "They wouldn't want us to know or anyone else."

"Why?" Nicholas asked.

"They're testing us to see if we're worthy," Marisha said. "Maybe they want to surprise the Germans, like in a surprise attack."

Once more, Father Kabos saw everyone voicing their opinions as to how they could discover whether they were truly angels in disguise. None of the children could come up with a suggestion that would satisfy all of them. One thing they did agree on, these men were different, something special, and easily could have been 'heaven sent'. Father Kabos could see the children were definitely not going to be receptive in their present frame of mind to something as mundane as the instruction of simple arithmetic, not when there were more exciting things to discuss, like the possibility that God had sent His angels to help protect them. This topic could be explored endlessly. He allowed them the time, even patiently answering many of the same questions again, as if the children by hearing the answers repeated might affirm to the majority their belief that these men called Americans were really angels. Finally, when he saw it was going to be hopeless trying to get the children to concentrate now, he dismissed them early.

51

Basha could not stop thinking of one of the men who was sitting off by himself, their leader according to Szabla. He was older and definitely different from the other Americans. The other Americans were men of various ages, yet they still had a boyish quality about them. The leader had a telling expression of a man with a past who had seen, and done much. She could see that they were tired and bloodied in battle, but she judged they would always retain that innocence so common to young men, who grew up in a land where people believed justice prevailed, that right won against evil. This one, she guessed, knew better. He would be more like Szabla and herself.

She became aware of his gaze and met his eyes boldly, and in that moment knew that like the children, she was committed to protect these strangers as well. She could read his interest and was quite surprised at the sudden surge of her own. Then she instantly dismissed it from her mind, considering even the inkling of an involvement with any man as pure foolishness. Yet when she had returned to the hut with Szabla, she once more thought of the American who had stared so penetratingly deep within.

She informed Szabla to keep the Americans at the camp with him until they could decide what they must do with them. In the meantime, the partisans would double the lookouts.

Basha returned to the community hut at the other end of the village. Immediately she became aware of some of the other problems these Americans were going to create for the villagers of Praznik. There was an air of excitement among the younger women in the hut. They were chattering away, discussing the Americans, who they were, where they had come from, and what this would mean as far as the war was concerned. She knew many of the women had lost husbands and lovers and had not seen any new or available men other than Partisans for some time. *True, a few had taken lovers among the partisans, but this was not the same.* Suddenly thrust into the midst of them was a handful of young robust men. Not only that, these men were from another world entirely. These Americans assumed a mythical aura that surrounded the land and its people. Just the mere presence of these legendary warriors was enough to excite any woman who grieved for the feel and taste of a real man.

Basha looked at Magda, the young girl whom Dunham had signaled out and caused to blush, she was now the center of a teasing and ribald attack by some of the older women.

They graphically informed her of the accoutrements of young stallions and the prodigious powers some of these Americans were supposed to possess. "A man like that would be too much for a young maiden," one said.

As Basha listened to the women laugh it reminded her of how quickly that innocence could vanish, causing Magda a great deal of anguished embarrassment. Then she heard some of the other women envious of Magda's youth, offer their services to relieve Magda if she needed any assistance. The teasing was good-natured, but like all jesting, there was a great deal of truth behind it. The women were frustrated, and the earthier of them had been denied too long.

The Americans had brought a waft of the rutting aroma with them, their strange arrival affecting many of the women, and for a moment even Basha. After a brief lull in their teasing conversation directed at the younger women, Basha watched as many of them suddenly began to address their suppressed needs.

"These men are different," someone said.

"Not too different, I hope," another woman added quickly, bringing laughter from the others.

"It is strange but some of them look as young boys."

"They are men, believe me. I can tell. Even the short one looks formidable."

"And clean."

"The tall one, the leader is handsome, is he not."

"They do not speak much, do they."

"I can make one talk, anyone of them. Oh, I could make him even sing, if given the chance."

"Since when is talk necessary for what we want," another said, with smiling intensity. "For me, he can be mute as long as he can toot his horn!"

This brought another great burst of laughter. After a few moments there followed a sudden reflective silence within the group, which surprised the younger women as they now observed their stirred up feelings. These feelings gushed to the surface by the ribald discussion concerning the Americans. Basha saw one of the earthier women speak up. She was a strong looking woman with a full figure, not easily hidden beneath her worn and heavy clothing. "It has been a long time since I lost my Jan. I still think of him often, when I awake in the morning, in the field when I work, and at night alone in my bed. But yet, I still like the Polish speaking American and feel attracted to him."

"They do say Americans are all great lovers. They treat their women like goddesses. They are tender, kind, and very romantic.

"May God have mercy on us!" Basha suddenly lashed out at them in anger, having finally heard enough. "You are all like a bunch of foolish chattering hens wanting a rooster. Do you know what would happen if the Germans were to discover them here? Have you forgotten? Or are you so filled with lust your minds have left your heads."

Basha saw one of the women looked up from her sewing, shaking her head. "There is no reason for your anger, Basha Mickiewicz. We have done nothing wrong. We are women who have been without our men for much too long. Why should we not be attracted to them? What is the harm? At least they are not Partisans."

Another woman came forward and faced Basha defiantly now. "Yes. Where is the harm of a little joy for once in a dreary existence? What's wrong with a little fun for a change. There are some here in the village who have never known of men other than Szabla and those animals of his in the upper camp. You may have lost your desire for a good man, but we haven't."

"Have you no shame with all this talk before the young ones here," Basha said loudly, indicating several of the other younger women. "You behave worse than hens. Now you are like a pack of bitches in heat! Insulting and stupid and I want no part of you!" She suddenly yanked up her broom and began flailing at the women. "Get out. Go about your business." She poked and smacked at them angrily, and they scattered in panic from the hut as she followed a few steps after them. Once outside, she immediately regained control of herself and gave up the chase, then turning, she stopped Magda and smiled at her.

"Pay them no mind, my lonely one. There is a good man for you somewhere. This madness cannot last forever, and good Polish men will return home. It is sometimes best to wait for the right love than to lose everything in foolish haste." Basha calmly put her hand to the girl's cheek and smiled at her with reassurance. Magda, still somewhat frightened, returned the smile nervously and then said, "Basha, how do you know when you're in love?" Basha thought about how sweet and innocent the girl still was among all these wolves, and the fact that she had yet to know real love. She was untouched and still girlishly romantic, Basha reflected with a touch of envy, *if only that flower of youth could remain protected from the worldly frost of reality. Magda was so young, hardly more than a child in her teens. Yet in these mountains, women matured early and the current madness of the war would certainly keep many young women from the illusion of romantic love. Their time and thoughts spent on the rigors of getting through the day-to-day hardship of life without families, without enough food, without their fathers or brothers, or the normal companionship of the men that afforded protection to women.*

"Basha, you must have been in love sometime?" Basha looked down and still did not answer her. In these mountains and in these times, one learned quickly, or one did not survive. Basha considered herself a survivor, and she worried about Magda, the girl who reminded her of all she had lost in the reality of her growing years in this hard country. Then Basha stared off in the direction of the Americans. She recalled the man taken with her in a way that had not occurred since those days so long ago.

"I thought I was once."

"What was he like?"

"I had returned from the rolling hills and low mountain country on the border where Szabla had kept his camp during his foraging days before the war. My father's business had continued to expand until finally it had become important for him to find larger quarters. So he moved to Kracow for more cosmopolitan surroundings. In my father's employment was a new man, young, dark-haired, and strikingly handsome. His name was Adam Pasek.

"What happened?"

"In time, for whatever reason, he was falsely accused by his employer of stealing."

"Your father accused him?"

"Yes, but that's another story. Go on get home and be careful. Don't get involved with anyone, now is not the time."

52

Marvin and the rest of the crew stood up and prepared to move out. It was apparent to him they were not going to remain in the village. The partisans resumed their previous positions and again, the entire group found themselves heading for the even higher mountains forming the majestic background of the village.

In only minutes, Marvin found himself going through some thick brush at the edge of the forest with the village already behind them. Marvin was on a narrow trail that was growing steeper with every step. Forced by their burden, and the thin air, they stopped many times, taking turns at carrying the litter. The trail took a sharp bend and Marvin found himself facing backward toward the area they had just climbed, and further down in the distance was the village. From this height, it looked unreal to Marvin, almost doll-like, as if he were back in his plane.

The partisans paused for rest, careful to stay well within the forest overgrowth of great trees, which amazingly flourished so high up in the mountains. They all sat on the cold earth, all except Szabla, the moisture of Marvin's breath creating many bursting patterns of condensation.

"Look at that tough son-of-a-gun," Haply said between breaths.

"Nothing fazes him."

Marvin was about to reply when he heard the sound of a low flying plane. He listened and Szabla barked a command at the men. They all quickly scattered, working themselves back deeper into a thicker stand of forest. Marvin stared up at the sky, searching for the plane. Then he saw it. Coming from an easterly direction, with the sun, a lone Stuka, a type of plane he had yet to come up against but had heard much about.

Marvin watched it with clinical appraisal as it circled in an apparent reconnaissance pattern. Marvin concluded the plane was directed by a ground controller, and then realized there must be troops in the area!

He quickly turned to relay this information to Szabla through Novak when the frozen expression of hate on Szabla's face let him know that Szabla had already seen something beside the plane. Marvin glanced down the mountain toward the village and then directed his scrutiny even further on down until he saw them. Coming up the mountain road was a slow moving column of vehicles.

"Germans! The Germans, sir. They're moving up to that village we just left," Ballard said. Marvin watched the German plane circle once more, and then continued on a straight line flying off southwesterly.

Szabla was now intently watching the village through binoculars. Marvin could see they were an excellent and expensive set of field glasses, probably taken from some captured or dead German officer. Shaw started to speak to Haply, but Szabla's menacing command cut him off. Putting his index finger across his lips, Marvin motioned the rest of the crew to remain silent.

They were there on the trail waiting silently and immobile for the better part of an hour, when Marvin began to feel the cold. He wondered if the rest of the men felt the same way. No one had spoken. Szabla still crouched at the edge with his eyes peering through the binoculars, glued to the village. The Germans had entered thirty minutes ago and Marvin half expected to hear the sound of guns. He wondered just what was happening down there. From this distance, it was difficult to tell how many Germans there were. If there weren't too many, would Szabla attempt to do anything about it? Marvin began to grow impatient, and whether it was the cold, their long immobility, or the tension of just waiting for something to happen, he couldn't be sure. Then Marvin did a surprising thing. He stood up and asked Szabla, by means of hand-signals to borrow his binoculars. Szabla handed them to him without a word.

Peering thought the glasses, Marvin could see about thirty German soldiers moving about the village. In the center of the village, the vehicles turned around to face down the mountain road, but the machine guns on the half-tracks were facing the village, and particularly on a small knot of people standing in front of one of the houses. Marvin immediately discerned the lack of children. He could also see that some of the Germans had passed on through the village and had gone into the forest beyond it. He was shocked to observe two of the German soldiers now coming from the forest escorting a figure in a black cassock to the center of the village, prodding him toward a soldier who was not wearing a helmet, obviously an officer. The man had what looked like a weapon in his hand. He watched as the figure in black stumbled. It was then Szabla took the glasses from Marvin and began to watch again.

Marvin squinted down toward the village, but could not see the detail of what was happening between the moving figures.

They remained on the trail for another hour and then the sound of starting vehicles reached them and they all stared back down toward the village. The Germans had climbed back aboard their vehicles and were pulling out of the village square, some of the motorcycles already starting down the mountain road. Marvin understood as Szabla sent one of the men back to the village, and ordered the rest to continue toward the camp again. This time as they moved, several of the-partisans left the Americans bunched together in small groups, engaging in low rapid conversation. Except for the two partisans bringing up the far rear, the crew was almost alone. They walked very slowly; Marvin sensed the partisans no longer seemed so anxious to reach the camp. The ominous tone and the surreptitious glances the partisans were now directing towards them disturbed Marvin.

"Novak, get closer and see if you can understand what all the talk is about."

Dunham had heard Marvin's command and joined Novak, pretending to be speaking to him but only mouthing his words. In minutes, Novak dropped back, his face gone pale.

"Sir, they're discussing whether or not to kill us."

"Are you sure?"

"Absolutely, they're talking about shooting us just as soon as we get into their camp. Some of the men are saying we brought the Germans into the village, and will soon bring them up to the camp. We are too dangerous. They think the village is already doomed now that we have been there. The crazy looking one, Yanov, he wants to march us all back down to the plane and blast us there. That way they won't have to carry us."

"What's keeping them from doing it now? Just Szabla?"

"No. They're worried about the priest."

"What happened to him?"

"Nothing, they're just worried about his reaction. What he might do if they were to knock us off."

Marvin bit his lip and made the decision. "Well, that about tears it. I guess we really don't have much choice, do we. Drift back and inform the rest of the men what's going on. Tell each of them to get as close as possible to a partisan, nothing suspicious, and wait for me to make the first move."

He saw Novak drop back and while he told Ballard and the others near him, Marvin moved forward and told Dunham. Marvin could see the new alertness in the crew as their pace quickened and they began to close up ranks. However, the trail was too narrow for them to mingle in with the partisans and they began to give up hope again when the trail suddenly broadened, and they entered a very craggy, rock-strewn series of jagged mountain crests.

Marvin nodded and the men moved up quickly. If the situation weren't so deadly, Marvin would have laughed watching Haply and Shaw in their almost ludicrous struggle with the litter to get close enough so that when they put Ryan down, they could put the rush on the nearest partisans.

The men were just about ready now and Marvin picked up his pace to reach Szabla and get behind him. He observed the trail up ahead and saw the sharp turn as it passed between the jagged peaks. That would be the spot. At the turn between the peaks, he would give the signal. They reached the turn and he raised his hand to grasp Szabla when he heard the shouts.

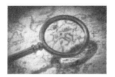

53

Emerging from between the peaks up ahead, Marvin saw several heavily armed men step out from hiding followed by a host of children. The forward group of partisans enthusiastically began greeting the men coming down to meet them and there was much embracing and backslapping.

Marvin rounded the bend and carefully threaded his way from behind a large rock formation, he found himself squarely facing the partisan camp. It was well hidden from the air, skirting the edges of the brush. He could also detect several camouflaged sod huts that blended cleverly into the mountainside.

A number of people occupied the camp working at various chores, all of which had become suddenly unimportant when compared to the sight of the partisans bringing in the Americans. Marvin realized now what had happened to the majority of the children they had seen earlier in the village. *How had they gotten up here so fast, and without passing them along the way?* He guessed there had to be a more direct trail.

Marvin and the rest of the crew staggered into the camp and the children began to surround them. Once again, they were staring with that intense peculiar interest, completely ignoring the sharp calls of the partisans to get out of the way. This strange continued fluttering of the children around them was now beginning to make the Americans uneasy. Their behavior was unnatural, beyond curiosity, and the men couldn't figure it out. Some of the partisans signaled the crew they were to move on to the area of sod huts, constructed simply from mud, grass, and tree limbs. Marvin could see that even up close it was difficult to differentiate between the huts and the actual mountainside. When they arrived at a particular dilapidated hut, they were informed this was to be theirs and the partisans dispersed, and for the first time left the Americans unguarded.

Haply and Shaw put Ryan down with loud groans of relief. They were about to flop in despair with the rest of the crew, when Marvin, studying the tired men sprawled about the hut, suddenly began to address them in a commanding tone. "Look, why be lambs and allow these people to think they can do what they want with us. Either we can continue to be helpless or we can change our behavior and maybe show them who we are, or at least try. Let's bluff it out."

The men looked at him without understanding. "What I mean is let's stop behaving like prisoners and start acting as if we were really allies of this bunch. Ballard, get out there and get some of that firewood. Dunham, see if you can scrounge up something to eat. If you're stopped, pretend ignorance. Laugh it off. If they get rough and start shoving or threatening, give them the other cheek and play dumb. And this goes for all of us. Don't do anything sudden or suspicious that would make it look as if we're trying to escape or cause any trouble. We just want them to accept us for who we are allies in a common cause. Okay. Shall we try it?"

The crew remained unsure of this new strategy of Marvin's but after taking some moments to think it over he saw they causally began to saunter out in different directions.

Dunham had no difficulty. Some of the partisans were glad to share with him. Ballard was stopped, but quickly flashing a friendly smile, he pointed to a large woodpile and continued. He returned with an armful of wood and even went back for more, this time completely unmolested.

Marvin watched Shaw and Haply make the mistake of walking out together. At the first indication of trouble, Shaw played it smart and came back but Haply stubbornly kept on. One of the partisans called to him but Haply acted as if he were deaf. Angrily the man hurried to catch up, then, grabbing Haply's arm, spun him around. Haply smiled and tried to walk away. This made the partisan even angrier and he raised his voice in some unintelligible command. With an angry gesture, he indicated Haply was to head back in the opposite direction. Haply smiled again and tried to walk on. This time the partisan slapped his face, hard, the sound muffled by the man's glove. Haply's eyes watered but he continued smiling, then suddenly his hand lashed out and he slapped the partisan, the sound of Haply's bare hand cracking loud across the cold air like a shot.

Marvin, had been a witness to Haply striking the partisan, and felt his heart constrict-in momentary fear for Haply. *We've had it now,* he thought.

The partisan looked at Haply in disbelief. Yet Haply was still smiling and even attempted to put his arm around the partisan's shoulder, but the partisan shrugged it off violently and slapped haply again, motioning for him to get back with the other Americans. Incredulously, Haply slapped the man back. A great silence fell over the camp; tenseness permeated everything as the feisty sergeant hung between life and death.

In a rage, the partisan stepped back to aim his rifle. Haply grabbed it, fell backwards, and pulling the partisan forward by the rifle, threw him over himself, and sent the man sprawling in the dirt.

Haply now had the rifle in his hand as he stood up and the partisan froze, expecting any moment to receive the bullet he had intended for the American. Still smiling, haply tossed the rifle away, and extending his hand, faked what had to be one of the best and most appreciative laughs Marvin had ever heard. The partisan stared at Haply's extended hand and slowly brought his forward. He accepted it with a grin as Haply pulled him up.

From a corner of the camp, a great roaring laugh echoed out over the two men as Szabla came forward and enthusiastically pounded Haply on the back in admiration.

Marvin thought whatever he was saying had to be favorable because they all kept grinning and nodding.

Finally, he watched it break up and the three men resumed heading for their original destinations before Haply's remarkable performance. Marvin silently promoted Haply on the spot, raising him one notch in rank and forgiving him for everything.

Marvin watched Haply reach the hut where the crew had assembled out front, several of them gave him a thumbs up sign of a job well done, nodding their approval. When Haply looked over at Shaw, the tail gunner spoke up quickly, the scowl on his face showing his displeasure.

"Haply, you've got to have mush for brains. You know that. Just who do you think you are, risking my life with a stupid stunt like that?" Marvin shook his head on observing Shaw's anger at Haply. He was never going to understand the strange camaraderie that existed between these two men.

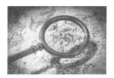

54

Szabla was not fooled by the American's sudden display of camaraderie, but he was nonetheless interested in the cleverness of the strategy, and much impressed with the cool courage of the short American, wondering whether any of the others possessed this seed of stealth and courage.

Witnessing the scene between Yanov and the American troubled him enough now to make it twice as difficult to decide on whether or not to kill these Americans. One does not kill courage, especially if there is a possibility this courage could be used in his own band for his own purposes.

As he mulled over the difficulties he might face in a decision made either way, he realized how much simpler it all might have been for both himself and the village if he had listened to the Czech's original advice and killed the Americans at the plane. The Czech always voted for killing; therefore, Szabla tended to discredit the impartiality of his advice on certain occasions.

Szabla decided to go on down to the village and find out what had happened with the Germans. If it appeared the Germans had even a grain of suspicion that these men were nearby, then he would kill the Americans as soon as possible, regardless of what it might cost him with the priest. Thinking of the priest brought him again to face another of his nagging difficulties, for the priest was the one person he still could not read.

Szabla found it difficult to maintain a consistent opinion concerning the man's character. He was like one of those jewelry stones of many colors, forever changing under different light. There were times when Szabla thought the priest a complete ass behaving as no real man with any pride would ever allow himself to. Then there were times when he thought the priest might be too clever, masking an entirely different person behind the cassock of his religion.

Now Szabla had discovered a new and surprising aspect of this Father Kabos, courage. What he had witnessed through his binoculars from the trail above the village had greatly impressed him, for it was obvious the man had deliberately provoked the attack upon himself. He was certain Basha would be telling him about it this evening, the great courage of the priest.

Strangely, Szabla was prepared to believe it, his attitude much changed from his first suspicions of Father Kabos. He recalled how at the discovery of the priest's apparent excellent medical skill, better even than any ordinary doctor, he had been amazed and thought the man an imposter. For Szabla had nothing but contempt for priests, convinced their only skill was in taking from the poor. But later when the priest had settled in to live as simply as the other villagers, and his healing ability soon taken for granted, Szabla no longer thought of the priest as a man who might ever again impress him. The other day with the Americans, then again with the Germans in the village, he had succeeded in doing just that. Twice the man surprised him in less than twenty-four hours.

Szabla promised himself to give this priest serious reflection at some future date, but for the moment he was now concerned with other matters. Szabla called Durcansky to accompany him, and they started down the trail to the village. They took the short cut, the hidden steep trail that led to the back of the village through the gully where the children were normally concealed. He and Durcansky skirted the village just in case the Germans might have left behind a few men to catch any careless visitors. Then, moving swiftly, and keeping themselves low, they went from house to house peering in, searching for traps and listening intently for unfamiliar sounds that might warn of danger.

When they reached the apartment of Basha Mickiewicz, Szabla entered up the back, telling Durcansky to wait outside and keep alert.

Szabla saw Basha at a small table slowly sipping at a mug of hot soup. She didn't appear startled at seeing him in her apartment, having gotten used to it long ago. He spoke quickly, his immediate concern being whether all the Germans had gone. When she nodded, he reopened the door and quietly told Durcansky it was safe. Durcansky headed for the village tavern as Szabla closed the door. Looking at Basha in the dim light, Szabla could see that she was upset. He was surprised at how her appearance still caused concern for her in him. He knew that to have any feelings or emotions in these evil times was the worst kind of weakness, and he tried to suppress them.

Looking at Basha, he knew this hard intelligent bellicose woman was unbeatable, inspiring a mixture of conflicting emotions within him just at her mere presence. Anyone with any brains could see she was a great woman, more than enough for any man to handle.

It all rushed back to him, those feelings so close to the surface of his emotions, the burning unquenchable passion he had once felt for her, still felt in spite of the fact she would have none of him in the way he had once known her. His passion had manifested itself in that terrible anger which had caused him to kill the count's son, her fiance, for the way he abused her years ago. It had turned Szabla into the bandit he became, forcing him to kidnap her, escaping into the hills where they had lived together.

He recalled the crushing despair he had struggled to overcome when finally she had left him to return to civilization again. Those memories welled up within him now, threatening to engulf his emotions and prevent him from speaking as he stared at her.

Gently, he asked her, "The Germans, did they mistreat you? Did they do anything to you?" Basha slowly shook her head and looked at him with watery eyes.

"Then for God's sake, woman, what is it? What have they done?"

55

"The priest. It was the priest."

"The priest?" He looked at her dumbly. Thank God it was the priest and not Basha. A sense of guilt quickly overcame the relief he felt at discovering she was untouched. "What have they done to the priest? Did they take him?" he asked, already aware of the answer because he had seen the Germans leave while standing on the mountain trail. He did not see them take the priest.

Basha shook her head in grim despair. "They beat him, without respect, and badly. They claimed to look for partisans. They meant to deceive us. For I know it was the Americans they sought."

"The Americans? So soon? Why did they come here? Did they suspect them to be in Praznik?"

"They know nothing."

"Did they follow our trail? They must have a reason to search here on the mountain."

"I tell you, they are ignorant."

"Then why did they beat the priest?"

"What reason do blasphemers need? They tried to frighten a village of women and old men, thinking to make the weak ones among us reveal the presence of any Americans. They threatened to kill him before our eyes if we did not speak. We could see they knew nothing. We cursed the day they were born; they saw we were not fooled. Frightened yes, but not fooled, which made them even angrier." He watched her take another slow sip from the mug, and then continued.

"One of them wanted to kill us all, but another said this might warn away their quarry if they were nearby in these mountains. It was then that they decided to pursue a different mischief. They asked Father Kabos what he was doing here in such a small village. And he said . . . he said simply serving God. 'What are you doing here?' He asked that German pig, so they beat him. If that un-Godly filth had not been so anxious to find the Americans, they would have killed him, and maybe the rest of us as well. I think if they do not find them, and they return, they will kill him. I feel this inside me."

"God will protect him," Szabla said, unexpectedly sounding pious, but only to calm her down. It had the opposite effect. "What do you know of God? All you know of is killing and more killing. Do you know what he did every time they struck him? Do you know? He blessed them! Yes, every time. Once when they struck him so hard he fell into the dirt, his mouth covered with mud and bleeding, he still blessed them! The filthy swine!"

Szabla looked silently at Basha and thought of Father Kabos with amazement. He didn't think a pale-faced, thin priest, had it in him. *The quality of bravery is strange,* Szabla thought. *It could be found anywhere. Weren't all men of God considered strange? He knew many who believed and all of them seemed to have this natural inclination to blind stupidity. Maybe it was a sort of courage, a kind of madness.* It was too deep and complex for Szabla to understand.

Once again, it was apparent he had underrated the priest. He wondered just how long before this strange man with those glazed over eyes would cease to amaze him. There was no escaping it, someday when the time was propitious; he would make a serious effort to understand him. *Who was the man under the cassock, the real Jan Kabos, not the stranger no one really knew. The Jan Kabos who revealed himself under stress was obviously a man not to be taken lightly.*

"Where is he now?" Szabla asked.

"The sisters. The sisters are caring for him."

"I'll go see him. Maybe there is something I might do to help."

"Leave him. There is no reason to disturb his solitude. He needs rest, not a stinking mountain goat to stare at him."

Szabla, hurt by her reference to the perpetual odor caused by his fondness for pungent mountain herbs and spices, hid his feelings. "What of the children? Did they ask of the children?"

"No. They were only interested in the Americans."

"They will be back then, huh? They are thinking we have them here in Praznik?"

Basha shook her head and rubbed her hands for warmth.

"No. as I told you, I am convinced they know nothing. They only guess. They will look elsewhere and keep looking until they find them. When they are through searching the mountains and the villages, and scouring the flatlands below us, then once more they will return. When that accursed moment is upon us, we will tell the pigs nothing. Not one person in Praznik will speak. Not one person will even let the Americans enter their minds so that even a thought cannot escape and reach the Germans. From Praznik, they will never know of their presence among us."

"I will kill them," Szabla said simply. "No need to worry. I will kill them and make certain they are found in the lowlands."

Basha turned to him, stunned. "What are you babbling now!"

"I have made up my mind. These Americans are not worth the trouble. It was a mistake to spare them. It is now clear to me, if one person anywhere in these mountains, even a child, were to speak when they should not, these Germans who are searching will return and destroy the village."

"Since when have you ever cared for the village?"

Basha said in anger. Always it is killing. Will there ever be anything in that stupid jelly you call a brain?"

"Do you think the Germans could not find our camp as well, if they continue to search these mountains?"

"Aah!"

"And what of the children? Because of the Americans, they could discover the children." She eyed him scornfully.

"Do you worry for the children or do you worry for Szabla. Listen, you don't fool me. I know you better than you do. Szabla, the patriot; Szabla, the bandit; Szabla, the hero of Praznik. Listen to me carefully, you rutting goat. You know me, Basha Mickiewicz. You know I am one who speaks the truth always. I say this to you. You will not dishonor Father Kabos with your stupidity."

"What has the priest to do with it?"

"You blind fool. Have you become so ignorant in your concern for yourself that you no longer think? The Americans have everything to do with Father Kabos. It was for them he suffered. It was for them and the children that he put himself on the cross and stood up to the Germans. And it is because of them he lies in his bed, bruised and beaten, and prays for deliverance."

"Yes, but . . ."

"What of Praznik? Do you think we stood, watched, and said nothing because we were afraid? Heaven forbid that we should let this man of God be destroyed before our very eyes just for the sake of the village. No. We remained silent only because of Father Kabos, for his honor and for his faith, and because he gave us courage. And you would take that from him now by destroying the Americans?" I give you warning, if you do such an evil thing against this priest, then I, Basha Mickiewicz, swear before God, I will kill you myself and pay the penalty of damnation for it! Do you understand? Do you believe me? Answer. Do you think I would not?" Szabla, moved by her emotional outburst, shook his head quietly.

"Good. Return to that camp of yours and wait. When Father Kabos is well, I will send Bronislaw to inform you. Then it will be time to discuss the Americans and what should be done."

"And the children? The camp is not a school."

"Then let it be a school. A few days only to be certain the Germans do not return again in their search and find the children."

Szabla faced her dejectedly; realizing it would be hopeless to oppose her now. He leaned closer, setting his jaw defiantly, and said, "So be it, but not for the Americans, or the priest, or for the children either. For you, and what we once were. Only because of you!"

Szabla became silent and his mouth suddenly felt dry. He swallowed painfully as he thought of how much he really wanted this woman. In spite of everything, he still found himself having to suppress the overwhelming desire to reach out and hold her again, have her laugh with him, feel the surging excitement they had once shared. He wondered how much of the past she still remembered, and if she did recall any of it, what feelings toward him still remained within her.

Then he saw Basha take a step forward and her face softened toward him. "Whatever the reason, see that you remember what I have said." Szabla stared into her eyes and spoke softly. "Woman, your heart is still made of stone for me. Someday the truth that you hide will cause it to break, and you will see me as I am. Then you will know what you have done to us." He saw Basha shrug as he closed the door silently behind him.

56

Ernst Von Reinstock had already covered an incredibly large area of territory within a short period in spite of the freezing cold, the ring closing tighter in his search for the Americans. He had cleverly created a separate department to handle the effort within his own organization. This allowed him to keep track of his singular goal, which constantly occupied his thoughts. By tightly monitoring the operation of his continuing search, he effectively eliminated any duplication in the tasks of the various units reporting to him. This rigid control also gave him the freedom to personally follow up promising leads and investigate anything that struck him as suspicious.

He decided to build an impenetrable steel ring around the suspected territory of where the Americans might be, quickly closing it about them and sealing the entire crew inside. He molded and built his steel ring like a deadly spider weaving its web for dinner. Day by day, he sent patrols and searches out, adding to it by the constant monitoring and marking of his maps.

He made a systematic check at the end of each day of all the various units involved. He evaluated, and then recalled units back, only to send them out again the next day. Just like an Anachrid would recycle its web by eating it each night, and then remake it the following morning. Even with the reporting system he devised, and its smart efficiency, it was still too slow a process for him. As the days progressed, he felt a growing concern that the Americans were somehow slipping away from him, getting through his steel ring.

Impatient during a day when his old wounds were troubling him again, he ordered out a plane, and had a pilot assigned to him. It was a two-seater; the fighter was converted for observation duties. Flying as an observer this time, he directed the flight over another area of mountainous terrain, once more flying over the route as he had finally determined the Americans must have flown.

They skimmed the trees and scanned the snow-covered valleys, checking gullies and ravines, at times barely avoiding the sudden rock outcroppings. There was no tangible sign of either men or plane. In fact, nothing seemed to be moving in the mountains this time of year, yet he knew better. From the reports he had been studying there was still partisan activity in the lowlands in many areas of the country. In addition, there was activity along the southern mountain ranges, with various bands from Czechoslovakia to Russia surviving the bitter winters and the occupying forces.

Reinstock continued to study the passing landscape, carefully using his binoculars, several times having the pilot dropping to treetop level to circle suspiciously flourishing overgrowth that might serve to conceal a large downed aircraft. Finally, after many hours, and the fuel becoming dangerously low, Reinstock directed the pilot to the SS military headquarter in the area and landed at a nearby field.

Riding in a motorcycle sidecar, it took him to the headquarters building, a former factory that easily converted to a perfect police compound. With suitable surrounding grounds, it was now a formidable armed camp.

Inside the building, Reinstock visited the commander of the special SS forces occupying this area. Reinstock had read the dossier of the man in charge, SS Major Otto Hassman, an effective old time party member whose primary purpose was the liquidation of all undesirables. He had a reputation for "getting things done". Earnst heard his current pressing concern was the difficulty stamping out a particularly vicious partisan movement in his district.

Reinstock entered the major's office, it had no door on it, and several lower-grade officers were standing uncomfortably before him. Reinstock stepped to one side of the room and waited unobtrusively, watching the hulking movement of Major Hassman before his men, who suddenly halted and faced them.

Reinstock saw the Major was quite angry, his face flushed as he stood before the silent officers. Hanging behind him on the wall was a large detailed map of his responsible territory, which went deep into the mountains and covered several military installations established in the occupied country.

"You mean to tell me that a heavily armed supply convoy was openly attacked and that these bandits escaped?" he said, scowling disgustedly at them.

"That you have no idea how many of them you killed or how many of these barbarians were involved in the attack?" He paused, glancing at a paper on his desk, reading the figures. "Thirteen of our men dead, slaughtered by incompetence. Six trucks destroyed including materials which they carried, two armored cars put out of action, and eight more vehicles in for repair. Unbelievable!"

"The convoy followed the normal defensive procedures," one of the officers said nervously. "We were on open ground and taken completely by surprise."

"That is obvious."

"We sent out another motorized detachment immediately," the officer went on. "Twice we made contact with the partisans who left men fighting a rearguard action. We overran their positions, of course, and the pursuit continued into the mountains. Then they just seemed to vanish."

"Not vanish Heir Hoffman, they are not magicians. Only more clever because they know the country. They are hiding somewhere, probably right under our noses. I don't like it Hoffman. I don't like it at all. They must have informers, spies among the local population who knew about that shipment. I want them."

"What about hostages, sir? In reprisal for the attack."

"The taking of hostages is futile. It only depletes the work force. I suppose we must follow policy. Round up one hundred and have them shot this Sunday. Spread the selection among the town and the factories. We don't want to have a work stoppage."

"Yes, sir."

"Somehow we must discover where those partisans are hiding, and who their friends are. I am determined to put a stop to their barbarous attacks on our people. We must have information. I would like to have an informer amongst them."

"What about the prisoners, sir?"

"Exactly what I mean."

"Sir?"

"How many."

"Two of them. One wounded, but not critically."

"Good, bring them down to the basement. And Hoffman, try not to kill them this time. I want to know where they came from and who their friends are."

"Yes, sir." Hoffman saluted and quickly left the Major's office, followed smartly by the other officers.

Reinstock pleasantly watched Major Hassman pull an almost full bottle of Cognac from his desk drawer and set two glasses before him. He filled the glasses then set the bottle down. He handed one of the glasses to Reinstock, and lifted the other. They both nodded and drank deeply.

"Trouble?" Reinstock finally asked, indicating the officers that had just left.

"The usual Partisans."

"Really? I had thought this area had been cleaned."

"The local population is completely subdued. Believe me, we have no real trouble from them; trouble is created from the outside. These bandits come down from the mountains. We've been successful against many of these fanatics already, and eventually we will get them all. There is a group that I have been after for some time. A particular brute of a man leads it. A real savage who goes by the name of Szabla, have you ever heard of him?"

"I Can't say that I have Major."

"He's quite notorious in these parts, and very clever."

"Was he responsible for the convoy?"

"I don't think so. It's not like him."

"Why don't you just go in and clean them out?"

"Believe me, I'd like nothing better. But, I'm spread too thin now." Reinstock thoughtfully watched Major Hassman pour himself another drink and refilled Reinstock's glass then he indicated the stack of on his desk.

"Jews, Gypsies, Saboteurs. Spies and escaped prisoners. There is no end to it. I have been killing enemies of the Reich since 1933. And where do I end up— in this pestilent hole of a country dealing with a population of sub-humans. And doing what? Listen." He held up a sheet of paper that Reinstock could see had the official stamp and letterhead of Berlin. "Over sixty Jews escaped from a derailed train. They were children. Imagine the incompetence, allowing children to escape. With the problems I have to face with this ugly population on my hands and the partisans in the hills, and now the sabotage that is increasing daily, what do you think Berlin keeps writing me about? Jews. Jews. They want those brats and any others we can get. It says they've recaptured almost half from the train. Do you think it matters that my men are being wasted now to be continually scouring the countryside for Jews that might be in my district? No. The orders still stand."

Rienstock, somewhat amused, now watched Hassman shake his head and drink, forgetting for a moment Reinstock's presence. He finished his drink and continued.

"You see the problem, Colonel. How can I find and destroy those partisans if I must spend my troops finding Jew brats." Reinstock glanced at his drink, studying it in his hand. "We do what we must," he said formally. Hassman recognized the official tone of Reinstock's response. "Of course, that is what we all do, what we must. Only I have been doing it for almost ten years."

Reinstock rose stiffly to his feet and placed his untouched second drink on the side of the desk. Leaning on his cane, he stared somberly at major Hassman.

Hassman saw the way it was, and put the bottle of Cognac away along with his empty glass. Then unashamedly, he reached over and drained Reinstock's drink, finishing it easily then giving a shutter of satisfaction at the response of his body before placing this glass beside the other and closing the drawer. Then he sat down behind the desk and looked up at Reinstock, Hassman's expression all business now as he wore his official attitude. "Well now, Colonel. What may I do for you?" He asked, already knowing what the answer would be. Reinstock said, "As I have been telling you daily on the phone, it is urgent we find the American Bomber."

Reinstock saw Hassman attempting to manage and contain his annoyance. This priority was painfully taking up his valuable time. Reinstock realized his constant harassment for information over the last few days had taken a toll on Hassman. He deduced that Hassman must have controlled his feelings, not so much out of respect for how great a flyer he was, but out of fear for his high placed connections among the powerful in Berlin.

"My friends in Berlin are anxious to hear of my success in this matter."

"You are right, what have I been thinking. With all those Jews still eluding me after all these months, and the partisans growing much bolder these days, maybe it is time to take the offensive again. Strike some terror into the local peasant population and those mountain villages."

"Good thinking Hassman, now have any of your prisoners revealed anything of any significance."

"No, they usually just die after they are tortured. But I am sure we will find out more this time. Then I will know how we can root them out."

Reinstock quickly approved of Hassman's idea to renew the sudden unexpected forays into suspicious areas and he proposed to put his plan in finding the American Bomber into action immediately. Reinstock discussed with Hassman several maps hanging on the wall behind his desk, and zeroed in on an area that included Praznik.

Just before Reinstock was about to leave he was interrupted by Hoffman who entered and spoke to Hassman. "Sir, the partisan prisoners taken during the raid on the convoy did not *tell us* anything, and in the basement during interrogation they apparently died while being tortured."

57

Joseph stumbled over a large bush root sticking out of the side of the secret gully trail. He felt Nicholas grab his coat from behind, and keep him up from a bad tumble. He turned to give Nicholas a glance of gratitude and saw him raise his eyebrows in amusement. Not speaking, he continued down the trial with his trusted friend back to the village. He knew returning to Praznik was risky, but he had to see Father Kabos.

Just outside the chapel, Joseph gave a worried glance around the area for Germans. Then he tapped Nicholas who accompanied him from behind and they both darted to the door. Joseph still was not sure whether the priest was all right and all the children had asked him if he was. He knew the children had come to love the priest almost from the first moment they met him. Nevertheless, he felt his love for the priest was different. It was obvious to him Father Kabos shared a special love for both he and Nicholas. Joseph let Nicholas go first as the startled Sister Theresa quickly ushered them into Father Kabos's little room. When Joseph first saw him, he fought back tears. The priest's welts and bruises covered and shined all over his face. He looked at Nicholas who could not bear to show his face of tears, and turned the other way.

Joseph had come to love the priest not only for his good advice, but also for the trust he showed in them. Wiping his wet cheek, he thought of how Father Kabos always spoke the truth regardless of the pain his words might cause, but attempting continually to give them hope. Joseph and Nicholas spread their newly acquired knowledge amongst the other children pertaining to such things as; how they should treat their adopted parents, the respect to be shown them, ways of dressing, eating, saying grace without giving offence to their Christian benefactors. He helped them understand the loyalty owed to the villagers and partisans, and their duty now as citizens of Praznik to protect its existence, and do nothing foolish to jeopardize all of them. Father Kabos treated the two of them with respect as the leaders of the children.

Joseph watched Father Kabos blink at them, and then give a painful smile. "It takes more than a few Germans to keep Gods servant down. Right boys?"

"The Partisans told Nicholas and I what they did to you Father."

"I'll be back on my feet in no time, but what about my two great leaders of the clan? Why aren't you with them? It is very dangerous for you to be here."

"We are thinking of leaving Praznik. It's not safe here anymore, not even for a priest." Nicholas blurted out.

"Boys, Boys, you are much better off at the camp than anywhere else at the moment."

"You said we should hope for the best but be prepared for the worst." Nicholas replied.

"Father, will you be alright, have they done any permanent damage to you?" Joseph said with concern.

"I will be ok. But now you must think of your departed loved ones who would still want each of you to survive and grow up to live good and decent lives, not bent by thoughts of bitterness and revenge. The best gift you children can give your parents is to have strong minds with a will to survive, learning the skills and education required to succeed in the new world that is sure to come. You must continue to love your fellow beings, and not succumb to the hate directed at you by so many deluded minds. The real victory for your parents and us is for you to succeed in becoming happy, God-loving grown-ups."

"How can we forget what they did to you and our loved ones Father?"

"You should never forget what has happened to you or your loved ones, because someday as adults you must do whatever possible to prevent this type of terrible calamity from ever happening again to any group of people." Joseph affectionately put his hand on Father Kabos shoulder and said, "We won't Father, thank you for helping us."

"Thank you for your concern for me, but I am quite alright. I have gained great strength with God's help."

Joseph reached out his hand to Father Kabos who had extended his to the two of them.

"Father, are 'The War Angels' an answer to prayer?"

"Yes, my child, I believe it could be. Moreover, if they are, we certainly must be thankful. Let us pray and thank Jesus for his infinite wisdom in sending us 'The War Angels'." Joseph had a problem. He did not know why he should thank Jesus. He was happy to thank God. He could see Nicholas felt the same way when Father Kabos said Jesus.

"Father, you know we are Jewish." Joseph said almost apologetically. "We don' t believe in Jesus." Nicholas said sternly, backing up Joseph.

"It's alright, then pray to God, he will hear you." Joseph bowed his head and Nicholas followed. "Dear God show these boys your love and protection, and let them understand the preponderance of evidence you have shown me that Jesus is the Messiah who returned to save us. Lord give us all the strength to be brave and believe you have sent us 'The War Angels' to protect these dear children and the village of Praznik. Thank you Lord, Amen!"

"Amen!" Both boys said together.

"And now dear boys, forgive me, I must get some more sleep, please tell the rest of the children I am ok."

With that, Joseph signaled Nicholas and they left.

58

All the way back up the secret gully Joseph wondered what evidence Father Kabos could have been talking about, that Jesus was the Messiah. He and Nicholas reached the village late that night and Joseph could see that miraculously no one had seemed to miss them except the few children who were impatiently waiting for them and their report on what they had discovered.

As the two boys joined the group, they looked brightly at the somber faces of the children crowded before them.

"Father Kabos will be all right," Joseph said with assurance. "He is sleeping and we will see him soon." Joseph saw immediately the children respond with their own smiles at his good news, and he encouraged them by going forward, squeezing arms, and patting several of them on their backs touching the heads of the younger ones. The children happily broke into individual conversations; Joseph let his gaze slowly move over them, observing each child affectionately as he continued to smile in warm possessiveness. While he did so, Nicholas casually leaned on his shoulder, waiting for his best friend to finish his silent reflection. Joseph knew this was something Nicholas had gotten used to as Joseph's companion during their adventurous travels together.

Joseph's attention went to Marjan, the red—haired boy and his younger sister, Hester, actively conversing with the children beside them. Both skinny to the point of emaciation when they had first arrived in Praznik, they had lately begun to gain a slight amount of weight, as had all the children. Their color had also begun to improve. He remembered

Marjan was a boy of about ten and Hester claimed to be seven, although Joseph had his doubts and suspected her of being much younger. For some reason, the little girl would hold her hands out and display seven fingers when anyone asked her age and protest violently when accused of being younger. She too was red-haired, and always kept close to her brother, both children happily taken by the same family.

Then, he fondly looked at Marisha standing nearby. She was also engaged in conversation, and unaware of being observed. The blonde-haired girl about the same age as Joseph was attractive and intelligent. Her influence with the children was almost as strong as Joseph's, yet like Nicholas, and the older children, she found it easy to defer to Joseph in any situation concerning their survival. If Nicholas was not already his best friend, Joseph was certain that Marisha would have been, as he found a great deal to like in this girl.

Joseph now let his gaze rest on Paul Geller. The boy returned his look without expression, without curiosity, just waiting for anything Joseph might command or reveal.

Paul Geller was the boy whom Marisha had taken such a sisterly interest.

He was tall; with hair so black, it almost appeared blue. He was strikingly handsome for a boy, with his dark curls, pale skin, and blue eyes. Yet he was a mute. He had no obvious physical impairment that any of the children could discover. He could hear and he could respond. He could not talk, no matter what. Several of the children had tried various strategies in an attempt to make him speak, only to give up in the belief his ailment must be in his mind, and only the healing of it could ever cure him.

Joseph had come to this same conclusion about Paul Geller. He had discussed this with Father Kabos. After gaining Paul's confidence and thoroughly examining him, the priest also came to believe the boy's problem was of the mind. Undoubtedly, he believed it was caused by some experience that had occurred in his recent past.

Father Kabos had confided to Joseph, Nicholas, and Marisha his plan to heal the boy and had asked these three to help him in his efforts. "My children. Paul is suffering from a wound inflicted on his mind," Joseph recalled the priest telling them." Moreover, when the mind is hurt this way, it needs assistance in helping it to get well. We must show him our love, which we are already doing. We must draw him out in gentle ways, not so obvious, until we can discover what this terrible thing was that is causing his present behavior."

Joseph's attention was now attrackted to a little girl, slightly more animated in her conversation, her small hands making wild gestures. He shook his head at the girl. It was Gilda, standing before Hester, her closest friend. She too, like Hester, claimed to be seven. It seemed to Joseph and the others, as if she were already older in her behavior. She always acted the little mother to anyone who would allow it. Of course, it amused everyone to let her play the adult, scolding them over any little misdeed. Joseph had never given a great deal of thought to how much he really knew about each of the children. He simply had grown to feel toward all of them as joined in one large close-knit family or clan, with the children still looking to him for leadership.

He continued to let his gaze wander over the relaxing faces, this time studying some of the children standing further away from him, many of whom nodded at Joseph in return. There was Nannette, and Pierre, another brother and sister who spoke French and Yiddish, and a smattering of Polish.

Joseph discovered there were still a few children he did not know as well, but only recognized. He felt a pang of guilt yet he considered the youngsters who were only familiar to him just as important as the other members of his growing family.

There were now twenty-five children in all, including him, twenty-three who had survived the escape to the mountains, and the hazardous trip to Praznik, and two more, which had been added to the group by the villagers. They were gentiles, non-Jews who were welcomed by the children into their family. Quickly they were accepted, and held in friendship but not as close as any other members. These two youngsters, a boy and a girl, were Stach and Wanda, rescued when found wandering from another village destroyed during a German bombing attack.

As Joseph watched his active little flock, some of the old fears returned, brought on by the surprise at his sudden awareness of the priest's mortality. Joseph never before considered the wellbeing of Father Kabos, thinking of the man as indestructible. What happened to him in the village gave Joseph pause, reminding him of the fearful truth that against the menace of the Nazi horde no person was safe. The fact that Joseph was unable to speak to Father Kabos, and see him when he needed, made him realize once more how dependent he and the rest of the children had become toward the priest. He thought of how even Basha looked to him for solace and advice. Father Kabos surely had to be sent by God, and now he was in deep sleep, recovering from a clash with the minions of Satan. The incident caused Joseph's security to be badly shaken. Joseph knew the Germans would come back no matter what Father Kabos said. He wanted to believe, but his few short years on the street made him decided he must also have a plan of his own to protect his clan.

PART IV

THE LONELY LOVERS

59

Marvin picked a stick of straw out of his sock that was irritating his ankle. He was propped up on a wooden cot built into the wall of a small lean-to hut he and the crew were gathered in. He smelled the damp wood and hay mingled with smoke from the fire. Leaning his head back, he stared into the burning embers of the fire-pit. The entire crew in the tiny lean-to were engrossed in conversation that was gradually building in volume, and Marvin realized he could no longer allow himself the luxury of intermittent dozing.

The men were definitely agitated and pissed off about something. He focused on the conversation and listened to their expressions of dissatisfaction. They felt like virtual prisoners by the Partisans. He could hear the men were feeling the derisiveness of the laughing and jokes continuously directed at them by the partisans. They were always telling them what to do, never asking. They prodded them with their rifle butts, and pushed and shoved them around. They remembered even having to ask if they could urinate, that really riled everyone. When they were hungry they were either laughed at or thought weak, but rarely fed on any regular basis. It was obvious the crew wanted to go home and this time they were ready to take action to get there.

"Well, what about Spain, or Switzerland?" Dunham chimed in. "Yeah, maybe we can get these Polacks to take us," Shaw said. "Are you kidding. I wouldn't trust 'em for spit, they wanted to kill us," Haply replied.

"But we're allies," Dunham said.

"Go tell them that," Haply responded.

"Maybe they won't cut your throat—not right away."

Marvin rose up and calmly brushed off more straw while he calculated all the facts. The Partisans had certainly contemplated killing them all, and even though things had settled down the Poles had not shown any sign that these men were comrades in a common cause, nor did the future feel promising for an equal alliance of any type between them. "Then we'll do it ourselves," Shaw said. "You're dreaming," Ballard told him. "You got any idea where we are? Or, which way to go? Or, what we'd use for food? Or, how to keep from freezing our asses off while we're doing it?" There was a pause and they turned to Marvin. "Frank's right, without the help of these partisans, we couldn't get ten feet in these mountains. Not without some German patrol chewing us up."

In spite of the facts, Marvin started to feel the formulation of an idea way in the back of his mind, which was shelved as soon as Father Kabos, and then Basha entered the hut doorway. "I'd like to look at your men and see how they are doing" Father Kabos politely asked. Marvin turned and looked at Basha then nodded his head all right to Father Kabos. "Sure father" he replied. Basha stepped aside as Marvin came out of the hut and stood next to her. "How are they doing"? She motioned with her head towards the men.

"They all want to go home" he replied.

"Like children," she said with a sigh, and took a few steps away from the hut. Both of them slowly walked toward a large pine tree and stopped underneath. Marvin looked directly at her dark eyes for the first time. Her soft brown hair hung over one of them and he wanted to brush it aside so he could see it better. As he looked at her, he hesitated then she said, "Did you eat today"? Marvin thought for a moment, he hadn't eaten anything since last night when he had a bit of bread and some old cheese. "I'm alright," he said with a smile, "Back in the States I probably would have pancakes and eggs this morning, and— its normal to eat three square meals a day."

"Ah, . . . Americans," she said in half wonderment, and in half disbelief. Marvin could see by her face it was hard for her to fathom a land where everyone was free to do as they wished, and eat as much as they wanted. "I felt the joy of freedom one time in Kracow. I learned some English from a man I thought was so different from other men."

Then, she asked, "Is it true, you can walk into any store, and buy anything you want any time?"

"Yes, —yes it is," Marvin said as if he too almost didn't believe it. "And, you can drive down the street a little further and see a movie if you wanted, or just drive around town." She had heard about movies but cars, . . .

"Does everyone own a car?" She had to ask.

"Well, almost every family does."

"Everyone must be very rich in America."

"No, but if you work hard anyone can become rich if that's what you wanted." He saw she was genuinely amazed at it all. Marvin watched as she got caught in the ether of this wonderland far across the other side of the world. "Maybe it's just making believe to give people hope that somewhere, someplace was protected and safe. You are a real person who came from what seems like, how you say, a utopian society? The women of my village are all curious and want to know about these strange men from America." Now he felt comfortable with her being so close and looking at him the way she did, and he wanted to tell her more. Just as he was about to speak she said, "Do all the men from America look so—" He could see her struggling with an English word, and she said, "scrubbed." He laughed, and looked at her grappling for another word.

"Do you mean, —washed"? He asked.

"Yes, something like that." She said, still searching for the word.

"In America we like to shower or bathe once a day, sometimes twice." He saw her hide consternation at this idea. "We would like to bathe once a day too, but it's not possible." She said while looking off into the forest. America and Kracow now both seemed worlds away she thought.

"And the women, what are they like?" she asked, this time looking directly into his eyes. He stopped and thought for a moment, and then looking down at his muddy boots he remembered Betty. She wasn't his first girlfriend, but she was the first girl he had started to feel real love for, then the war came and everything changed. "They're —kind." All of a sudden he didn't want to talk about other women so he changed the subject and continued with a growing smile,"—and very, very curious!" A bit of a smile forced its way onto her face. "So, they're not that much different from us" She said, and they both laughed. Marvin felt her starting to relax.

"It seems every man I have been with somehow let me down, mistreated or abused me. But I still have hope that someday there will be better times for all, and maybe then, . . ." her thoughts faded as Father Kabos came out of the hut and signaled for them to come over.

Marvin was on his way to the hut in the instant Father Kabos called them and Basha followed. He wanted to know how his men were. Father Kabos explained to Marvin, "Lieutenant Ryan's leg is showing signs of improvement. The bandages need to be removed and new ones put on every couple of days. Ryan is still weak and needs care but if he keeps improving the wound will heal properly."

Marvin was grateful for that and saw Father Kabos look at him directly. "The temperatures will be falling down below freezing and will stay that way in this high country. It might be better for the men if they went back down into the village for the remainder of the winter." Marvin also realized if they did, there would be less room for confrontation with the partisans. Then he looked at Basha and knew this would give him more time to talk to her if they were all staying in the village. He readily agreed to move out of the camp as soon as possible. "What if the Germans come back?" He stared at father Kabos. Father Kabos said, "I don't think the Germans will come in the winter, and if they do we will see them in time, and know what to do."

Marvin made his final considerations. It would be futile to think of going anywhere during the winter in these mountains. If the Germans or Partisans didn't kill them, the wild animals, treacherous terrain, or the cold probably would. So, it was settled, they would winter in the village of Praznik.

When Marvin returned inside the hut, Haply and Shaw seemed to have something pressing and urgent to tell him. He told them it would have to wait until he explained the winter plans to the men. Out of respect for the Major, the two men waited impatiently while he told all of them the plans to move. The men were somewhat relieved that they weren't going to have to contend with the partisans the whole winter in the camp, but were dismayed as the reality sunk in that they were really stuck there, and out of the action of the war. "Sir," Haply burst out. He couldn't wait another second. Marvin looked at him. "I don't think I'm staying the winter," Haply continued with a shaky voice.

"What he means Sir, is we would like your permission not to stay." Shaw followed up in a more conclusive manner. Marvin looked at the two of them and then at the rest of the men in disbelief. Everyone had gone silent. "Do you mean what I think you mean?" Marvin asked incredulously.

"Yes Sir, we would like your permission to escape."

60

Marvin stared at all the men and said, "Does that mean all of you"? Most of the men's heads were looking down. Shaw replied, "No Sir, it's just the two of us, the two of us to Switzerland".

"Switzerland? You'd be lucky to make it out of this forest much less Switzerland," Marvin said, almost half-chuckling. Didn't we already talk about this? It's three countries away, almost 500 miles, unless you go straight through Germany, and wouldn't that be fun," he said to all of them.

"We've got it figured out Sir," Shaw explained. "I saw a large river just off the tip of my tail gun going to the south as we were coming in over the mountains."

"One of the villagers told us it goes all the way to the border." Haply chimed in feeling his confidence growing.

"And he said it wouldn't be hard to build a small raft and take it down all the way, and the Germans don't stop loggers and fisherman that much."

"The river is filled with loggers and we'd fit right in." Shaw added. Marvin, with a slight change in his voice said, "What happens if you're lucky enough to reach the border?"

"We cross and find the Czech underground, we know they have an underground, other flyers have told us many times." Shaw said.

"That's it? You just cross the border and hope to find the Czech underground?" Marvin said expecting more. There was a pause amongst them and then Shaw said, "The Czech's will know what to do, they've done it before with our guys". Marvin shook his head, "It sounds too risky, and there are too many ifs, if you get out of the forest, if you get to the river, if you can build a raft, if the Germans don't stop you, if you cross the border and the big if, if you can find the underground before the Germans find you!"

Haply jumped up to attention and finally said, "Sir, —with all due respect, doesn't the Army Air Force tell us it's our duty to escape and, we should at least try to cause the enemy as much trouble as possible?"

Marvin reflected for a moment while all the men were now looking at him for his answer. He had put himself in this spot and he could have nipped it in the bud at the beginning of the conversation and been done with it. However, these two men had pushed him to give an answer. If he said yes, he was opening up a real can of worms and jeopardizing everyone, his men, the village, the partisans, and . . . If they got caught too close to the village the Germans would surely be all over them in no time. If he said no, he would seem unreasonable and would actually be disregarding an Army Air Force directive to escape. It was up to his discretion to evaluate if it was safe to escape. *When was it ever safe to escape?* The men waited while Marvin grasped for time in his brain to think, more time that he didn't have, and then he said, "You're going to need some time to get supplies together from the Village."

"Then we have your permission to go" Haply asked.

"If you're crazy enough to go then I guess I might be crazy enough to let you." Marvin reluctantly replied. Then Shaw said, "Then it's agreed, we should be able to leave in the next few days or so." Marvin looked at the rest of the men and said, "The rest of us will stick together and dig in at the village for the winter and hope the Germans don't catch you two before you get to the border." It didn't seem like any of the others were interested in rolling the dice with the odds Haply and Shaw were up against. At least for the moment Marvin saw the men felt justified someone was going to try to escape. Marvin knew he couldn't let any of them go. Many things could happen in the next few days and he hoped he could find a solution to the problem before the two of them were ready to leave. Marvin watched the men react to the idea.

Haply and Shaw, with smiles on their faces, started soliciting from the crew odds and ends that they might need on the trip, a cigarette or two from Dunham, a piece of chocolate from Ballard, a pocket knife from Novak. The men patted them on the back and wished them well.

When they got down to the Village, they got whatever food could be spared, and some old clothes to look like loggers. They wished Tony Stiles was still alive; he could have given them better directions and maybe even shown them a way to follow the stars at night. They hoped the Major would give them some pointers before they left, "Sure, I know how to read the stars." Marvin replied.

He walked out of the hut in search of Basha. He thought better of telling her and Father Kabos what had happened with the men, it would just cause them concern, and besides he did not intend to let Haply and Shaw escape. His thoughts now went to the hike down the mountain.

He walked up behind a tree where Basha was sitting next to a fire-pit and Szabla was gazing into the burning coals. He unobtrusively listened to their conversation.

"Well—?" Szabla said to Basha. Basha poked a big stick in the fire pit and replied, "If the Germans come back the Americans and the children will have to go to the camp."

"No, if the Germans come they will be looking for the Americans, it's their fault, I say kill them and be done with it" he said emphatically. Throwing the stick in the fire Basha spun around and said in a burst, "Is that what you do to innocent men from another country who come to help us?'"

"Help us! They can't even help themselves" he spat, "They're just more trouble!" Basha walked towards him and continued, "And how would you kill them, shoot them so the Germans can hear the shots?" She was in his face now,

"Or maybe you could come up to each one and say, excuse me I am going to quietly stab you with my knife now!" She plunged her fist into his stomach. He stumbled back surprised more from his allowing her to get that close then from the punch.

"You push me too far woman, you never listen to me," he grumbled.

"Listen to you? You listen to me! They can be helpful in the village. They can mend the roofs, fix the fences, feed the ducks and pigs, clean up their dung, and do all the things that you and your men love so much to do in the village. Then you could be free to run around the country and kill," she yelled, throwing her hands in the air and continuing, "And if the Germans come, the Americans can come back and stay in your camp and clean it up—it can use it! You probably won't be there anyway while you're running around killing." He immediately replied back, "Is that all you think I do? Do you think I kill for fun? I take risks with my men to bring you and this village back things you need. If it weren't for me there would be no village." Basha replied with the same tone of voice, "Oh yes, and things you need too! Don't try to pretend you do this just for us. Every time you come back from one of your raids with all your plunder from killing and stealing, you put us all in danger with the Germans, and with God. Using your way of thinking, you're the one that is nothing but trouble; maybe we should all kill you!"

Szabla was too frustrated to continue. He waved his hand down and stomped off. Basha looked toward him as he left and said, "Good riddance!" Marvin wondered what she was thinking. Then he saw her get up and walk toward the hut where Marvin was supposed to be, but she stopped, turned, and walked away.

* * *

Basha felt compelled to be with Marvin. *For what purpose did I want to see him now? Maybe because he makes me feel comfortable, or maybe it was the newness —it's just a distraction. Can I afford a distraction now? No!*

She felt a little dizzy and sat down. Certain feelings rose up when she was emotionally charged. Szabla did that to her. She pondered and saw Marvin in her mind, then Adam, then Szabla, always Szabla. She wished she could get him out of her mind. *It's the high camp; this camp always has an effect on me.* She was glad they were leaving the camp in the morning and she resigned herself not to come back to the high camp anymore unless of course Marvin or the children were there.

She realized something was happening to her that was uncontrollable. She wanted to stop the feelings and the thinking, but she couldn't. In the past, she had always been able to stay in control of herself. She had mastered self-control a long time ago. *Was it self-denial? I must talk to Father Kabos about it. Maybe tomorrow morning I will talk to him. No, there would be no time while taking the trail down. Once they were all settled in the village I will talk to him about my feelings.*

She heard the wind blowing over the tops of the trees and watched the smoke from the high campfires climb up in columns through the still part of the forest, and then, when it reached the top it scattered and dissipated into the moonlit night. The camp was finally asleep.

From her straw bed, Basha stared up at the moon through the window of her little hut. The faces of the women in the village wafted through her mind like drifting photos, then scattered like the smoke in the trees, and then, there was Marvin.

Basha awoke the next morning, put her sheepskin vest over her wool dress, and tied her hair in the accustomed scarf most polish women wore. An early dawn mist drifted low on the forest floor as she walked to the horse pulled cart that was already loaded up and standing outside her hut. She reached for the reins, and the horse blew out its nostrils a small cloud of warm breath into the chilled air.

She saw the Partisans were ready to move down the mountain, and they were checking last minute preparations to leave, putting out fires, covering tracks, and removing all signs that anybody had recently been in the camp.

Marvin and his men were still asleep when she came to their hut to wake them. She brought them some sour milk, black bread, and mashed potato pancakes loaded with caraway seeds.

The men gobbled it down after she told them it might be the only thing they would eat all day. Basha looked at Marvin with a smile and said, "Sorry, we have no eggs this morning, but we do have some very good pancakes."

When they had finished eating the trek down the mountain began. It took a good part of the morning to navigate the rough terrain and she was glad when they arrived at the village a short time after noon

61

Marvin scrutinized everything as they passed by the Bakery, Tavern, Church, and a few small shops that were at the center of the village. The other sod and log houses stretched out down one dirt road then became randomly scattered around the adjacent hills and knolls.

He watched as most of the people of the village were milling about the street watching the strange Americans arrive with the Partisans. It seemed odd considering the dangers it implied, but they looked happy to see them again, and many had smiles on their faces. He spotted two old men sitting on a log bench in front of the tavern smoking pipes with sharply curved stems. They wore coarse white homespun trousers, sheepskin coats and felt hats with bands of beads and seashells.

Marvin listened to Novak explain to the crew that the two old men were wearing the old traditional garb of the Gorals 'Mountain Men' of the region. One of them had a Ciupaga, which was a combined walking stick and ax.

"They come from the High Tatras where it is said one finds the true Poles. This strain escaped the invasion of the Tartars who had camped in the nearby Carpathian Mountains many generations ago." Then Novak continued, "The elders of the village said most of these bold mountaineers never knew serfdom in the old days, but lived as highwaymen, robbing merchants and the Aristocracy as they crossed the Tatras."

Marvin and the crew were impressed with Novak's knowledge of Poland and his easy command of the language. Then he noticed the women of the village clustered about and gawked again at the strange

American men wondering what it would be like to know them. One of them picked Dunham out, then they made eye contact, and she gave him a shy smile.

Marvin recalled it was the one Dunham had amused when they first came into the village. She wove in and out of the crowd watching him as they marched down the road to where the men were to be quartered.

Beata, the full figured woman who earlier had expressed an interest in Novak caught his eye as she gave Novak an alluring smile. She didn't go with the crowd, but Novak saw a 'come back and see me' nod from her. Marvin hoped he wouldn't take the offer.

Marvin turned his head and saw Marjan, Hester and some of the other younger children closely following the men. Geese and ducks waddled after the children as they went on their way to the other side of town. The children kept looking at the backs of the men. One would dart up a few feet away, and then run back and talk to the others, and then another would do the same. Novak attempted to talk in Polish to the next one, which was Gilda, but she just froze in her tracks when he addressed her. Novak had heard them talking about wings, or flying, but wasn't sure. Marvin came up alongside Novak and asked, "What's going on?"

"I'm not sure Major, but there's something really peculiar about these kids"

"There sure are a lot of them"

"And no men anywhere,"

"Yeah. I noticed that before."

"Except for those two old hoots at the tavern and the partisans, it's just women and kids. And something else; I don't think these kids belong to this village either."

"Then where do they come from?" Marvin asked.

"Beats me," Novak responded.

As the group reached the end of the dirt road, a large sod hut jutted out of the side of a hill and they halted.

Marvin kept the men organized as the partisans grunted orders and shoved them towards the doorway of the hut. Novak saw the red headed Marjan and tried to ask him some questions, but the boy recoiled from him. Realizing it was hopeless Novak joined the men and entered the hut.

The children remained outside the hut as if they were waiting to see something happen which they didn't want to miss.

Marvin was happy to see the inside of the hut was larger than the one at the high camp. The men had much more room to stretch out and there were enough cots for everyone.

"When do you think we're going to eat Major?" Haply asked.

"I don't know. Novak and I will go talk to the partisans after we settle in here and get Ryan squared away."

The men began finding their own little niche in the hut. They had all acted as if they were just trying their cots out with a make believe nap, but after a while they dozed off into real sleep, and one by one started snoring. They were snoring so loud that Marvin could see the children outside sneak up to the shutters on the windows and peek in to see what was happening. Then Gilda said, "I didn't know Angels snored."

That night Marvin observed that Haply and Shaw ate only a small portion of their dinner, and saved the rest in a leather bag. He witnessed Magda and Beata earlier bring the crew their dinner hoping to talk with Dunham and Novak. At Novak's request in Polish, the two women later came back with some clothes altered to look like loggers with big felt hats and a Ciupaga. Then it became clear to Marvin, Haply and Shaw weren't wasting any time, they wanted to leave, and they did.

When everyone was asleep except him, he watched Haply and Shaw sneak out of the hut, past the Partisan guard, and across the road headed into the forest. With much angst, he let them go.

The next morning he awoke with the sound of scuffling feet and loud shouting. He saw Ballard looking out the window and what he saw made him yell for Marvin. Marvin jumped up and headed for the door with the rest of the men following.

Opening the door, he was immediately confronted by two partisans with rifles, past them he could see other Partisans gathered in a circle on the road. The Partisans were yelling and grunting as if they were at a boxing match.

Haply broke through the circle and came sliding into the dirt in front of the cabin as the partisans cheered. They shoved Shaw on the ground next to him. Haply, though bloodied and bruised, seeing Marvin at the door, and the crew at the window, got up and took a flying leap at the Partisan who had shoved them. He knocked him down and the crew all cheered. Immediately the furious Partisan was up brandishing a rifle bayonet and took a wide swipe at Haply.

Marvin struggled to get out of the hut, but the two Partisans at the door held him back. Haply seeing the struggle ran up to one of the guards who had pushed Marvin and grabbed his knife. The partisan with the bayonet and Haply began to circle each other and all the men became silent. Just when the fight looked like it was going to get ugly Szabla jumped in between them drawing his wicked looking knife and stopped the confrontation. The Villagers had come to see what was going on and quite a crowd gathered at the edge of town. Szabla, with his knife still out, stomped into the hut and pulled Novak into the middle of the crowd. He loudly told Novak something in Polish and pointed to Marvin. Marvin stepped out of the hut and Novak translated. Szabla said, "I will not allow stupid Americans to get captured and lead the Germans back to Praznik. One of you will die next time."

Marvin attempted to reason with Szabla, arguing they are supposed to be allies fighting on the same side. Szabla spat contemptuously at this and threw his knife into the wooden door next to Marvin. It was apparent the conversation was done. Marvin waved the men to disperse, and the guards left the hut.

It seemed the crew was free to go into the village. The ultimatum from Szabla was enough to keep any one from attempting to escape again, and Marvin didn't need to say anymore. No one else was seriously contemplating escape before; now it was absolutely out of the question. Marvin wondered why Basha had not come to their rescue during this altercation and decided to go with Novak to find her.

62

In the village everyone stared at them, they were friendly stares, but still it gave Marvin a prickly feeling in the back of his head as they continued towards the center square. Just before they reached the center, Beata came out of the bakery and intentionally crossed the street to greet them.

She smiled at Marvin and handed them each a piece of black bread from her basket, then Novak spoke to her in Polish. He asked where they could find Basha, with a surprised look, she pointed behind them. Novak turned around and looked at the shop. They had stopped directly in front of the apartment Basha was living in. Then in Polish Beata said, "Why don't you let your Captain go see Basha, and you come home with me".

Novak, with a big smile, explained where they were to Marvin leaving out Beata's wanton plea. Marvin turned around and looked at the shop. There was a big ornate bell above the old carved wooden door at the entrance to the two-story shop. A small dusty pane of stained glass just above eyesight stretched across the outside. Under the glass on a wood panel, a painted name with a half washed out Star of David could not be read. The shop, boarded up and unused for some time, smelled of dust. Marvin rang the bell. Its deep resounding ring surprised the Americans. It wasn't just the first tone, but the many harmonic over tones that kept ringing in their ears that enchanted them. When no one answered the door Beata suggested that they go to the Tavern, drop Marvin off, and then she and Novak could go to her hut. Just then, Marvin looked up and saw the wooden carved shutters of the second story swing open, Basha stuck her head out of the window and stared at them, then went down stairs.

She opened the front door letting them in. Inside they could see that the front room had been a business at one time, but seemed deserted now. Violins, Italian and Polish guitars, as well as religious carvings covered the walls. Marvin thought the artisan who had done this handiwork was obviously no longer here, otherwise dust would not have covered everything. Novak immediately touched one of the guitars on the wall. He asked Basha in Polish if he could look at it. Basha asked if he knew how to play, and he said his Grandfather from Poland had taught him back in the states. She told him his Polish was very good and he could stay, but she and Marvin had to talk.

Grabbing a loaf of black bread from Beata she told Marvin to follow her as she went upstairs. Marvin hesitated, and then Basha said, "Come up, for breakfast" and she held up the bread. Marvin followed Basha up the creaking staircase and glanced back at Novak and Beata. Beata had decided to be patient, sat down on an old stool, and watched with great interest as Novak gently dusted off the finely carved Polish guitar.

Marvin liked Basha's room, it was simple and clean. It had a table, a chair, a bed, and some shelves. The only piece of luxury was a small handsomely carved bookcase in the corner with an oil lamp on top. Everywhere books filled nooks. Marvin wondered if Basha read them, or the artisan who owned the shop left them there. He wondered what her relationship had been and why he wasn't here, then he said, "Where are the men of this village?"

"The Germans came and took or killed them. They left us with nothing." She replied.

"Did they say where they were taking them?"

"No, nothing."

"Then why didn't you leave and go down to a city?"

"It is the same all over Poland; we hear in some places it's even worse. The Germans come; they rape, kill, and burn whole villages leaving nobody. They have no conscience, they are evil." She tore the bread in two putting one piece on a plate in front of Marvin. He stared at it but didn't eat. Basha put a teakettle on a burner and continued. "If it wasn't for Szabla we would all be dead."

"He is a bully and a brute," Marvin said.

"You don't understand him American, he and his men saved this Village! They brought food, helped with the harvest, and gave us the strength to stay alive. He has brought us much and we have much to thank him for."

"What about the children?" Basha flinched at the question. After a reticent pause, she began to tell him, slowly, the whole story. Marvin tore off a piece of bread and just listened.

Basha explained what had happened with the train, and what the trains meant. How all over Poland, trains shipped people to the death camps. Death camps from which no one returned. It was part of a plan for systematic extermination. She told him how the Germans mowed down the children with machine guns and how Szabla had saved them, bringing them back to Praznik.

Then finally, after all the bread had been eaten and washed down with two cups of tea, she said, "Before the children came, we were a village without hope, without men, without a future —just waiting to die. Then an act of God brought them to us, gave us back our future—-— and there is nothing we would not do to see that future protected. Do you understand that, American?" Marvin nodded his head in understanding. "All the more reason for us to get out of here," he told her, looking at her with questioning eyes. *Would she help them?* That was the question he was thinking and he asked, "Will you help us get to the border?" Basha studied him for a moment then replied, "It will not be easy, and if I can I will help."

The sun was squeezing through the top portion of the stained glass windowpane when Basha and Marvin came back down stairs. The light was throwing colors all over the carvings and instruments on the walls. Novak was playing guitar and Beata was at his side in awe. He had just finished playing a mazurka from the wild Oberek, and now he started to play the Zbojnicki, the fire dance song of the Gorale's that his Great Grandfather had taught him.

Marvin could see that the two women wondered how it was possible he could play music like that, especially their music from Poland. Even Marvin marveled at the sound of it. There was no question; Novak had more than a talent for it. It came from a deeper place, and for just a brief moment, there in the mid-morning colored light dancing in the shop, the four of them were transported to another world, forgetting their troubles and the war going on with the world outside.

* * *

Later that afternoon, Basha paid a visit to the tavern where Szabla and many of the Partisans had gathered to celebrate. She walked inside the tavern were there was an abundance of beer and vodka being drunk. The partisans had acquisitioned it on one of their raids somewhere near Kracow and the tavern wall behind the bar had row upon row of the same labeled bottles. Basha preferred the Miod, a local fermented honey drink, served steaming hot in the winter. It was similar to Old English mead. She took her drink and sat down next to Szabla and said, "We need to talk." He looked at her and replied, "So talk." Then Basha asked, "How long do you intend to keep the Americans here in the village? Szabla sidestepped her question and replied, "The Germans will be back, and it will be because of them that they come back as I have told you. There have been many German planes buzzing like birds of prey over these mountains. If just one of those vultures' swoops down and sees them what do you think? Or, if they try to escape and are caught? The Germans will come and rape all the women, kill everyone, and burn the village to the ground, do you doubt that?"

"That is why we must get Greg and his men out."

"Gregg?" He exclaimed, "Oh, so you are worried about him, don't think I haven't noticed the way that tall one looks at you. When are you going to show some feelings for me? Basha shrugged. "To tell you the truth," he finally admitted, "I am thinking of the best way to kill them!"

Basha became angrier. "You know you have been living in these mountains for so long you have become like one of the wild animals in it. Do you even remember what is right and wrong anymore? We must find a way to help the Americans."

"I'm not about to risk the lives of my men for these outsiders." Basha insisted they must help. Szabla had enough and angrily responded so the whole tavern could hear.

"You want to help them? Then do it yourself! I want no part of them!" Basha stared at him contemptuously then abruptly turned and headed out of the tavern, a great and proud peasant woman with a will as strong as iron.

Szabla sat there for several moments, clearly uncomfortable, then fuming with anger he rushed out the back door. A heavy snow was falling. He threw his beer bottle down the path towards Basha who headed towards the church. He called after her, "Woman! You always push me too far." He ran a few more feet and in his frustration picked up some snow and threw it towards her, "You hear me!" he shouted.

Basha continued walking staunchly towards the church, ignoring him. Her thoughts now were only of what she was going to say to Father Kabos, and how she would explain all her feelings to him. Feelings that felt natural, but only God could help her hold back.

63

The Argos inverted v8 air-cooled single engine sputtered its reliable drone as it kept the German 156 Storch in the air just above tree top level. It was slower than the other planes Reinstock had been using, and his FW was in for repairs. The Storch had short takeoff and landing capabilities, and was used to ferry officers, and medevac's in the area. It was now a recon observation plane, and Reinstock had requisitioned it and its pilot for the day.

He peered out over the mountainous terrain below with his Ziess binoculars and signaled the pilot to turn. He made the pilot circle an area, then crisscrossed over it making a grid formation for many hours. This went on until he was satisfied nothing was in the area after carefully studying the ground. Then they went back, refueled and did it again over another area. The particular section they were buzzing was very suspicious to Reinstock; he intuitively felt something that made him anxious. He wondered if he was flying over the same exact route as the B-17 bomber? If he only knew, he would keep the pilot going for many more hours.

The pilot signaled to the fuel gauge. Reinstock cursed and made the signal to go back. He continued looking for signs on the way. *I would much rather be in my Focke Wulf 189,—the "Eye in the Sky,"* as the Luftwaffe called it. It was easier to fly, had twice the range, and a huge RB50/30 camera. He could later review photographs and it would have picked up anything he had missed. Such was his luck; none had been in the area. The airport commander said that most of the 189's went to the Eastern front in Russia.

Reinstock remembered training in an FW-189 in his earlier years as a pilot. It was a superb plane and the winner of a concourse by the Luftwaffe in 1937. He decided he would demand one from the front, maybe even two. *Goering himself had given me authority, and the Fhurer had personally commended me, so I could certainly demand a plane or two for my disposal.*

The Storch quickly descended onto the short mountain airstrip. Upon getting out of the plane, he was greeted by Kramer, his military attaché, who saluted and immediately handed him an important communique. The note informed Reinstock reports of partisan activity in the area, and prisoners captured. Reinstock was now rolling down the mountain road in his Mercedes-Benz on his way to the flat lands heading for the local SS headquarters in the area.

An hour later, Reinstock pulled up in front of the SS headquarters. Stepping inside the building he saw several officers standing uncomfortably before their commander, SS Major Otto Hassman, the same man assigned to stamp out the partisan movement in the district. They were reporting another recent partisan raid on another of their supply convoys. The officers were explaining how easily the enemy again seemed to vanish. They took hostages in reprisal for this last attack, which they claimed was unusually barbarous. Hassman told them the idea of taking hostages was futile. "What does it take to find and destroy the partisans responsible," he bellowed. Hassman dismissed the officers and turned to Reinstock, who silently had observed the interview, and said, "You see Colonel Reinstock; I have been diligently directing most of my efforts in locating that particularly hated band of partisans led by that man I told you about, Szabla. He is of course a most elusive man, and I believe he has been the cause of your troubles as well as mine, and for many disturbances in the area. It won't be long before we find him."

"Of course, so I have heard you say, but in the meantime I would like to see your prisoners you captured in the last raid."

"Yahvoel, Herr Reinstock, please follow me."

The two men went outside the building where several partisan prisoners were dragged before them. "Try not to kill them this time." Hassman told one of his officers. "The Colonel and I would like to know where they came from." The officer saluted and turned to the worried-looking partisans. Hassman looked at Reinstock and asked in an almost obsequious manner, "Herr Reinstock, is there anything else I can do for you to accommodate your stay with us." "Yes, do you have a direct line to Berlin?" This question made Hassman a little nervous and he said, "Of course Herr Reinstock, but may I ask what is your purpose in calling Berlin?"

"You may ask Major, but I do not have to tell you my business, However, since you are assisting me in this important matter, and it is in both our interests, you may listen to my conversation."

Rienstock saw Hassman was relieved by the fact that it hadn't seemed to be a call about him, or his performance, but he looked like he was not sure he wanted to be any part of the conversation he was about to hear. Communicating with Berlin always opened one up to misinterpretations that could lead to unforeseen consequences in the future. Rienstock was sure it was hard enough to deal with Berlin concerning his own operations. He knew Hassman must be treading a thin line, and to be involved in any other complications would surely not be in his best interest. They entered Hassman's office and shut the door. "I assure you this is very private, please use my personal line." Hassman motioned Reinstock behind his desk, and Reinstock called Goering's office at Luftwaffe Headquarters in Berlin.

"This is Colonel Ernst Von Reinstock calling,——Yes, Yes thank you for remembering. Yes, it was a great day and the Fhurer was so generous . . . Yes, you can help me. I need two planes sent to SS Major Otto Hassman in Poland. I am on a most important mission for the Reich . . . Yes, I need two 189 Ohm's (Owls), . . . of course I know most of them have been sent to the Eastern front, I need two of them here now! —I understand your position and the paper work, now I want you to understand my position! I also want your best pilot. Get me that hero pilot who crashed in Russia, and who bravely escaped back to our lines by himself. What was his name? Oh yes . . . Lothar Mothes, I want him! —I want to make myself perfectly clear, I do not wish to disturb director Goering with these minor details, but if I don't have those planes here in 48 hours I will personally call him, and I will explain your new position to him! . . . Good, I hope there is no need for that also. Good, good bye."

Reinstock coolly hung up the phone and smiled at Hassman. Hassman displayed an expression that he was truly impressed. Hassman reached for a box on his desk and said, "Cigar, Herr Reinstock?"

"No, please inform me when my planes arrive, and give me any information you extract from your partisan prisoners." Hassman jumped up as Reinstock came around the desk and headed for the door. The two men parted with a salute, and a "Heil Hitler."

64

Marvin stood in front of the Chapel; Father Kabos wished to discuss several things with Marvin and had asked him to come by. They chatted about what they were going to do after the war and how the men were. Father Kabos had a way of bringing things out of people in a natural easy manner. Marvin wondered if Basha had confessed her feelings to Father Kabos.

Just as he finished that thought, Father Kabos asked him what he felt about Basha.

"That's very personal." Marvin replied,

"Oh, I see. That is alright my son."

Marvin and he were ending their conversation as they stood in the doorway of the church. "Ryan seems to be improving." Father Kabos exclaimed. From the corner of his eye, Marvin could see some partisans on a hill just outside the village. They were laboriously carrying several large crates over the rise. Marvin didn't remember seeing a house, or anything for that matter, over that rise. He looked at father Kabos curiously. Father Kabos tried not to show he noticed what he was looking at. Marvin excused himself and started to leave. "Well, thank you for coming, and God Bless you my son," Marvin quickly departed and headed towards the rise.

Marvin was lying in a patch of snow just at the crest of the rise watching the partisans loading crates and supplies off a cart. He watched as they carried the contraband half way up the mountain then seemed to disappear into the snow. Marvin wanted a closer look and slowly crept towards the place where they were unloading the cart. He glanced behind him making sure no one was following and saw Father Kabos trailing behind.

The partisans had finished, covered up their tracks and were heading down the mountain when Father Kabos finally reached Marvin. "Father, what are you doing? Get down!" Marvin whispered loudly. As Father Kabos crouched below Marvin's perch he said, "I might ask you the same question my son, what are you doing?"

"I'm going over there to see what is in that mountain." Marvin observed the last of the partisans leave and stood up. "I don't think that would be wise my son." Father Kabos pleaded. "Why father?" Father Kabos stood up next to Marvin, looked him in the eyes, and said, "They would kill you if you were not with me."

Marvin was going over to investigate no matter what but now decided it might be better to go with Father Kabos. The two men crossed a small barranca and climbed half way up the mountain. Marvin could see that behind the little glade of snow-covered trees was a rock formation, which seemed to be growing out of the mountain. Behind one big rock, looking like part of the mountain itself was an entrance to a cave.

Large icicles hung from the top of the entrance covered with the light falling snow that was now everywhere. Marvin looked in all directions to see that nobody had followed them, or watched as they went in.

He was not sure what to expect, and Father Kabos took the lead. He realized immediately that Father Kabos had been here before as the priest reached behind a rock and found a torch, lit it, and proceeded through a short maze of overhanging ledges and entranceways. Suddenly he stopped by one at the end. It opened up into a large cavern. Inside, he lit two other torches and a lantern.

What the light illuminated in the cavern totally took Marvin by surprise. Marvin felt he had entered a treasure trove of various and sundry supplies. Crates and boxes were stacked in the middle of the cave. Food cans and rations were everywhere. "These must be captured goods taken during various raids by the partisans and hidden here until needed", he said. "Yes, my son." Beside foodstuffs, Marvin rummaged over many truck items, auto parts, and equipment. There were things like B-17 radios; .50 caliber mounted machine guns, stacks of aircraft ammunition belts and several first aid kits. In a dark corner, he saw a large lump with canvass draped over it. He lifted the canvass and saw two large chests with ornate carvings and handles that looked polish, and then he quickly covered it back. Marvin asked Father Kabos, "Where did all this American aircraft equipment come from."

"From all over, The Americans and English have lost many planes and their wreckage is everywhere. The partisans just-simply take what they can use. They say Poland is an airplane graveyard." Marvin stared thoughtfully at the scavenged aircraft parts.

Now the formulation of his past idea was starting to solidify in the back of his brain.

"My son, we must go now, it is not safe for you to be here, and you must not tell anyone we were here."

"And, these, what are these Father?" He pointed at the decorated chests and lifted the canvass again, which seemed out of place nestled in with the ammunition boxes. "They look like dowry chests, come we must go!" Kabos said.

Marvin felt the danger of all this knowledge, and the two men cautiously left the cave making sure no one had seen them. As they descended down the mountain Father Kabos reiterated to Marvin, "Now that you know this vital secret of Praznik, it would not be wise to tell anyone!" As Marvin covered their tracks in the snow with a piece of brush he assured Father Kabos he would not divulge Prazniks secret, and that his intentions towards the village were always for its safety. Then he thought; *now my plan made much more sense and I can now certainly explain it to the men.*

65

Marvin warmed himself next to the fire in the crews hut. He broke his thoughtful gaze into the fire when some of the women of the village brought the crew a dinner of cooked goose, garlic potatoes, caraway seed bread, and steaming Moid. The men ravenously devoured all the food and settled down, lit up cigarettes, and were about to listen to what Marvin had to say when Haply started in again. "I don't care what you guys think, I still say we ought to get outta here" Shaw again chimed in with the same reason, "It's our duty to try and escape".

"Here we go again" Ballard exclaimed. Then Marvin changed the subject and began to tell them why he had wanted them all back to the hut.

"I think I have a way to get home!" he said. The men listened as he continued. "There is one way, but it's a long shot and dangerous. A lot more dangerous than if we tried walking out of here. But it's a way that could bring us all home together." Dunham, sarcastically said, "We could pretend we're a flock of birds and just fly outta here."

"That's right," Marvin said. "That's exactly what I had in mind." The men all stared at him, not sure they understood. Marvin looked in the men's astonished faces. He saw Harper wasn't surprised.

"We'd never get it off the ground." Harper said.

"We don't know that,"

"It would fall apart."

"Maybe."

"Gregg, it's too badly damaged. We could never repair it."

"We don't know that either." Then Haply jumped up and looked at them incredulously.

"You mean fly?" Haply asked. "You mean there's a chance we could fly the Queen out of here? How could we do that?" Marvin explained what he had in mind. His idea was beautiful in its simplicity. He proposed to simply repair the Sky Queen and fly it out!

At first, the crew reacted with some skepticism. Harper continued to think it was impossible. In his mind, Marvin actually had his doubts, but he had to find an activity to keep the men busy during the winter. "The Queen is dead. It's just a pile of junk now"

"She's not dead," Marvin responded. "She's only wounded; we could patch her together again —at least long enough to get her flying."

"Where do we get the parts?" Ballard asked.

"All over," Marvin explained. "Poland is a graveyard of downed American and British planes, a real storehouse of parts. We'll scrounge whatever we need off those wrecks. The repairs can't be that extensive, after all, the ship was still flying when we brought it down." The crew slowly began to warm to the idea that it was possible.

Marvin could see Ballard's mind racing. He knew Ballard was quickly making a menu of items in his head and was checking them off. As the flight engineer, he of all people knew what it would take to repair the plane. He would be the one most responsible for getting the Sky Queen flyable again if they were to go ahead with the plan. Then Marvin listened as Ballard began mumbling each part under his breath — "Stabilizers, tail fin, control cables . . ."

"What do you think Frank?" Marvin asked, breaking Ballard's concentration.

"Well —it's pretty wild, but anything's better than trying to walk across Europe, or . . . just sitting around here hoping we don't get caught." The men moved in closer around Ballard as he began to explain what they would need, and how they could put the plane back together. After listening to Ballard some more, Marvin started to believe, maybe it could be done.

Late that night Marvin and Novak were in the tavern sitting and drinking with Szabla and a few of his men. Marvin and Novak had been working on Szabla softening him up for what he was about to ask him. It was the first time Szabla allowed the Americans to approach him on any friendly level. Marvin reminded him about the toughness of Haply and the fighting; the Americans might be useful in some way if the Germans came. Marvin then asked Novak to tell him he and a few men want to go back to the plane. Then he asked if Szabla would take them.

Marvin watched Szabla react by staring at them strangely. "Well, will he take us?" Marvin asked Novak. Novak spoke in Polish again. Szabla continued to remain silent while he tried to study the two men. Marvin said, "Tell him we promise not to burn or destroy the plane, we only want to examine it for useful parts. We won't cause him any trouble."

Marvin looked at Szabla and realized he needed to consummate the deal with a gesture of good faith. He reluctantly took off his wristwatch and slid it across the bar to Szabla. "Is it a deal?" Marvin then asked Novak to translate in Polish. Szabla picked up the watch and rolled it over in his hands. Marvin knew it was worth keeping by anyone's standards and a definite souvenir. Finally, Szabla nodded his agreement.

Marvin saw that Szabla's curiosity had been aroused and he wanted to know why these men really wanted to go back to the plane. He knew that the only way to find out would be to bring them to the plane. Szabla thought, *They could tell me anything while sitting in the warm cozy tavern, but would it be the truth? I could always kill them if I don't like what I find out.*

The next morning, just before dawn, Marvin, Ballard, Novak, Szabla, and five partisans left the village. They followed the mountain road a short way that lead out of the village from below. Then, they cut off the road and went up a stream, walking in the ice-cold water to cover their tracks. The site of the plane crash was surprisingly close. It was nestled in the next valley over from the village.

The first sign of light came as the sun inched up over the rise and filtered down through the pine trees almost directly onto the plane. The rays hit part of the broken windshield, and a mound of snow covered the plane just at the right angle, and gave away its position. It was probably the only time of day to see the plane at the end of the field. The rest of the time, the plane was completely obscured in the snow.

Szabla watched with interest as Marvin, Ballard and Novak cleared away the snow and climbed into the plane to examine it. They looked at the control cables, the rudder, the fuselage, and the two engines. Ballard made mental notes as they went along. Marvin at one point patted the plane affectionately on the Queen of Hearts emblem painted on the side of the plane, which was partially burned from the hit on the nose. The wings on the Queens portrait were still visible even though the borders were no longer there, making the playing card now look like just an angel. "You really took a beating, didn't you," he told the Queen.

A short time later Marvin dropped out of the forward entrance hatch after reviewing the cockpit, and Ballard buttoned up the feathered engine nacelle. The two men looked at each other. "Well, with enough parts, I can fix it up some." Marvin stared at him and smiled. "Good enough," he said.

They looked at Szabla taking drags on his cigarette. He had come over to the plane and was acting as if he was inspecting it. He was actually trying to see what the two of them were looking at.

Marvin and Ballard both realized the next problem to overcome was Szabla. How would they get him and the partisans to go along with the plan? When Marvin returned to the hut, the men told him that Ryan had been moved to the church to be warmer. They said father Kabos and the sisters could look after him easier that way. Marvin decided to pay father Kabos a visit and tell him the plan. He could also check in on Ryan while he was there. As he made his way to the church, it started to snow again, and he thought of Basha and actually longed for a cup of her hot tea. He felt certain she also would be positive about his idea.

66

The sisters fussed over Ryan who was enjoying the attention. With smiles, the two nuns left the room. Father Kabos started to leave to let the two men talk, but Marvin held him back until the nuns were gone and then said, "I want you to hear this too father." Ryan sat up and asked, "What is it Major?"

"I have a way to solve many problems at once."

Marvin then explained what his plan was and how they had just checked out the Sky Queen to see the damage.

"It is an ambitious plan Major, but can you really do it?" Father Kabos asked. Ryan liked it, and approved of the plan, but also said, "How will you get the parts?" Then Marvin explained the one obstacle. "We need the help of Szabla and his partisans. Without it, we couldn't possibly accomplish what we need to do, especially scouring the Polish countryside looking for parts." Marvin looked at father Kabos and asked, "Can you help us convince Szabla and the partisans Father?"

"Well my son," he said to Marvin, "They are a primitive people, but basically good. You cannot appeal to their generosity because they have never experienced anything like it from anyone. Appealing to their hatred of Germans is wasted because it is something they would expect of everyone. When you deal with this kind of peasant, a man like Szabla, you must appeal to his emotions. You must never show weakness. For like any peasant, he respects only strength and courage. I will pray for your guidance in this matter."

The words 'strength and courage' were still ringing in Marvin's mind when he rang the bell at Basha's apartment late that night. He hoped she was in and would help him find a way to convince Szabla. She seemed to have the most influence on him, more so than anyone else in the village.

Basha opened the door and in that brief moment Marvin thought he detected a slight smile on her face. Saying nothing, she opened the door a little wider and let him in.

As he walked by the wall of violins and guitars he noticed that the one Novak had been playing the other day was gone. Just the hook where it had hung was left. Ascending the creaking stairs, he wondered if he was there to get advice, or just to be with her. It didn't matter; he had to find a way to get the partisans working with them. His priorities had always been his crew and The Sky Queen.

Marvin watched Basha pour them some tea while she looked at him in a very disarming way. Then Marvin explained the plan and observed her face go through several emotions. First, she seemed relieved but disappointed, then very interested. "I understand your need to have the partisan's complete cooperation or the plan won't work. To convince Szabla will be the toughest part of the plan. If he could be convinced it would be a matter of letting him decide how best to help you. That is not an easy thing to do." Basha said.

"Tell me something more about Szabla, I must find a way of dealing with him." He looked at her pouring more tea and then she said, "Szabla, what is there to tell, —Szabla is Szabla."

"Father Kabos said he only respects courage and strength." She smiled shaking her head in agreement, and began to tell the story of Szabla. "Yes, it is true. Strength and courage are also good words to describe Szabla. He has lived by them all his life. When he was a young boy, Count Gustaw controlled most of the great land holdings in southern Poland, many of which the count received through ill-gotten means. Gustaw, and his sons Gregory, Henryk, and Iqnacy, feared no one. Their greed was as notorious as their fathers were, and they were forever hungry for more land.

Szabla was called Pawel Pajak at the time, a name now lost in the legend of that period—Pawel Pajak, a handsome young man, wanted nothing more than to be a farmer like his father, and to till the rich soil of their land.

"Szabla a farmer?"

"Yes, hard to believe, but when his family was killed by the count to get his land, the government did nothing. He thought that somehow he would get his land back in spite of God and the government, who did not listen to his pleas.

It was then my father felt pity for him, took him in, and taught him a trade as a merchant. The count still lorded over our small town in the lowlands, and the lands as far as the eyes of anyone in the area could see."

"That's when he met you?"

"Yes, we became close, and he did very well showing much promise for being a merchant, but his heart wasn't into it. I became his only passion along with his vows. He only talked of marrying me and settling down on his farm that was right-fully his."

Basha paused as Marvin let the story all sink in. "Even though Pajak was my favorite suitor, I never really felt what you might call 'the grand passion'. Yet I had deep feelings of fondness for Pajak, even sexual desire. At that time, I think I was still convinced of my own romantic destiny, of a particular someone who had the key that would open the gates of my innermost being, and I wondered if he would be the one to break me in."

"You mean make love to you."

"Yes, but my father saw what was coming between us and cleverly tried to break us up. My father was very ambitious, and a poor orphaned farmer's son did not fit into his plans for me. My father realized where the power and wealth was, and he thought that eventually it could be part of his family if he negotiated it correctly.

My father managed to arrange a marriage with the counts eldest son, Ignacy, promising him an excessive dowry. Father commissioned two beautiful dowry chests made of oak and poplar with decorative iron handles, locks, rollers, and hinges. Carved and painted on the outside with birds of brightly colored plumage, vases filled with tulips, and roses tied with ribbons, it represented high quality folk art. Silk and finely woven linens filled the drawers, and the final touch was the secret compartments stuffed with gold coins. I had to comply with my father's wishes, even though I was against it, I was after all my father's daughter. It was a nightmare for Pajak, and the news crushed him."

"That's unbelievable; your father was selling you?"

"It is a common custom for a father to better his family by marrying a daughter into a higher class."

"And you went through with this?"

"I didn't know what to do, but then the count's son performed a courtship of contempt and abuse with me that finally ended in rape before the marriage." Marvin watched Basha look down and stop talking. "Where was Szabla, I mean Pajak, when all this happened?"

"My father had sent him away to sell goods in Kracow."

"Did you tell your father Ignacy raped you?"

"Everyone knew the transparency of the counts motive for marriage, and the only interest his son had in me was for my dowry. When my father finally realized what a terrible mistake he made by agreeing to the marriage, he attempted to get out of the contract, offering to pay a great deal of the dowry money. Then, to add insult to injury, he threatened him with the loss of all his good fortune, and even physical abuse by the counts abominable sons until I stepped in and said, 'I intended to go through with the marriage.' My motive was certainly not one of love, but a burning desire for revenge, administered later at the right time and place. "Did you tell Pajak what happened?"

"On his way home through the mountains with the money from selling our goods, Pajak was set upon by a band of outlaws whom he bested in a knife fight killing the leader. In a rare gesture, because he thought now he had money enough to marry me and get me back, Pajak released the other two outlaws. They all knew he could have easily killed them because of his size and strength, or he could have taken them into town to let the law administer their warped justice.

In their gratitude and admiration, they asked him to become the new leader of their group. He told them of his love for me, and how he must go back. They wished him luck and even promised to bring gifts to his wedding for letting them go.

When Pajak finally returned, the town's people told him the events of my courtship from hell. I was tight lipped, and my father too ashamed to talk of it. Pajak went to the authorities in Kracow and told them of the unconscionable acts the count's sons had committed, and the continued excessive greed of the count and his family. It was for nothing; as usual, they refused to act against the count. Pajak came back and pleaded with me not to go through with my dangerous plan, but it was too late; I was determined and set on my course."

"You didn't go through with the marriage did you?"

"This story is not about me, you wanted to know about Szabla. You wanted to understand him better. Well—"

"So the rumors in the village I've heard are true, he did kill the count and his family?"

"True or not true, that is not the point; he did what he did, what he had to out of love for me, and to right the terrible injustice done. No one blamed him for that."

Marvin looked at his wrist, but his watch was gone, the timepiece was now Szabla's. He thought of his parents for the first time since the crash. He glanced over at a dim light, the sun pierced the windowpane with its early stream of morning rays, and then it reached behind some patchy clouds. The sky painted the clouds magenta as he stood up and looked out the glass. He stared at Basha, she finished her cigarette, and ground it into the ashtray. "That is something of Szabla. He was different then. I'm going to bed now."

Marvin was shivering in the cold morning walk back to the hut, but he didn't really feel it; he was deep in thought about his feelings for Basha. In addition, he considered how to approach Szabla, a man of action. Somehow, he must demonstrate the Americans strength and resolve to Szabla, and the partisans. That's what they understood strength and courage, he had to take some kind of action.

Now he knew what to do. He would take the men back to The Sky Queen without the partisans. He knew the way and could find the plane. That would show initiative, some courage and resolve on their part. He was exhausted when he finally reached the hut. He quietly crawled into his cot and before he closed his eyes, he saw Ballard prop himself up and look over at Novak's bunk, it was empty. Marvin watched Ballard look around for Novak, and then he fell fast asleep.

67

At dawn the next morning, Marvin woke the crew. He cautiously led the men through the village gripped in a winter freeze, and headed to the mountain road. The road took them to the cut-off up the frozen stream and to the plane.

Just before they headed out of town, Marvin noticed a partisan watching from the trees. He signaled to another group of partisans hidden behind some rocks at the edge of town. They had anticipated his movement from the time Marvin left the hut, and were waiting for them. Szabla stepped out onto the road in front of Marvin surprising them.

Marvin turned to look for Novak and then remembered he wasn't there. He walked up to Szabla and said, "We're going to the plane, plane!" He made a plane with his hands. "No!" Szabla grunted and motioned Marvin to go back. Marvin thought the only thing Szabla would understand was strength and resolve so he pushed Szabla out of the way taking him off guard. Szabla, surprised by the action, shoved Marvin into some snow. Marvin got up and hit Szabla square in the jaw knocking him to the ground. Szabla immediately whipped out his knife. Someone else threw a knife in front of Marvin. He couldn't back down now, he was committed to the inevitable confrontation, so he grabbed up the knife and turned to face Szabla.

Marvin now found himself in a deadly fight, the men jeering, their shouts waking the village up. Out of the corner of his eye, Marvin saw two children viewing the event while doing their morning feeding of some chickens. They were horrified at the sight of Szabla's big ugly Tartar knife, and they ran to get Father Kabos.

At first, Marvin did surprisingly well. He used his jacket to keep Szabla's knife in check with jolting left hooks, but Marvin was at a disadvantage because he had no intention of killing Szabla.

Szabla first seemed to be playing with Marvin, but now that a crowd had gathered it was a matter of face, and a good excuse to do what he had been saying he would do all along, kill Marvin. Szabla lunged forward and sliced open Marvin's jacket, then part of Marvin's arm. Marvin started to bleed, continuing to get sliced up much to the delight of the partisans. More children had come out and were now yelling in a terrified manner for them to stop, but it continued.

As Marvin reached the point of exhaustion, Father Kabos and Basha arrived at the scene. The children babbled to Basha about the Angels, the Angels were leaving and that if anything were to happen to Marvin the rest of them might just fly away without taking them. "Take you where?" Basha asked, "Take us home in their great holy ship, that's where!" the children yelled out. "Father Kabos said they are going to fly home in it soon!" Basha stared at Marvin in disbelief, then at father Kabos.

Marvin was now on his last legs, and then down again on all fours. He watched Szabla walk towards him with his knife poised to cut the final deathblow. Basha stepped out in front of him just before he could finish Marvin off, unafraid and even prepared to take the knife thrust herself.

"What stupidity is this woman?" Szabla complained angrily on the verge of exploding.

"Yours fool! Only your stupidity would kill the answer to all our problems!"

Everyone grew silent with Basha's conviction. Basha turned to Marvin as he crouched panting on the ground, "Are you certain your machine will fly?" He weakly answered, "Yes, were going to fly home." She then turned to Szabla and with great resolve said, "The Germans are everywhere now, the war is getting closer, it is time to think of the children. Eventually the Germans will come and then what of them? What will happen? The children must be given a chance to live!" She pointed to Marvin and his men as she spoke her final words.

"These men must take the children!" The words were ringing in everybody's ears,

"They must take the children!" Not everyone understood what that meant. Szabla backed down and the crowd started to disperse. The fight was ended.

Marvin could see the children had understood and were ecstatic. Father Kabos calmed all the children down as they yelled, "War Angels, War Angels, War Angels!"

Marvin was helped up by his men, then, Ballard asked him what Basha was talking about, "-taking children with them?" Marvin was too weak to answer as they dragged him onto his feet, and then back to the hut. He heard Basha and Szabla in a heated discussion as they left.

Back at the hut, the men patched Marvin up and asked many questions. They were all incredulous at the thought of taking any children with them. Marvin heard Ballard say,

"Basha could not have meant for them to take the children on the plane." As they were conjecturing, the front door to the hut opened and Marvin smiled as Basha walked in. Two other women had accompanied her and immediately attend to Marvin's wounds. Basha sat down next to Marvin, but turned so all could hear what she was going to explain.

"You didn't exactly win his heart over! But, he has agreed to help you get out only on one very important condition!" Marvin looked up and all the men had become very attentive. "You must take all the children with you on the plane when you leave." Marvin couldn't speak he just hung and shook his head. Ballard said, "It's not possible, were not even sure we can get ourselves out, let alone a jillion kids." Basha replied, "It is 24, and most of them are small, and besides, this is not negotiable."

Marvin heard a silence fall over the group as the women continued to patch him up. Then Haply said to Ballard, "I've seen those kids most of them are about the size of a bomb and might even weigh less." Ballard, as if educating Haply, replied, "We can't stack and rack the children like bombs in the bombay, it's a question of weight distribution." Marvin looked up at Ballard and asked, "Can it be done Frank?"

"I've got to go over the numbers with Novak, he's our tech Sergeant." Haply getting irritated said, "Yeah, well where is he when you need him?"

Marvin looked at the men and then turned to Basha and said, "We have to accept, we can't do anything without the partisans and Szabla knows that." Marvin saw the men's discouragement and wondered if it would work. Basha asked, "How long will it take to fix your plane?"

Marvin turned to Ballard, "Frank?" Ballard was calculating, "Well, . . . if we can get all the parts, maybe a month or two, depending." Basha continued, "What do you need us to do?" Marvin stared at Basha, and then said with a tone of knowledge that only the two of them understood, "The first thing we have to do is find Novak!"

PART V

THE SKY QUEEN

68

It was so cold Marvin was wearing gloves inside the Americans hut. He stood in front of a rough diagram of The Sky Queen hung on the wall, and finished drawing a big gas can next to it. Underneath the picture, he wrote the words; 'Aviation Fuel.'

There were circles drawn around the areas of the plane that needed repair, and next to each section was a list of needed parts. He turned to the men gathered in at the meeting. Marvin listened to the men quickly realizing they needed certain tools, and added them to the list of things to acquire, or make.

It was obvious they were going to need the assistance of a blacksmith, although no one remembered seeing one in the village, and even if they had seen one they might still have to set up a smithy bellows at the site of the plane.

Marvin thought it would be easier to make parts right there than to trek them back and forth from the village. He considered the dangers of that course of action. So, it went for hours as Marvin and the men discussed various details of the parts required and the work to be undertaken until finally, it was time to decide who would go on the first 'search and scrounge' mission.

Marvin had many reasons for selecting Novak. First, he could speak to the partisans or any other Pole with whom they might meet. Second, he was the Tech Sergeant, and next to Ballard understood what was needed, and where everything was on the plane.

Marvin also wanted to get Novak back into the swing of things and away from his other most recent distraction. Few of the men understood why Marvin picked Haply to go with Novak. Marvin knew there was only one good reason to send them together. If they got into a scrape, Haply would get them out. It was a risk, but discipline needed restoring and everyone must pull his own weight.

Amused by the choice, the Partisans remembered the two men fighting all the time. Szabla made it quite clear to Marvin that if there was any fighting on this mission, other than with Germans, what he would do to them both without concern.

Marvin then let the partisans explain as Novak translated. The partisans showed them the areas they would cover, saying they had no maps. In addition, they showed them where they thought the greatest number of downed planes could be found. It seemed to Marvin that the region was near the German border, re-cognized by everyone as a high-risk area to be traveling.

They would have to travel by night, and try to sleep by day. It was not clear when exactly they would return; they hoped it would be within seven to ten days.

Marvin and the rest of the men bid their farewells to Novak and Haply as they quietly left the village that evening with the partisans shortly after sunset.

Father Kabos listened to Sister Theresa discuss details of making a pair of crutches for Ryan now that he was doing much better. Father Kabos was happy for the small distraction to work with wood in the back of Jarods old shed. At first, he went about fashioning a crude pair of crutches just to get Ryan up on his feet and walking about. As he refined them, they turned out to be better than he could have bought in a hospital. In fact, the whole process had been therapeutic for father Kabos as well as for Ryan. He remembered reading in the Bible that Jesus was a carpenter. It was almost as satisfying as surgery in the past, and he pondered his once renowned skill. If he were still good maybe someday he would practice again. He came to the realization that he had found great solace in helping people with spiritual matters, and the thought quickly vanished. He was in God's hands now.

Father Kabos saw that Ryan was thankful for the crutches and he walked around in the church for a day or two, then he went to the village for the first time. The two Sisters accompanied him there on a brief shopping expedition for some vegetables and bakery goods. It was slow going, but he was happy to get out and see where he was and what was around him. The villagers were all congenial and everyone was glad to see the American up and walking.

Marvin and the crew were at the plane every day. They had cleared away the snow and debris from around the fuselage and wings. They made a work area with makeshift scaffolding stands.

They had started the woman working on a mesh camouflage net to put over the plane. Just inside the forest nearest the plane, Marvin and some men were constructing an area for a blacksmith bellows to forge and work with metal. His thinking was that the smoke from the bellows would dissipate with the breeze that blew between the trees.

Szabla and the partisans came up to Marvin and expressed their dislike of bellows so far away from the village. They felt it would attract attention. One of the partisans had been the son of a blacksmith before the war and he was concerned that the black smoke from the coals, and the burning metal, would be spotted by a plane on some windless day.

Marvin and the crew had to agree only to work the bellows on windy days. The breeze blew into the forest almost every day lately.

Several days later, a light snow started to fall. It was beginning to build a small layer on the scaffolding when the wind kicked up. Marvin and Harper studied the short length of the prospective runway and glanced uneasily at the high trees near the end.

The snow was falling harder now making it more difficult to judge the distance. Marvin said, "We're just going to have to pace it off." Haply replied, "I would bet money it's not long enough." They looked at each other, got up, and started walking towards the trees counting the steps as they went. The snow swirled around in mini twisters, and started blowing harder. A bad storm was breaking as they looked up at the trees bending in the wind. "Damn!" Marvin exclaimed as they reached the edge of the trees. Harper turned to Marvin and said, "What do we do now?"

* * *

The gigantic map of occupied Europe, with Germany in the center, was the focal point for the room. A small red bulb showing the field post location emanated from which all distances on the map were calculated. This field post was a carbon copy of the one Reinstock ran near Frankfurt. He had mobilized his operations, and moved into Poland to be closer to his objective.

German aviators were busily engaged in answering field phones on their desks and rising to position small metal replicas of downed planes on the map. One aviator approached Reinstock with some field reports and handed them to him. He read them carefully and nodded, then limped over to another map to the right, in the corner, which was only half the size of the larger one. This map depicted the entire southern section of Poland where he personally had been searching for The Sky Queen and its crew.

Reinstock started circling various sections with a marker pencil and then stepped back to review them. Then he looked at his reports and went back to the map again. This time he drew straight lines on the map, which began forming a boxed in section that included Praznik.

He paused and looked over at the big board of downed allied aircraft, and especially at the single metal plane still hanging on a hook off by itself. There was still no name of the plane or list of pilots next to it. He picked up the phone and called Berlin.

69

Outside in the village street, Joseph observed Gilda asking Paul which one was his favorite Angel. Paul looked at her peculiarly, but didn't say a word. Gilda, irritated that he wouldn't answer her, started to tug on his shirt. He just stared at her while she continued to insist which Angel it was.

Marisha, like a big sister, came over and put her arms around Gilda. She calmly explained to her that Paul was still sick and couldn't talk right now. "Why is he sick?" She asked, "Because of all the bad things that happened to him." Marisha replied.

"What happened to him?"

Joseph saw Marisha look at him for help. She took Gilda's hand and walked over to him away from Paul, and Joseph compassionately said, "We don't know exactly, but maybe someday he can be made better." Fortunately for Joseph, Gilda's attention turned to several other children gathered at the entrance to the back alleyway, and was curiously watching something. Joseph watched Marisha and Gilda, hand in hand, slowly wander over to see what everyone was looking at.

The baseball made a clunk sound against the wall every time Shaw would pitch it. It would land right back into his mitt at the same place each time much to the interest of the children. Then he would mix it up throwing the ball closer to the ground on the wall, but still he would catch it in the same place each time. The children knew he had some kind of skill with whatever this game was, and they were curious like most children and wanted to know more.

Joseph saw Father Kabos walking towards the Church, and then he saw Marisha and Gilda standing in the middle of the street looking at the other children. "What is it Father?" Gilda asked. Father Kabos blurted out with some amusement, "Its baseball, an American game!"

Shaw turned at his sound and said, "Hello Father, have you ever played?"

Soon Joseph, Father Kabos, and Shaw were behind the shed and had fashioned a crude baseball bat out of the wood left over from the crutches. Now Joseph gathered all the children together and let Father Kabos and Shaw teach them how to play baseball. Shaw was pitching snowballs to the children showing them how to swing the bat. Father Kabos was behind home base calling the pitches. In short order, the children had taken to the game, and were enthralled by it. When Shaw finally switched to the real ball, instead of snowballs, they had more difficulty hitting it. "It's too fast," one of the children yelled. Father Kabos yelled to Shaw to slow it down. "It's a bit swift" he yelled and then translated the word swift in Polish for the children. "Yeah it's swift, yelled Marjan at bat, "Slow it down Swifteeee" he yelled back. He knew a little English from his parents. The other kids picked up quickly on the name and started to use it. "Yeah, slow down Swifteee, hey Swifty, Swifty" they were all laughing and calling him Swifty now.

Then Marjan connected with the ball and hit a high fly into the air, everyone was astonished and the kids yelled out calls with delight. Joseph joined the children having fun and soon it naturally attracted some of the partisans over, who were watching from a distance.

When Durcansky saw one of the children connect with another ball he insisted on taking a turn with this silly game. Shaw said he had to hit snowballs first. While the other partisans encouraged him, he cockily took a turn, and Shaw easily struck him out. He struck out again, and this time he went wild with frustration swinging the bat into the ground, and then smashing it repeatedly against a boulder as if he were possessed. Finally, he threw down the damaged bat and just trudged away, cursing in Polish.

Joseph walked over and picked up the bat. "Swifty, you fix?" he asked Shaw, while Shaw rolled the bat around in his hands looking at it.

Father Kabos walked over, took the bat, and said, "We can all help make bats."

Joseph and Father Kabos took the children to the back of the shed and he and Shaw started instructing them on how to form bats out of wood. Soon the boys of the group were working at making bats.

In the church, the girls and the two sisters were cutting pieces of cowhide in the shape of gloves the size of the kid's hands. They fit the new gloves with small wool mittens inside the leather. Gilda tried one on but complained that it was too hot. Back at the drawing board, Shaw explained to the sisters about smoother softer leather inside the glove and the process started over again. This time a better glove was made. Shaw was even teaching Paul how to follow a runner and lead his throw in front of the runner to get him out. Soon, boys and girls threw baseballs made of rags back and forth to each other with their new-fashioned gloves.

In the field behind the church, Joseph approvingly watched a line of partisans being pitched snowballs by Shaw as they each took a turn at bat. Joseph felt that Baseball mania was catching on. Everyone in Praznik was busy working on something, and as winter slogged forward, Marvin's concerns for Novak and Haply grew every day.

70

Almost three weeks after they had left, Marvin was standing in front of the tavern waiting for Basha when Novak and Haply, along with the partisans, arrived back in the village. The group was cold and hungry, so their first stop was the tavern for a drink and some hot food. Marvin was relieved and happy to see them.

Inside Marvin asked the old couple, who worked the tavern with two young girls, to put up a kettle of hot soup along with black bread and cheese. They complied, adding Moid, and a myriad of other Polish finger foods. They also made several pine tree concoctions that tasted of the forest. The brewed drink simmered hot, and the pinesap bread baked that morning along with roasted pine nuts served up nicely.

The men made short work of the food, and began to drink before they started discussing the contents of the two big canvas duffle bags they had carried in and set carefully behind the bar. Marvin felt everyone seemed to be in a good mood and talked about the highlights of their first 'search and scrounge' mission and its obvious success.

After a brief description of some of the more colorful aspects of their excursion, embellished upon by Szabla and some of the partisans, Novak and Haply went behind the bar and lifted the bags up on top of the counter. They pulled out and laid control cables, gauges and other small parts for all to see.

"There were many planes to pick from in one particular area. It must have been a terrible battle that chewed up that B-17 brigade." Novak said, and then went quiet.

"They all crashed in Poland, so far off their return course. One bellied in. There's a lot of stuff on that one." Haply added, looking at the parts.

Marvin watched the faces of his crew. He knew they were all wondering about the crews in those planes, and what their fate had been. He raised his glass, and all the men followed. "To the brave brigades and the crews that fly them." All the men repeated, "To the brave brigades and crews."

Back at the American's hut, Marvin and Novak prepared a rough map showing the approximate location of the planes they had discovered. Ballard was quite enthusiastic now, and his confidence increased as Novak explained the condition of the planes as well as the parts he had seen. Ballard looked at Marvin and said, "Well, we just might be able to pull this off."

"We only have till spring. Once the snow melts we'll be sitting ducks for the German planes to see." Marvin replied. Marvin, Novak, and Ballard discussed what remained, and realized they could probably get all the parts they needed in one more massive 'search and scrounge' trip. Marvin decided to use every man they could spare to go along.

For the next few days, Marvin and the men went repeatedly over the list of things they required, and Ballard rehearsed the crew in the proper methods of removing the needed parts from the crashed planes.

One of the partisans, whose father had been a blacksmith, fired up the bellows and began making the tools to rebuild everything. The black smoke filtered through the trees of the forest and disappeared just before the tops.

Marvin watched the work progress to the point where it was almost time to go on the second largest, and hopefully the last, 'search and scrounge' mission. Then something happened in the thread of events that were occurring, altering the plans they made.

One night Szabla and Basha called Marvin and Novak to the tavern for dinner, and at the table Szabla told Marvin, while Basha and Novak translated, that one of the villagers had given him some very important information. As Marvin listened, it seemed an elderly couple on a farm in the flatlands, at great risk to themselves, hid an entire airplane, intact and in good shape. Marvin and Novak were astonished at this news, but realized that if true, this could give them access to all the spare parts they would need for repairing the Sky Queen. They might even be able to fly the whole plane as is without repairing the Sky Queen. "When can we go?" Marvin asked. Basha translated Szabla's reply.

"It is not that easy, we will have to prepare things for the bargaining. They will not just give us the plane after all the risks in hiding it." Szabla continued to explain the difficulties and dangers to which the partisans would be exposing them in going down to bargain goods in the flatlands. Also, it was possible it could be a trap.

When they had worked out a plan, they finished off their dinner with drinks, and Marvin walked Basha back to her apartment. Basha decided to go with them, and help persuade the old couple. The next day they headed down to the flatlands.

Two days later, Marvin, Szabla, and the group approached the farm in the morning. From a short distance, everyone could hear the farm bustling with activity and animal noises from cows, chickens, geese, and hens blending into a pastoral symphony of sound.

The farmer's family ran here and there feeding animals and cleaning up messes. The farmer had spotted Szabla and his group coming, and started herding his family into the main house. Szabla and two of his men went first, and then signaled for Marvin and the rest to come.

It was a simple farmhouse, and inside the farmer's entire family sat around a long wooden table nervously waiting to see what was going to happen. Basha got right to the point. "What do you want for the plane?" In polish, the farmer explained that times were hard and things were not easy to come by. Then the farmer expressed all the trouble and risk he and his family had taken to hide the plane for so long. The bargaining went back and forth for some time, as Basha and Novak translated. Marvin wearily nodded his head. Szabla impatiently stepped in, and in Polish said, "We have food and some gold, you'd better take it, and that's that!"

The farmer trembling meekly spoke up and said, "My family and I of course appreciate Szabla's generosity, but do not want the goods." There was a silent pause from the whole group, all eyes went to Szabla expecting next to see the ugly knife that he was famous for come out of its sheath.

Basha put her hand on Szabla, and then calmly asked the farmer, "What is it that you wish for the plane?" Still trembling, but with confidence he replied, "I would like you to take my two daughters along with you. It is only a question of time before the Germans come and take them."

To everyone's disbelief, Szabla agreed, settling the deal. Marvin then asked if they could now see the plane and the farmer rose and led them outside to the barn.

The barn was very large, and the two big wooden doors at the entrance were heavy to open. The farmer and Szabla both pulled the doors together, the sun flooding inside illuminated the entire plane in the middle of the barn floor. The farmer wore a big smile expecting accolades from the group, but Szabla had a look of disgust and Marvin and Novak were speechless.

There before them, sat a small World War I Sopwith Camel bi-plane. Marvin and Novak wondered at the surprisingly terrific condition it was in, but of course, absolutely too old, to small, and worthless to them.

Marvin watched with some amusement as Basha prevented Szabla from beating the farmer to death as he wanted to, but instead, for the farmer's trouble she made Szabla leave some of the bargaining goods they had brought. Then, with quiet disappointment, they all headed back to Praznik.

As they marched up the mountains, Marvin was the first to realize the humor of the situation, and at the top of one ridge, he started to laugh. Then Basha laughed, and then Szabla, and one by one they all broke out with uncontrollable laughter. It rang out across the canyon with a jovial bounce to it. Marvin found the release rejuvenating, it had been quite a while since he had laughed, and it had been a long time for all of them.

* * *

Marjan, the red-haired boy, and his sister Hester, were talking with some of the other children who had gathered in front of the Americans hut to see if they were back yet. The children were expressing a keen interest and pride in various aspects of each crewmember, and possessively identified their own Angel. "Ballard is the smartest" Marjan said, "But Marvin is best because he is the leader." Hester replied, and some of the children nodded in agreement. "What about Haply?" Gilda blurted out.

"He is always angry"

"He probably didn't want to leave heaven because he liked it so much." Marjan said. Whatever they were, the children all agreed that the crew of the Sky Queen was a strange group, not at all like the 'War Angels' of the Bible.

A hush fell over the children as the door to the hut opened, and out walked Haply and the rest of the crew. The men smiled at the kids who were all grinning at them while they picked up various tools and equipment to bring down to their daily work at the plane.

As Haply started to leave, Gilda and Hester inquisitively followed behind him continually looking at his back for protruding wings. Haply was amused at their actions and just as they reached the edge of town he abruptly spun around startling the two of them. He yelled out, "What?" Hester was too scared to say anything, but Gilda cautiously asked, "What is it like?" Haply looked at her with a smile and asked back, "What is what like?"

"Where you come from," she replied.

"Ohhh, that! Well, it's pretty wonderful" Haply described the big city of New York, the tall buildings, hot dogs, elevated trains, jitterbugging and baseball stadiums. And when he told them about the great statue, which welcomed all newcomers, the kids were really confused.

"Why would a statue welcome people into heaven?"

"Well,—I've heard it called a lot of things, but heaven, . . . that's a new one!" Haply chuckled. He waved goodbye to the girls and headed down the trail.

A short time later at the plane, Haply told the other guys, "These kids really think we're Angels!" They stared back at him in amazement, but then smiles emerged on their faces as they continued about their work. "Maybe that's not such a bad thing." Novak said.

71

Basha walked towards the church to pray and ask for guidance on how to approach Marvin regarding the subject of Novak and Beata, and then there was Magda and Dunham's growing romance. When she rounded the corner, he was sitting on an old stone bench smoking a cigarette, and observing the brilliant stars that were so clearly visible in the cold night air.

At first, it was a bit awkward, but as usual, Marvin made her feel comfortable by his tone and conversation. As they looked at the stars together he said, "When you look at that kind of beauty it makes you forget there is a war going on. How can anyone imagine we are the only living beings in the Universe? It makes our individual problems seem petty in the whole scheme of things."

"Yes, that is true, but we still must face our situation here" she said. She was leading him into the conversation she wanted to have with him. Even though she wanted to give into her romantic feelings, he was bringing out in her. "I don't mean the war, I mean right here in this village." Marvin looked at her in a differentl way and smiled, "What do you mean?"

Basha started to blush, and it was the first time Marvin had ever seen her having difficulty saying what she felt. "Well, we are a village with an abundance of lonely women and a shortage of men, and if your crew were to remain here too long who knows what could happen. In actuality, she realized she was talking about herself and Marvin.

"Don't worry, we will be gone in a couple of months" he assured her.

"It will be when you fly away so easily out of the lives of these vulnerable women that the real problems will occur. And it won't be helped by the fact that the children will be leaving as well."

"Yes, I thought about that, all that missing love. It wouldn't be right for the women. I'll have a talk with Novak and Dunham." She looked into Marvin's eyes and realized how truly unique this strange man was, and felt all those feelings she kept locked up inside her that needed to be let out and expressed. For a moment, she wished he could stay with her and find a way to bring out those feelings. "Magda is very young, it would be worse for her, Beata is a women who knows the ways of the world. Some women can take the pain and still be glad for the experience."

Marvin reached out and touched her hand. She checked herself as all those feelings came welling up inside her.

"Can they?" He asked gently. She looked deeply into his eyes searching for the truth. Could he be the one? Could God have sent him for her? Then he said, "What about Szabla?" She pulled her hand back and said,

"Are you afraid of him?"

"No!"

"What will you say to Novak and Dunham?"

"I'm not sure yet."

"Well, you can say that women in this village want something long lasting, something more than just an experience. They are Catholic, they must think of the consequences of their actions. It must be more than just lust. If it is, why not let them get married in the church under Gods sanction?"

"I can't tell them what to do."

"You are their leader, are you not?"

"Yes, but that is something every man must decide for himself. No one can tell that."

"But you agree it is the right thing to do, no?

"I can't answer that for other men. For myself,—Yes!"

"You are a good man Captain Marvin."

"Thanks." He hung his head and chuckled to himself.

"I must go and pray in the church now." She held his hand and touched his shoulder. "I know you will do the right things."

The next day Marvin divided the men into two groups. They headed for two different parts of the area where planes had been found. That way they could cover the most ground in the shortest amount of time. Dunham, Novak, and Shaw were with one group of partisans, which this time included Joseph and some older kids, as cover and lookouts. Marvin had heard Marisha and Nicholas protest as Joseph explained why it was important for them to stay with the children. Marvin, Haply, and Szabla were with the other group.

The trek down the mountains seemed to go faster this time. The men walked with a sure determination knowing where they were going and what they had to do. This would be the last time they would have to do this. Marvin listened to the empty cart they had brought clunk along with its wooden wheels.

At the bottom of the mountains in the foothills next to the flatlands, they hid the cart for their return trip up, covered it with brush, and then headed to where the downed planes were scattered over a wide area. The two groups split up and went separate ways.

Marvin could feel a stillness hanging over the field where the first plane crashed. It was badly shot up, and it was obvious it had been a disastrous mission for some unfortunate bomber group.

"A lot of mothers and wives cried for this group," Marvin said. The whole plane seemed burned out, and had bullet holes everywhere. Miraculously, the only thing that seemed to be untouched was two of the engines. They found a good propeller, and proceeded to dismantle it. Then they took an entire rudder section. It was very hard to carry the parts as they made their way back to the cart in the foothills. They stumbled down an incline, and almost lost the rudder section. Then Szabla halted everyone, and gave the signal to get down.

While they crouched in the brush they heard the sound of grinding gears from a lone truck. Szabla could see only one driver in it. They all watched Szabla go into action signaling his men with hand signs.

Shortly, after a brief encounter, they were riding in a German truck on the way back to the village. They left the cart for the other group.

72

Joseph was glad to finally be doing something important. He and Marjan were walking together when they arrived at the crash site of their group's downed plane. He nudged Marjan and pointed to Dunham, Novak, and Shaw, who were busy dismantling parts, getting cables, taking out turbochargers, and everything else on their shopping list.

Joseph could see Marjan admiring Shaw as he stuffed his pockets with spark plugs when suddenly, just at the edge of the field where the plane was, German soldiers from Hassman's unit appeared.

The men quietly snuck into the plane to hide except for Joseph and Marjan. They had been rehearsed for this, and immediately Joseph knew what to do and took charge. They acted as if they were school boys playing on the wrecked plane. They almost managed to pull off the deception when the Germans slowly came over to the wreck. Some of them were talking to the children and seemed relaxed, but the officer of the group poked his head into the plane and saw Shaw. Joseph saw Marjans horror as the officer fumbled to unholster his luger. Then, they heard the shots as Shaw fired point blank at the officer blowing him out of the plane and into two other German soldiers. As the gunfight escalated, Joseph pushed Marjan down and dove for cover. Bullets whizzed over his head and Joseph watched the fire fight in awe.

Novak took up one of the bags of goods and ran out of the plane, and yelled for the kids to follow him. Dunham grabbed the other bag and went out the side window in another direction as Shaw started popping off shots at the German soldiers.

The German soldiers had regrouped at the edge of the forest and were crawling on the ground towards the plane. Shaw was covering for everyone, but Novak yelled back for him to come with them.

Joseph watched Shaw get up to make a run for it. Shaw caught a bullet as it ripped through the fuselage, and then into his leg, and another into his arm. He fired a few more rounds at the oncoming Germans, then dropped to the ground, and signaled Novak to get going without him.

Joseph realized that Marjan was beside himself, and didn't want to leave Shaw. Strange as it seemed neither did the partisans. Novak and some of the partisans stood up and started a barrage of firing picking off the front group of Germans as they made their way back to the plane. They circled back to the plane. Inside, they looked at Shaw's wounds and realized he wouldn't make it, the logical choice was for him to stay as more Germans started gathering at the edge of the forest.

Joseph was holding Marjan back from running over to Shaw. With tears in his eyes he yelled out, "Swifty, Swifty come back with us."

The partisans left Shaw with some ammunition, and then he waved goodbye to Marjan and Joseph knowing his fate.

Joseph through the loud firing saw Novak run up to them, he quicky grabbed Marjan as tears rolled down his cheek, then ran with him away from the plane. Joseph and Marjan waved as they left and said, "Good bye, Swifty"

As the group retreated into the nearby forest they heard Shaw putting up a fierce rearguard action, emptying his gun until Shaw was overwhelmed by the onslaught of Germans, then there were no more gunshots.

On the way home with the cart loaded up, Joseph and Marjan were crestfallen; they continually looked back on the trail hoping to see Shaw following after, but there was no one following them.

Joseph looked in Marjans face and remembered his last view of Shaw as the Germans closed in for the kill. The fading sounds of the fight in the distance reverberated in his mind, and seemed to be written all over Marjans face.

It was a sullen group that entered the village two days later. Joseph and Marjan went to their respective homes, but neither of them could really eat, and their surrogate parents listened to them tell the sad story of Swifty Shaw.

Joseph asked his parents if they could do something about Swifty, and it was decided to hold a church service for him.

The next day Father Kabos called his congregation together to bid the dead farewell in honor of Swifty Shaw.

* * *

The Focke Wulf 189 'eye-in-the-sky' with Reinstock, and three crewmembers, was headed through the patchy clouds for Hassman's headquarters. Glass windows completely surrounded the center of the wing where the crew quarters and pilot station was mounted. It looked like a bombardier cabin with glass encircling the entire front section. Despite its fragile appearance the aircraft was remarkably sturdy, and had returned from combat many times with one of its tail-booms missing, or an entire left or right fuselage shot to pieces.

Reinstock was calibrating the new RB 50/30 camera that had been installed, and was adjusting the lens. Then, he extracted the film canister when the pilot told him to, "Buckle up, we are going to land the plane Herr Rienstock."

Major Hassman was waiting in the Mecedes Benz at the edge of the field. Reinstock walked up and climbed in.

"Ah, Colonel Reinstock and the famous "Eye in the Sky" good, very good! I suppose I am going to continue my cooperation in tracking down that murderous group of gangster Americans?"

"I'm sure they are somewhere in your district. This film, when developed, should tell the tale and give us the signs we need to find them."

On the way back to headquarters Reinstock felt Hassman was somewhat reluctant in giving his full assistance to the Colonel, complaining that he had his hands full just finding, and fighting the partisans.

"I am sorry that you have not been able to control your partisan situation, however, this must take priority as you can see by reading this document!" Reinstock handed Hassman a document signed by none other than Goreing himself. Reinstock knew that Hassman now had no choice but to fully cooperate.

Upon reaching headquarters Hassman politely invited Reinstock into his office and poured him a brandy and offered him a cigar. "I don't really have time for these social amenities Herr Hassman. We need to find the Americans."

"Oh, but Colonel, what I am about to show you will give you much cause to celebrate." Hassman said, in a very beguiling manner. "In fact it will demonstrate to you and your beneficiaries in Berlin my complete cooperation in helping with your problem."

"What is it, get to the point?" Reinstock demanded.

"I believe I have an answer to one of your riddles." Hassman said, as he motioned Reinstock to get up and follow him out of the office and down the hallway. Hassman ushered Reinstock into a dark room where seated in the center, bruised, bloodied and beat up, but still very much alive, was an American airman.

As Reinstock entered the room he saw the airman look up at him grimly. Reinstock walked over to the table in the corner and examined the strewn out junk found in possession of the American. He picked up one of the spark plugs and rolled it around in his hand while looking at it, contemplating its meaning. "What were you going to do with this?" he said, as he started his intense interrogation.

The American steadily refused to reveal anything concerning the crew, or where they might be; in fact, he even denied knowing what Reinstock was talking about. He just repeated his Name, rank and serial number much to Reinstocks aggravation.

Some frustrating time passed and Reinstock decided to take a different approach. The questioning had become useless, and he knew it. Reinstock walked over to the American and stared at his bandaged arm. "This is your last chance Herr Shaw. You know it is going to be much more painful now." he said, while patting Shaws bandaged arm. Reinstock reached out and jabbed a fist into Shaw's wound. Shaw screamed out in pain, then passed out.

73

The geometrical crystalline structure of a snowflake quickly changed as it melted, starting a chain reaction with those connected to it. The light from the sun refracted off prism like colors as it warmed the interior of the clump of snow. The pine needles holding the snow began to sag under the weight of water and ice. It could no longer support the dissipating form now suspended precariously from a branch at the top of a tree. Finally, it slipped off the dormant pine needles and crunched into another branch below it, sending a cascade of snow that fell through the air to the ground.

There was no snow where the clump had landed, and instead of adding its countless flakes to merge with others, it splashed down into the leaves and pine needles that had been building up debris on the forest floor. It quickly transformed into water. Beneath the foliage, the water found several small rivulets in the dirt that carried it down to a stream. There, it overflowed and rushed at full speed through a gorge that headed for a larger creek somewhere at the bottom of the hill.

The sound of rushing water was constant and could be heard all over the mountains and down in the valleys. Vapors from melting snow filled the air with a misty haze that snaked through the canyons and rose to encircle the tops of the ridges of the southern mountain caps of Poland.

Small sections of grass and flowers dotted the hillsides. Szabla knew the changing sunny weather announced the coming of spring as he stared down the valley. The snow that had been on the Sky Queen was completely gone and a lean-to hanger with a camouflage net was over the plane. Another makeshift scaffold stand was propped against it next to one of the engines, and Szabla leaned on it. He watched as the crew climbed in and around the plane continuing their work.

Then Szabla, as if he was the forman, walked over to the bellows. He approvingly observed Yanov, the partisan smithy, teaching Branislaw how to pound metal from the hot forge. Yanov had his shirt off as he took the red hot metal propeller connector with a tong stick from the fire, and put it on the anvil ready to form. Branislaw quit pushing the bellows and came over to watch the part take shape. Szabla was happy the work on The Sky Queen was progressing nicely, and so far without any hitches.

That night Marvin walked into the smoky tavern where an intense card game between the partisans and The Sky Queens crew, was in full swing. Marvin knew that aside from facing death on an almost daily basis for a grand cause, playing poker bonded the American crew and partisans together. That is why he allowed it.

The next morning, as Marvin was walking with most of the crew to the plane, he saw Dunham and Magda duck into the bakery holding hands. It was obvious to Marvin, and the entire village, that they were in love. Marvin knew that Dunham had come right out and told Magda that he loved her, Magda had told Basha, and Basha told him. Though Basha didn't have to, Magada had told almost everyone else.

It wasn't Dunhams shift at the plane today so Marvin put in the back of his mind to deal with him later. When Marvin returned to the hut from another long day at the plane he wanted nothing more than to just lie down and gather his thoughts when Dunham approached him. Dunham struggled getting out what he wanted to say and stammered beating around the bush, which was beginning to annoy Marvin. "Why don't you just say what's on your mind Roy?" Marvin said in a half knowing manner. "I, well, I would like to take Magda with us when we leave on the plane." Marvin's attitude now became one of compassion for the boy's dilemma.

"I'm not even sure we can squeeze in the number of kids we're already committed to take with us Roy. I know you mean well, but I think your making a mistake getting involved with this girl, and I've been meaning to talk to you about it." He carefully chose his words as he tried to explain the pros and cons of their relationship in a sensitive manner, emphasizing the cons. He soon realized that Dunham was having none of it, and had already made up his mind, so he eventually said, "Lets wait and see how the numbers add up Roy, then I will make a decision." Dunham wasn't thrilled with that answer, but at least it wasn't a no! Marvin could see Dunham could live with that for now, and Dunham went off to relate his conversation with Marvin to Magda. Marvin wasn't as satisfied with his own answer, and felt the need to discuss the situation with Basha.

Marvin rang the bell out in front of the shop where Basha lived. As it rang it reminded him of the book he had read in high school, 'For Whom the Bell Tolls', and all the lives that were caught up in that plot. Now this strange girl whom he didn't even know, whose future was being held in his hands, was involved in the web of events taking place in Praznik. So much rested on getting the plane flying, and for a moment he felt that everyone was depending on him to make it all happen.

Basha opened the door and once again let him into her life. Marvin felt that she instinctively knew his anxiety over something that he wanted to talk about. They knew it would take some time for him to get it out so she boiled some tea that he liked and set the cups on the table. First they discussed America again. This was a subject that Basha always found fascinating and interested her. Then they talked about Dunham and Magda. Basha couldn't help herself and she said curiously, "Then it is true. You Americans are all romantics, huh?"

"Only the young ones, those without experience." Marvin responded. "And those that do —have this experience?"

"They look for something deeper, more realistic. They realize that things like duty and honor count for a great deal in times like these. Sometimes what a person feels is just better left alone."

"Why does it always seem to me Major, that you, how to say, you dance around what you truly mean." Basha was looking him right in the eyes. "I thought I was making myself pretty obvious," he replied.

"No. You are not. I would like you to tell me so I do understand. You see I have no shame or pride when it comes to true feelings." Marvin paused, now he stared into her eyes before he said with some difficulty, "Maybe somewhere else under different circumstances, I could tell you what I feel without fear of harming others, and you could respond as a woman with deep feelings might."

She studied him for a moment then said, "I was right, after all."

"About what?" he asked.

"You Americans are romantics." She smiled, and he could see she had already decided it was time for him to leave, or she might do something that they would regret. As she opened the door she smiled at him and said, "Good night my romantic American friend." On an impulse, Marvin took her hand up and kissed it, then she let him out. As Marvin left Basha's, he saw someone lurking in the shadows across the street. It was Sediva, the Czech. He had seen their exchange at the doorway, and Marvin was sure Sediva didn't like what it appeared to be. Marvin figured he would tell Szabla what he saw, or maybe he would confront Marvin on his own. Whatever happened, Marvin felt very uneasy and knew there would be trouble.

74

The sun was shining very bright the next morning. Father Kabos got up and had his final discussion with God regarding the two sisters. Not only did he take the sunshine as a sign that God approved of what he was about to do, having prayed many days about it, he too felt that God had personally given him the message to ask this selfless thing. He had originally wondered if this was even possible to do but then he remembered in the scriptures of the new testament, which he had just read again, in Mathew 19, verse 26 Jesus said, 'With men this is impossible, but with God all things are possible,' and his mind was at peace about it.

He dressed in his priest robes, which he now felt was as much a part of him as his arm or leg, and took his prayer book to breakfast. The two sisters had soup and bread ready on the small table and the three of them quietly sat down to their simple repast. Father Kabos said the prayer, and this morning he added, "And thank you lord for these wonderful two souls, Theresa and Anna, that you have blessed this village with, and the many things you have done through them for all of us."

The sisters bowed their head in humble embarrassment and respect for God, and father Kabos. Without saying anything else they ate their breakfast knowing what he was about to do. At the plane, Marvin was inspecting the windshield that had just been installed the day before to see if there were any leaks or cracks. He poured water on all the seams and watched for bubbles or leaks seeping into the co—pilots side of the cockpit where it had originally shattered.

The pine sap adhesive he had cooked up was hardening and holding nicely. How it would hold up under altitude pressure was another thing, *God only knows,* Marvin thought.

Marvin watched Ballard finish installing the turbocharger in engine number four. He would liked to have fired up the engine to see if it was working properly, but that would have to be done just once on the final check. With that realization, he told Ballard to check it again, and Ballard tugged on the hoses around it re-tightened some of the bolts and screws.

The two men climbed down from their respective positions simultaneously and looked at each other. Marvin raised his eyebrows at Ballard and said, "Well, what do you think?"

"I think were doing the best we can do." Ballard replied in a positive, but retrospective manner, shrugging his shoulders.

"Lets take a look at what's left to be done," Marvin said, as the two of them walked over to some drawings on the work table next to the plane.

"How is the pulley crane coming? Will it hoist the vertical tail fin up?" Marvin asked, as they both started to walk towards the back of the plane. Upon looking up at the half sheared away Fin Marvin caught a glimpse of Father Kabos coming down the path in the forest. Ballard pulled on a rope connected to some pulleys and a bucket of rocks rose into the air next to the tail section.

"It seems to be working, but we haven't tried it with the same amount of weight as the fin yet." Ballard said doubtfully. "Lets try it today" Marvin replied. Now Marvin saw Father Kabos approaching the two of them, and he came in out of the sun under the camouflage canopy. "Good morning Father" Marvin and Ballard greeted him. "I am sorry to disturb your work my sons, but I wonder if I might have a word with you?"

"Sure Father, we were just taking a break" Marvin replied and Ballard pulled up a chair for Father Kabos, and offered him some water. He sat down and took a sip of the water before continuing.

"You see, I do not ask this thing for myself."

"What is it Father?" Marvin inquired and Father Kabos said almost apologetically. "I ask you my son, if you would please take sister Theresa and sister Anna with you when you leave!" Marvin and Ballard both looked at each other and made facial expressions as if they were saying, what can we do? Both of them realized they had to turn him down, the plane would be overcrowded to the point of bursting.

"What about you Father?" Marvin exclaimed,

"Yes my son, what about me?"

"Do you want to come with us also?" Marvin replied as Ballard looked at him incredulously, then Father Kabos slowly nodded and said, "If it is possible, I would like to." Marvin knew in order to accommodate their heavy load they would have to make modifications to the bomb bay compartment. It was the only place designed on the plane to carry the biggest load. He also knew that Ballard and Novak had been working the numbers for a certain amount of weight and now would have to change it again.

After Father Kabos left, Marvin could see Ballard figuring in his head and trying to come up with answers. He wanted to say something, but Ballard blurted out, "We can't take the whole village you know!"

75

Marvin racked his brain, three of the crew were dead, Tony Stiles the navigator, Bob Miller the radioman, and Clifford Shaw the tail gunner, leaving seven men at about 150 to 175 pounds each. There were twenty-four children at about 60-80 pounds each and now the two sisters and Father Kabos was added to the weight distribution. Thank God, Ballard and Novak had figured out the modifications on the Bomb Bay, and it was completed. Now it was time to test the children.

He looked out the cock-pit window and saw Ryan, who was doing much better, hobbling down on his crutches to see the test. It was a rehearsal of the children getting in and out of the plane in a hurry, something Marvin thought might be necessary at the last moment of departure.

The squeak of the bomb bay doors opening was soon obscured by the sound of kids screaming and yelling as they poured into the plane through the modified entrance and up crude ladders to the rows of seats newly installed. But they didn't sit in their seats, and instead they were jumping up and down causing the plane to bounce precariously. Marvin cringed as he saw them touch the guns, climb in and out of the waist gun openings, and in general were driving the crew crazy.

The kids thought it was a great deal of fun and games, and the rehearsal was a total fiasco. Ryan, who was standing off to the side observing the whole thing, shook his head and sat down feeling a little weak. Marvin and the crew rounded up the kids and finally sat them in their seats. Harper was now sitting next to Ryan under the canopy both looking at the plane when Marvin walked up. There was no bandage on Harpers arm and he was completely mended. "Well what do you think Art? Will the kids cut it?" Harper asked. "I could always pull the emergency bomb release handle if they don't," he replied half-chuckling. "That's a terrible thing to say Art" Harper chuckled back.

Marvin appreciated the humor at his expense, and was now wathching the kids marching into the forest with Father Kabos at their lead. "Lets take a walk Dave". Marvin said. The two of them again started pacing off the prospective runway they would have to use. It was now without snow and bumpy and short. The biggest problem was that it still headed directly toward a stand of high trees at the edge of the forest. They stopped at the half—way point and discussed putting some kind of marker there, a spot where they must lift off if they were going to get over the trees.

Harper found a fair sized rock and placed it at the spot. They both looked back at the plane; the men had turned it around to face the lift off point and the stretch of runway. It appeared that it was the only possible direction to take off.

Later Marvin and Ballard, sitting in the cockpit, looked towards the marker on the runway. Ballard was expressing his concern over getting full power out of the two damaged engines. Marvin knew there was no way they would get over those trees. Ballard continued to inform him that he had completed work on a home made auxiliary power unit that would be needed because of the low charge of the aircraft batteries.

Marvin picked up the clipboard with the list of things that still needed to be done. Ballard looked at it, and then at Marvin, "We've still got problems."

"Yeah, I know!"

Basha set up a meeting with Szabla to discuss some of the problems that still remained, and late that evening they met in the tavern while the card game was going on. Szabla was sitting watching the game, having drawn out, when Marvin came in. He sat down and observed the game with Szabla.

It was an exciting moment in the game, and one of the partisans had gone all in with his money, Novak calling him. The atmosphere was intense at the show down.

Marvin was thankful when they showed their cards, and it was a high low split. Both of them won and it was a good time for Novak to leave the game in order to translate for Marvin and Szabla.

Marvin explained the problem concerning the trees, cleverly allowing Szabla to come up with what he thought was the best solution.

"Is that all that is bothering you? The solution is simple. Just cut them down!"

"What about German reconnaissance planes? What happens when they suddenly notice the trees are gone?" Marvin asked. Szabla smiled, "They won't. Not if we build a net. A great net. One that will hold the trees up. Then just before you go, down they come and up you go, good—bye."

Marvin pulled at his earlobe, thinking of Szablas idea. "Actually that's not a bad idea, and all we would need to open is a slot big enough for us to fly through. That should do it." Marvin exclaimed.

"Yes, then down they come, you fly through, its simple, and it's done!" Szabla finished his drink and returned to watching the card game. "Is there anything else I can do Sir?" Novak said. "No, that's it Sergeant, you can go back to your game."

"Thank you Sir" and Novak bought back in the game and again ended up the big winner of the night.

* * *

For the next few days Marvin, together with Szabla, directed everyone in securing the trees and making the net, including the children. The net was made of finely woven ropes, and was secured with supports around each of the trees. The men were cutting the trees at angles to make the trees fall just in a certain way. They were prevented from falling by the ropes. Then all the cut trees held by the net were secured by a main line on each side of the slot opening where the Sky Queen would fly through. All that would be required was for someone to cut each of the two main ropes, and then all the trees would come crashing down in the direction away from the oncoming plane.

The children wrapped vines around the ropes to hide them. The net had branches around them to look like part of the forest. The fresh cuts in the trees had pine sap smeared over them, and from a distance Marvin felt everything looked the same as before, —just a normal great line of tall trees on the edge of the forest.

When they had finished, Marvin brought everyone out into the field to view and admire their handiwork. With smiles and hand shaking the villagers, children, and men, headed back to the tavern for a celebration dinner for a job well done.

Marvin remained and asked Basha to stay for a moment. Marvin was concerned with another problem, and he conveyed it to Basha. He was worried she and the rest of the villagers who would remain may have to abandon the village after the Americans left.

"If the Germans see the cut in the stand of trees, or discover any tracks, they may figure out what happened. If they do, they are sure to destroy Praznik in retaliation."

Basha looked at him, thought for a moment and then said, "What if we cut down all the other trees on the other side, and use it for lumber to rebuild some of the houses. We keep the rest out in the open for firewood? The Germans could be easily deceived if we are clever enough." Marvin smiled at how her mind worked, and then told her what he really wanted to say.

"Basha, would you consider going on the plane with us?" He could see she was taken aback by the question. She stared at him without words to say. She seemed truly moved by his asking this of her. She sat down and looked up into the sky as if she were looking at images that were only dreams. After a very pregnant pause she said, "I cannot do this thing!" Marvin, with a bit of disappointment in his tone asked,

"Why not?" She bowed her head, but did not answer. Marvin asked one more time. She declined again, but this time she stopped him from going on, and put her hand on his shoulder. "My place is with my people. It is the same as with your duty to return to your military kind. Did you really believe I would abandon those I cared about for fear of my own safety?"

"Maybe not for fear, but maybe for something else." Marvin replied with hope, looking at her in the eyes and really seeing her. She looked at him in a kind way but said, "It is like you said before, in times like these, feelings like that are better left alone." Marvin noded his head in understanding, and instead of going to the tavern to celebrate, walked back to the American hut by himself.

Basha remained sitting on a stump by the edge of the field and was staring at the sunset when Szabla approached her. He was angry and snapped, "I do not like this constant talking and touching between you and the American". Basha stood up and forcefully reminded Szabla, "No man tells me what I am to do! Anyway, you are stupid to think what you are thinking!" Szabla kicked a pinecone into the air in frustration. Basha softened her tone and continued, "I am somewhat flattered by your display of jealousy, but there must not be anymore of it. We have enough to do then worry about personal feelings." She could see Szabla wasn't buying what he thought was an act, but felt it was better to remain silent for now, and he sulked off.

Once Basha was alone again, she found herself thinking about both men: Szabla and Marvin, trying to analyze her true feelings. *Was what she told Marvin the way she really felt? Was she passing up one of those moments in life that could change everything? How would it be, to go to America with a man she really did not know, but liked. Maybe she even had deep feelings for him? But, she knew Szabla all his life. There were no secrets about him that she didn't know.* She was at the point where she was actually going to draw a line down the center of an imaginary piece of paper in her mind, and list the pros and cons when Magada walked slowly up to her.

Basha immediately saw the anguished look on her face and asked, "What is it my dear?"

"I'm not sure how to say this," she started.

"Then just say it." Basha bluntly said. Magada then poured out her experience of the last few days she had spent with Dunham, and all the new kinds of feelings she was having. She asked Basha if there was anything wrong with that. She was deeply concerned that if it continued she was going to have to consummate her love in order to understand all the true feelings of love.

Basha marveled at the innocence of it all, and was gentle with her answers. She let Magda know that whatever she did was going to be the right thing if she was in love.

Then Magada said, "He asked me to go with him on the plane, if the Major will let him." Basha looked at her with a questioning glance of surprise then understanding.

"I don't know, I want to go, but how can I leave you and Praznik? You are like my sister and mother, and I care so much about you, I just couldn't . . ." Magda started to tear up. Basha put her arms around her and said, "Don't cry my foolish young one. Always choose love against staying with a dead past. Life will go on for those left behind. It always does." Magda looked up at her while sniffling, then smiled. Basha continued with a smile, "You were meant to follow this road where love leads you. Go with your American, if you can, even if it means much pain to you now. For this pain is easily overcome if you can remember one thing, love is also the same road which connects each of us to our past as well as our future. With this knowledge, wherever you may find yourself, you will have no regrets." Magda seemed relieved and threw her arms around Basha again, "You have always been so kind, I am going to miss you greatly. I must go and tell Roy to talk to the Major now."

"Yes, yes, you go." Basha replied, as she shooed Magda down her path. She watched her run and wondered to herself what her own choice might have been if Marvin had asked her when she was younger. *Would I have left everything behind to go off with this man?* She laughed and shook her head to make sense of it all.

Again, the threads and fluctuation of life's currents were changing, and so were the people of Prasnik. She always seemed to be moving at a pace that left no time for the calm of reflection. These sudden moments always swept the cluttered past from one's mind and revealed the present in all its dangerous clarity. Basha realized they were a people thrown unsuspectingly into events that raised them beyond their own expectations much to their surprise, and often times revealed the best in themselves.

Basha also realized; the approaching dangerous events could change the lives of everyone in a more permanent way. She hurried back to the church to pray for she knew only the hand of God would direct all these seemingly unrelated events at a precise moment in time to change the destiny of all involved, and she needed solice.

76

The reconnaissance photos developed in Berlin had taken three weeks to get back to him, and Reinstock found that totally unacceptable. He had gone through channels to expedite the process, but it was delayed in the delivery, somehow getting shipped to the eastern front where the Focke-Wolf 189 he requisitioned from Russia had been stationed. So much for German efficiency, the Russian front had put a glitch in the machine, and he wondered who was going to fix it.

The first batch of photos had revealed nothing of importance, and once again Reinstock was in the "Eye-in-the-Sky" with the RB50/30 camera clicking away while he flew over the valley where the Sky Queen was hidden. Reinstock thought about the German conquest of Poland and how in the invasion it had been so easy to pick off their targets. The Poles had absolutely been unprepared for modern warfare, relying only on diplomacy and a very antiquated army for their protection. Then he thought of Hassman's problem with his partisans. He continued to find himself amazed at man's stubborn will to resist, even against overwhelming odds, a trait characteristic of certain races, and totally absent in others. He wondered if his Americans had that trait.

Then, he began to assess his own will and persistence, reviewing his determination to find the plane called The Sky Queen. "Yes, The Sky Queen! Now I know what your name is," he said out loud. That was the name of the ship that had carried his elusive quarry into the deep mountains of Poland. He lifted his binoculars in another routine scan of the terrain below.

Reinstock again found himself thinking about who these men were that flew the ship. His search group had supplied him with a list of pilots assigned to this particular bomber squadron, and opposite the printed listing for the Sky Queen he had found the names of Major Greg Marvin, and Lieutenant Dave Harper. He had no names for the rest of the crew, but the identification of these two was sufficient for him as he tried to conjure up what type of men they might be, and just how resourceful they were to elude him.

Rienstock grabbed the handle above him in the viewing cockpit as the Fock-Wolf hit some turbulence. After all these months of searching he was still not discouraged. He knew that his net around them was drawing tighter, having combed and eliminated many areas where a plane could possibly land safely. He had all but ruled out a fatal crash for the Americans because of the skill displayed by this Major Marvin in keeping the battered aircraft airborne for as long as he had. He yelled out to the entire Folk-Wolf crew, "They are still alive!" No one heard him over the drone of the two engines churning up the air around them as he peered out of the glass observation bubble mounted on the front of the FW 189. Alive or dead, he was determined to find them, for all he knew they might even be in some hidden place watching him fly over right now.

Down below, Marvin and Ballard looked up to see the Folk-Wolf fly overhead. They were on their way down the forest path to inspect The Sky Queen and held their breath as the observation plane came in low enough to buzz the valley.

Marvin remained motionless until the plane eventually flew off in another direction.

"They know something." Ballard whispered to Marvin "I can feel it." Marvin looked at him with concern. Then he stared at the German plane as it disappeared into the distance.

It was a beautiful spring day and Ryan was feeling very chipper. He had made a miraculous recovery and was almost at the point where he could get rid of his crutches. He was grateful to Sister Anna Pulaski who had mainly been responsible for babying him back to health with father Kabos's guidance. She had to be the kindest, sweetest most genuine person Ryan had ever met. She had spent many unselfish hours with him talking about his guilt-ridden life as a bombardier.

"Art, there is a reason God has chosen you to drop bombs on this evil spreading across the land" she had consoled him. "What about all the innocent ones my bombs fell on? There had to be innocent Germans I killed?"

"God takes his children to heaven when he wants to; it was not your doing."

She had soothed him with sponge baths, and stories of war angels from the bible. There was also something wonderfully worldly about her wisdom which he found mysterious about her, and he wondered who she was before she was a nun.

When father Kabos had come and told them about Marvin's acceptance of the sisters going with them on the plane, Ryan became ecstatic and reiterated what Anna had said before about God having a plan for everyone. She had smiled that perfect smile at him and squeezed his hand.

Marvin had left Harper in charge of the final checkout of the plane, and Ryan went with the remaining crew to inspect every inch of the plane to make sure it was ready for the flight of it's life. It would hold the most precious cargo it had ever carried.

Ryan wondered, as he watched the men run their check lists. *Would The Sky Queen lift off with its heavy load? And, if they got airborne, what about the Germans? Wouldn't they chase them, and try and shoot them down? What about the town of Prasnik? What would be the repercussions the village would suffer?*

77

Ryan had now turned his thoughts to Anna. That had an immediate effect on him, and he practically exuded positive feelings out of every pour in his body.

He went around cheering up the nervous crew by bringing them water while they worked on the plane. He became annoying to most of the men, so he found himself gravitating towards Yanov. Yanov was chopping wood for the fire-wood piles being made around the field.

As he stood next to Yanov and watched the ax fall on each piece of wood with lethal precision, he remembered his conversation with Anna, about dropping bombs on Germans. Then, in between Yanov's chopping, Ryan heard something back in the woods.

At first, it sounded like an animal, and he looked at Yanov for some recognition. Yanov was intent on swinging his ax and obviously hadn't heard it. Ryan limped off the trail and went deeper into a little wooded area nearby. To his shock, tied to a tree, were two horses. They wore military saddles, and etched into their leather were un-mistakenly Nazi swastikas.

Ryan's brain cleared out all other thoughts, and he quietly untied the horses leading them away from the area to prevent the Germans from escaping. He sent the horses trotting down the trail towards the village, sure that the Germans hadn't gone in that direction. Then he hobbled back towards the plane to warn the others, but came upon a German soldier peering through binoculars at The Sky Queen.

Suddenly, Ryan felt arms wrap around his neck, grabbing him from behind, it was a second German soldier. Ryan reached up with both his hands and dropped his crutches. He managed to free himself from the grip, picked up one of his crutches, and jabbed at the German. The German soldier pulled the crutch, along with Ryan hanging on, into a tree knocking the air out of Ryan.

A brief hand to hand combat ensued, but because of his weaker condition Ryan was no match for the younger German. In the next instant, the soldier plunged his Hitler youth knife into him, and Ryan keeled over dead.

The two horses had turned and taken another path back towards the plane. They broke out from the rim of the forest trotting right up to the B-17 much to the amazement of everyone working.

Yanov had seen where the two riderless horses had come out of the forest. It was where Ryan had wondered in. He wasted no time motioning Ballard to join him as he raced down the path clutching his ax.

Yanov took a stealth position scanning around to see if anything moved. When nothing apparent stirred he approached the wooded area where Ryan had wandered. Just on the other side he could see Ballard squatting behind a log as if ready to pounce on something. Yanov whistled a partisan whistle to get Ballard's attention, and motioned him around to the other side.

They approached the horses from different angles. Yanov caught a glimpse of the Germans right where Ballard was heading. He crouched lower and signaled to Ballard that there were two of them, and to stay down, and go around the opposite side. They stalked the two Germans as if they were prey in a hunt. Just prior to reaching the spot only three feet or so from the Germans, Yanov felt something wet. To his Horror, and dismay, he had crawled over Ryan's blood soaked body.

Yanov jumped between the Germans and plunged his ax into the back of the younger one who was checking his rifle. With a surprised look, the German dropped his gun and staggered a few feet clutching for the ax in his back, and then collapsed.

The officer with the binoculars had been reading a map and dropped it when he saw Yanov. He reached for his revolver with trembling hands, but could not get it out of the holster in time. Yanov leaped on top of him. They tumbled down an embankment exchanging blows as they rolled.

Through the tumbling, Yanov saw Ballard go into action and snatch a large dead pine branch off a tree. He ran to the two men, but not in time. A shot rang out and blew Yanov off the German, they both looked surprised at the blood gushing out of Yanovs abdomen.

Ballard had just enough time, and kicked the gun out of the Germans hand. It flew into the air, and into the bushes. The German tried to scramble to his feet, but Ballard landed a crushing blow on his back with the pine branch splintering it into many pieces.

The blow to the German knocked off his helmet, but he kept crawling, and reached out for a rock next to the creek. He threw it at Ballard's head. It bounced off his thick skull and made him dizzy, giving time for the German to charge at Ballard taking them both over the embankment and into the creek.

Yanov couldn't believe he was dying as he watched from the embankment. The ice cold water splashed on Yanov as Ballard struggled, rolled over in the creek, and cinching the German in a headlock. Yanov's sight started to dim while he saw Ballard hold the German under water. It seemed like he had held him there forever, and finally he saw the body go lifeless.

Several partisans and the rest of the crew ran up to the creek, rifles and guns leveled. They saw Ballard in the water with the body stuck in his head lock. Then, Ballard released the Germans body, and it slowly drifted down stream with the current.

Yanov, with his eyes still opened full of surprise, watched the German float away, and then he let out his last breath and died.

78

The dawn gave no indication to Father Kabos of the momentous events that were soon to occur. He sensed a spiritual admiration at the spring sun rising clear and bright, illuminating the pine forest with great shafts of warm rays. Birds and chipmunks chirped away in the trees, and other animals darted about on the forest floor.

At the church, he had just finished an early mass with Sister Theresa and Sister Anna, and the three of them were taking a final look around the stone sanctuary they had come to know so well.

On this day Father Kabos and the two nuns were feeling a special closeness knowing they were about to leave Praznik probably forever. At the chosen moment, Father Kabos said something that had to be said, "Sisters, I hope someday-to confess something you should know, and I must ask your pardon for." Sister Theresa looked him in the eyes and touched his hand and said, "There is no need to ask pardon from those who long ago gave only God the divine right of judgement over their fellow human beings." Father Kabos, with a pang of guilt reached out to hold her hand, and she continued, "Father, I can only speak from my own experience. All of us, who eventually come to know God and worship Him, seem to travel down many different pathways with unexpected side roads. Yet the final destination is always the same. What really matters is that we enter into a relationship with Him, to live in His love in whatever position in life we are called on to serve him."

Father Kabos was moved, and he held back his tears knowing the full extent of what she said applied to him. "Thank you my child, those are very comforting words, let us now pray in silence." The three of them knelt before the alter and silently prayed for divine guidance.

Marvin and some of the crew were at The Sky Queen getting ready to do a final check and actually fire up the engines for the first time since the repairs had been completed. If all went well they could possibly leave in the twighlight of evening, so they would not encounter any fighters at night. They would fly low once they got out of the mountains and head for the coast.

Marvin was in the cockpit going over his preflight checklist, and the crew had started to remove the scaffolding around the engines. Marvin opened the wing window and poked his head out to tell them to clear for testing when he heard it. It was the buzzing of an airplane engine. He saw that the men on the wing heard it too. Everyone froze silent and listened.

In the distance the faint sound of many vehicles grinding up the hill could also be heard. Then the rifle crack of the Alarm rang out. "What was . . . is that . . . ?" Harper asked, as Marvin turned to him and said, "That is the sound of time running out. I believe this is the real thing not a test, get her ready to go Harper!"

Moments before, just below the village, a partisan lookout had spotted a German military column heading up the mountain with Hassman's Mercedes leading the way.

The partisan fired the alarm, and it was heard quickly through the village. Szabla gave the command that everyone had dreaded from the day the children had come to the village, "Evacuate the entire village and get the children to the plane!" Szabla had told Sediva and Bronislaw, who already knew the plan. The two of them headed for the cave to get the necessary arms, ammunition, and certain special items. Then, they would set the fuses and blow the cave. Everyone in the village went about his or her predetermined tasks that had been organized long ago for just such a grim possibility.

Basha organized the surrogate parents, and partisans, who were giving farewell kisses and embraces to the children, but didn't tell them this was goodbye for good. The children still thought it was a rehearsal like all the others as they hurried down the hidden trail to the valley below, and the Sky Queen.

Basha saw them to the trail head and watched the great activity through out the village as everyone prepared to leave. Szabla and several of the partisans were well down the road planting mines that had been hidden inside the forest for just such an occasion. He motioned for a machine gun nest back in the trees to be set up. In a few minutes Szabla would have his first line of defense in place. He was ready to hold back the Germans for as long as he could, giving the village, and The Sky Queen time to escape.

At the plane, Marvin supervised the crew frantically clearing everything away from it, all the scaffolding, the lean to's, and the camouflage. Then he saw the children come marching out of the forest in a playful mood, believing it was just another rehearsal. When they reached the plane, Gilda said, "I want to sit up front with the Captain this time." They hurried up to the bomb bay doors that squeaked open, and the crew started stuffing them in one by one.

In the distance an explosion was heard, then another. The children didn't pay any attention, as they were totally engrossed with getting into the plane, jumping, and running in and out of it.

Marvin and Harper sitting in the cockpit knew what the explosions meant and gave each other glances of concern. Harper gave Marvin the signal to start the engines. Harper said, "Please God!" Then the first engine slowly chugged and spit before it finally turned over, grabbed and held. It was a tense moment for everyone. Then the second started with a bang as carbon exhaust cleared out and got two engines going.

Back down the road, the lead German half-track in front of Hassmans Mercedes had traversed over a mine and blown away its tracks. Hassman jumped out of his Mercedes and into a tank behind him. He peered out of the slit in the tank window and saw the partisan machine gun nest in the forest open up on the Germans who were jumping out of the burning half-track. A fire-fight began and the Germans returned sporadic shots as they deployed into the forest, and up the hill to the valley next to the village.

The tank Hassman was in veered off the road. Hassman was talking on the radio to Rienstock who was in a Falk Wolf 190 circling above.

"I see them gathering at a clearing just over the hill from where you are. I will make a strafe run then circle back for a closer look," Reinstock bellowed into his radio. Then, Hassman heard the engines of The Sky Queen echoing across the valley over the sound of the gunfire. He struggled to listen more intently and was now sure it was a big plane.

Hassman ordered all the men back to the convoy and commanded the column to drive off the road and head for the valley towards the noise. He called Reinstock, "Large engine sounds, I hear them. Its coming from the valley to the left of us. I am taking my column through the forest."

79

Marvins hands were sweating, and the number three engine would not start. It kept backfiring, but wouldn't kick over. He decided to start the number four engine and turned it over. It started, but it was running very rough. At the same time he watched the nuns and some of the crew working frantically to get the rest of the kids in the plane and settled down. It became easier once they heard the roar of the engines and realized something new was going to happen. Some of the younger ones playfully climbed back out of the waist gun openings. Dunham and Magda were nowhere to be seen, and Novak was kissing Beata good-bye.

Marvin leaned out the window and looked around. Then he told Harper to tell Novak to find Dunham fast. Novak started to go back up the path, but Beata was crying and clutching onto him. Just then Dunham and Magda came running down the trail, and they made the dash over to the plane.

Father Kabos was waiting just outside the bombay doors when the four of them came running up. Marvin poked his head out the cockpit and told them to hurry up. Father Kabos and Dunham helped Magda up and then they both got in.

Beata, with tears running all over her face screamed over the engines "Take me too, I don't want to stay!" Father Kabos saw Novak was in great turmoil, and he got out and tried to get her up inside. Marvin stopped him and said, "There is no more room Novak." Beata's face was full of desperation. Then Father Kabos got out and gave her his place. Marvin and Novak looked at him in disbelief. Father Kabos smiled an assuring smile, then shoved Beata and Novak into the plane. He watched Novak button up the door and crawl to his position at the right waist gun. Everyone was in, and just as the bombay doors closed with a click, the third engine kicked over and started.

Hassman and the Germans reached the edge of the valley. The partisans were firing at them while working a hit and run guerilla tactic. The partisans stayed just far enough in front of the Germans, fired, and then fell back to a new position firing again. This slowed the Germans advance little by little.

Hassman now saw the plane on the other side of the field and gave orders for his soldiers to concentrate their fire on The Sky Queen.

"Rienstock, Rienstock, its them, the plane, The SkyQueen, I see it, on the other side of the field!" Hassman was yelling into his radio. Bullets were flying everywhere, but the Germans were still some distance away. "I see them, yes I've got them!" Reinstock dove his Folke Wolf 190 at the edge of the clearing and strafed the partisans, killing several in his first run.

As he started to climb out of the valley he caught a glimpse of dust rising from the engines back wash of The Sky Queen. Reinstock raised his nose of the FW to circle around for a closer look at The Sky Queen, passing over a hill with a large rock formation. Below he saw two partisans setting charges at what appeared to be an opening to a large cave entrance.

At the entrance, upon instinct, Sediva grabbed one of the 50-50 machine guns he and Branislaw were loading into a cart as Reinstocks FW roared just over their heads. Sediva mounted the gun on the rocks and took aim. Branislaw retrieved two boxes of 50/50 ammunition, and slapped a bullet belt into the machine gun, as Sediva followed the FW190 into the valley with the machine guns sight. He would have a clear shot if Rienstock made another pass over them, and he began to calculate the approach of the plane in the crosshairs.

Basha was the only one at the other end of the field at the tree net, and she struggled wielding the ax to cut the ropes to release the trees. The villagers, who had been assigned to help fall the trees, were no where in sight. Basha saw Father Kabos across the field and looked on in helpless dread as he and some of the partisans, under heavy fire from the German troops, raced for the tree net.

Two of the partisans were hit and fell dead while crossing the field of treacherous fire. Father Kabos was the only one left who made it to the net, picked up an ax, and started hacking at one of the heavy support ropes. The first rope was starting to fray as the two of them continued to chop away, bullets flying all around them.

80

Marvin, at the controls of the Sky Queen, didn't wait any longer. The plane was under heavy fire. He could hear Novak already using his waist gun, firing away at the Germans. He told Harper to crawl into the nose gun and help hold off their advance.

Marvin got the plane rolling and the Lockheed B-17F started rumbling across the makeshift field, picking up speed as it bounced over the bumps and rocks.

Suddenly, out of the forest, Marvin saw a German half-track come barreling onto the field right in the path of The Sky Queen. Harper saw it too, and began blasting away with the nose gun, exploding the gas tank just as the Queen lifted off the ground, and passed over the top of the burning half-track.

Dead ahead, Marvin saw the trees still standing as they flew straight for them!

Szabla had left the frontline fighting and ran out of the forest over to the tree net. He looked at Basha, who was near exhaustion, grabbed the ax out of her hands, and with one mighty blow hacked the first rope away. The first rope whipped into the air with a recoiling sound, and the trees started to dangerously sway. He furiously started chopping away at the last rope as The Sky Queen came closer to them. He felt the Germans all around and heard bullets zinging into the trees, flinging bark, and branches everywhere as they tried to kill him.

Out of the corner of his eye, he saw Father Kabos duck down to avoid a line of machine gun fire heading across a log towards him. Then a grenade fell right where Father Kabos was hiding. It exploded ripping the rest of the support ropes off at the last second, the trees fell away just as The Sky Queen flew through the slot and slowly started gaining altitude.

Szabla saw Father Kabos pop his head up behind the log and cheer, "Stay down you crazy priest!" he yelled at him.

Reinstock worked his way back towards The Sky Queen, it was in his gun sights as it flew through the slot in the trees. "I've got you now!" he screamed in a mad fury while blasting away at The Sky Queen with his machine guns, "This is for my brother Han's" he barked, with several of the rounds puncturing the right wing of The Sky Queen as it topped the trees. The Sky Queen was still to low to get a correct bead on, and Reinstock cursed at the plane.

Back at the cave entrance, Sediva looked through the end of the machine gun and imagined it was his lethal rifle-scope. He lined Reinstock up in his crosshairs. He had been waiting for the FW to come back around and try to finish off The Sky Queen, which was now easy pray as it struggled to gain more altitude.

Sediva led the FW 190 as it neared the cave and took the most important aim of his life, and fired. As shell casings flew into the air all around him from the 50-50, Sediva could see Reinstock in the cockpit as the plane roared up the side of the hill, then directly overhead. He could see the front glass of the plane shattering as he hit Reinstock in the shoulder and blood spurted up with a patch of his uniform. Sediva continued to fire as the plane and Reinstock passed over and continued up the mountain.

Reinstock looked back, and the last thing he saw before dying, was The Sky Queen, climbing over the first mountain peak. Then, Reinstock and his FW 190, on his last crash of his life, skidded up the top of the mountain in a ball of flames.

Hassman and his Germans realized their defeat, and retreated back into the forest to re-group. He called out loud to his troops. "We are not defeated yet, these Jews, and 'Piss Ant Poles' are going to pay for this. I want the village of Praznik leveled for this outrageous act!" Just as Hassman was radioing for more back up support the tank he was riding in exploded from a booby trap mine, igniting the ammunition compartment, sending him into a white flaming oblivion.

The remaining Germans razed the empty village of Praznik, shooting at anything that moved, and hitting many of their own soldiers in a macabre ghost like dance of death through the smoking streets. There was no one left in the village to kill.

Szabla had already put a retreat into motion as soon as he saw that The Sky Queen had made it over the first group of mountains. He watched the remaining villagers, along with the partisans and their wounded, stretched out in a column heading through a secret mountain pass away from Praznik. Behind them he could see the valley with several burning vehicles still ablaze.

As Szabla and the villager's climbed a little further up the trail great clouds of billowing smoke could be seen from Praznik. He saw Basha pause to look back at the smoke clouds, then she studied the sky where the plane had disappeared into the horizon. Szabla walked up and handed his binoculars to her. She took them and looked out over the hills for the plane. She and Szabla exchanged glances, and smiled. Basha came to his side, and he put his arm protectively around her pulling her close. He knew they were finally together as a couple once again. Branislaw was right behind them carrying the guitar from Novak on his back. He glanced over at Father Kabos who was helping some of the elders and wounded up the trail. Father Kabos looked up at Basha, and Szabla, and then towards the parting plane in the Horizon, and said, "It's a Miracle."

81

In The Sky Queen, the plane was vibrating with the engines running very rough. Marvin had to give total concentration to the control panel while flying full out at tree top level. As he skimmed the plane dangerously along, he missed trees, and an occasional mountain peak.

When they finally made it to the flatlands, he Looked down at the close landscape and saw a farmhouse with startled peasants staring up at them in surprise.

Marvin fought the controls staying low to avoid radar and German fighter planes. Harper was back in the seat next to him working the plane as his co-pilot. Dunham and Novak were on the waist guns. Ballard was mounted on the top turret right behind Marvin. He glanced at Harper scanning the sky above them for signs of fighters. Haply, was in the tail gun position, he was happy to have the last view of Poland as they crossed over into Czechoslovakia.

Marvin had charted a course to enter Germany right out of Czechoslovakia somewhere south of Nurenberg. Then fly the shortest distance across Germany between Nurenberg and Karlsruhe and into France. This way they would spend the least amount of time necessary over Germany. If they were lucky, they would be flying at night, and continue north into France along the border to Calais. If they were downed in France they would have a much greater chance of being picked up by the French underground than by the Germans. Then, they could cross the channel to the Straights of Dover, landing at home base in

England. It was daring, and if they didn't encounter any detours they had just enough fuel to make it.

Marvin had anticipated flying by the stars at night. He had always enjoyed traveling by the ancient symmetrical universe of Ptolemy. But now Marvin had to rely only on dead reckoning with his ground charts. It wasn't going to be easy, but he had spent a lot of time studying the maps and charts of Germany when they started making their runs into Deutchland, navigating France was going to be the hard part.

* * *

On the border of Germany and Czechoslovakia, in a small little cement building, Frauline Oaufmeyer had just finished a piece of German strudel, and was wiping the crumbs off her table, hoping no one would see them. As she turned around to throw them away a blip appeared on her new radar screen. She had just finished her training in Berlin, and was one of the few women who had passed the course on the advanced technology section. When she swung back around she caught a glimpse of the blip.

It was intermittent at first, so she did what most of her classmates probably would not have thought of doing, and had not been trained to do; she banged the side of the radar screen. Now the blip was constant. She immediately picked up the phone and called headquarters, who in turn called the nearest airfield to scramble fighters into the air.

Marvin wondered how the children were doing crowded throughout the inside of The Sky Queen. He asked Harper to take the reins and went back to take a look. Before he got out of the cockpit he could already see one of the little boys squawking about going to the toilet. His whining was driving Novak crazy. Novak picked him up, and for a moment it looked like he was going to throw him out the waist gun opening.

Instead of brining him back to the small chemical toilet in the rear of the plane, he held the kid up and let him urinate out into the slipstream. Some of the spray got on Novak and the other kids went hysterical with laughter. Novak angrily wiped himself off as Beata chuckled with the children.

Harper nervously scanned the instrument panel and looked out at the rough running number four engine. Marvin came back and took control, holding the plane steady. He looked back at Ballard behind him in the top turret who continued to intently scan the sky above as the other crewmembers were doing.

Novak rebuffed the children's attempts at conversation as he too watched the horizon. Suddenly from behind, Ballard yelled out, "Two bogies, twelve O'clock high out of the sun and coming at us."

82

Marvin tried to look up at the two Mishershmit 109s that had spotted The Sky Queen, and were diving to intercept them.

Marvin watched helplessly, like so many times before in real life, and in his dreams, the fighters came in rattling off quick bursts. *Thank God, it was difficult for them to maneuver because of our low altitude.* Ballard kept pumping short bursts at them as the fighters looped up and swung around. Everyone had become tense in the plane as Marvin took dangerous evasive action dipping and swerving to escape the fighters.

Now the Mishershmits came in from the side firing longer bursts. This time tiny holes ripped across the fuselage at the waist gun. Suddenly Marvin heard through the head phones, "Novaks hit!"

Novak, shocked and surprised, fell back into a sitting position mortally wounded. He watched as the children stared at him in horror, and Beata began to cry. Novak smiled at them, trying to cover up his spreading bloodstains.

His thoughts were now going back to Chicago when he was younger, and his grandfather was teaching him how to play Polish songs on the guitar. He started to sing to the children, but didn't have enough strength to continue. Then he said to the children and Beata, "I'm a little tired, I'm just going to sleep for awhile". He closed his eyes and quietly died listening to guitar music in his head.

Sister Anna turned to the children and told them that 'War Angels' like Novak were so special, they were the only one's in heaven that were allowed to play music for Him and other War Angels, and sometimes

God needed them back in Heaven. She assured the children that God wanted Novak to play music for Him and the other 'War Angels' to help them win the battle they were fighting. When she turned around to pray over Novak, Paul Geller, the tall mute, had jumped up and taken over Novaks place at the waist gun.

Sister Anna and everyone else were amazed when he screamed out, "German Bastards!" and fired away. Paul was no longer a mute. Sister Anna heard Dunham shout out to Paul, "Short bursts! Short bursts!" Then he hit one of the planes, and it exploded in the air in a fiery ball of flames. Sister Anna moved out of the way as Dunham came to the side of Paul guiding him as the last fighter headed in for the kill. She and all the children watched Paul follow Dunham's instructions, "That's it, short bursts, follow out just in front of him, that's it, steady, short bursts! You got him now!" The fighter caught fire then exploded. The children went wild and screamed for joy.

Dunham took one of Novaks wing medals off him and gave it to Paul; "He would want you to have it." Sister Anna put her arm around Paul as Dunham pinned the medal on his shirt, and tears started to well up in his eyes. She felt him turn back to the waist gun and he focused his gaze into the sky, it was clear now.

A short time later, Marvin recognized the city of Calais down below and the coastline of France ahead. The number four engine started to smoke as Marvin tried to gain altitude and head out over the water. He and Harper kept at it until finally the plane slowly responded and began climbing. As the plane started rising Harper could see a small thin stream of spray coming from the right wing. "My God" it's the Tokyo Tank, it's been hit. We have got to kill the number four engine." Marvin saw him reach up and automatically hit the kill button of the number four engine. Marvin looked out and strained to see the wing. He couldn't see it, but underneath the wing two holes were spewing gas where Rienstock had fired his last shots through The Sky Queen. Marvin looked at the fuel gages and his stomach knotted up. They were dangerously low as he tapped them to make sure they were working. Then, he looked out the window and saw his worst nightmare. Another large formation of planes were heading right for them; he counted at least nine. He got on the head phones and said to everyone at their guns, including Paul, "Cock and load!" Dunham yelled into the headphones, "Hold on, wait, I think they're RAF!"

Marvin radioed to the RAF squadron, and put it on speaker for all to hear, "Permission for a lost lamb to join your flock." Marvin said to the RAF commander, "Come on in lost lamb. The Good Shepherd will fly you home." All the children felt secure about what sounded liked their heavenly escort.

Thick black smoke poured out of The Sky Queens number three engine on the right side. Marvin didn't want to wait until flames started licking the wings where the fuel was leaking. He reached up and now hit the number three engines red knob just above him, and then trimmed the plane for a two engine landing. He watched the propellers on the number three engine slow down as the blades rotated to a full-feathered position into the slipstream. The smoke from the engine began to thin out turning a lighter color of gray.

On the ground in an airfield somewhere in England, a small crowd of mechanics, flight personnel, medics, and soldiers saw the smoking plane from a distance. They all began gathering near the runway in anticipation of a crash landing.

The Sky Queen started into a steep decent pulling to the right as it came in. The ground crews saw it lumbering, and thought it was unusual the way it was flying, as if it had a full load of bombs still on board. They considered that it must be from the damage. None of them felt the plane was going to make it, and they prepared for the worst.

Marvin desperately went through all the landing procedures, landing gear down, flaps, reduced speed, everything he was supposed to do, then he got on the intercom and said, "Crash landing positions." Everyone on the plane braced themselves.

The wheels touched the ground with a smack and screeching sound. He felt The Sky Queen shiver and rattle its aluminum rivets through out its structure as it bumped along the concrete runway lurching forward almost out of control, heading toward the ground crew.

Marvin instantly thought of his flight school training remembering the instructor saying, "That's what any landing is, just a controlled crash." He had to take back control. Marvin fought the controls; he glanced over at Harper and saw he had his eyes closed. He cut the engines and the B-17 came to a quiet rolling stop, *we made it!*

Marvin watched the ground crew drive along side and immediately attack the number four engine with fire extinguishers. Everyone on the ground watched curiously as the hatches to this strange-looking bomber began to open. He watched their expressions of absolute astonishment as The Sky Queen seemed to disgorge a million kids, two nuns, what appeared to be a few Polish peasants, and the remaining rag tag crew of airmen.

The medics carried Novaks body from the plane and Marvin was the last one out. He patted the ship affectionately and then joined the others. The children all talked excitedly standing together with the crew. The small crowd of onlookers gathered in closer to stare and gently touch the freshly painted name on the fuselage next to the scorched queen of hearts wings that looked like an angels. It read in bright golden letters: THE WAR ANGELS! The ship sat proudly, absorbing their appreciation.

EPILOGUE

ROY DUNHAM and **MAGDA** were married in England. After the war, Dunham brought Magda home to live on a farm somewhere in Kansas, and they raised three children.

MAJOR GREG MARVIN went on to a distinguished career in the air force. He never married.

SWIFTY SHAW survived to escape from a German prison camp, and did eventually reach Switzerland. He and **RALPH HAPLY** own a chain of successful hardware stores.

FRANK BALLARD is the vice president of a major airline.

DAVE HARPER became a writer, living in California.

THE CHILDREN were placed with the other thousands of English children made orphans, or homeless, by the madness of war launched against a world unprepared. After the war, where possible, they were reunited with relatives in various countries. As adults, many of them, who never forgot The War Angels, migrated on to America, and raised families of their own. **MARJAN** settled in Israel and became a soldier. He was killed in the Six-Day War. **HESTER**, Marjans sister, became an attorney. **PAUL GELLER** became a psychologist specializing in the treatment of mental disorders, particular to children. He lives in Chicago not far from the place where Novak was born. **SISTER THERESA, AND SISTER**

ANNA, returned to Poland where they lived long useful lives in the ministry of their love.

None of them would ever forget the great drama of the world conflict that affected their lives, nor have the millions of others who lived through the experience. Yet, by simply resuming their normal ordinary lives, each of them contributed their day-to-day experiences the necessary threads that go into the weaving of that vast mosaic tapestry called human existence by which only God knows all the reasons. **SZABLA AND THE PARTISANS**, including **BASHA MICKIEWICZ** and the priest, **FATHER JAN KABOS**, vanished into the mountains, and into legend, as did all traces of the village Praznik.

Author with B-17

CPSIA information can be obtained at www.ICGtesting.com
Printed in the USA
BVOW08*0241180214

345199BV00001B/1/P